PRAISE
The Comfort

"On its face, *The Comfort of Monsto...*
begs to be read quickly, compulsively. But page by page, this electrifying debut by Willa Richards weaves an increasingly complicated and dark tale of guilt, fury, and the danger of building
stories on that shakiest of foundations: memory. Every sentence is
a delight in this taut and thrilling debut by Willa Richards."

—Elizabeth Wetmore, *New York Times* bestselling
author of *Valentine*

"*The Comfort of Monsters* is shadowed by crime but cares more
about consequence—it pairs the pulse-quickening pleasures of
a murder mystery with a probing portrait of loss. Willa C. Richards's unflinching debut picks apart a tangled knot of violence,
shame, secrecy, lust, and fearsome love. A dark, elegiac exam-
ination of sisterhood that's impossible to forget."

—Robin Wasserman, author of *Girls on Fire*

"*The Comfort of Monsters* captivates with a cold case, and becomes
an unflinching, unapologetic story of sexuality, victimhood, and
the dangerous pull of memory. Richards exposes the underbelly
of grief, shows the heartbeat shaking that thin skin, and leaves
you, at novel's end, holding something raw, fragile, and essen-
tially human. A remarkable debut."

—Lydia Fitzpatrick, author of *Lights All Night Long*

"Novels that explore the effects and aftermath of serial murder,
especially over the course of decades, always capture my interest. Willa C. Richards's debut, *The Comfort of Monsters*, is a
particularly impressive example, setting its layered narrative of
sisterhood, tough upbringings, violence, and grief against the
backdrop of what happened in Milwaukee during the summer of
1991, when the city reeled after Jeffrey Dahmer was arrested for

killing a number of young men. Richards has flipped the usual narrative, centering not on the crime itself but on the loss that ripples out from it, on the grief that can't be relieved even with the prospect of so-called 'closure.'"

—Sarah Weinman, *New York Times*

"In her fiery debut novel, Willa Richards folds the electrifying zing of crime fiction into an exceptional study of character. This book begs us to consider why we blame and otherize victims of violent crimes—especially when they come from society's margins. Potent, gritty, and deeply comprehending, *The Comfort of Monsters* is written with a clear eye and an aching heart."

—Amity Gaige, author of *Sea Wife*

"In a glut of dead girl stories and true crime vehicles, Richards pulls a wrenching and rewarding twist on both."

—*Publishers Weekly*

"A wrenching debut. . . . Meticulously researched and atmospheric, this is a perfect pick for book clubs and true crime aficionados."

—*Booklist*

"Richards turns tropes of crime fiction on their heads in this gripping, deftly crafted debut novel." —*OprahDaily.com*

"Delicate and heartrending." —Molly Odintz, *CrimeReads*

"*The Comfort of Monsters* casts a powerful spell with its sharp, lucid prose and its urgent, irresistible pacing. Underneath this shimmering surface, however, Willa C. Richards has crafted a profound novel of depth, complication, and intelligence, exploring the inconstancy of our recollections and revealing the elusiveness of our deepest truths. This debut is both a thrill and a provocation."

—Jamel Brinkley, National Book Award finalist
and author of *A Lucky Man*

THE COMFORT OF MONSTERS

THE COMFORT
OF MONSTERS

A NOVEL

WILLA C.
RICHARDS

HARPER ● PERENNIAL

NEW YORK ● LONDON ● TORONTO ● SYDNEY ● NEW DELHI ● AUCKLAND

HARPER ● PERENNIAL

FIRST HARPER PERENNIAL EDITION PUBLISHED 2022.

Library of Congress Cataloging-in-Publication Data has been applied for.

ISBN 978-0-06-305303-8 (pbk.)

22 23 24 25 26 LSC 10 9 8 7 6 5 4 3 2 1

Memory is a mosquito
pregnant again
and out for blood.

—GAYL JONES

I have to say what is said. I don't have to believe it myself.

—ANNE CARSON

Memory, of course, is also a story. It feels like the truth, especially when there is no one to dispute your recollection of events. But it is a story nonetheless—some moments have been elided, and others have been emphasized and made either luminous or horrific or both. Who, or what, does this editorializing is not clear to me. I know it's not me or not exactly. And maybe that is what frightens me now: I can see how much of the story is out of my control. I don't choose what is carried along year after year and what is discarded. (My sister, Dee, once took her shoes off during a long road trip north and threw them out the car window. We craned our necks to watch her white tennis shoes bump down the highway behind us.) And because now, more than ever, my sister's case depends on these memories, I am terrified that crucial pieces of evidence have been lost along the way.

If you think of a torso as a box, you can see
how someone might want to open it with his fingers.

—BETH BACHMANN

Modernity has eliminated the comfort of monsters because
we have seen, in Nazi Germany and elsewhere, that evil
works often as a system, it works through institutions as a
banal (meaning "common to all") mechanism. In other words
evil stretches across cultural and political productions as
complicity and collaboration. Modernity makes monstrosity a
function of consent and a result of habit.

—JACK HALBERSTAM

Federal Rules of Evidence

Article I. General Provisions

RULE 102. PURPOSE

These rules should be construed so as to administer every proceeding fairly, eliminate unjustifiable expense and delay, and promote the development of evidence law, to the end of ascertaining the truth and securing a just determination.

Let me try to be clear about what this is: I have a layperson's understanding of the law. Until several months ago, when I was fired, I was a library and circulation services assistant at Marquette University's law library. I'd spent most of my five years there studying textbooks with anesthetizing titles like *Evidentiary Foundations.* (I often stole these books, stashing them away with the files from my sister's case, so I could keep studying at home.) But even so, all I can say with confidence is that the most compelling story is the truest story. Unfortunately, it's rarely the other way around.

What I've learned from Graham C. Lilly's book, for example, is that when lawyers argue a case, they aren't interested in the truth. Instead, they are concerned with curating a body of evidence that is favorable to their client. The fact finder, either a jury or a judge, is then tasked with evaluating that evidence and deciding what has occurred. During closing arguments, lawyers have one last chance to shape the meaning and weight of the presented evidence, and to construct a believable story, a series of plausible events, that is supported by the evidence. Legally speaking, evidence is any matter, verbal or physical, that can be used to support the existence of a factual proposition. In this particular case, I bear the burden of producing evidence that will persuade law enforcement of the following factual proposition: A man I knew as Frank Cavelli murdered my sister, Candace McBride. So far, I have failed.

This failure of persuasion, according to police, lies in the fact that I am missing the only piece of evidence that has ever mattered: my sister's body. *No body; no crime.* They've repeated this mantra so often over the years that I've begun to hear it at all times, like it's etched onto one of the very fine bones inside my ear. What the police mean to say is that my account of Dee's disappearance is inconsequential. It's not just that they don't believe me, it's that even if they did, without her body, my story does not legally matter. I'm sure this true. I'm also sure that they aren't inclined to hear my story because of the unofficial form it takes. So, I've tried over the years to engage in a process of translation: to transform these memories into evidence and to apply the federal rules of evidence to these memories. This is an impossible endeavor. The language of the law was designed to exclude, to be cold and unfeeling, and above all else, to confuse. I've done my best.

For decades now I've kept all of Dee's files crammed inside my one-bedroom apartment on Milwaukee's East Side. And I've been rehearsing my story. And recent events have convinced me I cannot wait any longer to argue this case. Otherwise I'm afraid Dee and I, and the rest of my family, will be forgotten, because our story will dissolve first into the annals of the local newspaper archives and then finally into meaninglessness. This has already happened once. Lately I've also become afraid that someone else will tell this story and their version will prove to be more compelling than mine.

Among the legacies of misogyny that live on today is a general distrust of women, a belief that we are conniving and cunning by nature. Still a fear exists that women are capable of controlling, using, and abusing men with their feminine wiles. Lest we believe that this hysteria peaked in Salem, Massachusetts, in 1693, the forty-fifth president of the United States has publicly propagated these biases saying, among other things, that he has seen women manipulate men with just a twitch of their eye, or perhaps another body part.

The social constructions surrounding gendered categories have had grave and lasting consequences. Consider, for example, early civil laws on the European continent, inherited from Roman codes, which were based on the inferiority and subjection of women. In these early courts, women were not allowed to be witnesses, and later, even after they were deemed legally competent to testify, their testimonies were almost ubiquitously cast as worthless.

Today, though the United States' Federal Rules of Evidence indicate that "every person is competent to be a witness," this language only calls attention to the courts' long and ongoing history of exclusion. This storied history is very much not behind us.

I'm somewhat embarrassed to admit that a few years ago, I became emboldened when the MeToo movement picked up steam and everyone started saying they were going to "believe women." *Excellent*, I remember thinking. I waited for Gary Wolski, Jr., the MPD detective who had been assigned to Dee's case twenty-eight years ago, to call and say let's hear your story. I waited for the MPD to call and say we're sorry we didn't believe you before, but we're listening now. I waited for the *Journal Sentinel*, for BuzzFeed, for anyone to call and say let us help you tell your story. No one called. No one checked in. I reorganized my files for the six hundredth time. Finally, against my better judgment, I called Wolski. He picked up immediately.

"Ah, Christ, Margaret. I thought you might call," he said, sighing. "I'm sorry."

My heart leaped. An apology!

"Should I come into your office now? I have tapes. And the files. Or I could fax everything."

"No, no, no," he said. "That won't be necessary. I just wanted to say I'm sorry for what happened between us."

"Between us?"

"Yeah, I know now, uh, it wasn't right."

I paused. I recalibrated. "I'm not calling about that."

"Oh." He breathed a quiet and incriminating sigh of relief. "I thought you were going to MeToo me."

"Should I?" I asked him sharply. We'd slept together once, a very long time ago, when I was in a bad way. I blamed him, of course, but I blamed myself more. He didn't take the bait.

"Why did you call, then?" he asked. He suddenly sounded bored and eager to hang up. I was disoriented.

"I thought maybe, with the climate and everything," I said, "maybe you guys could take another look at my testimony, my evidence."

There was a long pause. I held my breath. And then I hung up on him. I didn't need to hear what he was about to say because I'd heard it too many times before.

No body; no crime.

Almost thirty years after Dee went missing, and twenty-three years after she was eligible to be declared legally dead, my mother proposed that we hire a psychic to help us find her body. Three decades before, I would have said, and I believe my mother would have agreed with me, that we weren't the kind of people who hired psychics. But later I finally understood, given the right circumstances, anyone can become this kind of person.

For instance, I was initially resistant to hiring the psychic for all the obvious reasons: the expense, the fraudulent and unethical nature of their businesses, etc. But many of these reasons proved much less compelling than the only reason we had to hire him: We all wanted to find Dee's body. And at some point, perhaps after watching the video my mother sent me, or perhaps after she begged in her bed at the nursing home, I began to entertain the idea that the psychic *could* be successful. Local law enforcement had given up on us decades ago, and we'd exhausted ourselves by holding weekly, then monthly, then annual canvasses looking for her body. We'd exhausted ourselves by sorting through bogus tips and prank calls. We'd exhausted ourselves by begging local and state and national presses to cover our story. We were exhausted. It was a permanent state.

Here is a piece of evidence with many stories behind it and also without any story at all: In America over half of all murdered women are killed by a current or former partner.

Dee was always my father's favorite. Pete was Ma's favorite. And I guess I was nobody's favorite. Well, maybe I was Dee's favorite, or maybe I just believed that and was desperate to continue believing it. The idea was very comforting to me. My mother named my younger sister Candace, but my father quickly shortened this to Candy, which I quickly shortened to just Dee, and Dee stuck. Almost no one called her Candace, and only my father was ever allowed to call her Candy.

We were born thirteen months apart, so our father called us Irish twins. Dee and I loved this—we believed that we could read each other's minds and that our heartbeats were synced. But when we were older, our mother made it clear to us that though we could say we were Irish, on account of our father's grandfather, we were not actually twins. This was disappointing news to both of us. Even worse, we discovered that because of how our birthdays fell on the calendar, we would be two years apart in school.

So when I was a junior in high school, Dee was a freshman. And when Dee started high school, it became clear to me, rather quickly, that our experiences would be different. For starters, unlike me, Dee was popular. I knew this was in part because she was rather classically pretty (and I was apparently a bit odd-looking; people said that my brow ridge cast a great shadow over my face so it looked like I was always wearing a mask), but also because she had the je ne sais quoi that some popular people seem to be born with: that special cocktail of charisma and confidence. (I definitely didn't have that.) Sometimes this attribute doesn't follow people once they leave the social bubbles of their schools, but sometimes it does. Anyway, Dee had a large group of girlfriends in high school, many of whom prided themselves on dating older boys.

One day during lunch Dee was standing in a circle of these girls as they chatted outside the cafeteria. I was sitting alone at a picnic table picking at a peanut butter sandwich and writing little poems in illegible cursive all over my notebooks. Every once in a while a group of boys, standing a good distance from Dee's group, would cheer or hoot, and it took me almost ten minutes to figure out why.

It was a breezy fall day in Wisconsin. Though chilly, Dee and some of the other girls were still wearing short floral skirts with their Docs. Whenever a breeze came and lifted the girls' skirts, these boys cheered. I didn't know if the girls heard the boys or if they cared. Maybe they just enjoyed the pleasurable sensation of a cool breeze on the backs of their thighs. In any case, none of them seemed concerned, none of them clutched at their hems to keep them flat, and eventually one gust lifted Dee's skirt up to show her underwear and a sliver of her butt. The boys screamed with joy. I felt, with absolute certainty, that I hated every single one of them.

Watching, I was suddenly afraid another, larger gust would reveal Dee's underwear completely. This breach of privacy inspired a sinking dread in me. (As girls, Dee and I shared the same room and often the same clothes. I remembered her stepping into her underwear, our underwear, that very morning: an old ratty blue pair that had come in a cheap department-store pack of eight. She was fourteen.)

I leaped up from my picnic table and ran over to her. I gave her an aggressive hug from behind, wrapping my arms around her shoulders and pressing her spiny back into my stomach. Dee whipped her head around to see me. Some of the boys booed. Dee blushed. I kissed her cheekbone from behind and she shrugged me off.

"Pegasus," she whispered into my ear. "Can you *stop* being so weird?"

"Sorry," I said. She looked bewildered.

The lunch bell rang. Harried lunch attendants ushered us inside.

Later that day, one of the boys who'd apparently been particularly disappointed by my intervention keyed *prude* and *slut* into our parents' car. I wasn't sure how I could be both. Or maybe one was for me and one was for Dee.

"What did you do?" Dee screamed at me while we were inspecting the damage on the car. I stared at her with my mouth open, shocked that she would assume I'd provoked this treatment. I supposed that if one used the sick logic of our high school, I was, in fact, to blame.

"I don't know," I shouted back. "Maybe you should ask one of your blockhead fucking boyfriends."

"Let's go," Dee said. We were aware that a small, whispering crowd was forming in the parking lot.

I never explained to Dee what happened that day. Maybe she knew. Maybe she didn't. We never talked about it. I'd bet a lot of money that by the time we were both in college, she'd completely forgotten about the incident. I never forgot about it, though. And much later, after she disappeared, I would regret my unwillingness to even try to explain the dread I felt while I watched these boys watching her. It wasn't, I might have told her, about some paternalistic desire to protect her from them or to shield her from their sight. It wasn't a fear that they would hurt her or that she would be embarrassed. It's difficult to explain. I suppose the dread came from an understanding that even then I was losing *us:* this *we* that had once been solely ours.

When she was eighty-one, my mother suffered two strokes in one year. After the first stroke, she was unable to move the left side of her body and in need of full-time care. After the second stroke, she was *affected*. Or that's how she described the feeling. She felt she'd briefly crossed over to the other side, where, she explained to us, she saw a world she'd never believed possible. Among the visions she'd had in this other world were: her own death at the hands of a final stroke by the end of the year, and Dee's body decomposing in a handmade grave somewhere in the city of Milwaukee.

My mother first saw the psychic on the *Today* show after her second stroke. Thomas Alexander was featured in a long segment detailing his most recent success stories. One of these successes—a cold case the psychic claimed he helped solve—caught my mother's eye. A young woman's murderer was finally found, though the killer himself was by then dead too. My mother watched the woman's parents speak about what this discovery meant to them, and she was shot through with jealousy, then with a fresh spike of hope. The jealousy could be managed; the hope was more dangerous, because in our family, hope could travel like a virus we passed between us.

Though my mother wanted our support, logistically she needed it, confined as she was then to her bed at the Lutheran Home. Ma met with each of us (my brother, Pete, her sister, Suze, and Wolski) separately, in an apparent divide-and-conquer strategy. Though, in the end, she may not have needed to be so cautious. We were, every one of us, easier to convince than she expected.

My mother's right eye nailed me against the wall of her room. Her left eye was still and murky. She waited to hear my objections. It was telling that I couldn't think of many.

"He is going to be expensive," I offered.

"So bury me in a cardboard box if you have to."

"Ma," I protested. "Please."

"I'm serious. You know I don't care what kind of damn container I'm in, but I want her next to me."

"There are other options," I said. "Still." Though I knew this wasn't true and so did she. We'd known this for twenty years now. I pressed my back into a bookshelf full of framed photos of her children, her grandchildren, her sister, my father in his navy uniform. One of the pictures, of Dee in middle school, toppled off the shelf. The rubber bands in Dee's braces were magenta. I scrambled to set it right but couldn't and ended up clutching the photo awkwardly. My sister's twelve-year-old face shone up at me.

"Don't give me that crap," she said. "Not from you." My mother tried a shake of her head. She looked like a doll being tossed by a toddler.

I nodded. "I'm sorry."

"This is my last chance. I can tell, Pegasus," she whispered to me (using Dee's nickname for me was purposeful), and then she repeated, "This might be our last chance. I want her next to me and your father when I'm buried. I will not leave Dee's plot empty. I won't do it."

I squeezed my eyes shut. We'd buried my father in Forest Home

Cemetery after his heart attack. My mother had purchased a plot for herself then too, and after Dee had been missing for twenty years, she'd purchased a third plot for her youngest daughter with the hope that one day we might find her body and finally have a proper funeral for her.

She clutched frantically at the air with her right hand like she wanted me to go close to her, but a bout of nausea rose in my throat. I stayed where I was, so she clutched her own dead shoulder instead, crossing her right hand diagonally over her chest. Her left hand lay like a dismembered limb by her side. Outside the room there was another Lutheran Home resident yelling, *You're hurting me, you're hurting me.* I felt a little dizzy from the heat of the room, the smell of reheated food, the overlapping white noise of the residents' TVs on all at once.

"You owe me this," Ma whispered. The nausea continued to bubble. It had moved into the soft palate of my mouth, which now watered. Suddenly, my mother began laughing. It was unlike the laughs Dee and I had shared with her as children, though. There was something dull and metallic about it: a knife in need of honing. She clutched her dead shoulder and laughed and laughed. The doctors had said this was something that could happen too. It was called emotional lability: It caused her to mix up her emotional reactions, to express them without provocation, to be confused. I had the awkward instinct to laugh with her, but when I looked into her eyes, I saw a deep well of fear and confusion. I just reached for her right, feeling hand. Her whole body went limp.

"Watch that video," she said. "Just watch it."

"Okay, Mama," I whispered back. "Okay, okay."

She laughed at me.

Across the street from the nursing home, my aunt Suze was sitting on the curb, smoking a cigarette and rebraiding her long gray hair. She had just gotten off work—her cheeks were flushed, there was a sweaty dew on her brow, and she was wearing dirty sneakers crusted with diner-floor filth. As I'd gotten older, I'd become more impressed by my aunt's ability to waitress well into her sixties. Though of course she'd never looked at it like that: *It's got nothing to do with ability, Margaret,* she'd scolded me once, *it's about need.* Though she'd tried on a few different jobs over the years—a couple stints as a receptionist in various offices, some telemarketing gigs, even sales—she always seemed to go back to waitressing. She was an incurable extrovert, she was hugely anticipatory of her customers' needs, and she was most content when she was in motion. So she was very good at what she did. Still, I knew the lifestyle wore her mind and her body down, though she wouldn't admit it to us.

Though she was fifteen years younger than Ma, they'd always been close. When Pete, Dee, and I were young, she was like a second, much cooler mama to us. She'd watch us on weekends and sometimes take us camping or to the 7 Mile Fair, a big flea market near Illinois. She used to rubber-band big wads of her cash tips, tuck them into her fanny pack, and then hand the cash out to us at the flea market so we could buy whatever random shit caught our eye. These outings used to infuriate our parents, but she always laughed at the junk we brought home. She never had kids of her own, so she doted on us.

When she saw me, she crossed the street and then wrapped me in a tight hug. I breathed in her smell, which was mostly of the perfume called Red Door.

"How is she?" Suze asked. This was a question we rarely asked of each other anymore because the inanity of it was too overwhelming. Maybe my mother's deteriorating condition had made it seem more appropriate again.

I shrugged. "She's . . . animated." I hoped this would serve as a warning.

"So what did you say?" she asked.

"I said sure. She wouldn't hear much else."

Suze hardened her face like she was receiving a bad diagnosis. "I figured."

I wanted then to warn her about a shift I felt inside me. "Maybe she's right?" I said. "I don't know." I looked past Suze onto the stretch of North Avenue that ran from the swamps in the suburbs all the way downtown where it eventually spilled over the bluffs and into Lake Michigan. "Maybe we have a chance here." When I looked back at my aunt, she was gazing at me sharply. Though she tried to soften her face, I'd already caught an expression she hadn't meant for me to see. There is no word for the specific mixture of pity and pain one feels toward a beloved who is sinking.

"Maybe," she said, but it was obvious she didn't mean it. She cupped one of my ears and then tugged on the lobe like she used to do when I was a kid.

The year Dee went missing, she was a freshman at Mount Mary College, a small all-girls' liberal arts school run by nuns. She had applied on a whim after receiving a glossy brochure in the mail. Dee was charmed by the quiet, stately campus and the school's core curriculum, which, she explained one night at dinner, was rooted in humanity's search for meaning. Pete laughed, teasing Dee that she was sending herself to the nunnery. But when they offered her a partial scholarship and she vowed to pay the rest of her tuition by working part-time at a nearby hair salon, he stopped teasing. Ma enjoyed the idea of Dee studying at an all-girls' school: She felt Dee had gotten out of control in high school, lamenting her youngest daughter's love interests, whom Ma described as a slew of degenerates. She thought maybe Dee would be more focused at Mount Mary.

Though I was not under any such illusions, I also supported Dee's decision, because I had been disappointed in my own school of choice. I was a junior at UWM, on the East Side of Milwaukee, a school that felt large and impersonal, full of brutalist concrete buildings and dimly lit, orange-carpeted libraries. One rampant rumor held that UWM's libraries were populated by perverts who sat and waited underneath the tables to fondle girls' feet.

In retrospect, we both ended up at the wrong school. I would have been much better suited to the verdant humanism of Mount Mary, and Dee probably would have enjoyed those aspects of UWM that I abhorred: the larger classes, the boozy house parties, the proximity to Brady Street.

I hadn't made many friends at UWM in my two years there, in part because I'd taken up a serious relationship when I was still a freshman. Dee was also trying to find her footing that year. Between work and school, she struggled to find a group of close friends like the one she'd leaned on in high school. So we were close then, maybe closer than we'd been since we were girls, I think because we both felt out of place. She spent a lot of nights at my place in Riverwest, and we often spent weekends together back at home. Maybe this lack of belonging had pushed us back toward each other, even while I could see that the contours of our new adult lives didn't necessarily have room for the same kind of relationship we'd had as girls.

During her second semester at Mount Mary, she began seeing a man whose identity, to this day, remains opaque to me. It's frightening now to consider how little I knew about this person. These are some of the facts I thought I knew: His name was Frank. He was thirty-five, he was recently divorced, and he was training to become a firefighter. He said he had worked most of his life for his parents, who owned a small cemetery in Menomonee Falls. He seemed to have a lot of money, or enough money to splurge on gifts for Dee, but he didn't seem upper class. I thought that he was crude and that he was a bigot.

Was that all? Why didn't I know more? What did I think then? Probably that I had *time* to get to know him. Probably that *eventually* I would understand what she liked about him. (It turned out that I had no time at all, and that fact still haunts me.) Or maybe I didn't get to know Frank because, off the bat, I hadn't liked him, and so I guessed he was a fad, another phase Dee would leave behind when she felt she'd gotten what she needed. She could be ruthlessly utilitarian.

The way Dee always told it was that she had met Frank at a bar at the beginning of her spring semester. She had liked his confidence but also his composure. She said most men in the bars had a desperate, hungry air about them, like they'd steal you away if they thought they could. She said Frank was different. They'd gone on a few dates: coffee, then a Bucks game and a late dinner at his buddy's Italian restaurant, where they got the whole candlelit dining room to themselves. Dee felt the whole thing was very adult; she liked that.

When she first told me about him that spring, I said I was happy for her and that I was excited to meet him. She said we'd definitely hang out together, but then she always seemed to find an excuse to put it off. This stung. And honestly, it got to the point where I wondered if she was making him up, and I said so once, while we were out to breakfast together.

"He's an adult, Pegasus," she said smartly. I rolled my eyes at her. She was a college freshman—she barely knew what that entailed. "He doesn't have time to barhop like you and Leif." This was a deliberate slight against my then-boyfriend, Leif, who admittedly did enjoy barhopping.

"So? Leif's an adult too," I told her. Leif was twenty-eight and gainfully employed at Ambrosia, a local chocolate factory. We'd recently moved in together: We paid our rent on time. What could be more adult than that? "He seems to make time for me. And for you."

She shrugged because she knew I was right. Leif often cooked simple dinners for me and Dee. He'd been to Sunday dinner at

Ma's, where we'd watch the Packers game together. Sometimes Leif even watched long, boring Brewers games with Pete while they both crushed cans of Schlitz. "Yeah," Dee said. She studied her eggs. "I'll ask."

I didn't know at the time if he was refusing to meet me, or if she was reluctant to introduce us for some reason, but either way, something felt off. I tried to explain this to her, but she got defensive. "I said I'll ask, dammit."

When I did finally meet him, I could see why Dee might have wanted to keep us apart. He proposed we meet for custard, which I thought was kind of creepy, because it seemed like the type of outing an uncle or a brother would suggest. But I loved custard, and I loved Dee, and so I tried to push the thought away. But then he chose some Podunk custard stand in West Allis that I'd never heard of, which also annoyed me because everyone knows Kopp's is the best.

Frank hugged me when we met. I didn't like the feeling of his body against mine. I kept my arms awkwardly by my sides. When he pulled away, I felt like he was looking through my clothes. Some men seem to be able to do that—to make you feel totally naked. How did he make Dee feel?

"Finally!" he said. He clapped me on the back and grinned. He had dark, wavy hair that stayed glued in place even when he moved, on account of copious product. He smelled like cedar chips. He wore a gold chain that seemed too tight for his neck and a large gaudy graduation ring. He made a big show of paying for our custards, which came out to a whopping eight dollars. He seemed able to keep a part of his body touching Dee's at all times. He didn't look like her boyfriend, he looked like her boss. I made a note to tell her that later. We sat outside on the damp cement benches, even though it was chilly, and ate our custard in relative silence. I shivered and tried to hide it.

"Dee tells me you're a writer," Frank said. I nodded. "Have you published anything?" I shook my head. I tried to eat my custard faster, but my head ached already with cold. My mind was numb. I wished I were drinking. I knew he was trying. I locked eyes with Dee, and I could tell she was begging me to try too. Plus, while I'd heckled her for weeks about meeting him, I couldn't think of a word to say to the guy. I knew I'd hear about that later.

"How is firefighting school?" I said. I didn't know what it was called, but once I'd said that, I felt it was wrong. My cheeks went hot even though my brain still felt cold and slow. I pictured the vast glaciers that once crawled over North America. I felt much younger than I had in a long time.

He laughed. "It's hard, honey," he said. "It's really hard."

I refused to say anything after that. I threw the rest of my custard away too.

Damn, did I hear it after. Dee said I'd been rude, which stung, because it wasn't true, and also because he was the one who'd been rude. She said I'd acted like a half-wit, which also stung, and made me self-conscious. I told her I didn't like him, and she said I didn't even try to get to know him. I wanted to tell her the things I had intuited about him, but I was scared she would stop talking to me. I was scared she would hate me. I thought she'd figure it all out soon enough. It was obvious to me that he wasn't the right person for her, but if she wanted to enjoy the gifts he bought her and the adult trappings of their fling a little longer, maybe that was fine. That was my position on him at the time. But things only got worse from there, and I felt less and less certain that keeping my mouth shut was the right thing to do. And now I can't believe I ever felt that way.

Leif and I met at a house party my sophomore year of college. He was a real wallflower type at big parties—nursing room-temperature beers or a finger of whiskey near the turntable, or spending long minutes examining the bookcases and leafing through chapbooks. But in smaller groups, or one-on-one, he was charming, boisterous, quick to joke. Later, this made me suspicious that the wallflower behavior was an act meant to cultivate a sense of mystery, but at the time it impressed me—I'd never seen someone so content to be alone at a party. Wasn't mingling the whole point? Plus, we shared a sense of humor, which was rare in my world. I'd never met anyone except my sister who laughed at the same things I did.

I could tell Leif had been eyeing me from the moment I got there, but he waited until much later in the night to approach me. "You look like a poet," he said to me. He offered his hand. "Leif."

I took his hand and rubbed my thumb up and down the thick ligaments attaching his wrist to his fingers. His hands were cool and in need of lotion. I imagined myself rubbing cold cream into his skin. He smelled oddly of cocoa and Lysol. My mouth went a little dry. "Peg," I said. "Why do you say that?"

"The way you're noticing everything."

"Why are you noticing what I'm noticing?" I asked. He had a messy mat of auburn hair that I wanted to put my fingers in, and his eyes reminded me of a set of green marbles spilled across a wood floor. They stayed moving.

He shrugged. "It's the most interesting thing happening at this party."

"Who's your favorite poet?" I asked him.

He raised his eyebrows. "Bob Dylan," he said. I laughed because I thought it was a joke. Leif frowned.

"So you mean Rimbaud?" I asked.

"I believe the term is *intertexuality*." He made air quotes around the word.

"I think actually it's just *plagiarism*." I made air quotes back at him.

He laughed. "What about you, then?"

"Oh, I don't know," I said. "Kurt Cobain?" We both laughed.

"No, really," he said. "Come on."

"Lorine Niedecker," I said without hesitation because it was the first name that popped into my head and because I'd read these lines about her earlier in the day: *Niedecker lived in southern Wisconsin for the rest of her life. She scrubbed hospital floors, read proof for a local magazine, and worked other menial jobs to support herself and her writing. She endured near-poverty . . .*

"*Grandfather / advised me: / learn a trade / I learned / to sit at desk / and condense / No layoff / from this / condensery,*" Leif recited. Very quickly I learned this about Leif: Lines of poetry stuck to his brain the way gum, once hardened, will stick to the underside of chairs. I tried not to look impressed. He knew.

Thirty minutes after we'd met, he tried to kiss me on the mouth, and I backed myself against the wall.

"Too soon?" His eyes were dopey with beer.

"Much," I said.

He held his hands up by his face like he'd been ordered to do so. "You got it, baby," he said.

I was under the spell of an intoxicating sense of invincibility, which is to say I was twenty. Leif and I dated for about a year and then we moved in together, a secret to which only Dee was privy. Leif was twenty-eight, which was much too old for my mother's and Pete's tastes. I suspected Pete was particularly worked up about it because Leif was only a year older than he was. *Why can't you date someone your own age?* Pete had whined when he found out about Leif. *Because men my age are animals,* I'd told him smartly. Over a series of laborious Sunday dinners, Leif gradually charmed my mom and brother (or so I'd thought), but I knew they'd never come around to us living together in Riverwest. So, after we moved in together that spring, I told them I was living with two friends from school in a flat on the East Side.

When I look back now, I see how it was over almost before it began, but at the time I felt the whole hot promise of a life with him. I still remember our belongings on the sidewalk outside that apartment building. There was trash everywhere. Springtime turns the city of Milwaukee briefly into a landfill; the snowmelt from the most stubborn snowbanks reveals heaps of trash: cigarette butts, dog shit, shredded newspapers and magazines, vomit, crushed cans, and plastic bags whipped into stringy ropes. Each year, after resident weatherman John Malan has determined the city won't be visited by any more snowstorms, they send inmates out to collect all the winter trash in white plastic bags. Afterward they cart the trash away to the landfills west of the city, and they bring out pressurized hoses and spray down the sidewalks and the streets with water pumped fresh out of Lake Michigan. I love the smell of cold water on concrete. That's spring to me, not tulips or daffodils or rain, but Lake Michigan's cold bathwater washed over the whole city.

There were still blackened snowbanks in front of the building in Riverwest when we unloaded our furniture. We were young enough then to be thrilled by things like a kitchen table belonging only to us. Our first night we spent there, Leif made steak and we drank red wine out of the bottle and ate on the living room floor, which was filthy, and then we fucked on the floor. We were covered in dust. At the end of the night, the soles of our bare feet were black. It's hard to believe now. Showering without a shower curtain, air-drying our damp bodies in that dirty apartment, Leif shaking sheets out for us to sleep on top of the mattress on the floor, the way he held me that first night to make sure I knew it was safe in there. He checked and rechecked the locks.

Riverwest was, and remains, one of the few somewhat mixed neighborhoods in Milwaukee, a city that is intractably segregated. And Riverwest was, and still is, often described as dangerous. As far as I could tell, though, the reputation was unearned and due mostly to the fact that the neighborhood's western border was Holton Street. This street, to many Milwaukeeans, represented a kind of tenuous border between the wealthier, mostly white East Side and the poorer, mostly Black communities on the North Side of the city. Riverwest was like a long, funky, porous borderland between these two parts of the city. So, of course, Leif loved it there. He said it was like living in a liminal zone: a place with its own rules and its own separate zones of possibility. I teased him that he was only glad it was safe for him to smoke weed on the streets there, although I knew that wasn't what he meant.

Frankly, I often felt more afraid on campus than I ever did in Riverwest. Once during my first semester as a freshman at the University of Wisconsin–Milwaukee, I left the library after dark and walked across campus to my dorm. I had gotten in the habit of spending long afternoons that blurred into late nights reading, or doing homework, or writing in the library. I avoided my dorm room, which wasn't conducive to studying and which also smelled permanently dank, like the primate house at the county zoo. I would stay at the library until I couldn't stand the hunger anymore, and then I might walk to Oakland Gyros and flirt with the boys behind the counter who sometimes gave me extra fries for free. On this particular night, a Friday, I was trying to avoid being witness to the excessive alcohol consumption I knew was taking place in my dorm room, but as usual, by nine-thirty, my stomach was growling and my focus was shot.

The fall chill had just sunk its teeth into the city, so that already layers upon layers of clothing were necessary in order to be outside. I'd forgotten a hat, so I pulled the hood of my sweatshirt up over my head and went out to brave some kind of disgusting sleeting rain.

I hadn't decided what to eat or where when I saw a group of boys, already absolutely loaded, headed in my direction. I thought maybe I could cross the street to avoid passing them, but cars whizzed by in both directions. I stuffed my hands into my sweatshirt pocket and focused on the cement. *Probably harmless,* I thought. *Probably you will be fine.* They were loud, though, and judging by the way they were walking and monopolizing the sidewalk, the case of PBR they'd just drunk had them all feeling like kings. I inched to the edge of the sidewalk. When they got close, one of them, whose face I never saw, bumped into my shoulder with his whole body, even though I was taking pains to be as far away from them as possible. I stumbled off the sidewalk and into the wet grass. Rain and mud leaked through my canvas sneakers and soaked my socks. The boys laughed. They passed, and when I thought that was the worst of it, and I was already letting out a breath, the same boy turned around and said loudly to my back, "Your hood won't keep you from getting raped, you know."

I didn't make any sudden movements. I walked like I hadn't heard a thing. They kept walking too. I made myself keep moving. Down the block, I spotted a pay phone, and I called Peter.

He picked me up ten minutes later and drove me to Ma's. During those ten minutes, I tried to make myself very small. I pretended I was invisible. I didn't say anything in the car, and Pete didn't ask. I studied his movements: the assuredness with which he drove, which was the same way I remembered my father driving when I was a girl. Was Pete capable of this kind of behavior? It seemed impossible. Pete squeezed my knee. I jerked away from his hand. He tried not to notice.

"Ma and Dee will be thrilled to have you home," he said.

I said nothing.

At home, Ma fed me a reheated slice of Cornish pie, a meat pie in a buttery crust that I slathered in ketchup and practically inhaled. Then Dee and I curled up on the couch together with her head on my legs and my hands in her hair and we watched *Full House* until we fell asleep.

Later, when I told Leif about this incident, he was shocked: *He said what to you?* I was often confused when men were outraged by these stories; I assumed so many of them had witnessed or participated in some degree of it at one time or another. Maybe the outrage was a performance for my benefit? Or maybe fewer of them participated than I suspected? Or maybe these stories manufactured, in their minds, some scale of heinousness that easily reassured them that their own transgressions were comparatively minor. Was it in this way that the men I knew often didn't see themselves as the problem? Sometimes I worried that telling these stories would only assure them of their superiority rather than forcing them into reflection: *Jesus, well, at least I've never done that.*

The psychic's face appeared out of a headline I clicked on. He was small and blond, with bones like a bird. Television beautiful, Dee used to say about people whose faces appeared too smooth, too perfect, to believe. *But we must believe.*

Television beautiful had become Internet beautiful. When I clicked on the boy's face with my own tiny computer, a different man appeared in the video. A freelance reporter for *Vox* stood grim-faced in tight khakis and a denim button-up in front of a vacant lot. (Most people who'd never been to Milwaukee underestimated the unpredictability of the weather and came either underdressed or overdressed. He was the former; he struggled to keep his teeth from chattering.)

"This is 924 North Twenty-fifth Street," he said, "where the famed cannibal and serial killer once lived." He motioned behind him where a crowd of people had gathered with homemade signs. "A celebrity psychic, in collaboration with the popular Netflix series *Dark Tourist* and a local cigar bar and former whorehouse (also reportedly haunted), will be hosting a special series here in Milwaukee commemorating the twenty-fifth anniversary of the serial killer's death."

A few weak boos from the crowd gathered behind the news

anchor. A bead of sweat formed on his temple despite the spring chill. Dried, pulverized leaves blew through the alley next to the empty lot. A garbage can tipped over and the wet contents spilled across the cement. More boos. A block away, a siren. Photos of young men on the posters. Old photos. Ages frozen. Fourteen, eighteen, twenty-five, nineteen, seventeen, twenty-two. Signs that said: *Grief vampire, just stay away.* The families, the anchor reported, were protesting the psychic's show. An old woman holding a baby girl on her hip spoke into the anchor's mike.

"Those men," she said, "none of them, none, have ever gotten the respect, in death, they deserve. They're going to let a serial killer speak from the grave before they'll let us speak."

I recognized her. From almost thirty years ago. She'd protested the murderer's insanity plea outside the courthouse. One of those dead men's sisters. She looked as if she'd been crushed down by time, an aluminum can that had been pressed flat by a giant hand. I supposed that was how I looked too.

"We won't see one cent of this damn money. They're selling those tickets for two hundred dollars. So they can walk around and continue to glorify this monster? So these people can drink old-fashioneds and hear what he did to my baby brother? To talk to that monster from the other side? That damn cigar bar sells T-shirts with his picture on it. Now, you tell me that isn't exploitative."

A gust of wind blew a flattened cereal box against the anchor's shins; he was anxious to finish the segment. I thought I saw snowflakes caught up in a gust of wind. They wouldn't land. "Thomas Alexander, Netflix, and the local cigar bar have put forth a joint statement reiterating that they have the utmost respect for the people of Milwaukee, they understand the sensitive nature of their enterprise here, and therefore they will proceed with absolute deference. Local businesses have also noted that the exposure could be good for tourism. A spokesperson for Thomas Alexander has said that the special-edition tours will run every other Friday and Saturday through the summer. The show will air on Netflix on November twenty-eighth, the day the Milwaukee Cannibal was killed in a Wisconsin prison by fellow inmate Christopher Scarver."

After this video ended, another began, and I knew immediately that it was the video my mother had wanted me to watch. Four point two million people had recently watched this clip. The family had that average-American look going for them—the man wore a baseball cap and a blue pocket tee, and the woman wore a white blousy button-up and tasteful silver hoops in her ears. The couple was graying, though not completely gray yet, and they were plump in their middle age. I wondered if only I, or someone like me or Ma, could see the few things that were really different about them: the almost imperceptible sag of the shoulders, a few uncontrollable nervous tics, and most prominently, the deadness in their eyes.

The most remarkable part about the video was that, by the end of it, after the psychic told them who had murdered their daughter, this deadness disappeared. It had been either destroyed or replaced, temporarily or permanently. I wasn't sure it mattered what had happened to it or where it had gone. All I knew was that I wanted the deadness gone from my mother's eyes; I wanted her to be like these people. Hell, I wanted to be like these people. I began then to become wed to the idea that this was possible. Apparently, so did Pete. He watched this video too, and after, he called the psychic, and just like that, Thomas Alexander was hired.

I once believed Pete named his eldest daughter, Dana, in homage to Dee, though he denied this. In the end I began to believe him, if only because my niece Dana turned out nothing like

Dee. For starters, Dee had a head full of messy blond curls she was constantly teasing out, whereas Dana had dark brown hair that she wore in long straight greasy strands. Her mother, Helena, was constantly begging Dana to wash her hair. Dana's refusal was a kind of stand, though against what none of us were entirely sure. I supported it, which endeared me to her, though it did me no favors with my brother or my sister-in-law.

And where Dee had always seemed to be at the center of attention, no matter the setting, Dana was perennially reserved. She spoke only if someone spoke to her first, and even then she often seemed eager to end interactions with adults. She abhorred eye contact, and she rolled her eyes at most things people said. In these ways, Dana reminded me more of myself, though it pains me to admit this because it would be a great tragedy for her to become anything like me at all.

But even though she looked nothing like Dee, and acted nothing like Dee, her presence always called my sister to mind. It's difficult to explain. When Dana was near me, my memories of Dee, and of our girlhood, seemed to float easily, almost heavenly, to the surface of my consciousness, where they became suddenly clearer, more accessible, even more honest, than they often were when I tried in vain to recall them on my own: lying in bed drunk, or staring at a data-entry form at work, or stuck in traffic on I-94. I don't know why, but I felt closest to Dee, or to what I had left of her, when I was near Dana. I never told anyone about this, maybe because it embarrassed me, or because it was too difficult to explain. I wondered if the same thing would happen with my youngest niece, Sophie, as she grew older, but though I loved Soph desperately, she did not bring Dee to mind the way Dana did.

Though it sounds strange, I was aware of this effect from the minute my niece was born. The night Helena went into labor, I hoped, prayed, even, that she would give birth to a boy. I'm ashamed to admit this, but I couldn't bear the thought of trying to love a girl child who was not Dee. But of course my "prayers" were neither heard nor answered, which I did not take personally, because I'd never been much of a believer. True faith is not a fair-weather practice. I, of all people, know that.

At the hospital fourteen years ago, when Pete handed the baby to me and I looked at her face, how unbelievably alien and ugly, the raw pink vulnerability of her, still wet with her mother's insides, I cried. And it wasn't just because she was a girl and not a boy, but also because I sensed that night, already, that I needed her. There is no word for the feeling of finding something you didn't even know you needed and realizing you've found it, that before, you had been just barely alive. I cried too because I understood then that we aren't even *born* unburdened: Already at birth we carry so much.

Perhaps more profoundly than any of us, Dana understood the gravity of our involvement with Thomas Alexander. No one in our family listened to her except maybe me, and I don't think even I heard what she wanted me to hear.

Pete and Helena had given her an iPhone at twelve. Not long after, she boasted an Instagram following of thousands, and she followed thousands more. Apparently, this was "typical" for people her age, or so she told me. I didn't know if all her followers were real. I'd read an article about bots which I sent to her, but she never responded. I knew many, maybe even most, of the people she followed were celebrities. One of these celebrities was Thomas Alexander. When she heard the news of our mother's plan to hire him, she scolded Pete and me and rolled her eyes. I was at dinner at Pete's when Dana tried to tell her father what she knew about the psychic.

"You have no idea how famous he is," she said. She looked to her little sister, Sophie, who was twelve, for confirmation.

Sophie bobbed her head. "He has, like, millions of followers."

"So?" Pete asked. "Why do I give a damn about his followers? That doesn't matter."

"No," Dana said. She made eye contact with me briefly, frowned, and then studied her food. "It does. Look at it this way: Followers are like money. The more you have, the more powerful you are."

I laughed at this, but Dana cut her eyes at me, glaring.

"Dana," Pete said. "Enough. It's already done. I don't want to hear about it."

I did want to hear about it, so after dinner, as I was on my way out, I nodded for Dana to walk me to my car. She mindlessly twirled the ends of her dark hair between her fingers. Dee hadn't had that habit, exactly, but the way Dana was doing it made me think of Dee.

"So what's the deal?" I asked her.

Dana looked past my right shoulder and into the street, where a group of boys were tossing a football. I hated the noise of them. I wondered if she did too. "I don't think you guys get it," she said.

"What do you mean?" I felt sometimes like Dana spoke in code purposefully, in order to frustrate us, though maybe it was just the years between us.

"Whatever he says, millions of people will hear it, and they will probably believe him." One of the boys threw the football in our direction, and it rolled toward Dana's feet. She kicked the ball back into the street, and the boys snorted and laughed. "That will be her story."

"I'm sure your father can write a nondisclosure agreement for us," I said. She shrugged. "That means—"

"I know what it means."

I raised my eyebrows at her.

"Okay. Still. What if *you* don't like what he says?"

"I've been doing this my whole life, babe. I've grown accustomed to hearing things I don't like," I told her. She put her hands on her hips. "I'll be fine. I promise."

She was unconvinced. "Just get *your* story straight," she said. "That's all I'm saying."

I once read that watching a video right after an event can overlay and alter the actual memory of the experience. I wondered if that was true for photos and stories too. Can looking at a picture of a moment replace the memory of the moment with what you see in the photo? What is the difference between the memory and the photo of the remembered moment? I don't think I know. (What do I remember of the moment Dee left me for good—Leif's hard hands on the sharp part of my cheekbones, the sour taste of my own saliva dripping from my open mouth, the sweet rush of wetness between my legs, Dee's face folding in on itself like a paper fan snapped shut, her small hand opening to show me an acid tab, the crush of a camera shuttering open and closed.) Could telling a different story of what happened replace your original memory of the event? I felt, after Dee disappeared, my memories from that summer beginning to drip and harden like stalactites forming in a dark cave. Dana didn't know it, but I'd spent most of my life guarding these fragile formations fiercely, even though I hated many of them. I was not eager to allow anyone to replace them—they were all I had left of Dee.

We'd been dating for a year and living together for two months when I first met Leif's brother, Erik. Though they had been close as kids, their relationship was strained that year because, at the age of seventeen, Erik had run away from their parents' house and revealed to Leif that he was gay. Leif had called Erik and asked if they could meet to talk. Erik proposed some seedy bar in Walker's Point, and Leif said he didn't want to go alone. I suspected he was using me as a buffer. I wanted a buffer too (though for what, exactly, I wasn't sure), so I asked Dee to come along. I was relieved when she said Frank was busy.

Leif wasn't particularly thrilled about Dee coming along, and though he acted like he didn't care, he told us he had no intention of spending the night babysitting. Dee narrowed her eyes at Leif from the backseat of his car, where she'd pulled her knees tight to her chest. Her shoes were on the seat, which Leif hated, but about which he said nothing.

"Okay, honey," she said. "We'll see who needs babysitting at the end of the night."

Erik was waiting for us outside the bar in Walker's Point. The highway overpasses bisected Milwaukee in odd ways, cutting off entire neighborhoods from one another. Walker's Point, for example, was hemmed in by the highway and the confluence of the Menomonee River, the Milwaukee River, and the Kinnickinnic River. This part of the city once was home to heavy industry, but at that time it was full of empty warehouses with their glass windows punched in. Since the sixties, Second Street in particular had become known for its gay bars. Some of the old warehouses were converted into clubs, but others had been torn down, leaving large empty lots full of gravel. The streets were poorly lit except for flashing Schlitz signs and the flickering neon signs for the clubs: La Cage, Club 219, M&M Club. Beautiful boys loitered outside bars they were too young to enter, and groups of men shared cigs on the curbs and blew kisses at honking cars as they passed. The smell of cheap weed hung thickly in the summer air. A boy, a child almost, was trying hard to talk to Erik, who was laughing and shooing the boy away.

"You good?" Leif asked his brother when we got close.

"I'm good," Erik said. "Go on," he told the boy, who huffed at us, hunched his shoulders, and walked to the bar across the street. "In your dreams!" Erik shouted to the boy's back.

"Your loss," the boy shouted over his shoulder.

Erik laughed and drew me into a tight hug. When he pulled away, he held my shoulders, keeping me at arm's length as he inspected. "Hello, gorgeous," he said.

I blushed hard, and I felt the heat of it when I put my hands up to my cheeks

"This is my sister, Dee," I told Erik. He took up her hand. I'd never seen two people love each other faster. Their gestures, almost instantly, became imbued with the confidence that they should and would love each other absolutely. I was initially a little jealous of their quick bond, and afraid that it diluted my own lifelong bond

with Dee. But what they had was too true to resent. Their friendship made me believe that probably, in another life, they had been
friends then too, and that maybe (God, how I hoped later that this
would be true) they would find each other again in other lives they
might lead in the future.

"I love you," Erik said to her as if saying something much more
banal, like *Nice to meet you.*

Dee laughed and squeezed his hand. "Okay," she said. She
threw her hands up. "I love you too."

Leif grunted and hugged his brother. He seemed uncomfortable with all the impromptu professions of love.

"I'm glad you made it," Erik said.

"Yeah, we'll see," Leif said.

Inside, there were only two other women, and they were both
behind the bar. I felt awkward and anxious until Erik bought us a
round of drinks and found a booth for us near a stage at the back of
the bar. It was a small place with a lot of heart and a lot of grunge;
there were sticky vinyl booths lining the walls, a tiled dance floor
in the center, a DJ booth, and a jukebox. It was obvious to me that
many drinks had been spilled here. Dancing was a priority. There
were fishbowls full of brightly colored condoms on the bar. A fish-
bowl was also something you could order to drink. The crown
jewel of this particular bar was a large horned devil bust that occasionally blew smoke from its nostrils onto the dance floor. This,
plus the cigarettes, turned the air thick and cloudy.

"Things should start up soon," Erik said.

I sipped my PBR; how was it already warm?

Whitney Houston filled the lulls in our conversation, and there
were many of them.

"You good?" Leif asked his brother again when we were seated.
Leif was shaking his knees like he was on speed. He might have

been on speed. I put my hand on his thigh, but he just squeezed it and then nudged it off. He wasn't the kind of man who liked to hold hands in public.

"I'm good," Erik said. "Sick of my job already, but c'est la vie."

Erik had gotten a job as an usher at Uihlein Hall downtown; he said he was mostly in it for the free shows. We didn't ask where he was living.

"I hear you there," Leif said. "Ambrosia's a shit hole."

"You still doing third shift?"

Leif nodded and sipped his beer.

"Amen," Erik said. He raised his glass.

"Makes me want to go back to school, you know?" Leif said.

Erik shook his head and tousled my curls. "School's for fools. What about you, beautiful?" he asked me.

"Just living the dream," I said.

And wasn't I? Leif and I had moved in together. School was almost out for the summer, and I'd taken a job at the Milwaukee Public Library erasing patrons' annotations from the library books. It was easy, mindless work, and I loved reading the sentences that had compelled a borrower to underline, or to add exclamation marks, or to write their own personal grief into the texts. *All is lost. Yes! Humanity is doomed. Unbelievable . . . No! Help . . .* And there was something satisfying about erasing all of it. Leif slept late into the day, and we spent lazy afternoons drinking pots of coffee and writing and making love and walking around the city aimlessly until our feet hurt. I felt my life peaking.

Erik shook his head at me like he knew. "Poets dating poets," he said. "I can't wait to see how this one ends."

I think I blushed again; I'd had the same thought when Leif and I had started dating.

"How about you, love?" Erik asked Dee. "What do you do?"

"Dee's a—" I said. She elbowed me in the ribs.

"Wait," Erik said. "Let me guess . . . you're a painter."

We all looked at him, surprised, and he grinned. He leaned across the booth and touched the side of Dee's neck gently, like he'd done it many times before, where there was a swatch of mint green paint dried on her skin. We all laughed. Erik did a fake flourish of a bow.

"I'd love to see your work," Erik said.

"I'm hardly a painter," Dee said. We had been raised to be humble. Even to consider oneself an artist, to our mother, was a kind of embarrassment. That was one reason why, as a young woman, I claimed the title of poet so adamantly and perhaps so prematurely. I wanted to defy that humility.

"She's really talented," I said. Dee shook her head, blushing a little.

"I also dabble," Erik admitted.

"You do not," Leif said. He laughed at his brother.

Erik frowned at him. "What do you know about me?" he said. He punched Leif in the arm. "You don't know shit."

"I'd love to see your work too," Dee interjected, probably sensing a bad shift in the conversation.

"You're an angel," he said. I didn't disagree.

The lights dimmed, and the devil blew smoke from its nose. Leif looked around. "Seems empty," he said.

Erik pulled out a copy of a newspaper I'd never seen before called *The Wisconsin Light* and threw it down on the table. He tapped his finger on the headline: "Slew of Disappearances in Walker's Point Leaves Community Concerned, Police Apathetic." He leaned in toward the center of the table and motioned for us to do the same. "People are disappearing. Ask anybody around here."

Leif snapped to attention; his recent poems were very much interested in conspiracy theories. He'd affected a constant air of paranoia. Although maybe he had always been that way. (When we'd moved in together, he'd wanted to buy a gun. That was our first argument in the apartment. I lost.)

"See that board?" Erik pointed at a corkboard near the entrance of the bar. "Those are all men who've gone missing recently." There were about fifteen faces on the board, each with a list of identity stats: height, weight, eye and hair color, tattoos.

"But the police know about it?" Dee asked.

Erik snorted. "They say we're a 'transient' group of people; we come and go so often that it's hard to tell the difference between someone who's gone missing and someone who's left town. They said there's no law against picking up and starting a new life somewhere else."

Leif frowned. "Mom and Dad think you're missing," he said.

"Already with that?" Erik looked at an invisible watch on his wrist. "It's so early," he whined.

"I'll get the next round of drinks," I said.

I went to the bar, put our order in, and then went to look at the pictures on the board. Some of the men were very young, under twenty, maybe; many of them were Black men.

"You missing someone, baby?" the bartender called to me. I turned back to her. She had set our beers in a line at the edge of the bar.

I shook my head. "I was just looking," I told her. I collected the sweating glasses.

She eyed me and ran her hands through her heavily moussed hair. "Some of those boys . . . those men. You know, they were sick, or are sick. But a lot of times they won't ask for help, you know, when they need it."

This felt like an invitation to a longer conversation I didn't want to have. Instead, I only nodded, tipped her generously, and carried the drinks back to the booth.

"You get lost?" Leif asked me. Erik punched him again.

Onstage, a drag queen in a platinum-blond wig and a red se-quined dress was singing. This was a ruse, because soon the song faded into a dance number during which the dancer began to tear off layer after layer of panty hose. This pleased the crowd.

"Dragstrip," Erik yelled at us over the crowd. "You gotta strip from girl to boy."

At the end of the performance, there were at least ten pairs of panty hose littered across the stage, and a man danced in a tiny pair of underwear. The crowd cheered. There were probably six or seven different numbers and at least that many rounds of drinks. At one point, Erik took me and Dee backstage, and he put a thick layer of makeup on us. He glued fake eyelashes on top of my real ones, and when I blinked, I felt like a doe. I felt like Dee. I thought maybe we were the same person; maybe we could blend into one, more superior woman. Dee's eyelashes were so long they fluttered against my face when she kissed me. But when I looked at myself in the mirror, I didn't look like anyone I knew. And Leif agreed. When he saw me, he spewed beer across the booth. "Jesus, Peg, if I go home with you looking like that, we'll both get arrested."

"Oh, stop," Erik said. "She looks gorgeous."

I pursed my lips at Leif. He cupped my face and then withdrew his hand, which was now sticky with foundation and blush.

"Yuck," he said. He wiped the makeup on the booth. He was flushed, ruddy from his eight beers, and sweating.

Erik got onstage then. He was three sheets to the wind for sure, but who wasn't? His lips were too close the mike, so there was a lot of feedback. Mostly, people kept dancing.

"I just want to say I'm so happy my big brother is here tonight." Clapping, cooing, aw-ing. "And his beautiful girlfriend. And Dee, my soul mate. I love you all so much. And Leif? I just want you to know I'm so proud of you, man. So proud. Yeah. You're following your dreams. I couldn't be prouder. Guys, my brother's a poet. And he's really talented. Leif, would you read us some poems?" I got embarrassed for Leif, because I knew he was just drunk enough to agree. The setting wasn't right, though, which was putting it mildly. A small chorus started up. Erik and his friends chanted, *Poems, poems, poems*. The music was still loud, and some people were patiently ignoring Erik. Leif staggered to his feet. I put my head in my heads. Onstage, Leif dug his hands deep into his pockets and pulled out a wad of papers. It was just like him to have a bunch of poems on his body at all times. He said he liked to keep poems in his pockets while he worked at the chocolate factory because they helped him remember he was human. He was swaying, but it wasn't to the music. Someone turned the music down a notch, and there was some grumbling, but those who wanted to keep dancing did. I suspected everyone was listening at least halfway.

Leif chose to read a poem about my pussy. Although he'd be mad if he knew I said that. There were other aspects to the poem, it's true, but none so prominent as my pussy. It was a long poem. No one booed or threw anything, but someone turned the music up incrementally, and people began talking quietly over him. The devil blew more smoke from its nose. The clouds of smoke wound around the dancers' legs and hid their feet. The men were floating. My face was as red as a tomato; I could feel the color. Dee laughed and laughed. I wanted to live and die inside her laugh. I stumbled to the bar and ordered a tequila shot; the bartender looked ready to refuse me. A man approached me while I was buzzing from the tequila and licking lime and salt from the corners of my mouth.

"You've got a really nice ass," he said to me. "Like perfect." I swayed. The bartender rolled her eyes. I suppose in any other context, I would have been irate. Maybe I was too drunk, or maybe I felt it was more honest or less loaded, because it was coming from a gay man. Was it?

"Thanks," I said. I leaned in to see him better. He had very long eyelashes; they reminded me of Dee. I put my face next to his, and he didn't pull away. I brushed his nose with my own, back and forth, and it tickled, and I waited for him to blink, to feel the brush of those lashes against my own, but before he did, I felt a hand on my arm. Leif.

"What the hell's this?" Leif asked.

The man eyed Leif, up and down, up and down; he grinned a toothy grin. "Your girlfriend's got a really nice ass," he said. He craned his neck over Leif's shoulder. "So do you."

"I know," Leif said. I swayed. "I mean, I know about her."

The bartender had her hand on the phone.

"What's it to you, anyway?" Leif asked.

"Just making sure she knows," the man said.

"She knows," Leif said.

The man turned to me. "Now you know," he said.

"I knew," I said.

And then I threw up into one of the fishbowls full of condoms.

Leif and Erik sat me down in one of the booths, and I tried to get less dizzy. The more I thought about it, the dizzier I got. Everywhere I looked, the smoke swirled. Dee plopped down beside me and put a cool, damp piece of paper towel on my forehead.

"I knew I'd be the babysitter," she said.

I stuck my tongue out at her, and my stomach somersaulted. "Don't," I said. "Please." She shrugged.

Around us, there were men dancing, and men in dresses parading on the stage, and men with their hands deep into other men's pants. In the booth next to ours, Leif and Erik were having a conversation that sounded like the chorus of a song; they kept saying the same thing over and over.

"I've missed Mom," Erik was saying. "It's not that. It's not that."

"Well, she's worried. Real worried. I think you oughta see both of them, and I think you oughta explain yourself."

"Explain myself? They won't understand. You know that."

"You told me."

"Yeah. Do you understand?" Erik's voice wavered like, even drunk, he was afraid to ask. I imagined a man on a tightrope strung between skyscrapers. Leif said nothing for a long time. I was dizzy, spinning circles in a big green field with my eyes closed.

"No," he admitted.

The circles stopped. The lights came on. I blinked into the fluorescence. A bar with the lights on is a real sobering sight: the grime, the garbage, the pallid faces, the melting makeup, the sweat on the backs of necks, the stains from decades or more of vomit. Piles of sheer panty hose lay coiled on the stage like soft slippery skin just shed. Bar close. Dee helped me up from the booth and let me wobble into her. I wasn't the only wobbler. Erik and Leif clung to each other, and the weight each put on the other's body seemed to destabilize them both. They looked like little boys running a three-legged sack race. The bartender ushered us out; Erik kissed the one I had spoken to earlier in the night. She, like many other people, it seemed, was smitten with him.

When we emerged outside, I wished we hadn't. Two squad cars had their high-powered spotlights on, and they shone harshly into our eyes. Some of the men cried out and shielded their eyes with jackets or shirts. A hot flash of pain lit up my brain and I threw up on the sidewalk. The cops were shouting at us from their megaphones: *Hickory dickory dock, some young blond is sucking my cock. You're all sick fucking faggots!* This inspired laughter from some other men who were leaving an old blue-collar Polish bar at the same time. Down the block, some of these men started throwing small stones and bits of garbage at our backs as we filed away from the bar. The cops kept their lights on our faces. Easy targets. Erik ran down the street and shoved one of these men, who then swung hard at Erik but missed, probably because he was drunk but also because he was out of shape. Leif ran over, and before I could stop her, Dee followed. Where had she gotten this astonishing store of courage? Erik saw Dee charging after Leif. One of her sandals fell off, but she paid no mind. Erik grinned at her. The men noticed Dee too and seemed, momentarily, to lose focus. Leif took the opportunity. He punched the guy who had tried to hit Erik. The whole group mobbed Leif then, and a few more men from the club started to run over to help, so the cops got out of their car and started prodding the groups apart with their billy clubs. *Who wants to sober up in holding? Move it!* The energy in the air seemed to fizzle. There was some half-hearted spitting. The cops jangled handcuffs at the men who wouldn't quit, ushering them apart. The sound of old engines turning over and over. Wheels on gravel. For my part, the more I tried to see, the less I could make out; the storefronts began to blur into the streetlamps.

Dee and I sat down on the curb. She combed my hair with her fingers. I shivered, blinked into the loudness of the night, and panicked.

"I can't see anything," I told her. "I think I'm blind."

"You're perfectly fine," Dee said. "Look at me."

She took my face between her hands and pulled my eyes wide like she knew what she was looking for: obvious signs of blindness. Then she gently closed each eye and kissed both eyelids. I imagined her lipstick leaving rose-colored stains. I leaned in to her for a second.

"Everything's all there," she said.

"Thanks, Doc." I shoved her away.

Leif and Erik came to sit down next to us. Leif lit a cigarette that we all shared. Dee coughed her way through it, and we teased her. She was a sport about it. She always was. The crowds were thinning out. Leif once told me he'd loved to carry Erik around as a baby. Leif was eleven when they brought Erik home from the hospital. He toted Erik all around the house, supporting his soft head the way his ma had shown him, and he gave his baby brother the grand tour of their little apartment. *Here's the fish tank; when you're old enough to pinch, you can feed them. Here's the kitchen; when you're old enough to chew, you can eat Cocoa Pebbles. Here's the living room; when you're old enough to crawl, you can wrestle me.*

Erik's nose was bloodied. "Sorry," he said to us. "That's never happened before."

I suspected that wasn't true. I put my hand on his knee. "I'm still glad we came," I said to him. I hoped Leif would say something that would support this sentiment.

"I wish," Leif started. He swallowed two times. "I wish you were different."

Erik put his head between his knees. Dee rubbed the back of his neck.

Sometimes I wished Dee had been different too. She was twelve when she began to grow tiny budlike breasts. She itched them mindlessly when it was just the two of us. My own breasts had come in at thirteen, and by fourteen, they were already about as large as they'd ever get—the girls at school called me a washboard. Dee's breasts outgrew mine quickly, and this, among other things, was part of the reason people always thought she was older. She also had an air of confidence about her, which, later, older men would like. When I tried to adopt this affect, it seemed to scare them away. Apparently, it was sexy on her.

Once we were waiting for Peter to pick us up from the local pool. We had towels wrapped around our waists, and we were sitting on top of a picnic table with our feet dangling on the bench. I stretched out long on the wood and let the sun warm my stomach. Dee tried to tickle my ribs, but I shoved her hand away. There was a group of boys riding their bikes in circles around the parking lot. It was obvious to me, even from minimal observation, that they were working themselves up to do something stupid. At the time, I figured it was some dumb trick on their bikes that would land at least one of them in the hospital. But when they pulled their bikes up to our picnic table, I knew immediately what they wanted. I had a hard time deciding what age they were—fifteen, maybe sixteen, definitely older than we were. The leader of the group was jostled forward by the others, and he dramatically wiped his forehead with the back of his hand.

"Hey," he said stupidly.

I said nothing, and tried to look everywhere except at the boys, but Dee stuck her neck out as if to say, *Go on* . . . Where had she learned these postures?

"Oh," he said. "I just wanted to say I like your boobs."

Dee rolled her eyes. The boys behind him hooted and whistled. I could tell by his reddening face that he had not executed the original plan. Dee had scared him—caused him to veer from his original course. She turned her head slightly toward me and started twirling my wet hair between her fingers. I shivered. The boys retreated like a losing army. It was as if she did not believe men could hurt her, or maybe she just acted that way. Somehow she made men feel like she was always out of reach, as if she contained many secret parts of herself that no one could control.

Article IV. Relevance and Its Limits

RULE 401. TEST FOR RELEVANT EVIDENCE

Evidence is relevant if (a) it has any tendency to make a fact more or less probable than it would be without the evidence; and (b) the fact is of consequence in determining the action.

I was fired from my last job at the law library, in part because I often missed weeks of work without explanation, and also because my boss suspected I was stealing books. Though, as he put it when he fired me, "We're not *accusing* you of anything per se, but we are letting you go." He would have been right to accuse me, because I did steal books, compulsively and without remorse. Rumors of my kleptomania followed me during my subsequent search for work. Henry, the last man I'd loved, had secured that job for me, and my dismissal from it was one among many reasons he cited for ultimately ending things between us.

The first book I ever stole, a tattered copy of Edith Hamilton's *Mythology: Timeless Tales of Gods and Heroes,* was from UWM's library. It happened like this. It was a few days after the anniversary of Dee's disappearance: She had been gone four years at that point. I was having a very bad day. I woke up from a terrible night of sleep during which I was unable to tell if I was awake or asleep but all the while certain I was having nightmares, which could have just been bad thoughts, or memories, of the summer Dee disappeared. (It was common for memories of that summer to play on a never-ending film loop in my mind even when I wasn't interested in viewing them. I attributed this phenomenon to my efforts, immediately after Dee disappeared, to petrify these memories in my mind and body.) I went to work feeling angry and anxious, and prone to rehearsing my list of reasons I hated my job and my life more generally. I was pushing a large cart of books to be returned to their shelves when I noticed Edith Hamilton's book. I am certainly no mythology buff—in fact, though I once tried to get interested in it on account of Dee's passion for the subject, the material honestly bored me. I never could remember the names or the stories associated with these names, which I know seems crazy, given their oral nature, but I just never loved the stories the way other people did. So much slaughter, and incest, and rape, and suicide. Anyway, one day in middle school, Dee stumbled upon Edith Hamilton's book, which she'd found abandoned on the school steps. Though she would have happily returned it, there was no name written on the inside cover and no indication that it was a library book. So Dee kept this tattered copy, and for years it seemed she brought it everywhere with her. She became obsessed with the book, and of course, that was how she began to call me Pegasus, and how the nickname took off with some of the rest of the family as well. She told me to imagine I was a beautiful winged horse.

"But what are my powers?" I asked her.

"What do you mean?" she whined, already annoyed with me. "You can fly!"

"But what else?"

She humphed and thought, and then her eyes went wide. "You can make magical springs appear with your hooves. Oh, and you're an inspiration to the muses," she said. I shrugged, not particularly satisfied, but the nickname stuck. Later, she would tell me that my mother was Medusa, and I liked that, and we both laughed.

Anyway, when I saw the book on the cart, I grabbed it and rushed into the nearest bathroom, where I picked off the bar code. I threw this bar code into the toilet and flushed it down. Then I hid the book in the front pocket of my sweatshirt until later in the day, when I had the chance to put it in my bag. After I stole that book, I got into a bit of a habit. If I saw a book that reminded me of Dee, I would take it in the bathroom, scratch off its bar code, and take it home to my apartment on the East Side, where I added it to my sad illicit library. Sometimes the book would not remind me of anything at all, but I still felt I had to bring it home with me. I piled these stolen books in gravity-defying stacks inside my apartment, and I never, ever opened them once I brought them home.

After Henry got me the job at Marquette, I began stealing law books. These were the books I did open. I tried to study them at home, particularly Graham C. Lilly's *An Introduction to the Law of Evidence,* but they were so dry and inscrutable. I felt I needed to steal more books to help me explain the ones I'd already stolen. It was a vicious cycle, and I guess I got careless. People whispered. I wasn't embarrassed. Who knows why they didn't follow up— maybe out of respect for Henry, or maybe because I was too pitiful to punish. Either way, by the time I was fired, I had amassed hundreds of dark green and burgundy law books.

Shortly after I was fired and Henry and I split for good, I was watching a movie when Dana called. It was late. I saw her name flash on my phone, and I felt a sickening lurch of fear. I grabbed the phone and pressed pause on the movie.

"What's wrong?" I said. I mashed the earpiece against the side of my face, fearful that I wouldn't be able to hear her.

"I need . . ." She stopped. "I need a ride."

"Drop me a pin," I said. "I'm coming."

I followed the directions to the pin and found myself west of the city in an unfinished housing development. I parked the car in front of a locked gate. A harsh floodlight flickered on, and the blinking red light of a rotating security camera shone in the dark. A danger sign posted on the gate depicted a prone stick person being electrocuted. Beyond the gate, the skeletons of half-built homes were scattered across several acres of grassy knolls. I called Dana, but she didn't answer. I couldn't get out of the car. I kept my hands on the steering wheel. In the distance, I thought I saw a flare of blue light erupting from a pipe. Another flare of light flashed on the horizon; I couldn't have imagined it twice. I fixed my gaze beyond the empty houses and tried to see where the light was coming from.

When Dana rapped on the car window with her knuckles, I spooked. She had the hood of her sweatshirt pulled tight over her face, so at first I wasn't even sure it was her. When she turned to look back the way she'd come, I could barely see the outline of her face. I unlocked the car door, and she threw herself into the passenger seat and then relocked the doors herself. Her clothes were wet, and water dripped from her fingertips.

We agreed that she could stay at my place, because she didn't want to face her parents that night, but that I'd have to call her father. Pete was harried and short with me, as if the whole thing were somehow my fault, but he was okay with her staying over as long as she came back first thing in the morning.

While she showered, I tried to tidy up the place. This mostly involved throwing shit away: empty wine bottles, candles burned down to their last grimy, unlightable layer of wax, cartons of cigarettes, takeout containers. Then I tried to shove all of Dee's files into my makeshift study. When I'd first moved in, I had hoped to use the small room to write, but I never bought a desk, and over time, I stopped writing completely. Until I started writing this, I hadn't written in over two decades. I housed all the files on Dee's case in the study: transcripts of the interviews we'd conducted, the various iterations of her missing-persons report, the paltry *Journal* articles that ran and were mostly ignored. I'd absorbed Ma's files when we'd moved her into the Lutheran Home, as well as the ones that Pete no longer wanted at his house. Now I was the only keeper, and the files had begun to spill out into the living room.

I was still trying to shove the files back into the study when Dana came out of the bathroom. Her hair was wet but combed now, and she was wearing a pair of my pajamas. We'd hung her wet clothes on the backs of the kitchen chairs. She seemed calmer.

"What's all that?" she asked, motioning at the files.

"Nothing, nothing," I said. I shoved a box of papers past the threshold of the study and shut the door with effort. "Come on," I told her. "Come sit with me." She nodded. We sat on the couch together. She pulled her knees into her chest. Her feet were still pink from the heat of the shower.

"I can't swim," she whispered to me as if this explained everything.

"Oh, you know how," I protested. I remembered summers when she and Soph had splashed for hours in the shallows of Lake Michigan.

"Not well," she said.

"We can get you lessons."

She glared at me like I was missing the point. Probably I was.

"There is an old quarry out there," she said. "But a long time ago, they filled it all with water. It's deep. Miles deep, I think. I mean, that's what the boys said. I was afraid . . . I mean, the boys said they were going to throw us in. So I kept thinking about floating down to the bottom. How long it would take to sink. I felt like if I fell in, I would just be floating down to the bottom, like . . . forever."

I had the urge then to hide her. I didn't say anything back to her for a long time. A bus sputtered in the street below my apartment. We did not look at each other.

"What boys?" I asked her finally.

She shrugged like she was sick of the whole conversation, though we'd only just begun. Like I'd disappointed her with the wrong kind of question. I was embarrassed.

"It doesn't matter," she said. "Where's Henry?"

"What?" I said stupidly. I was trying to buy myself time to think. I hadn't told my family yet that Henry had finally left me for good. I couldn't bear to hear their objections. Pete especially was concerned that I'd end up alone, so he'd thrown his unequivocal support behind Henry, even though he'd barely known the guy. Besides, Pete had never understood that I had always, since Dee disappeared, been alone.

"I mean, why aren't you with him?"

"Henry and I," I started, and then stopped. "Hey, I'm tired. Okay?" She nodded. I gave her a pillow from my own bed and tossed a knit throw over her. When I leaned down to kiss her forehead, she squirmed away and shoved her face into the crack between the couch cushions. I kissed her wet hair. She pulled the blanket over her head.

In the morning, I found her sitting cross-legged in stacks of Dee's case files. She had begun to organize them.

"Stop," I said.

"Why?" she asked. "This stuff is a mess. Everything is all over the place."

"I don't care."

She looked up at me. Her hair was messy from sleeping on it wet, and her eyes were dull and still a little sleepy. I felt for a moment like we were in some twisted Christmas-morning nightmare—a child in her pajamas surrounded by stacks of missing-persons reports.

"Get dressed," I said. The sharpness in my voice made her spine go a little straight and I regretted it. She didn't mind, though. She was probably used to it from Pete. "We have to go."

In the car back to her house, she harassed me about letting her come back to go through the files. She said her dad never let her look at anything related to Dee. She felt she had a right to know. "I'm old enough now," she told me confidently. I didn't say anything. There was no minimum age that would make Dee's case fathomable. I was forty-eight and still couldn't understand the whole of it. "Plus," she kept going, "I could help you."

"Help me how?" I eyed her.

She shook her head at me, amazed. "I told you. You need to be ready."

I knew Pete had done his best to keep the details of Dee's case from his girls, but as these things go, it had only made Dana more invested in discovering these details. I didn't know if keeping the story from the girls was truly for their benefit, or if it was for Pete's own peace of mind. I guessed he needed to compartmentalize, which I understood. But even when they were young, they sensed more than Pete presumed.

One night I was babysitting them when Dana brought it up. Dana was seven and Sophie was five. The girls had refused to fall asleep alone, so I climbed in Dana's bed and sandwiched myself between them, one under each arm. We haggled for a while about the number of books to be read, and by the time we'd settled on three and the girls had made their selections, Sophie was almost asleep. By the end of book two, they were both asleep. I carried

Sophie to her own bed, and I was just about to leave the room when Dana bolted up.

"Auntie Peg?" she cried.

"I'm here," I said. "Close your eyes."

I went to sit with her on the bed. I reached for one of the books we hadn't read yet and started to open it, but Dana put her small hand on the cover so I couldn't. She shook her head. I could see her forming the words in her mind before she said them.

"What if I disappear?"

My mouth went dry.

"What do you mean, baby?" I said. "You're not going any-where."

"But what if I do? Where will I go? What will happen to me? What will happen to Soph?" Across the room, Dana's sister was sound asleep on her back. One of her arms was flung above her head. Even in the dark, I could see her small hands twitching in her dreams.

"Baby." I tried to keep my voice light. "You're not going to dis-appear."

"But Auntie Dee did."

I chewed on the inside of my cheek and waited and waited for the metallic taste of my own blood to flood my mouth. "She didn't disappear."

"Daddy says Auntie Dee disappeared and she never came home."

"He told you that?"

She shook her head. A string of hair near her neck was plas-tered with sleep sweat against her skin. "I heard him say it."

"She didn't disappear," I repeated.

"What happened to her? Where is she?"

I paused. "I don't know," I told her. "We don't know."

Dana cried, "That's disappearing. I know it is." She wrung her hands. "I want Mama." She began to cry louder, and I worried it would wake Sophie.

I climbed back into the bed and got under the covers with her. I hugged her tight against my chest, where she was working herself up to cry louder. I tried to muffle her against me. "I know, baby," I tried to say. "I know. You're not going anywhere. I promise."

Dana pulled away from me. She put her hands on my shoulders to keep a distance between us. Her eyes were massive and still pooling hot tears. "You don't know that," she said.

And that was the truth.

The exhibition was sparsely attended. I felt relieved I'd made it and ashamed that, when Dee had asked me to come a few hours earlier, I'd considered skipping. The Milwaukee Art Museum had selected student work from five different colleges in southeastern Wisconsin. Dee was ecstatic that they'd chosen two of her onion paintings to represent Mount Mary's student artists. I didn't particularly want to go because we were in the midst of a demoralizingly late-spring storm—heavy, slushy sleet blew from the lake and turned the streets and the sidewalks into slick death traps. It was cold, wet, and dark; winter was making one last desperate fight for its life. I was just as content to stay in my apartment, drinking day-old red wine and reading until I had to pick Leif up. But Dee worked her magic on me, as usual. She called me an hour before doors opened. *I need this. I need you, Pegasus, please. Please* without the question. That was one of her signatures.

All the student artists wandered around awkwardly holding sparkling water and complimenting one another's pieces; it was painfully obvious to me who they were. A few parents and friends milled around; most of them affected interested, engaged expressions.

The gallery itself had the feel of a great open mouth. Sleet thrashed the windows, creating a loud, frantic atmosphere despite the relative silence of the attendees. I felt my pulse with my thumb, but the beats were too quick to count. I scanned the place for Dee. Even from a distance, I could tell there was an energy suck in the room, that there was a leader or two toward whom everyone had trained their attention. I knew one of these people would be Dee.

As I got closer, I saw the other one was Erik. They had their arms around each other's waists so tightly they looked like con-joined twins. I was surprised by their closeness, embarrassed by it. They were aware of how closely the rest of the group was watch-ing them. Throwing their beautiful heads back and laughing with their throats shining up to the ceiling, dramatic flourishes of their wrists, hands cupped to each other's ears. A performance. I almost didn't want to say hi, because I sensed that my presence would alter this dynamic, change it, and something would be lost. But Dee caught me watching from a distance. She broke away from Erik and rushed to me. He followed. She hugged me and her body was warm against mine, cozy from the heat of Erik's body pressed against hers.

"I didn't know you invited Erik," I said when she pulled away.

Dee blushed. "You said you weren't sure you could make it."

"I said I'd be here." She frowned. It wasn't what I meant to say. I added, "Hey—congratulations, babe." I tried to shake the edge in my voice, but I could tell it had already affected Dee. "I'm so proud of you." She nodded at me and let herself get led away by some fellow students who wanted to talk technique. Erik patted my arm. I shirked his touch, but he stayed close nonetheless.

"How's Leif?" he asked me. I glanced at him. His expression seemed genuine. I scanned the gallery for Dee's paintings and be-gan to make my way toward them. Erik followed. He had a skittery energy—he moved like Leif but more concentrated and frantic, like he felt he had no time at all.

"He's okay," I told him. "He's fine."

"He's crazy about you," he said. I didn't take my eyes off Dee's paintings. They hung side by side, two purple onions, which in the stores they call red onions, though ever since Dee started painting them, I've thought of them as purple. In one piece, the onion was fully intact and floating against a dark green background; in the other, the onion was splayed in half on a green countertop.

I noticed Erik watching me. He was waiting for a reply. I nodded.

He went on, "Like, really crazy. I've never seen him like this before."

"What do you mean? Like what?" I said.

"Like . . . in love."

"Oh, stop. I'm sure he's been in love before."

"No," he said. He leaned in to me. I didn't want to turn to him, so I kept staring at Dee's paintings. "This time is the real deal. Don't you think I can tell? I know him. It's like you with Dee. I'm sure you'd be able to tell if she was in love."

I thought on that. Would I? My mother always said when you're on the outside, you can never know what goes on between two people in a relationship. I very much agreed with that sentiment, and I also wondered if we could ever truly *know* what goes on in our own relationships. Given that the bonds with even our most beloved contain such unknowns, such gaps, such vast spaces of inaccessibility, what can we ever truly know about those smallest of spaces where we overlap and come together?

"Do you think Dee's in love?" I asked him.

His face took on a pained expression. I felt awkward for asking.

"With . . . with this Frank guy?" He said the name like it tasted bad. "As I'm sure you've guessed, he's a phase. I think she's trying to impress you. And between you and me . . ." He hesitated, and I made a gesture like, *go on*. "Don't tell her I said so, but he's an absolute fucking nightmare." This was the most pointed Erik had ever been to me. I wanted to know what he knew, but just then two guys brushed by us. One of them checked Erik with his shoulder and muttered something I couldn't hear.

Erik's body took on a charged energy. He made himself bigger, which was a considerable feat given that he was already a tall man. Though he was quite thin, he had the ability, under certain circumstances, to grow and to loom. I felt myself shrink in comparison.

"What did you just say?" Erik shouted into the back of the kid's head.

The kid had a baseball cap on backward and a stiff polo with large Tommy Hilfiger logos on the sleeves. He turned around to look at Erik. He drove his eyes up and down Erik like a steamroller flattening a massive mound of dirt. He smirked. "I didn't say anything."

"I heard you." Erik's voice echoed through the gallery. People began to turn their attention to us. My cheeks were hot. I checked my pulse again. "I heard you say something about my friend's painting." He was shouting. Some people began to leave through the wide-open doors—out into the disgusting Milwaukee night. I wished I could go too.

"Come on, man," the kid said. His smirk was fading. "I didn't say anything. You heard wrong."

"You better apologize to my friend," Erik said. "Dee! Dee!" he shouted across the gallery. More people started leaving. The kid's friend took a step away from him. "You better fucking apologize," Erik said again.

"Or what?" The kid laughed in dry spurts. "Are you going to fight me, you fucking fairy?" The kid's friend took a second step back. A big betrayal that he'd hear about later. Dee rushed forward, and I watched the kid become a different person once she was in his purview. I felt sick. His eyes took on a dumb glaze.

"What's this?" Dee said. She looked at me desperately, trying to take stock of the situation. I looked away. Erik took a step toward the kid, but Dee moved in front of him.

"Apologize," Erik said again.

The kid was ignoring Erik now and staring at Dee, who'd planted herself firmly between the two men. He shrugged heavily, like they'd only been arguing about what the Brewers' chances were that year. "Sorry," the kid said. He walked away.

"What the hell. Come on," Dee said. Her face was flushed and shining. She shoved Erik playfully. "Let's get a drink."

She tugged on Erik, who had turned back to her paintings and who didn't seem ready to stop looking.

I don't remember anything else from that night. What bar did we go to? How late did we stay up? Did we talk about Frank? Did we talk about the city whose seams had been, or were always, unraveling rapidly? What songs did Erik and Dee sing together while we walked back to my apartment in Riverwest? Did our fingers get numb from the cold? Were Erik and Dee there with me, laughing and laughing, when Leif came home from work?

Are you ever afraid of how much you've forgotten? Entire days slip by—the contents of which could just as easily have been a dumb drama or a sitcom or an inane advertisement—with not a single discernible moment to hold on to. You don't even know what you've lost unless you're like me, and then every day you think about how much might be gone, how much you wish you still had, how difficult it is to mourn memories that don't even exist.

think my parents blamed me for what they perceived as Dee's excessive promiscuity, because I was the older sister, and I was supposed to be a good model for her. I was supposed to set *standards*. But the truth was that I was as shocked as they were by some of her behavior. I was especially baffled by her early preoccupation with sex, or maybe, more aptly, her preoccupation with her own sexuality, though in front of her, I did my best to hide this. In fact, I often made an effort to seem much more knowledgeable than I really was.

Once, when I was a freshman in high school and Dee was in seventh grade, I came home from school to find her sitting on our porch stoop with her face flushed pink. Her bike, a pale blue Schwinn our father had bought her for her twelfth birthday, was lying on its side by her feet. Later, when she moved into her dorm at Mount Mary, that bike was stolen. Dee mourned it for weeks. She never had the chance to buy another one.

I sat down next to her. Her thigh was warm against mine. I pressed in to it. She smiled at me conspiratorially. She was drinking a glass of Ovaltine and shoveling popcorn into her mouth. I reached into the plastic bowl for a handful. I tossed a few kernels in her hair, and she pretended to be annoyed.

Then she turned to me seriously. "Do you know what orgasms are?" she asked. I didn't have time to hide my surprise.

"Sure," I said confidently, though I'd only read about them in books, or heard about them on TV and in movies, and I wasn't convinced at the time that they existed for women. Once while reading a graphic sex scene, I'd reached into my underwear and been surprised to find a filmy wetness there. I'd since made a few half-hearted attempts at masturbating, but I had yet to experience anything miraculous beyond agitation.

I hadn't told Dee any of this. She nodded at me like she knew, though.

"Well, Nicole told me that she had one when she was riding her bike on a gravel road," Dee said.

I eyed the bike at her feet. "Uh-huh," I said. "And?"

"She said it was the best thing she's ever felt. Ever." Dee whispered the last word, which I found a little creepy. She tossed her head at the bike and then kicked the wheel so the spokes spun thin shadows on the concrete. "So I gave it a try too."

I felt the need to laugh, because I was suddenly uncomfortable in my skin. Or maybe I was just more aware of it than I'd ever been. Everything on me felt electrically charged, like I could shock anything I touched. I thought about how our comforters would spark with static charge, bright bolts of light in the dark, when we shook them out at night. I moved my leg away from Dee's. She didn't register it. She just kept kicking the wheel of her bike.

"Did it work?" I asked her.

Dee shook her head. "I couldn't find any gravel roads."

I nodded. "Did Nicole also tell you that you can lose your virginity if you ride your bike too much?"

Dee's eyes widened. I'd read this in a book, though I didn't believe it.

"Really?"

I shrugged. "Maybe," I told her. "Why? Do you want to lose your virginity to a bike?"

We laughed. She threw the rest of her popcorn at me.

When I finally did lose my own virginity, and I was shocked at the sheer force required to break inside me, I remembered this moment. It became unfathomable to me that some women could lose their virginity to something as gentle as a bumpy bike ride, when it took so much effort on the part of the boy, and involved so much pain, for me to lose mine. At the height of this pain, when the boy was finally inside me, all I could think about was the pretty pale blue of Dee's new bike, and those spokes spinning as she kicked the wheel absentmindedly with her bare feet.

The protestors in front of the now vacant lot at 924 North Twenty-fifth Street began to thin when most of the cameras left. The news crews went to stake out spots at General Mitchell International Airport, where famed psychic Thomas Alexander would be arriving shortly. The media had never been interested in the protestors anyway; they had been interested in the protestors' tangential relationship to the psychic. NPR was barely interested. The protestors were asking community leaders to come out and support their efforts.

But a lot of people had forgotten about the serial killer altogether, and even more had forgotten about the young men he'd killed. It had been easy for people to forget, because most people didn't know who those men had been. After the arrest, one man's sister said, "They could put *these* boys on the front of *Newsweek, Time,* and everything to show that these boys were real. If it wasn't for these boys, he wouldn't even be existing."

But the serial killer did exist. He persisted in his existence, and in death, he became truly famous: the Milwaukee Cannibal, they called him on episodes of shows like *Truly Terrifying People.*

"Now, isn't it odd that the majority of his victims were Black or Brown boys?" one of the protesters asked an NPR reporter. "You reporters have all kinds of reasons for this. None of those reasons have anything to do with the relationship between the police and the communities where these men lived in. Nobody wants to hear that story. And that story certainly won't be told on these tours, especially not right now."

The group put out a statement requesting that the mayor stop the show. The mayor's office declined to comment.

When I typed Thomas Alexander's name into Google, his baby face shone in a strip of headshots at the top of my browser. He had wispy blond hair, pearly teeth, and the upper body of a yogi. He probably could have been a model or an actor. I stared into his eyes—they were a different color in almost every picture: ultraviolet purple, bright blue, hazel. Maybe he had a rainbow of differently colored contacts in his medicine cabinet. Beneath his photos were hundreds of links to news articles about celebrities who'd used his services to contact dead loved ones. I noticed a link to his website, which was a flashy page full of glowing testimonials from celebrities. He said he was a medium, a clairvoyant, and a medical intuitive. According to his bio he was twenty.

Thomas Alexander had garnered attention most recently for predicting the death of some B-list actor. The actor's wife begged her husband to do a reading with Thomas Alexander. During the session, Thomas Alexander contacted the actor's dead grandmother, who said she wished she'd been at her grandson's wedding. The actor rubbed his scruff. He got a little misty. The psychic also mentioned that some of the actor's ancestors wanted their progeny to take better care of their hearts. The ancestors told Thomas Alexander that high blood pressure or something was an issue. The actor threw back his head and laughed. He said something like *Thanks, Doc,* and Thomas Alexander laughed too, so all of his immaculate teeth shone. He looked like he still had all his baby teeth.

Two weeks later, the man died of a dissected aorta. He was playing basketball with his son when his heart literally exploded. A few months after that, the widow asked Thomas Alexander to come back and do another taped reading at their home. Thomas Alexander walked around the woman's sprawling property and told her that her husband wanted her to date again. He wanted her to move on. He told her she was still a beautiful young woman. After this episode aired and earned a record number of viewers, the television series, despite terrible critical reviews, was renewed for a second season.

I hungrily read the skeptics' takes on him—he taped all of his readings; he used a combination of hot-reading and cold-reading techniques to convince his clients as well as his fans that he could speak to the dead; he employed flattery. This worked, apparently, because of a psychological phenomenon known as the Barnum effect, which occurs when people believe that what they are told applies specifically to them, despite the fact that it could apply to almost anyone. This phenomenon is the reason people hungrily consume horoscopes and the reason why Thomas Alexander's readings worked so well, especially on people who were grieving.

Meanwhile, the kid refused to do live shows. He refused the skeptics' calls. He refused requests for interviews. He smiled his *Mickey Mouse Club* smile and tweeted *Haters gonna hate* memes on repeat. He was a twenty-year-old millionaire.

I called Peter.

"Yeah," he said in a huff. Pete was partner at a swanky law firm in downtown Milwaukee. Sometimes I felt like most of his job was acting very busy.

"Are we sure about this?" I asked him.

He knew immediately what I was talking about. "Of course not," he said practically. "It's a terrible idea, but we're doing it anyway. You talk to Ma about it?"

"Yeah . . . she had one of her fits."

"They're happening more often now." This was hard for him to admit. I tried to get the conversation back on track.

"The truly terrible television award." I read from one of the many articles about the kid. "In acknowledgment of the extraordinary ongoing deceit of the American public represented in his television program."

"I know, I know," he said. "You watched the video, though?"

I swallowed some bad-tasting spit. "I did," I said.

"So you know."

"I do," I whispered. I realized then that I didn't know which prospect frightened me more: the psychic's success or his failure.

"You saw their faces?" I could hear it in his voice: that contagion of hope. I was scared to breathe for fear I might catch it, but it didn't really matter. I'd already been infected.

"What about the money?" I asked.

"I'll draw up a contract."

"A contract? This kid doesn't care about a contract."

"I suspect he will," Pete said. "Oh, and Dana wants to start spending a couple of hours, maybe a few days a week, after school with you. Is that something you'd be okay with?"

I was surprised. I looked around my filthy apartment. A slant of sunlight electrified the layers of dust on the baseboards.

"Sure," I said. "I'm not very . . . entertaining."

"She'll bring her homework. It's something she wants to do. So Helena and I are going with it. Besides, she seemed to think you could use some help around your place."

I felt my face redden and was glad Pete couldn't see it.

"Help?" I asked. "With what, exactly?"

"I don't know. She said it's messy there, I guess. So it's okay?" He had sensed my defensiveness and become eager to end the conversation.

"Sure," I said. "She's always welcome."

Pete and Helena felt that, given the incident at the quarry when I'd had to pick Dana up in the middle of the night, and a few others which I never learned about, she was getting into too much trouble. They hoped that spending more time with me would keep her out of this trouble. I didn't particularly enjoy the idea of being some kind of community service project, but I also felt my heart hiccup pleasantly at the idea of having her around more. She said she wanted to organize my study. I wasn't thrilled with that idea either, but I didn't think she could do any harm. The only rule was that she was not allowed to throw *anything* away. I stressed this strongly and received a look I was very familiar with—her face, even her lips, were full of pity. Beyond that, I didn't mind how she "organized" the files.

Sometimes we worked side by side in the study. I had begun, at that point, another round of revisions to my case against Frank. It turned out Dana's reorganization of the files was actually helpful in these efforts. A few times I caught her trying to read the documents I had open on my computer, but she usually averted her gaze when I noticed. And a few weeks in, I noticed that she had begun to take her own notes in a composition book. I was tempted, a few times, to read the notebook while she was in the bathroom, but I just didn't have the heart to go through with it. Once she looked up from her work and said to me, "Have you ever seen the show *Hoarders*?"

I shook my head. "I don't watch much TV anymore," I told her.

"I think you're a hoarder," she said. She gestured at the boxes and the stacks of library books and the copies of the *Journal* and the *Wisconsin Light* I'd kept over the years. Things that seemed important to have and to keep, though for what reason, I couldn't definitively say.

I shrugged at her. She was maybe right. "So?" I asked her.

"Well, it's like a disease, and stuff," she said. This time I laughed and she shrugged. "Like, why do you have all this stuff about Dahmer in here?"

"They broke the case that summer . . . the summer Dee disappeared," I told her.

"I know," she said. "But why did you keep it all?"

"I'm just saying it was all mixed in."

Dana thought on this. "Still," she said quietly. "It's kind of creepy." She waved an advertisement I'd torn from a magazine: *Buy your copy of the exclusive confessions copied DIRECTLY from the files of the Milwaukee Police Department. For the low price of ONLY $13.95,* True Police Case *magazine readers can learn how he lured, drugged, killed, had sex, and dismembered bodies. Gerald Boyle, the Milwaukee Cannibal's lawyer, says his client's confession is "the longest confession in the history of America."*

These are the names of every man the serial killer confessed to murdering between 1978 and 1991: Steven Hicks, eighteen; Steven Tuomi, twenty-five; James Doxtator, fourteen; Richard Guerrero, twenty-two; Anthony Sears, twenty-four; Raymond Smith, thirty-two; Edward Smith, twenty-seven; Ernest Miller, twenty-two; David Thomas, twenty-two; Curtis Straughter, seventeen; Errol Lindsey, nineteen; Anthony Hughes, thirty-one; Konerak

Sinthasomphone, fourteen; Matt Turner, twenty; Jeremiah Weinberger, twenty-three; Oliver Lacy, twenty-four; Joseph Bradehoft, twenty-five.

Edward W. Smith was nicknamed "the Sheik." Steven Hicks grew up in Coventry, Ohio. Ernest Miller lived in Chicago and attended the Golden Rule Church of God and Christ; he was a talented dance student. Raymond Smith went by the name Ricky Beeks. Curtis Straughter called himself Demetra and belonged to Gay Youth Milwaukee. Joseph Bradehoft was married and had three children. Errol Lindsey sang in the Greater Spring Hill Missionary Baptist Church choir. Anthony Hughes was deaf-mute and could read lips. Oliver Lacy had a two-year-old son and a fiancée named Rose; his family called him "Birdie." James Doxtator's mother called him Jamie. He liked to play pool and ride his bike. Anthony Sears was an aspiring model who also managed a restaurant. David Thomas was a father. Matt Turner was born in Chicago; he lip-synched at a bar under the name Donald Montrell. Jeremiah Weinberger worked as a customer service rep at a cinema. Steven Tuomi worked at a restaurant in Milwaukee. Richard Guerrero was the youngest of six children. He worked at a pizzeria and often babysat his nieces. Konerak Sinthasomphone was the youngest of eight children and enjoyed swimming, soccer, and drawing the Teenage Mutant Ninja Turtles.

often liked to have Dee over to my place if I got lonely during Leif's long night shifts, and sometimes she'd come by of her own accord when she was annoyed with her roommate, Felicity. We'd drink wine and smoke some of Leif's weed. One night, we were two bottles of wine in when Dee confided to me that most times, after she had sex with Frank, she went into the bathroom alone and made herself come fast with her own index finger. I laughed when she told me, though truthfully, it made me sad.

"I'm not an engineer," Dee said.

"You mean a rocket scientist?"

"Whatever. What I mean is that I just don't understand the mechanics. How am I supposed to come?"

I shrugged. "Practice?" I shook my head and tried again. "Perseverance?"

"This isn't a motivational poster, Pegasus," Dee said.

"In the meantime—" I stuck my tongue out at her and wiggled it between bared teeth.

She shoved me away and laughed a throaty laugh. "Frank says only pussies eat pussy," Dee said.

I slammed my wine down on the table between us. Some of it spilled from the glass down my forearms.

"That is some bullshit, Dee." I took her chin in my hand and squeezed her face so the fat of her cheeks collected around her lips. I wanted suddenly to put my own tongue on her lips, tracing their lovely outline, if only just to show her what gentleness could feel like, the way we used to play when we were babies finding our bodies. But I felt gross for even thinking of it, and I let her go. Chalked it up to the wine and my growing dislike for Frank. "I think you need to ditch him," I said. She was nineteen, and she could have anyone she wanted, though she didn't seem to know it. Do we ever?

"I didn't say the sex was bad. I like it."

I wondered if she'd seen my thoughts about her lips pass over my face. I figured she could read my mind, because I believed I was capable of as much when it came to her thoughts.

"Of course. It's a spectrum, not a binary, babe. But look, you give him head?"

She nodded, gulped at her wine. There was a rose-petal-pink stain on her glass.

"Then it's only right that he return the favor, otherwise it's some bullshit. Sorry." I was proud of myself. Though I was only just discovering the vast joys of cunnilingus, I felt I had asserted myself as the expert in this situation. And I felt Dee was taking me seriously. I got up to roll two joints, one for Dee and me, and one for Leif. He liked one ready after he got off work.

"Oh, and Dee—you better not let him catch you in the bathroom."

"Why?" she asked. She rolled her long neck in circles over her shoulders.

"It's an ego thing," I told her. "I suspect he would not be pleased."

The TV was on low in the living room, and its gray light shone through into the kitchen. I watched a local news segment about a piano prodigy, a young Black jazz musician who'd been visiting from Chicago and had recently gone missing. They showed a picture of him: another man Milwaukee had swallowed. The reporter said he was nineteen. Dee clucked her tongue. "He looks about fourteen, if you ask me."

I eyed her. Dee looked about fourteen herself—her primped hair, her tight, high chest, the skin of her face like a Revlon ad. Dee was a painter, but she was in cosmetology school at Mount Mary College, which she hoped would one day pay the bills. Dee told me once that she did not like to indulge in impracticalities. I took this to mean she didn't believe she would ever make any money from painting (and, by extension, I would never make any money from my poems), and in the end, I suppose, she was right about all of that. She could do hair, nails, and makeup, turn you into one of those magazine women with no rough edges. I was twenty and still had no idea how lipstick worked.

She noticed me watching her, and her eyes widened. "It's just like Erik said," she whispered. "They're disappearing."

Later that night, almost morning, Dee left and Leif came home smelling like disinfectant and cocoa powder. He picked up the joint I'd rolled him and kissed me on the nape of my neck. He took the ashtray into the bathroom with him and set it on top of the toilet; he liked to smoke in the shower. I followed him in there, sat on the toilet lid, and snuck some puffs while he was soaping up and rinsing off. The paper was wet, and I chewed the bits that stayed in my mouth.

He poked his head out from the curtain, inhaled on the joint so his cheekbones went sharp. "Come on, then," he said.

He exhaled slow and beckoned me in. He ducked behind the curtain, and when he popped back out, he spit a thick stream of hot water in my face. I stripped slow and watched him get hard. I loved that my body had that effect on him. He pulled the curtain back for me and I stepped in beside him. There was a dark brown slush, cocoa powder and milk chocolate and some white paste, which had washed from his hands and forearms, collecting on the shower floor. It swirled down the drain, and I put my toes in it. Leif put his hands around my neck and felt between my legs. He said I got wet faster than any woman he'd ever known. I'd learned that men thought being wet was the same thing as permission. I'd warned Dee about this too.

In the shower, Leif pinned me against the tile wall, but I turned back to him.

"What do you think about men who say *Only pussies eat pussy*?" I asked him.

He paused. He was hard, and maybe it was difficult for him to think then.

"Their loss. Pussy is delicious." He put his hands on my shoulders and tried to turn me back around. He wanted me from behind. He moved a rope of wet hair from my ear. "Who the fuck says that, anyway?"

I didn't let him turn me. "Frank," I said.

"What the fuck. Is he Italian or something?"

"Leif!"

He laughed at his own joke. "I'm just teasing," he said. "I heard that about mobsters."

He turned me for the third time, and with my chest against the wall and his hand on the back of my neck, he came inside me.

It occurred to me then I was a hypocrite, preaching to Dee about egalitarianism. Her bullshit was not so different from mine. Was it any different? Once, when Leif and I were falling asleep after sex, he pulled me to him and whispered against my neck, "Sometimes I just want to beat the shit out of you."

I stayed very still. Felt my heart leaping against his palm where he cradled my right breast.

He continued, "Just when we're fucking, I mean." He squeezed me.

GLENDA CLEVELAND: I wondered if this situation was being handled. This was a male child being raped and molested by an adult.

OFFICER: Where did this happen?

[Transferred to another officer.]

OFFICER: Hello, this is the Milwaukee Police.

GLENDA CLEVELAND: Yes, there was a Squad Car No. 68 that was flagged down earlier this evening, about fifteen minutes ago.

OFFICER: That was me.

GLENDA CLEVELAND: Yeah, uh, what happened? I mean, my daughter and my niece witnessed what was going on. Was anything done about this situation? Do you need their names or information or anything from them?

OFFICER: No, I don't need it at all. No, not at all.

GLENDA CLEVELAND: You don't?

OFFICER: Nope, it's an intoxicated boyfriend of another boyfriend.

GLENDA CLEVELAND: Well, how old was this child?

OFFICER: It wasn't a child. It was an adult.

GLENDA CLEVELAND: Are you sure?

OFFICER: Yup.

GLENDA CLEVELAND: Are you positive? Because this child doesn't even speak English. My daughter had, you know, dealt with him before and seen him on the street, you know, catching earthworms.
OFFICER: Yeah—no, he's—it's all taken care of, ma'am.
GLENDA CLEVELAND: I mean, are you positive this is an adult?
OFFICER: Ma'am. Like I explained to you. It is all taken care of. It's as positive as I can be. I can't do anything about somebody's sexual preferences in life.

OFFICER JOSEPH GABRISH interviewed in the *Milwaukee Journal* 1991: "We're trained to be observant and spot things. There was just nothing that stood out, or we would have seen it. We've been doing this for a while, and usually if something stands out, you'll spot it. There wasn't anything there."

FORMER MILWAUKEE POLICE CHIEF HAROLD BREIER (1964–1984): "There is no substitute for strong law enforcement. First, a police officer doesn't have the training to take care of all the social ills of the city. And second, he should be so busy maintaining law and order that he doesn't have time for all that crap. When I was chief, we were relating to the good people, and we were relating to the other people too—we were throwing those people in the can."

When Thomas Alexander began his ghost tours, I felt deeply embarrassed for my city and outraged on behalf of the serial killer's victims and their families. Milwaukee, having failed these families in the seventies, the eighties, and the nineties, seemed poised to do so again. Perhaps, as Dana suggested, I had been obsessed with the serial killer coverage. But it wasn't an obsession born out of a dark interest in the gruesomeness of his crimes. Rather, it was rooted in my belief that the serial killer's fame proved something about my family's case: We weren't special. There were many families, in the city of Milwaukee, in the state of Wisconsin, in the country and the world, just like mine. These families had lost loved ones whom city officials were eager to forget. Maybe these people had been murdered by a serial killer, or maybe they had been murdered by a jealous boyfriend or by a cop, but either way, these people were not special. That is what the news taught me. That's what it is still teaching us. But a serial killer? Now, that was special.

Originally, the consensus among Milwaukee's civic and business leaders was that the serial killer was bad for the city's reputation. Local leaders were appalled when, in 1996, a lawyer representing some of the victims' families wanted to auction off the killer's estate for roughly $1 million. A judge had awarded the families the estate after they'd sued for damages, and the lawyer hoped the auction would provide some additional remuneration. Local leaders said the auction was "morally reprehensible." They feared the belongings, which included, among other things, a drill, four knives, a handsaw, an eighty-quart kettle, a freezer, a hypodermic needle, pornographic movies, and letters received while in prison in Portage, would end up in carnivals and traveling road shows. They vowed to stop the auction and to destroy the serial killer's belongings. They raised about half of what the families were asking for, bought the estate, destroyed what they could, and buried the rest in an undisclosed Illinois landfill.

The vice president of the city's tourism promoters summed up these sentiments when she said, "No one in the U.S. or the world can disagree that this is a catastrophic tragedy. But I don't think anyone is holding it against Milwaukee."

In the end, popular opinion on the subject was slowly reversed, in part because, it seemed to me, Americans had an unusual appetite for stories about serial killers. Sometimes the appetite was just for the killers themselves. Netflix, for example, was full of shows about serial killers and the detectives who tirelessly pursued them. The actual people these serial killers had murdered were often an afterthought. Maybe a couple of naked women poised in gruesome crime scene photos. Maybe some smiling headshots. The kind of photos I'd seen posted on the doors of bars in Walker's Point or on the *Journal's* missing-persons wall.

A phenomenon called dark tourism was gaining popularity at the time when Thomas Alexander came to Milwaukee. Sometimes people paid to sleep in hotels where other people were known to have been murdered or to have committed suicide. Sometimes people visited the childhood homes of serial killers. Sometimes people traveled thousands of miles to visit famous cemeteries.

Specter's, a prohibition-era bar and former whorehouse, was one of the Milwaukee businesses that truly capitalized on people's appetite for stories about the serial killer. One of their ghost tours, devised in the late 2000s, was advertised as a guided walking tour through his old *stomping grounds*. On their website, they noted with unabashed pride that their tours had been *banned on Groupon— twice!* The tour covered roughly two blocks of mostly shuttered storefronts along Second Street. The guides stopped at three of the bars where the serial killer had picked up victims. Only one of these, La Cage, was still open. La Cage had banned the tours from coming inside, so the groups strutted up and down Second while Walker's Point residents occasionally heckled them by imitating ghostly noises.

When the tours first started, everyone hoped they would flop. Or everyone said that they hoped the tours would pan. But in the first few weeks, Specter's sold out of tickets. I read the news coverage and watched in horror as family members of the victims protested the tours. They stood outside in February with poster board signs onto which they'd pasted blown-up pictures of their loved ones. It was easy to forget how young some of those men were. According to Milwaukee, it was easy to forget that the victims described by the guides had been real, living people with real, living family members who still missed them every day. Milwaukee was keen to keep the serial killer's dark story alive, but the families were furious: The victims hadn't gotten any tours. Meanwhile, his Wikipedia page was a novella. The victims were mentioned only to describe the way he killed each of them. The families argued the tour was glamorizing the serial killer, just as the media had done (and continued to do), while exploiting the victims. Sympathy, even praise for the serial killer, was nothing new. An anti-gay group in Oregon had once printed and sold posters that read: *Free Jeffrey Dahmer. (He only killed homosexuals.)*

Indeed, the guides spoke to the tour groups about the serial killer's care and concern for his victims: "He hadn't wanted to hurt them. He just wanted them to stay." They spun stories of the killer's historic loneliness. To hear the Specter's tour guides tell it, the man had become a murderer because he'd once given his teacher a bowl of tadpoles as a gift, and then later, he saw this bowl at another child's house. Apparently, the serial killer was tortured by this regifting episode, which meant the teacher didn't like his gift and didn't like him either. He was seven or something. Or, another guide argued, he'd become a murderer because his parents had taken away his dissection kit that he'd been using on roadkill. Or, another guide argued, he'd become a murderer because his parents had lied to him about an operation "down there" he'd had as a young child and he associated any and all feelings "down there" with confusion, shame, and guilt. These were the beginnings of his problems with his sexuality. I, like many other Milwaukeeans, read these accounts voraciously, but I think most of us knew how thin they were. None of them made any sense, but we needed sense, we had to have sense. The tours continued as a number of the historic gay bars in the area shuttered. Purple Door, a trendy ice cream place, opened a few blocks down from Specter's.

And that's how Thomas Alexander came to make some quick money in Milwaukee. Tickets for the Thomas Alexander special edition of this ghost tour sold faster than anyone predicted. (We'd thought better of one another, but as usual, we disappointed ourselves. Some Milwaukeeans were too proud to admit we were buying the shit they were selling. They said it was Chicagoans or other tourists, but most of us knew better.)

Rumors began to circulate about what exactly went on during these tours. Some people said that Thomas Alexander used long divining rods to reach out to the serial killer. Thomas Alexander, for his part, took his job very seriously and so, reportedly, was disappointed by some of the recent disturbances on the tours. Apparently, some of the protestors had begun heckling the tour groups by dressing in white sheets with eyeholes and making ghostly noises while following them around Walker's Point. They would cut those people out of the Netflix show. (This is to say that it never happened.) Once, allegedly, a ghost was arrested for public intoxication and resisting police orders, and after that the ghosts stopped following the tours altogether.

Leif and I hung out with Dee and Frank exactly once. Dee suggested we go bowling and we did. Frank was big into bowling; he had his own ball, which he carried in a special leather bag, and his own shoes, which he shined himself. He knew the owner, so we got to play for free. My shoes pinched, and Leif sucked down warm light beer that turned his mood sour very fast. Dee bowled strikes consistently. She was very good, and Frank took credit for that. While Dee lined herself up in front of our lane, the ball close to her chest, Frank turned to Leif. "So, what's your story, man?"

Leif narrowed his eyes and pretended intense interest in Dee's immaculate form. "Story?" he repeated.

"Yeah. The whole nine yards. What do you do? What makes you tick?"

I felt suddenly I was in a play, but I'd not been given the script for this scene.

Leif sipped his beer. "I'm a poet," he said. It was like the whole bowling alley heard and cringed. Frank looked like Leif had admitted he worked for the IRS.

"Yeah? What's that like?" Frank asked.

Leif turned back toward me for help. I shrugged and leaped up. It was my turn.

"Agony, Frank. It's agony," Leif said. "What about you?"

"I'm a firefighter. In training, actually."

Frank tilted his chin toward the ceiling. Dee came back to us. She grinned and I leaned in close. "Jesus, Dee. Are you sweating?"

She laughed and dramatically wiped a bead of sweat from her forehead. "Frank takes this seriously."

"Noted," I said. I put my sweaty palms under the stream of cool air, which blew from the machine that returned our balls. I chose a deep maroon one, threw two gutter balls, and slunk back to my seat. Leif rubbed my shoulder and I tossed his hand off. He went to get another beer. Frank stood up and offered his hand to me. I stared at it.

"Come on," he said. "I can give you some pointers."

I shook my head. "I'll study from here," I told him.

"Go on, Peg," Dee said. "He's a great teacher."

Frank's face was sweaty and eager. He was handsome in a stiff way; he reminded me of one of those dickless Renaissance statues. I nodded. "Okay," I told him. He grinned like he'd just won the fucking lottery. I followed him to the lane. "I'll ruin your impeccable score, though," I teased.

Frank didn't take it as a joke; he just nodded grimly. He set his body up slowly so I could see everything. He had that dramatic poised form: His right leg ended up crossed behind his left; he followed through. He bowled a strike. "See?" he asked. He was too close and I took a step back. "Now you."

I'd brought my maroon ball and I held it up against my chest. Frank stepped back toward me. He took my elbow in his hands, moved my body a little here, a little there; I could smell his Old Spice, which made me feel sick. He breathed on my neck not inconspicuously, and I thought, *Fuck this*. I dropped the ball and it rolled, painfully slow, toward the pins. Near the end of the lane, it careened into the gutter and stayed there. A buzzer sounded and a young man came to retrieve my ball, and the machine wiped the pins away and then began to set them back up again. I walked back to the chairs and sat next to Dee, whose face was trained on the grainy television near the bar. She hadn't seen Frank's lesson.

The TV was tuned to WTMJ. An anchor in a tight bright pink dress was interviewing a conservative radio talk show host. The segment's headline scrolled across the bottom of the screen: "Local WISN-AM Talk Show Host Asks, Should Dentists Be Required to Treat AIDS Patients?" *What we have here is a group of people who are responsible for their conditions. Ninety-five percent of people with HIV are personally responsible for their infection and should not complain. Look, if you're a person who has anal sex with gay males and uses IV drugs, if this is your lifestyle, you're to blame.*

I wished there were a mute button. The anchor asked the talk show host about allegations that his words were harmful, even a serious threat to public health. He said he was only using "uncommon common sense."

Dee shook her head. "Why do they give these people a platform?" she asked.

"Because they know we'll watch it," I said. She nodded.

It was Leif's turn. It was obvious to me he was taking all of this much too seriously in an attempt to match Frank's fervor. Frank came back from the bar and sat between Dee and me; my left thigh touched his right. He reached his long arms behind us and brushed my shoulder with his fingertips.

"What are you guys talking about?" Frank asked.

"The news," Dee said. She gestured toward the TV, where the radio host was still talking and the headline still scrolled. Frank's eyes narrowed and then he laughed.

"Who gives a shit about a bunch of fags," he said. Leif was poised to release his ball, but there was a hiccup in his elbow. The word shook him. I had a memory of the cops' blinding lights as we all exited the bar in Walker's Point that night. The ball fell heavy from Leif's hands, bounced once, and then picked up momentum near the end of the lane. I think we were all surprised to see it was a strike. Leif turned back to us before the ball hit the pins, though. Dee clapped her hands together; I saw her baby self for a split second, and it made my heart ache.

"What did you just say?" Leif asked.

Frank laughed. I stood up.

"You've got another ball there," Frank said. He motioned at the lanes behind Leif.

"Stand up," Leif said.

And Frank did and Leif punched him in the nose so he fell back into the seat. Dee put her hands in her hair but didn't make any noise.

"And don't you ever fucking touch Peg. Understood?"

Frank said nothing, but he scrambled to get out of the seat and on his feet. When he tried to move toward Leif, Dee grabbed his arm. He threw her off and she stumbled back, surprised. A hard knot formed in the pit of my stomach. She refused to make eye contact with me. A large man appeared from the back office and shouted something about the police.

"We're going already," Leif shouted at him. Leif and I grabbed our things and I didn't look back at Dee.

"Was that entirely necessary?" I asked Leif in the car back to Riverwest. He was chain-smoking through a crack in the window, and the car was practically hotboxed.

"That guy's a certified asshole."

"You're the one who hit him."

"Maybe if you hadn't let him grope you. I mean, Jesus H. Christ, woman."

"Let him?"

"You know what I mean."

"Fuck you." I pressed my body against the passenger window. "You're drunk." Neither of us had the energy to sink our teeth into the argument. At a stoplight, steam from an open storm sewer coiled up and choked a lamppost. I wondered what Dee would do tonight, if Frank would be angry with her or if he'd be gentle with her, if he was even capable of gentleness. I felt everything then was make-believe, like we were playing these women who dated these kinds of men in one long, bad game of truth or dare. Everyone was choosing dare every time.

Later that night, Leif woke me as he climbed into bed. He made a C shape to cup his body around mine, slipped his arm underneath my neck. He took my earlobe into his mouth and sucked on it; I breathed slow and deep to mimic hard sleep, but still he put his hand between my legs to see if I was wet, and I was.

After that, I didn't see much of Frank, but I saw signs of him all over Dee. Once, in her dorm room, she pulled off a tattered paint-stained tank top, and there was a nasty wound on the washboard of her ribs. She put on a flowered top and smoothed it over her lovely stomach, but I pulled the shirt back up and pointed. "What the hell's that?"

Dee inspected the wound. "Frank's dog bit me."

I raised an eyebrow and let the shirt fall.

"He's training his St. Bernard to attack, but the dog got confused," Dee said. She shrugged, like, *No big deal*.

"Why?" I asked her. I resisted the urge to pull her shirt back up, to get close to the wound, to try to fix it.

Dee gave me an incredulous look. "You heard about that woman who got raped: The guy climbed right in her first-floor bedroom window."

I had heard. So had Leif and almost the entirety of Milwaukee. Leif had bought me a knife, and he'd taken to keeping his loaded gun next to our bed at night. Frank, apparently, had bought himself an attack dog. I repeated something our mother once told me: "Watch out for the overprotective types."

Dee huffed. "Well, I like that he's protective of me."

I almost said, *No, you don't,* but I stopped. I was reminded suddenly of our conversation about her sex life. She'd said the same thing then: *But I like it.*

"Maybe he could start by protecting you from his damn dog," I told her.

Erik often showed up at our apartment in Riverwest late at night with a busted lip or a bruised eye; he said he got in fights at the clubs. We patched him up and fed him each time. He'd take long showers at our place, and sometimes I thought I heard him crying, but Leif said he was praying. I think we both knew he wasn't the praying type, though. In late May, he showed up with a badly swollen lip, and Leif finally asked where the hell he was living. Erik said he'd been staying with his boyfriend, a man who owned a bar in Walker's Point. Leif had a lot to say about this. Erik tried to use our own living situation as collateral.

"You live with Peg, though," he said to Leif over one breakfast at our place.

"That's different. We've been together for a while."

Erik sounded like a baby, and Leif sounded like a dad.

"You're so closed-minded," Erik whined.

"Can't you get something on your own?"

"I can't afford something on my own."

"Have you looked around here?"

I eyed the apartment. With morning sunlight, and the plants

I'd started from seedlings growing on the windowsill, the place looked less depressing than when we'd moved in, but there was still so much dirt.

"I don't want to live around here; these places are so crappy. Plus, people are always getting robbed here." Erik turned to me. "No offense."

I shrugged. "I haven't been robbed," I said.

"Yeah," Leif said. "Also. Beggars can't be choosers, man. Have you talked to Ma?"

Leif's response stung me for some reason.

"What good will it do?" Erik asked.

"Fine. I can't let you stay here anymore. I mean it. I'm sick of fielding Ma's calls. I'm sick of lying for you. Do it your damn self." Leif pushed away from the table and slammed the bedroom door. Upstairs, someone beat on the floor with a broomstick. The neighbors complained that Leif and I were loud. And they'd told the landlord they'd seen young men coming and going at all hours of the night. We had received a formal warning.

"What about you, huh?" Erik asked me. He grinned; he was as beautiful as his brother, and infinitely more charming, though I never would have told Leif.

I wrote my work number down on a napkin. "If you need me. But don't tell Leif."

I slid him the paper and he pocketed it.

Leif was true to his word. He didn't let Erik back into our apartment, and he refused to answer his brother's calls. I knew Erik was in and out of trouble. He liked to come by the library to see me after he'd been on benders. He'd show up strung out and sometimes still coked up, and I knew he hadn't eaten in days. He worked fifteen hours a week, and I assumed he spent the meager money he made on drinks and drugs. His cheekbones grew sharp. Sometimes I'd buy us sandwiches or hot dogs, and we'd eat on the benches atop the bluff overlooking the lake. There was a historical reconstruction of the *Denis Sullivan*, complete with billowing white sails, anchored in the harbor that summer. From atop the bluff, the ship was a white speck in Lake Michigan's gray froth.

"I heard people are paying five hundred bucks for five-course meals on that ship," Erik said. "Can you believe it? They've turned the damn thing into a restaurant."

He'd devoured his sandwich and was licking mustard from his fingers. I handed him my second half. He didn't refuse.

"Sounds nauseating," I said.

"I have to tell you a secret," he said.

"Okay," I said.

"I'm . . . homeless," he said, spitting the word out like it was thick phlegm.

"Jesus," I said, because I didn't know what else he expected.

"Don't tell Leif, please."

"I can't make any promises."

He nodded. "What should I do?"

I thought about what I would do. "What about Dee?" I asked him.

He nodded. "I know," he said. "But she lives in a damn closet."

"I bet she'd make room."

"It's not just that," he whispered.

I leaned closer to him. "What is it?"

"Frank," he said. "He won't have it."

I bristled. "Well, fuck him." Erik made a face, like, *Don't go there*, so I backed off. "Look, I'll talk to her, okay?"

He didn't object. I wiped a bit of mustard from his chin. He put his head on my shoulder. I breathed in the smell of his hair, which smelled just like Leif's.

Article IV. Relevance and Its Limits

RULE 405. METHODS OF PROVING CHARACTER

(a) By Reputation or Opinion. When evidence of a person's character or character trait is admissible it may be proved by testimony about the person's reputation or by testimony in the form of an opinion.

On the day of the consultation, the psychic arrived at the Lutheran Home with an entourage, which included two bodyguards, a stylist, and his PR rep. He was an hour late. He had also brought along a camera crew; the psychic reassured us this was standard procedure, it didn't mean anything would be filmed. I gave Pete a look, but he refused to catch my eye. I caught Dana's eye and she frowned at me.

Dana had strong-armed her parents into letting her attend the session with Thomas Alexander even though Pete and Helena had tried repeatedly to discourage her interest in Dee's case. Gary Wolski, who had once been our assigned MPD detective but had become, over the years, more of a family friend, had also insisted on attending, though Ma had told him it wasn't necessary. I suspected Wolski carried around the same kind of crushing, debilitating guilt that I did. (Though I didn't know the true source of his guilt then.) We didn't believe he was totally to blame for botching the crucial early days of the investigation into Dee's disappearance, but he had made at least one massive and ultimately formative mistake. My family was quick to point out that his classification of Dee's case as noncritical was largely the result of us having concealed her relationship with Frank. This meant that if Wolski was to blame for underestimating the suspiciousness of her disappearance, I was to blame for the fact that he had reached the conclusion in the first place. We were linked. Wolski noticed me watching him and he tried a half smile. I only nodded back.

My aunt Suze held Ma's hand, and they both watched Thomas Alexander's entourage rush around the community room. Thomas Alexander knelt down in front of Ma's wheelchair and put his hands on her knees. Suze knitted her brows at him. I felt embarrassed and wanted to look away from the scene, but I didn't. The psychic was dressed in a baby-blue cashmere cardigan, dark-wash jeans, and those low-cut leather boots that were popular among both men and women.

"I'm so sorry we're late, ma'am. We got a little lost."

I supposed he had taken forty-five minutes to get his hair just so—it was baby-fine and swept over his forehead as if his own mother had brushed it minutes ago.

My mother appraised him. "Well," she said. "You certainly are pretty." This time I did catch Peter's eye, and we both stifled a laugh. Even Dana produced a half smile.

The kid didn't miss a beat. Many people had probably told him this during his short life.

"I thought we might speak privately," Thomas Alexander said. Pete looked like he wanted to say no, but he didn't. I just shrugged. Suze made a face, like, *Why not?* Thomas Alexander rolled Ma through the automatic sliding glass doors that opened into the community center's courtyard. It was a little too cold for Ma to be out there without a coat and a blanket, but I said nothing.

Pete attempted small talk, but none of us were up to the task.

"How's Henry?" Pete asked me. My family didn't know that Henry and I were now officially, and I believed permanently, separated. Dana frowned at me. I tried to make a meaningful face at her, but she looked away.

"Fine, yeah," I said to Pete. "Thanks." He nodded.

When Thomas Alexander rolled Ma back in, he shook everyone's hands, saying our names loudly one by one: Alice (my mother), Wolski, Pete, Dana, Peg. He lingered with me and frowned slightly. His hand felt soft and small in mine. I assumed he'd had more manicures in his short lifetime than I'd ever have in mine. He looked slightly sweaty; there was a light sheen on his forehead. I wondered if his stylist would powder his face dry in the car when they left. He said he'd be in touch. And next time he'd be prompt. He winked. Ma loved him. I could tell.

Ma motioned for me. I crouched down next to the wheelchair. It was getting late and golden-hour light was dappling the leaves of the trees in the courtyard. It looked warm, but I knew it could still snow at any moment.

"I need you to do something for me," Ma said.

"Okay." I waited.

"He needs something that belonged to Dee. From the storage locker. It doesn't matter what. Just something she used to use a lot or keep close to her. Can you get it?"

The thought of the storage locker made my stomach turn. Peter paid the bill for it each month, and we all tried to pretend it didn't exist. It hurt just to think about all her stuff in a dark ten-by-ten cement block. The contents of her dorm room. Her paintings. The hope chest she curated for her wedding. The storage locker was filled with things like that—the stuff of Dee's life that Ma used to say she kept so Dee could have it when she came home.

"I don't want to go in there," I told her.

"I know," she said. "I know. But he needs it."

"Okay," I said. "I can do it. What else did he say?"

She looked back out the window to the courtyard, which was filling in with shadows.

"He knew something," she whispered, and then she laughed

harshly, like I'd made a dirty joke, and I cringed. Her eyes went wide.

"About what?"

"About me. Something only I know." She laughed again, and I slumped over and put my head in her lap. I felt her thighbones through her skin. She rubbed my back, but it was so light I barely felt her touch.

The item from the storage locker was not the only thing Thomas Alexander required to begin his sessions. Two days after he met with Ma privately, he sent Pete an invoice for six thousand dollars. He said this was to get started, but after that, nothing would be due until the sessions were over. Pete tried to get a sense how much each subsequent session would cost, but the psychic said he never quoted because there wasn't any way to tell for sure what would be required of him. Every session was different. I could hear Pete grinding his teeth as he told me over the phone.

We didn't tell Ma about the money Thomas Alexander asked for to get started, or about his suspicious billing procedures, not only because we didn't think she would care, but also because we became embarrassed to talk about it at all. The sheer amount of the money made me nauseated and unable to speak, and I sensed Peter felt the same. We divided this in thirds between me, Suze, and Pete, and we said nothing else about it to one another or to Ma. I used the remainder of my savings to pay for my portion. The bank called to ask if I'd like to close the account.

Dee was living in the dorms at Mount Mary College and planned to stay on through the summer because, she said, she wanted to take a few summer classes. I also suspected she didn't want to move back in with Ma for those few months. Ma wasn't pleased with this arrangement, but seeing as Dee was paying her own room and board, Ma couldn't really say much about it. Technically, Mount Mary students weren't allowed to have men stay with them. Maybe, I thought, she could say Erik needed sanctuary. It was a Catholic school, but they were what Ma called those liberal kumbaya Catholics.

I borrowed Leif's car and drove to Mount Mary to tell her about Erik. The phone lines at her dorm were shoddy and usually jammed with girls calling long-distance lovers or whatever. Everyone knows those conversations can last hours. When I got there, though, I knew she wasn't alone. She'd marked the chalkboard on her door with a small, polite X. This was the code she and her roommate used to indicate the presence of male guests. I entertained the idea of knocking but instead pressed my ear to the door. I wondered what Frank sounded like when he came. Dee would have chided me for the thought, but I was fascinated by the noises men made when they came. The first time I heard that kind of noise

(I lost my virginity when I was fifteen, and he couldn't have been inside me longer than a minute), I couldn't discern whether the kid was in pain. The cry sounded so desperate. Men, and maybe women, are their most animal selves when they're coming; I'd seen it with Leif. He always seemed so vulnerable in that moment, and sometimes I wondered if he resented that part of it, if other men did too. I couldn't hear much because those doors were so thick.

A girl walked down the hallway and narrowed her eyes. "Do you have a visitor's pass?"

"This is my sister's room," I said.

"You still need a pass," she said.

"What the fuck are you, the hall monitor?"

The door swung open and nearly hit me in the forehead. The girl looked like she wished it had.

"What the hell's this?" Frank's sweaty forehead was inches from mine.

I peered over his shoulder to see Dee slipping her jeans on. "Frank," I said.

"Margaret," he said. He reached out to touch my lower back and I jumped backward. "I was just leaving."

He looked odd in the hallway. His body was too large and too grown for the dorm. It was early afternoon, and he looked like he already needed a shave. The girls' doors were decorated with pastel-hued paper flowers.

"See you," I said.

"Good to see you."

I said nothing.

He smelled sweaty. Dee padded to the threshold, her clothes askew, and he leaned in and grabbed her behind the neck. He pulled her in for a showy kiss with a lot of tongue. "Bye, baby," he said.

The hall monitor stood there the whole time. "She needs a visitor's pass next time," the girl told Dee.

"What about him?" I said. I pointed at the back of Frank's head as he left.

Dee laughed, pulled me inside, and slammed the door. I imagined the paper flowers floating to the floor. Inside the room, I choked on the smell of sweat and cum. Rooms that small keep everything inside. I threw open a window, and Dee lay back on her skinny bed, her legs hanging off, bare toes brushing the dirty carpet. Mount Mary let the students decorate their own dorm rooms. Dee had repainted hers in dark purple and forest green. They were beautiful colors, but they kept sunlight at bay and made me anxious. And there were canvases everywhere. I think she had more canvases than clothes. Most of them were facing backward, so all I could see were the wooden skeletons of the frames. Paint was splattered on the carpet.

"Don't you have a studio?"

"I like to keep them close to me. What's up?" she asked. Her breath was heavy. I had the sudden urge to be close to her, right near her, shoulder to shoulder, but I stayed where I was. I touched my fingers to my sternum and felt the bruise there that never went away. This was where Leif put the heel of his hand when he was on top of me, the whole of his weight concentrated on a few of my flimsy bones. The spot stayed sore. Touching the bruise could be a strange comfort to me.

"I saw Erik today," I told Dee. She ticked her head to the left, like, *Go on*. "He needs somewhere to stay."

She sprang up. "Why? What happened?"

"He said he's homeless."

"Fuck," she said. "He's still fighting with Leif, then?"

I nodded.

"He can stay here," she offered easily, as if inviting him to dinner.

"Yeah. He's worried—"

She stopped me. "He probably said there wasn't any room here, right?"

I paused. I didn't know how to say it. *Frank. He won't have it.* "Something like that, yeah."

"We'll make it work. Felicity is never here anyway," she said. This seemed true; her roommate's side of the room was relatively empty of personal belongings. Still, I knew I should bring up Frank, but I didn't know how. Or maybe I was just afraid of her reaction.

"Thank you, babe." I sat next to her on the bed and hugged her. She shoved me playfully.

"It's not a big deal," she said. "Of course, he *should* be staying with Leif."

I curled up on the bed next to her, and we lay together with our faces close. It was hard to imagine Frank's big body on the skinny bed. I shrugged. "I know," I said. "Leif's fed up with him, though."

Dee humphed.

"Plus his ma's on his case about it."

"Look at you. Making excuses for Leif. Family's family. You know that."

"Nope. I've been trying to disown you since the day you were born." I tickled her rib cage. I knew, from when we were little, the spots she hated: touchy tissue between the bones. She laugh-cried and shoved me away. Her ribs felt small between my fingers.

After all three of her children left home, Ma liked to make sure the four of us still met at least once a week to share a meal. Sometimes this was Sunday dinner (and usually the Packers game) at Ma's; other times we liked to meet at a Milwaukee establishment called Ma Fischer's. This was a 24/7 diner known for its pies and its recurring grease fires. Aunt Suze waitressed there, so she could comp small items for us. Sometimes, if we went when it was slow, Suze would share a couple of pieces of pie with us and catch up.

I remember one of these meals at Ma Fischer's the spring before Dee disappeared because the conversation, at the time, felt fun and clandestine. Dee and I worked together to keep each other's secrets. I still didn't want Ma and Pete to know I was living with Leif, and Dee wasn't ready to tell them she was seeing a grown Guido.

We tried to focus Ma's attention back on Peter. Ma loved Peter in a way Dee and I knew she would never love us, because he was her only son, and because he'd filled our father's shoes after he'd died. In another sense, I knew Ma would never love me the way she loved Dee because Dee was her youngest, her baby, and the only one of us who had been a surprise. Or that was how she told it. Over breakfast that day, Ma asked Dee if she was dating anyone at school.

"What's this I hear about an Erik?" Ma asked Dee. My sister smiled at me, and I looked away. "Last time I dropped you off, your roommate was telling me he's been around quite a bit."

Dee shrugged. "He's just a friend," she said.

"We've heard that one before," Ma said.

I laughed because it was true. Dee used to have lots of "friends" in high school.

"So you're not seeing anyone, then?" Peter asked with an air of authority that had a bad effect on me; it made me want to spill Dee's secrets. Had he learned this affect in law school? I had the sudden urge to tell Peter and Ma about the jagged wound I'd seen on Dee's ribs, and I looked at her across the table, where she held my gaze like she knew. She kicked my shin, and I spilled my coffee on the paper place mat in front of me. I watched the stain spread. Suze rushed over, whisked the place mat away, and with one fluid motion, wiped the table down and refilled my coffee. She ruffled my curls and gave one of my earlobes a tug. Then she rushed away again.

"No, no," Dee said. "I'm not seeing anyone right now."

"Well, that's smart," Ma said. "Focus on school. Right, baby?"

Dee nodded smugly. Peter blew on his coffee. Neither of our parents had attended college. After getting out of the navy, our father had inherited a filling station from our grandfather. The gas station, and the repair shop he ran out of the station, kept our father busy and away from home a lot. My mother was hired as a typist at a local paper straight out of high school. When computers had made her job obsolete, her union continued to pay her a decent stipend while she worked as a rep.

"And how's Leif?" Ma asked me.

"Good," I told her. "He's still working third shift, but his boss told him if he gets through this summer, he'll have his pick of shifts in the fall."

"That's honest, hard work," my mother said. I nodded. "Where does he live again?"

"Riverwest," I said.

She clucked her tongue. "You be careful when you're visiting him. You're liable to get robbed over there. In broad daylight."

I said nothing. Dee smiled at me sweetly. Pete picked up on something there, but I could tell he didn't know what it was. He eyed me suspiciously.

"So are you still planning on being an English major?" Pete asked me. He said the word *English* like it was a food he hated.

"I don't know," I said. "Are you still planning on being an asshole?"

Dee giggled. Our mother frowned. Suze's timing was impeccable. She bustled over with four slices of pie and a bowl of ice cream that she placed in the middle of the table. She spooned a healthy scoop onto each plate.

"When are you taking the bar again, Pete?" Suze asked.

Under the table, Dee rubbed her foot against my shin where, minutes earlier, she had kicked me.

My father used to always say, "Poetry isn't a job, Peg." After he died, Pete took up that refrain as if he were afraid I would forget it. Ma and Dee were always more gentle with me about my writing—Ma because I think she dabbled herself, and she understood what writing meant for me, and Dee because she was an artist too, and though she was more realistic about her job prospects than I was, I knew she harbored the kind of dreams that would make a high school guidance counselor shudder. The last summer we lived together in Ma's house, we liked to trade some of these dreams back and forth. We liked to hear how they sounded out loud. Sometimes we'd be lying in our matching twin beds just staring at the ceiling and dreaming out loud. The dreams we really liked, we used to write in pencil on the part of the ceiling that slanted down toward our beds.

I'm going to paint a mural in New York City.
I'm going to learn the name of every native bird in Wisconsin.
I'm going to write a book about birds.
I'm going to paint birds.
I'm going to go to Italy and eat nothing but bread and olives.
I'm going to live by the ocean.
I'm going to write a book about living by the ocean.
I'm going to do makeup for famous people.
I'm going to be a famous person.
I'm going to be a person no one can find.
I'm going to have four children.
I'm going to learn how to sculpt.

I'm going to open my own salon.
I'm going to write a book about you.

I sometimes suspected that Dee kept many of her crazier dreams to herself. We both understood, at an early age, the difference between words in the world and words in our own heads. But the thing with me and Dee was, I sometimes felt like we shared the same head, especially when we were younger. This theory was tested when we got older and we started to lead lives that intersected only because we forced them to and because we fell in love with people whose mere existence created such massive clouds in each other's head, it was difficult to make room for much else. I sometimes wonder if that's really what happened that summer—we were pushing each other out to make more and more room for Frank and Leif in our own heads. We didn't leave any room to let each other back in.

At home we had a large library, which was filled not just with classics but also with poetry and science fiction, memoir and nonfiction. Ma read to us often, and often it was poetry because it was short and had the feeling of a lullaby, even if the meaning was not there. I started writing poems at eleven. Ma was thrilled, but my father was less excited. I read lots of poetry, but I didn't understand most of it. Instead, I focused on the feeling of the words in my brain. They made a mark there like they were characters pressed into soft clay. They stayed. I would reread the books I'd read as a child when I was older and living with Leif for the first time. Those imprints in my brain buzzed and came alive anew. You can understand something new about yourself, about the way the world works, how other people's minds move, any time you read a book of poetry. I learned it was only important to keep your appetite for the words alive. Leif disagreed. He thought this was a ridiculous way to read poetry. He had dog-eared copies of chapbooks with Post-it notes and bookmarks. He looked up every word and allusion. He took apart syntax. He ferociously memorized lines. He read poems like he was wrestling them, trying to pin them to the ground. It reminded me of the times he and his brother used to roughhouse in our flat. Using force to feel.

When we moved Dee's belongings into the storage locker, the company had been selling the contents of a unit whose owners hadn't paid the bill in months. I tried not to survey their property too closely: family portraits in extravagant frames, jars of rocks and sand, kids' artwork, a messy box of rusted tools, a set of expensive kitchen knives. Where were these people, and what had happened to them? Did they know that strangers were picking through their things? Did they know that after today their photos would end up in a landfill? I wondered about the contents of every single locker. I wondered about the people who had put their belongings in these boxes. Now I was one of them. We put Dee's stuff away seven years after she disappeared. Ma wouldn't have anything to do with it because she didn't approve of us breaking down Dee's room and carting her belongings away. Pete and I had both hoped out of sight would help push Dee a little further out of mind for Ma. But as with everything else we tried, she interpreted it incorrectly. She thought we were giving up. She thought we were accepting Dee's fate.

I toyed with the idea of driving to the storage locker but decided I couldn't do it. Instead I opened a bottle of wine and began sifting through a box of Dee's stuff that I kept at my apartment but hadn't looked at in years, maybe since I'd moved there. It contained an odd assortment of things that I'd kept with me over the years: some photos of the two of us, some of Dee's jewelry, little notes she'd written me. I sat on the floor of my apartment with the box and my wine and tried to find something suitable for the session. I didn't really know what I was looking for. I found a picture of Dee painting in her studio at Mount Mary; I thought I'd taken it, but I couldn't be sure. Dee stood in front of the canvas with her back to the camera. The camera had caught her just as she looked over her shoulder. She was surprised or maybe about to laugh. The backs of her knees looked oddly childish in the photo; she'd had the tendency to hyperextend her knees when she stood still. I put the photo back in the box. My mouth went sour. I found a string of fake-looking pearls that I remembered Dee wearing in high school. She had loved things like that—dainty country-club shit that always looked elegant on her but phony on me.

I closed the box and was about to shove it back into a corner when I noticed a box Dana had organized and relabeled in a swooping script—*Transcripts*. Tentatively, I flipped open one of the cardboard flaps to find a neat stack of witness interviews we'd conducted shortly after filing Dee's report. I wasn't sure if I had read all of them. I'd often preferred to get someone's recap of the interviews rather than reading through them myself. It was odd to think of all the documents I'd kept in that room, files I'd never even read, maybe.

I opened another bottle of wine, and when I was drunk enough, I called Henry. He picked up after the fourth ring. Like he'd been deciding. I breathed into the phone.

"Peg?" he asked. His voice pierced me with a spike of longing. The last time we'd spoken, he'd been angry with me, but in a restrained way, like he felt I was too fragile to truly admonish. This in turn had made me very angry. I had tried to hurt him. I supposed I'd succeeded.

"Can you come over?" I asked him.

"No," he said without hesitation.

"I think we're going to find her, Henry. I'm feeling ready this time."

"I'm happy for you," he said. He had written a script out for himself. A playbook. I didn't mind.

"You're sure you can't come over?"

"Take care of yourself," he said, and hung up.

Once when Henry and I were having dinner at Pete and Helena's place, Pete had pulled me aside while Henry was in the bathroom. He'd grabbed me by the upper arm. He could almost fit his whole hand around what passed for my bicep.

"What the hell are you doing?" Pete asked me. His voice was low.

"What are you talking about?"

"You're using Henry like some kind of emotional punching bag, and it's really uncomfortable."

I was taken aback. "Am I?"

"I don't know how many times we have to tell you. You don't get to treat people like shit just because something shitty happened to you."

"Happened to us," I corrected him. He let go of my arm, and I massaged the place where his fingers had gripped me.

Henry specialized in dystopian literature. Though his classes were very popular, I cringed to imagine him teaching. We'd met at UWM, where I had been an assistant librarian for a time. He had a spacey, aloof handsomeness, the kind of attractiveness one acquires from being totally unconcerned about personal appearance. For some reason, I had been quite attracted to Henry's wrinkled clothes, the ink stains on his fingertips, his overgrown facial hair, the bewildered way he sometimes looked around as if to say, *How the hell did I get here?* He pursued me with a confidence that did not seem to be supported by his appearance. I thought that was funny. It's only men who can get away with that kind of thing—the unabashed swagger in the very average body. Though he'd asked me to marry him twice, I couldn't entertain the thought of a wedding. During the six years we'd dated, Henry never saw my apartment, and when he finally did, a few weeks before Ma decided to hire the psychic, he officially ended things.

If, during our time together, I had used Henry as an emotional punching bag, I think we evened the dynamic out because generally, and with a few (very few) limits, I allowed him to use me as an actual punching bag in bed. One of the greatest pleasures and surprises of our time together was discovering Henry was a little kinky.

We were fooling around late one night after a considerable amount of wine, and I was lamenting how bad my day had been, how little I'd gotten done, how much a piece of shit I was. Usual writer stuff. Henry stopped me. He got very close to my face and kissed me very gently. He kept his lips close to my face so that they brushed against me while he whispered, *Tell me every bad thing you did today*. He kissed me lightly and I tried to move toward him. *Everything,* he said. So I began: *I ate pie for breakfast*. He bit my bottom lip hard but then licked both my lips. I was instantly wet. *What else?* he whispered. *I procrastinated on the Internet for an hour after that*. He took off his belt, flipped me around, and hit me hard once. The sound of it scared and delighted me. He crawled on top of me and brushed the hair away from my ear. *What else?* I said, *I smoked two cigarettes*. *Oh dear,* he said, *that's very, very bad*. He went to his drawer and got out an old tie. He tied my hands behind my back and made me kneel on the ground. He hit me twice with the belt. The second time I cried out. He pushed me down so my shoulders were on the ground and my ass was in the air. He put his face beneath me, between my legs, and he licked me from anus to clit, and I cried out again because it felt so good. Then I think he lost his patience with the game and the moaning noises. He fucked me harder than he ever had before, and when he came inside me, he collapsed on top of me, and we both fell down onto his bedroom carpet. He left my hands tied.

We sometimes called this little game *what did you do?* I was allowed to say anything during these games, and Henry would never bring it up outside the game. The punishments were mostly of a sexy nature. They rarely hurt or left a mark. Often I felt refreshed or cleansed after we played. I don't know if catharsis is real, but I swear I felt the guilt sloughing off me like dead skin after we fucked like this. Sometimes I wanted to say the real stuff, not the petty things I knew I shouldn't be doing (smoking cigarettes, drinking during the day, buying lottery tickets, eating Taco Bell) but the stuff I carried around. How I'd lost Dee, and Leif, and Erik, how I'd given up on writing, and mostly on living. How I wanted to live stagnantly, dumbly, mutely, like a fish in a glass bowl or a mosquito larva hatched into a dirty puddle and doomed to stay a larva living out its days in muck, because that's what I believed I deserved. Sometimes I wondered if the real punishment for these things should be death. That, I would think, only seemed fair. I remembered what the serial killer had said when he'd finally been caught. *I should be dead for what I've done.*

We were sunbathing on Bradford Beach when Dee told me Frank had taken her on a date to a cemetery. Lake Michigan was still cold then, and entering the water was an icy shock to the system, but the sand was already summer-warm, and the sun was hot. Dee said his parents worked at a cemetery, so he'd grown up around it; he found those kinds of places peaceful.

"Come on," I said, exasperated with her. "Talk about a red flag."

"Well, it doesn't look like a cemetery anymore," she said. "There aren't any grave markers, and it's a bit elevated, so you can see Milwaukee and the lakefront below. It's beautiful now. It's one of his favorite spots."

"I don't know. He seems morbid."

Dee sniffed. "You don't know him."

"I don't know him, true. But I *know* that kind of guy."

"Yeah, just like I *know* what kind of guy Leif is."

"What kind of guy is that?" I asked her.

"He's dark." She paused. "And emotional."

I sensed this was supposed to sting. "Well, that's how I like my men," I teased her.

"Why?"

"The sex is better that way," I said. (Did I even believe this? I still wanted to say things to shock her, because she was *so* capable of shocking me.)

She rolled onto her back then, and I stared at the wide flare of her hip bones, the sharp projection of them through her swimsuit.

"Not me," she said. "I like my men light and airy. Like they're walking on clouds."

That didn't seem an apt description of Frank, but I didn't say it. Even then I knew we saw our lovers through poorly adjusted lenses. Is it the responsibility of our loved ones to help us adjust that vision? What do we risk if we try? What do we risk if we don't try?

Dee folded her hands behind her head. I wanted to keep asking her questions about what she liked and why, but she put her headphones in and threw her shirt over her eyes. It seemed important for us to figure this out *together*. I needed so badly to be able to relate to Dee, I was willing to lie to her about what I liked. I had a fear of us developing such different tastes that we'd be stranded worlds apart. Now I wonder if that's a fear born only out of what happened, a fear I've mapped onto the past and onto our conversations about men and love and sex. Maybe I was listening for myself, and I never heard the important things Dee said to me about Frank.

Or maybe I never knew what the important things were. I read later about something called subjective validation, a psychological phenomenon that humans are prone to, wherein we believe a few unrelated or even random events must be related because a belief, expectation, or hypothesis demands a relationship. Is that what I've done here? Is that what I've built?

Later that same day, when Dee and I had begun to get sun-drunk and loopy, Erik stopped by. He brought a Styrofoam cooler full of Milwaukee's Best. He was already loaded, and while what Dee and I really needed was water, we didn't refuse the beers. We opened one after another after another. The edges of the day faded; the sun sank behind the bluff and cast a dark shadow over the lake. We paid no mind.

Erik had a jagged cut under one of his eyes. When he handed Dee another beer, she brushed the cut with the soft pad of her thumb. He pulled away.

"What's this." It wasn't a question, which was maybe why Erik did not feel the need to say anything back. He took a pull from his beer and burped loudly. Dee laughed and tried to do the same, but her burp was pathetic in comparison. She kept trying.

"You guys are disgusting. And drunk," I said. "We've got leftovers at my place. You guys hungry?"

"Frank doesn't want Dee going over there anymore," Erik said matter-of-factly.

I paused mid-sip and hiccupped. Heat rose to my cheeks. "What the hell does that mean?" I asked. Dee shot Erik daggers. The corners of her mouth went hard.

"Frank says it's too ghetto. Where you live. It's not safe," Erik said stiffly, as if he were a TV reporter doing a segment on "crime in *your* neighborhood." Though he was clearly poking fun at Frank's assessment of Riverwest, I seemed to remember that Erik had said a similar thing about our neighborhood to Leif. *People are always getting robbed.*

"Will you shut up?" Dee said. "Just let it go."

"What the fuck does Frank know, anyway," I said. I felt a wave of anger.

"He doesn't know shit," Erik said. "He's a bigot." He burped again.

"Well, fuck you both," Dee said. She tossed her beer away and it spilled into the sand. She threw her dress over her swimsuit and started running away. I got up to follow her, but Erik stopped me.

"I'm sorry," he said. "It's my fault. I'll handle it."

"Have you met him?" I shouted at Erik as he started after Dee. He nodded and puffed his chest out. But beneath his bravado, I could tell he was afraid.

I watched him jog after her. To an outsider, they might have been a young married couple having a fight. Dee had already made it a long way down the beach, so when he finally caught her, they were just two dark specks against the lake.

On the day of the first session with the psychic, I called Peter to pick me up because I'd woken up with a splitting headache. I had been subject to nightmare after nightmare, though when I woke, the specificity of them faded fast, and I was left with only a sense of foreboding and the thick taste of rot on my tongue. I scrubbed my tongue vigorously with the back of my toothbrush, grabbed Dee's pearls from my kitchen counter, and went outside to wait for Pete.

When Pete pulled up, Dana hopped out of the passenger seat, brushed her cheek against mine, and climbed in the backseat. I knew instantly Pete was in a sour mood, which clouded the atmosphere inside the car. Dana put her headphones in and leaned her forehead against the window. Pete glanced at his daughter in the rearview and then turned to me.

"I heard back from the *Journal Sentinel*," Pete said.

"Oh."

"They said they would send a reporter to the next session with the psychic."

He darted his eyes at me. Pete had been particularly supportive of Ma's decision to hire the psychic in part because he believed it might get us a fresh dose of press. It was odd how we'd traded these roles over the years. When Dee first disappeared, I'd tried desperately to get my family to take exposure more seriously. But as the years wore on, and I became less and less convinced it would ever matter, I gave it up. Pete had taken up that torch in recent years, perhaps emboldened by his perceived status. Even so, it hadn't mattered. No one really picked up the story the way we hoped they would. He thought the psychic might be a new angle to get the press and the pressure we would need to reopen the case. From my perspective, the case was solved, but we desperately needed to find Dee's body in order for law enforcement to take us seriously again. I was long done dealing with apathetic journalists over at the *Journal Sentinel*. They always focused on the wrong thing.

"It's a mistake," I told him. I tried to keep my voice light, because I didn't want Dana to think we were fighting. We weren't fighting. We never fought anymore. What was the point?

"Exposure," Pete said, like it was a mantra for him. "We've always said, *you've* always said, this is what we need. Now we're going to get it."

"What's the reporter's name?" I asked.

"What's it to you? Like you know every fucking guy over there."

I could feel Dana's eyes on the backs of our heads.

When we got to the Lutheran Home, Wolski was outside smoking a cigarette. I followed his gaze to two MPD patrol cars parked across the street. Two shadowy figures shifted inside one of the cars.

"What's all this?" Pete gestured at the cops.

Wolski shrugged. "The kid asked for police protection."

"MPD's for hire now?" I asked him.

"Certainly looks that way," he said.

"They really don't tell you shit over there, do they?" Pete said. Wolski let this one go.

At the doors, two more cops drank the shitty nursing home coffee and cracked jokes with each other.

"This is, hands down, the most boring detail I've ever been on."

"Aw, shit, man. I don't know. You ever done suicide watch? That shit is brutal."

Wolski flashed his badge at them and they clammed up. As we passed, one of them let his eyes linger on Dana twenty seconds too long. I glared at him. His eyes glazed over and he sipped from his Styrofoam cup.

In the community room, Thomas Alexander was running his long thin fingers over the piano's keys as if dusting the instrument. When he noticed us, he leaped up from the bench and attempted awkward hugs with each of us. Pete stuck his hand out instead, and Wolski merely sidestepped and patted the psychic on the shoulder. He tried to kiss Dana on the lips, but she turned her head away. I held the pearls out to Thomas Alexander so as to avoid physical contact, but he pulled my hand in and closed his dramatically over mine. The pearls hung out the sides of our clasped hands. I squirmed. Wolski's face turned a bit white when he saw the necklace. Thomas Alexander's eyes lingered on Wolski's coloring. Then he turned back to me. He let my hand drop and brought the pearls close to his lips like he was going to kiss them. He inhaled. He frowned.

"Thank you for doing this," he said. "I know how hard it must have been."

I nodded. Wolski elbowed Peter in the ribs. "Would you excuse me and Pete for just a minute?" Wolski asked.

I glared at them. I tried to make a face that perfectly meant *Do not leave me with him*. But Thomas Alexander smiled. I imagined he spent many hours a day in front of a large mirror practicing this smile. The sheer stamina of it astounded me.

"Absolutely, gentlemen," he said. "We're still getting set up here."

I wasn't in any kind of mood to make small talk, so I went to where Ma was seated at a table.

"Hi, Mama," I said. She looked up.

"Did you bring the item?"

I nodded. "Thomas Alexander's got it," I told her. She breathed a sigh of relief. It was clear she hadn't thought I'd bring it.

"Where are the boys?" Ma asked.

"They had to step out for a minute, apparently," I told her.

She frowned. "They just got here, dammit." I didn't say anything. I couldn't think of anything useful to say. Ma waited. I waited. A windstorm started up outside. It whipped tree branches against the sliding glass doors. I had to work not to hold my breath. Something felt wrong. No. Everything felt wrong. Eventually, Pete and Wolski hurried back in. They gave me identical glares. I made a face back to them, like, *What did I do now?* They shook their heads.

One of the assistants arranged Thomas Alexander's chair in front of Ma. The chairs were close enough that Thomas Alexander could easily reach out and touch my mother. There were only a couple of inches between their knees. That seemed too close. The assistants started shepherding us away from Ma and the psychic. We waited near the walls.

Ma sat quietly with her ankles crossed and her hands in her lap. She was wearing a flowery dress I hadn't seen on her in a long time. It hung off her shoulders so she looked a shrunken version of herself. Thomas Alexander had a large drawing pad out in his lap, and he clutched a black felt-tip pen tightly in his right hand. In his left hand, he held the string of fake pearls. It was quiet. No one spoke, and the only noises I heard were the storm whipping outside and the dull whir of several hundred televisions running at the same time. Thomas Alexander began to draw on the pad. He drew large looping circles without much thought. He closed his eyes. He fingered the pearls. Once again he put them up to his lips like he could taste them. He let out a long sigh. He mumbled. Ma leaned in. I couldn't hear anything he was saying, if he was saying anything at all. The circles on the pad got smaller and smaller so it looked like he was drawing a dark tunnel which we were all falling into. I thought for a minute I would explode for wanting to end the scene, but Thomas Alexander did it for me. His eyes snapped open, and he threw the pad and the necklace on the ground. "Stop," he yelled.

"What the hell?" Ma crossed her arms over her chest. "What the hell is going on?"

Pete and Wolski glared at me. Thomas Alexander stormed toward the door. "The necklace was not hers," he said to me. Thomas Alexander's entourage rushed after him, and they did so in a manner that told me this was not the first time they'd set everything up just to break it down minutes later. The wind kept up outside.

Wolski took me by the arm. "I gave you that fucking necklace," he growled.

"Are you sure?" I asked him. He nodded. "I thought . . . Dee . . . They were in the box . . . I remembered . . ." I choked out. Peter pinched the bridge of his nose. Ma was still sitting in her wheelchair with her good arm clasped over her chest. I backed out of the room. No one tried to stop me.

Wolski had developed a thing for me over the past ten years. I hadn't done anything to encourage it, except one bad year on the Fourth, when I'd stumbled to his place and drunkenly fucked him. I didn't remember most of that night, and I especially didn't remember the part when we slept together, but Wolski did remember. He still remembered. I didn't know who, in our family, knew. But I had guesses. Peter, for one. Suze, maybe. I didn't call Wolski or talk to him for a good seven months after that, but he left me long voicemails and he wrote me letters and I thought about reporting him as a stalker because it wore on me to keep saying no. But he was so much a part of my family's life by then that it didn't seem feasible to avoid him anyway. I told him he had to stop, and he said he would try. He got married and had a kid, a girl, Kelsey, and he got divorced and then married again, and the whole time he slipped in and out of love with me, or that's what he said. I tried not to think about it too much. He was like a brother or an uncle to me. I assumed the proximity of our lives had just spun us into too tight an orbit with each other: Now we couldn't escape even if we wanted to.

That's how I felt about much of my life. I'd thought about leaving Wisconsin before. But as long as I was in Wisconsin, I kept some irrational hope alive that Dee would turn up, and I knew I'd never forgive myself if I was gone when she made it home. I was attached to the state with a heavy anchor. I figured I'd die, like Ma, without ever living anywhere else, maybe without ever leaving the city again.

Once, one of my friends from school, Veronica, had submitted some of my poems to a writing residency in Bulgaria. If you were accepted, the whole trip was paid for; you spent a month writing and workshopping your work with other writers, presumably looking out over the Black Sea and drinking copious amounts of wine. It was the kind of thing that Dee and I would have dreamed about. I was accepted, and Veronica came by my apartment with a bottle of sparkling wine and my plane tickets. I was so angry that I refused to speak to her for a year. She didn't understand how I couldn't ever leave. Not many people did. I don't think she really ever forgave me for giving that fellowship up, and I certainly never forgave her for submitting my poems. I lost a lot of friends this way. Hell, I had lost Henry this way.

Late in June, Erik showed up at Mount Mary with his arm hanging sickly from his shoulder and a mouthful of blood. Dee was tougher than she looked, and the sight of a lot of blood had never been enough to make her queasy. Besides, she'd always been more maternal than I was. Though I'd never learned the art of comforting people, Dee always knew what people wanted to hear. I never said the right thing or the thing that was needed. *It will be okay. We'll figure it out. I'm here for you.* But as she told me on the phone, "I'm not a damn doctor."

Leif was at work, and I was pulling on jeans with one hand and tripping over the phone cord. "I'm on my way, baby," I told her.

"You better be," she hissed. "It is four-thirty in the damn morning, and I've got campus security on my case for routinely letting 'a suspicious person' into the dorm."

I held my tongue. (I wanted to say maybe they meant Frank.) "Be there in ten," I said.

We were lucky Dee's roommate was out of town, because the room wasn't built to hold more than two bodies at once. Erik was splayed out on the dirty carpet. He looked like he was part of some modernist art exhibit. Dee's paintings threatened to topple down on him from all sides. He cradled his left arm tight against his chest, and his eyes were squeezed shut. There were thin lines of blood dripping down his neck and pooling in the hollow of his collarbone. Dee looked ready to fight me.

"He needs to go to a hospital," I said. Erik flung his head wildly from side to side. He was in a bad way. He smelled like he'd drunk a whole bottle of whiskey.

"Thank you for that astute observation, Margaret," Dee said. I flinched; I hated it when she called me Margaret. "I already told him that."

"Best we can do is clean him up, and then we'll get Leif to help us take him to the ER."

She nodded and began to get to work. She got Erik to sit up and swish some water and then spit it back out. We eventually coaxed him to drink water. Dee dabbed away the blood on his face and neck and tried to get a look in his mouth, but he wouldn't let her. We didn't touch his twisted arm; I guessed it was dislocated or broken. Dee cooed while we worked, and though it would have annoyed me, Erik seemed to respond to it. He relaxed at her touch, and he put the ice she'd pilfered from the cafeteria on his swollen jaw. When we took his shirt off to throw it in the wash, we saw his arms were bruised in the shape of long thin fingers. He cried a little bit when we eased his bad arm out of the shirt, and this seemed to exhaust him so much that when he laid his head back down on the carpet, he fell asleep fast and hard. Dee propped his head up with a pillow and threw her comforter on top of him.

I had only a couple of minutes before I needed to pick up Leif at Ambrosia, but Dee and I went outside and sat on a bench underneath some old grapevines. The summer leaves had only just begun to grow back, and we could see the sky getting light through the arbor. The sun was coming up now, and there were nuns on their knees in the chapel singing, we could hear them; Dee said they sang every morning. We leaned in to each other and listened. I wanted to say I was sorry, not just for mixing her up in this but for every ugly thing in the world. I've never loved someone the way I loved Dee; I loved her so much I wished I could make the world more deserving of her. I wished I could get rid of all this muck. And that wasn't even the whole of the way I loved her; it's a difficult thing to explain. The only thing I can say for sure is that I would never love anyone else in the same way.

"Do you know what happened?" I asked her.

"He wouldn't say, but I think it's pretty obvious," Dee said. She examined the blood underneath her fingernails.

"He says he gets in fights at the clubs," I said.

"Every night? Peg, don't be dense. His boyfriend beats him up," she said.

I flinched; she was rarely so frank.

"I'm getting scared," Dee whispered.

"Of what?"

Dee hesitated. I thought of Erik's face on Bradford Beach the other day: a stripe of fear he'd tried to hide from me.

The singing had stopped. The nuns filed out of the chapel and walked through the grapevine. I was acutely aware of the blood under my own nails. The nuns' robes brushed our bare knees as they passed us, and Dee stayed quiet.

The truth about that summer, at least the part of it before Dee went missing, and after too, I suppose, is I was so caught up in my own sad state of being in love that all I could do was play a dumb game of comparison with her. Dee and I were competing to see who could be the most adult, which was only proof that we were still children.

When we were girls, we used to play a game we called *next-door neighbors*. We'd pretend the upstairs of our house was a little town—the separate rooms represented our own homes, the grocery store, the coffee shop, the library, or whatever other locations we needed for that day's game. We'd pretend we lived in that tiny town together, and every time we played, we were caught up in all kinds of small-town drama—fighting over fences or tree lines, gossiping over whose son was dating whose daughter, planning parties for town events: festivals, and markets, and parades. I'd told Leif about this game, and he'd been shocked. He seemed embarrassed for me. He said there was no imagination in that kind of play. He said we'd chosen a boring imitation of reality to play in. But we never saw it like that. I think for Dee and me, when we were girls, almost nothing was more exciting than the prospect of being grown.

One "grown-up" habit Dee adopted when she moved out of Ma's house, along with the purely aesthetic cigarette smoking and beer drinking, was dieting. Dee had always been skinny. She had an obnoxiously tiny waist above round, beautiful hips. She'd always wanted the Twiggy figure, but I'd told her men were crazy for bodies like hers. She never did believe me. When I went back to Dee's dorm to check on her and Erik a few days later, I found them lying in bed together, sipping from red SlimFast cans.

"What the hell is that?" I asked them. Erik giggled and took a big gulp. He had a chocolate mustache.

"I wrote the company a letter, and they sent me a bunch of promotional samples." She hopped out of bed and opened her tiny dorm closet. Inside were three cases of the cans stacked beneath her dresses. She pushed aside several long, shimmery gowns, getups I didn't think she had any reason to own, and fished inside an open box. "It's really good. Here, try it." She handed me a can, and I sniffed it. I tried to read the ingredients, but I didn't know any of the words. I took a sip.

"Tastes like chalk," I said.

Dee shrugged and finished off the can. She closed her closet and stood in front of the mirror on the back of the door. She rose up on to the balls of her feet and lifted her shirt, turning this way and that way in front of the door.

I shoved her away from the mirror. "You ought to eat some real food. You're both too damn skinny as it is." Admittedly, Erik looked better than when I'd seen him writhing on Dee's floor a few days before, but he still had the look of someone climbing out of a hole. His left arm was snug inside a hospital issued sling and his eyes were heavy like maybe he was popping painkillers.

"Frank says I have a billion-dollar body."

I laughed despite myself. "A billion dollars, huh? Not a million?"

"Frank says Atlantic City strippers have million-dollar bodies."

I wanted to kick him in the nuts, but Dee liked him. I didn't know why, but she did. Maybe she sometimes felt the same way about Leif. I pulled her shirt back down over her stomach. "Bodies aren't for sale, Dee."

"Oh, come on." She tousled my hair. "It was just a compliment."

"Fucked-up one, but sure."

"Jealous?"

"Not in the least. That's a white-trash compliment."

"You want to talk about white trash? When's the last time Leif took you out on a date?"

Erik's face reddened. He attempted a laugh, but it came out choked and ugly.

I tried to remember my last date with Leif; after we'd moved in together, the idea of dates hadn't made much sense. I thought I remembered a meal we'd had earlier that spring at a Mexican restaurant with a patio. We'd drunk a lot of tequila and then put our numbed toes in Lake Michigan's winter water. The city left the lifeguard towers up on the beaches all through the winter, and we'd climbed one together and huddled in the wide chair, watching the tiny white lights of the shipping freighters floating on the horizon.

Dee must have seen something sad in my face, because she came close to me and nuzzled her nose in my neck. "It's not a contest, Pegasus," she said gently, though of course she knew it was.

It took me a long time to admit, but Dee was always more adventurous than me. Even when we were much younger, she enjoyed proposing ridiculous dares, teasing me while I agonized over consequences, and then finally, in frustration with me, completing the challenge herself. It was in this way that I learned a defense mechanism that ultimately established one of the crucial dynamics of our relationship—at some point, I began returning her dares with even more outlandish dares of my own.

NAME: Felicity Hale
RELATION: Roommate
INTERVIEWED ON: July 10, 1991
INTERVIEWER: Peter

PETER: When did you last see Dee?

FELICITY: July third.

PETER: She didn't stay at the dorm on the Fourth?

FELICITY: Dee did not stay here on the Fourth. I didn't either, but I knew she hadn't spent the night because her bed was still made up, and it was full of shit, and if she's spent the night, that shit's usually on the floor.

PETER: When she doesn't stay here, where does she usually stay?

FELICITY: Uh, Frank's? Peg's? Your ma's place?

PETER: How often did she stay at Frank's?

FELICITY: Maybe a couple of times a week.

PETER: Did she say where she was going on the Fourth?

FELICITY: She said probably Peg's. She packed an overnight bag. And then I saw Peg in that red convertible come to pick her up. That's a nice car. Dee said it belonged to Peg's boyfriend, but she also said he worked at Ambrosia, and I don't know how someone affords that kind of thing on a factory salary.

PETER: Did you notice anything unusual about Dee's behavior on the third?

FELICITY: Dee's an eccentric woman. What exactly do you mean?

PETER: She wasn't emotional?

FELICITY: We're artists, Peter; we're all emotional.

PETER: But she didn't mention anything to you about Frank?

FELICITY: What do you mean, *about Frank*?

PETER: Did she mention a fight with Frank?

FELICITY: My understanding is that their relationship is relatively low-stress for Dee-Dee.

PETER: Have you met Frank?

FELICITY: In passing. I think. Maybe.

PETER: What was your impression of him?

FELICITY: He didn't impress me much at all. But boy, is he into Dee-Dee.

PETER: How so?

FELICITY: Oh, you know. He dotes on her. He buys her lots of gifts. A Walkman and dresses and jewelry sometimes too.

PETER: Did Dee say anything to you recently about fighting with Peg?

FELICITY: Well. You know Dee and Peg. They're always fighting about something; they don't see eye to eye on much. But they always make up.

PETER: But did Dee mention if they were fighting on the third? Or what they were fighting about?

FELICITY: I don't remember. I don't know. I don't think so. Maybe they weren't fighting, then.

PETER: Did she say what she and Peg were going to do for the Fourth?

FELICITY: I think the fireworks at the lakefront? Oh, wait, that was the third. I don't know if she said.

After the first session with the psychic, I drank a whole bottle of wine and paced around my apartment like I was practicing for an afterlife in which I would haunt the building. I had truly believed the pearls belonged to Dee. The realization that I'd misremembered this small detail was disorienting. I felt confused. Knocked out of time. I needed to take back control, but I wasn't sure how.

I stared out the window overlooking the street, where groups of students drunkenly paraded up and down Oakland. One teetering boy shouted: *Who wants to have my babies?* A car honked at him. He blew kisses into the night. I thought of the night Dee and I went to Walker's Point. I searched my inbox for the psychic's contact info, which Pete had forwarded a month ago. I dialed Thomas Alexander's number and a woman picked up. She asked who was calling. I told her. She said to hold.

"Hello? Peg?"

"Hi," I said. "I was wondering if we could meet."

"Why?" he asked.

"I need to explain some things."

There was shuffling, almost like the sound of tissue paper being crumpled. "Okay. One drink. I'm at the Hyatt."

I hung up the phone, put my coat on, and drove to the Hyatt. The top floor of the hotel rotated slowly to give viewers a panoramic experience of the city's mostly meager skyline. Lake Michigan's black expanse stretched out behind the city.

I felt dizzy after the first rotation, but Thomas Alexander claimed that was impossible because the rotations were extremely slow. *It's all in your head*, he said. I felt like the sloppier I got, the more composed he became. I imagined him sucking every sober fiber out of my body and internalizing it for himself. Magic. The bartender was serving him whiskey lemonades muddled with extra sugar. I asked how he could be drinking in public, aged twenty, as he was.

He flashed a fake ID at me. "But this is just a formality, really." He slurped his drink loudly and laid down a forty-dollar tip for the bartender. "Also," he whispered, "I'm famous."

"I've heard."

"From whom?" he asked jokingly.

"My niece," I said.

He nodded. "I'm very popular with Gen Z. They have a great appetite and appreciation for the psychic sciences, for alternative forms of healing, and for astrology." He sounded like his own infomercial. I didn't bother telling him that Dana wasn't exactly a fan. Instead, I nodded.

"I wanted to apologize for the necklace. I really thought it was Dee's."

He shook his head. "Don't worry about it. I understand." This reaction surprised me: He had thrown a tantrum at the nursing home. He slid to the edge of his stool so he was closer to me.

"And I . . . I really want this to work," I told him.

"Of course, of course," he said.

"So what can I do?"

"You've got to get me something of hers that isn't all gummed up with your own psychic energy. You know? Like something untainted. Do you think you can do that?"

An image of our storage locker loomed large in my mind. I thought of Dee's paintings piled up almost to the ceiling in that dark room. I nodded and took a drink. The spherical space of the bar seemed to be closing in.

"What did you tell my mother?" I asked him. "What does she think you know about her?"

"She had a miscarriage," he said easily, like he was reporting the weather. "Between you and Pete. No one knew. Not even your father." I didn't know if this was what he'd told my mother, and I knew also that I'd never, ever ask her or try to confirm it. He was a smart kid. "What about you? The first one is always free."

"No, no, thank you," I said.

"You're hiding something. Some kind of behavior. Destructive behavior. And what about this photo?"

"Please," I said. "That's enough."

"Okay," he said. "But the more you hide from me, the harder it makes my job."

I drained my glass and motioned for the bartender to pour another. "I thought people couldn't hide things from you. Isn't that the whole point? Isn't that what you do?"

"Oh, no, not at all. Willing participants always present clearer channels and better access, you know? Those who are resistant can easily create confusion for me. A messy, distracting aura can complicate my readings. Cause me to make mistakes. That's why I always tell people to be absolutely sure they're ready. Otherwise the process can be . . . dangerous?"

I caught the bartender's eye as he put down my vodka soda. Our fingers touched as I picked up the drink, and I thought he looked like he wanted to ask if I was okay. I hated those kinds of men—the ones who wanted to intercede on my behalf.

"I'm not scared of him," I said to the bartender.

The bartender frowned at me, confused. "Sure," he said. He left to help another customer. I'd maybe said the wrong thing. Thomas Alexander looked like he might laugh.

I turned back to him. "Dangerous how?"

"Like with this photo. I'm sensing it means a lot to you. But you're blocking my path to it. With something. I can tell you're all caught up in it. Was it . . . the photo . . . was that the last time you saw your sister?" Without realizing it, I had edged closer to him, to hear more clearly what he was saying. To try to understand what he meant. I wanted to shake myself awake. I realized our knees were touching, and I jumped back.

"What the hell are you talking about?" I muttered, but without conviction. It was too late; I felt I'd already folded. My vision wavered. The photo bloomed in my mind like I was watching the images come alive in developing solution—my own body taking shape in the dark. I finished my drink in two gulps, threw down some cash, and left.

Once, when we were girls, we took a family trip to Washington Island, a small island off the Door Peninsula accessible only by ferry. It was the middle of winter, and the surface of the lake had frozen unevenly in massive ice floes that crashed against one another in the waves. We drove our car onto an old ferry, which then began to make its way across the strait. There was a terrible splitting noise like a band saw put to concrete. Dee held her mittened hands over her ears, and we ran up the stairs to see what was happening. From the top deck, we saw that the bow of the ship was breaking through the ice as it moved. The noise was the sound of the ship clearing ice from its path. Dee and I stood on the top deck the whole trip, even though it was below freezing and the tips of our noses burned with the cold. I couldn't stop watching as the ship moved and cracked the ice, and the fissures in the largest ice floes rippled out and away from the ship, out farther than we could see. *It's so pretty,* Dee mouthed over the sound of the ice breaking beneath us. I smiled at her, but I didn't think it was pretty at all.

When Frank walked in on Dee and Erik cuddling in her bed one afternoon, he didn't ask any questions. Dee said Frank grabbed Erik by his shirt and threw a punch that Erik ducked. She said Erik tripped and fell as he tried to get out the door, and Frank kicked Erik in the gut and the neck, and pinned him down by holding his knees tight against Erik's hips. Dee called me at work; I was gently erasing pencil from some very delicate yellowing paper. Dee was hysterical and barely making sense. In the background, I heard the soft, sick sounds of one body caving into another. I thought of the wound on her ribs. I told her to call the police; I tried to use my calm voice. It didn't work. The nub of my eraser tore a hole through the paper in front of me.

"Dammit," I whispered.

"Please," she screamed at me. "Help."

When I got off work, I drove to the dorm, but there was no sight of Dee, or Frank, or Erik. The angry hall monitor who'd chastised me before paced in front of Dee's door. Pastel paper flowers crunched underneath her shoes. I was about to ask her where they'd gone, but she beat me to it.

"Dee went in the ambulance with that *other* guy." The girl

lowered her voice. "The *gay* one." She seemed impressed with herself for saying the word.

I drove to the closest hospital and checked in at the ER's reception. A tired nurse motioned down the hallway behind her. There were stretchers lining the hallway and people standing over these stretchers waiting for rooms. Some of these people were very sick; some of them were handcuffed to the metal rail of their bed. Erik and Dee were curled up in one of these beds together. They were holding hands. I felt a pang of jealousy and then a wave of nausea. I tried to shake it off.

Erik had his eyes closed. His face had already begun to swell up badly, so I almost didn't recognize him. When I got close, Dee narrowed her eyes to slits and put her finger up against her lips. "They gave him some morphine," she whispered. "He's dozing now."

"Are you okay?" I asked her. I took her free hand into mine and kissed it.

"Frank thought we were fucking."

"He's an idiot," I said. "Erik tried to tell you . . ."

Dee bristled. "You're an idiot," she croaked. "You're the one who suggested he stay with me!" The tone of her voice was changing fast. She tried to take her hand away, but I kept it and squeezed hard.

"You said it was okay!"

She paused and breathed a labored breath like she was trying to calm herself down. Her tone stayed strained, though. "Look at him," Dee said. I couldn't. I looked at Dee's thin pink fingers threaded through my own. "Look," she said again. I did and I felt the nausea rising in me again.

"We have to fix this." She gently released Erik's hand and used her opposite hand to pry my fingers away from her own, one by one. It hurt. She took Erik's hand back up and buried her face in his neck. I'm ashamed now to admit I didn't tell her that from where I stood, it looked like she was the one who needed to fix things. She needed to get rid of Frank.

That night there were fifteen-foot waves off the shore of Bradford Beach. When I picked Leif up at Ambrosia, I told him about the waves before I mentioned anything about Erik. I didn't know how he would react. It occurred to me that this meant I didn't know Leif well at all. He wanted to see the waves, so we drove to the break wall, but there were fire trucks and neon-orange fencing blocking us from the beach. The waves had begun to wash up into the street, and the officials were working on blocking that off too. A policeman waved us back. He came up to Leif's car and rapped his knuckles on the window.

"We're closing this all off until the waves die down," he told us. "I'm going to have to ask you to turn around." He shone his flashlight into our car and then pointed it out toward Lake Michigan, where the black waves ate the light. "I've never seen waves like this," he admitted.

"We just wanted to see them, Officer," I said.

He nodded. "Leave your car here," he whispered conspiratorially. "You can walk to the edge of the fence if you want."

Leif was ecstatic. We hurried out of his car. The lake was so loud it drowned the noises of the city: the sirens, and the cars, and the groans of buses and trains, and people everywhere making it known they were unhappy. It was late, but there was some purple light left in the sky, so we could see the waves as they collected themselves high and then crashed heavy on the white rocks of the break wall. There was a desperate energy to the scene, and it had the effect of making me want to confess. But to what? I looked at Leif, his face wind-whipped and tired from the slow slog of his shift at Ambrosia, and I told him I was sorry. He took up my hand, maybe because there was no one to see. It was hot and wet.

"For what?" he asked.

"Erik's been staying at Dee's. Frank found the two of them there together and got the wrong idea. He beat Erik up bad. He's in the hospital."

One of the waves rushed through the holes in the orange fencing and kissed our feet. The water still felt like winter. I shivered, and Leif, to my surprise, collected my body in his arms.

"You can't fix people," he whispered. I wished he would speak loudly; I could barely hear him.

"What do you mean?"

I tried to pull away from him, but he held me against his body. Our feet were soaked.

"Listen to me," he begged. "You can only ever make it worse."

SUZE: When was the last time you saw Dee?

TODD: God, it had to have been almost a week and a half ago.

SUZE: How many hours was she working here?

TODD: Oh, maybe ten to fifteen.

SUZE: Do you remember the last time she worked?

TODD: I can check. But off the top of my head, I think it was July first. She told me she wanted to reduce her hours here the last time she was in.

SUZE: Did she say why?

TODD: Yeah, uh. Something about wanting more time to paint. And she had some hotshot boyfriend who was taking care of her.

SUZE: She told you that?

TODD: In not so many words. She told some of the other girls. Her boyfriend bought her things. Took her out. I think she thought they might get married. Or that's what she told the other girls, like I said.

SUZE: Did you ever meet this guy?

TODD: Not directly, no. He came by here a couple of times to pick Dee up after work.

SUZE: What was your impression of him?

TODD: Looked like a real Guido type if you ask me. I think she could have done better. But he was clearly crazy about her.

SUZE: Why do you say that?

TODD: Oh, I don't know. He did a lot of totally pussy-whipped shit. Over-the-top gifts. Like he was scared to lose her.

Article IV. Relevance and Its Limits

RULE 405. METHODS OF PROVING CHARACTER

(b) By Specific Instances of Conduct. When a person's character or character trait is an essential element of a charge, claim, or defense, the character or trait may also be proved by relevant instances of the person's conduct.

On the day I went back to the storage locker for the first time since we'd moved Dee's things there, I woke up with a powerful hangover. The predictability of it was a comfort: I lay in bed late into the day and my mind fed me a slow, sad diet of memories: Dee and me being followed by a car full of boys. They ride the bumper of our parents' station wagon while I try to drive. Dee sticks her middle finger out the window, and my face burns so red it hurts. *Dee,* I choke out in fear. Dee sobs on the Fourth of July. Her whole body is cast in fluorescent firework hues. Me and Dee and Pete splash in the shallows of Lake Michigan just north of the city. Dee takes her shirt off when Pete does. *Don't do that,* Pete tells her. *Why?* She puts one hand on her waist and juts her hips out to the left in a perfect imitation of our mother. With the other hand, she rubs her flat baby chest. He shrugs. Dee climbs onto Peter's back and wraps her legs tight around his waist. I try to tackle both of them. Dee throws her mouth open to the sky, laughing. Henry stands over me while my knees burn against the carpeting in his bedroom floor. *What did you do?* he asks me. He brushes the pad of his thumb over both of my lips and opens my mouth.

I tried to focus. What did I want? We all wanted different things. Ma wanted to find Dee's body so she could be buried next to her baby and her husband. Suze, I think, wanted her sister to finally find some peace. Pete wanted more press in the hopes that this might reenergize local or national interest in our case. Wolski probably wanted to assuage his guilt. And I still wanted to nail Frank. At that point I hoped, and was edging dangerously into the territory of believing, that whatever the psychic discovered, it would bolster my own evidence against Frank. It would prove that he murdered Dee and tried to disappear her body. Maybe it was the psychic's comment about the photo, vague as it was, that had pushed me toward this notion. I tried to rationalize his knowledge of the photo— but there weren't many people who knew. (Wolski was one of them.) Maybe I needed to commit, like the psychic said. Maybe, in order for this to work, I needed to believe, without reservations, that it would work. I decided to go to the storage locker. Suddenly, though, the hangover began to overwhelm me, and I felt sick, so I dragged myself into the kitchen, forced down the lone beer in my fridge, and called Wolski.

"You busy?" I asked him.

"What do you need?" I heard some voices on his end, but I couldn't make out what they were saying.

"I wanted to say sorry about the necklace. I didn't remember you giving it to me. I'm sorry."

"It's fine. Is that all?"

"I need some help."

"When?"

"Whenever you can."

"I'm a little tied up here." The voices got louder. The tenor of it sounded like an argument, but it was hard to tell. Wolski got louder too. "Text me. I can be where you need me in an hour or two."

He hung up without saying goodbye. I texted him the address of the storage locker where we kept Dee's stuff. He never responded to the text, but I knew he'd be there. I closed my eyes and lay back down for another half hour. All I could see were Thomas Alexander's baby teeth shining in that tiny, immaculate forever smile of his. Then I brushed my teeth and fixed my hair. I avoided the mirror. When I pulled up to the gate of the storage locker, Wolski was already there, smoking and leaning against his car. I thought for a moment I felt something unnameable for him, and then the thought was gone, and as was the case more often than not, I felt nothing.

"Rough night, eh?" he shouted while I was still getting out of the car. I wondered if I should have been braver and looked in the mirror. "You look like shit."

"Yeah," I said.

He squeezed my shoulder. "We're gonna get through this," he said in a low voice. He tried to make his voice like an anchor. Usually, this tone worked on me, but I wasn't attached that day. A heavy gust of wind could have carried me away.

"I know," I said. I stood straighter and shrugged his hand off my shoulder. "I just didn't want to go alone. It's been a while."

It had been two decades since we'd boxed Dee's stuff up and locked it away. I didn't think Peter had been in here since, and I certainly hadn't.

Wolski nodded. "Well. Let's make it quick," he said. "I need to get back." I was tempted to ask him what was going on back at the office, but I needed to focus. I hung back while Wolski took the key from me and opened the sliding door. I imagined a large steel mouth with Thomas Alexander's tiny teeth lining the top and the bottom. Dust flew from the door and into Wolski's face. He coughed daintily, pretending he hadn't inhaled it. I stepped over the imaginary row of teeth on the floor and into the locker, which was hot inside even though it was brisk outside. I looked up into the cement cell.

Dee's paintings were stacked like pallets on top of one another along the walls of the unit. I took one down from a stack near the door. It was a painting of an onion cut in half: deep purples and reds on a dark forest-green background. The paint was smudged and faded now. It was one that had hung briefly on the wall in the Milwaukee Art Museum that spring. I put it back on the stack. I opened a box near the door and found a set of art supplies. I picked up a dirty paintbrush. She used to let me watch her at work, though often she would make me promise not to talk, because I was a distraction; she, however, was allowed to talk. Once she turned to me, her whole body lit up by a long shaft of light spilling through the high studio windows, and she said, *You can never really mix the same color twice, but that's okay.* And I remember repeating in my mind, *But that's okay, but that's okay, but that's okay,* like it was some brilliant bit of Buddhist wisdom. It occurs to me now that Dee was the type of person who seemed to float, without effort, but also without judgment, above all the rest of us sad, rooted people.

I grabbed the paintbrush and was about to leave when I noticed her old Walkman in a box of tapes. It was one of the bright yellow ones that had SPORT written in large block letters across the side. Flimsy headphones, the foam now crumbled, were still plugged in. I remembered Frank had given the Walkman to her. At the last moment, I chose the Walkman instead of the paintbrush. I rushed out of the unit and motioned for Wolski to help me slam the heavy door shut again. The lock was sticky, and I fumbled with it. Wolski took it from my hands, his large fingers brushing the backs of my own, and I stepped away. He snapped the lock into place with a terrifying click, and I jumped back. Wolski moved to keep me from falling backwards. I let him. He nodded into the top of my head. I put a hand on his chest.

"Hey," I said. "Did you tell the psychic about the photo?"

Wolski looked hurt, or like he was pretending to look hurt. I was suddenly saddened, and very exhausted, by the fact that I couldn't tell the difference.

"You know I wouldn't . . . I couldn't do that."

I wasn't sure about this. "Okay," I said.

"He knows?"

I shrugged. "I don't think so, not really."

Wolski left in a hurry, and it wasn't until later that I realized he, along with his MPD brethren, was dealing with another crisis.

News of Thomas Alexander's request for police protection had only stirred up fresh outrage over the city's clear support of the psychic's tours and the mayoral office's historic apathy regarding police brutality. More people were now joining the victims' families in protesting the tours and the police presence in that area of the city. Besides the victims' families, most people hadn't been particularly interested in protesting the tours, but people were eager to protest the MPD. They had been doing so for years. Because every year there were more police killings of Black Milwaukeeans. Many of these cases failed to make national news, and I'm sure there were many that never made the local news either. The coverage of Terry Williams's murder stayed with me. Maybe because he was the same age as Dee when she disappeared, or maybe because it happened near Bradford Beach, a place that is, for me, inextricably linked to that summer. Or maybe it was the way they assassinated his character after he died. All of it disarmed me. Made me feel like we were living on overlapping loops of loss that circumnavigated one another. I couldn't see how we would get out. But I could see the years stretching out in either direction and understand that all of this had happened before and it's still happening now.

On a summer night in 2017, a Milwaukee County deputy fired several rounds into a car whose driver was fleeing from a traffic stop. That driver, nineteen-year-old Terry Williams, was murdered across the street from Bradford Beach. The young woman in the passenger seat was gravely injured. The deputy said he had feared for his life, even though the car was not headed in his direction. In the days that followed, the news pored over this young man's history, reporting on his rap sheet. The reporters seemed eager to explain the teenager's death, and in order to do so, they needed to make him irredeemable and deserving of his fate. I saw this happen again and again. They'd done the same thing to Sylville Smith a year before Terry Williams.

After these murders, protests spread and flourished on the North Side, in Riverwest, Harambee, and Tosa. People marched up and down MLK Drive. UWM students joined the protests and helped organize community events. In those days, the news almost never used the word *protest* or *protestors*. They preferred the word *riot:* They sought out small-business owners to interview in front of damaged storefronts—people who gave impassioned descriptions of looting and destruction. During the last set of protests, the police department sent cops in riot gear into the streets and enforced curfews. The governor sent in the National Guard. They arrested dozens of protestors. People marched downtown and stood in front of the Milwaukee Police Department headquarters with their hands in the air for hours on end.

Whenever protests erupted, I had memory flares from the summer Dee disappeared. Activists had held multiple rallies in front of the serial killer's apartment after learning that officers had automatically trusted a white man more than the Black women who had tried to flag the killer's suspicious activities. Just like in 1991, protestors made demands and the city made promises. Olive-branch stuff. For example, the previous police chief resigned, and they brought in a new one. The protests would die down when it started to get cold again, kids went back to school, and the national news outlets that had covered Milwaukee finally left, but only after almost everyone ran some version of the following head-line: "Milwaukee Remains One of the Most Segregated Cities in the Nation." Many white people in Milwaukee were shocked to hear people say this about their city, though they had only to look at their neighborhoods and their children's schools to know it.

As far as I could see, the police reaction to real or perceived problems was to add more police. That was what they'd done in Walker's Point when the psychic arrived. They'd tried to quietly squash the protestors by restricting access to Specter's and other establishments on Second Street. They added horse cops, and bike cops, and motorcycle cops, and cops walking around with their fingers looped through their belts. Two helicopters noisily patrolled the neighborhood from the sky. But the more police the depart-ment threw at the situation, the angrier people got, and the more the protests' popularity grew.

I sensed Thomas Alexander was nervous but hopeful about the situation. Though the optics weren't ideal, they still put him and his show in the spotlight. Who cared what was in the spotlight with him if he was the shiniest thing in it?

Wolski grumbled about the whole situation. "Only way this will die down without somebody getting killed is if it snows. Nobody likes protesting in the snow," he said to me and Pete once.

"It's April," Pete told him.

Wolski shrugged. "Crazier things have happened."

On the same night he'd been admitted, Erik checked himself out of the hospital while Dee was out getting something to eat. When she got back, she dropped the bag of takeout she'd bought for the two of them, and the tomato soup spilled across the hospital floor. The nurses did not have a forwarding address, and they admitted that they'd recommended he stay another night, but he'd requested the wheelchair, and they'd brought it and rolled him outside. He'd limped away. Dee left a voicemail about it all on my work phone, and I listened to it while sorting books. My boss eyed me warily from the door of his office. I hadn't picked up because I'd known it would be about Erik, and I'd missed so much work that summer, and done such a terrible job when I had been there, that I sensed I was dangerously close to losing the job. I assumed I'd been hired in part because my boss thought I was cute, in part because I played the poet-needing-work card well, but I'd missed several days in a row during the past week and I knew I wasn't that cute. I wasn't Dee-level cute, anyway. It was a good job, an easy job, and I needed it. I listened to the voicemail and acted bored, like it was a message from my mother or the landlord. I could still feel my boss's eyes on me while I deleted the message and quietly put the phone back on the receiver. I picked up my sorting pace and kept my head down.

When the clock struck four-thirty, I rushed to Dee's dorm. I had to walk and then take the bus, so it was almost an hour before I was knocking on her door. I was sweating from the walk, and I felt empty and hungry, like I could drink all of Lake Michigan or eat six meals at once. Dee didn't answer, so I gently opened the door and found her painting. She looked so beautiful, I had the urge to run to her and wrap her up. Dee had this effect on me sometimes; I needed to be near her body. She was sweating too, but just lightly, and it gave her whole body a glistening pulse. She ignored me, and I allowed her that. I sat down on the floor and watched her paint, and I could feel time passing by the way light pooled and evaporated and pooled again in the corners of the tiny room and on her bed and in her hair. She was painting more onions. It was getting dark when she finally turned to me and said, "What?"

I felt like I was waking from meditation. "You called me," I said.

"You didn't answer." She wiped her forehead with the back of her hand unselfconsciously and smeared a streak of purple paint on her nose.

"Babe," I started. "I was at work."

She rolled her eyes, and then they got large and dark and began to well. I stayed on the floor. I lost the urge to touch her when the tears started to flow.

"He's gone," she said. Her voice broke. I wanted to turn a light on in the room because the space seemed suddenly, dangerously dark, even though summer light still lingered in the sky. Leif's words echoed in my head: *You can only make it worse.* I was making it worse.

"He's a smart kid. He'll be okay," I tried.

Dee threw down the paintbrush she'd been holding. Paint splattered on the carpet. "You're dumber than I thought," she said. I cringed. "Okay?" she repeated.

I didn't really think he was going to be okay, but I needed to say something. I was bad at saying the right thing, even when it came to Dee, whom I knew so well. Whom I thought I knew so well.

"We need to find him," she said. She pointed at me. "You need to find him." I nodded and nodded, but I had no real hope we would. The nodding seemed to calm Dee, though, so I put some heart into it. She sat down next to me on the carpet. I wished she would turn the light on. Her bare shoulder touched mine, and I felt our skin stick together for a second while she leaned in to me. "You saw those pictures at the bar. What if Erik . . . What if he goes missing too." I was ashamed I hadn't thought of this possibility. Or that Leif hadn't.

"Right," I conceded, because I was tired of fighting. This was the way I lost all arguments—appeasement. "You hungry?" I pinched her arm, and she shoved me.

"Whatever," she said.

"Let's go to Walker's Point," I said. "We can ask around."

Dee eyed me. Her face was hard to see in the dark room. I put my forehead against hers, but she still wasn't having it. She pushed me back. "Fine," she said.

I scrubbed Dee's nose harshly with a washcloth to get the paint off, and then we took the bus down to Walker's Point. I was starving and wanted to kill two birds with one stone, so I decided we'd check out the bar right next door to the one where the devil blew smoke out onto the dance floor. This bar was famous for serving cheeseburgers that would change your life. I'd heard this from Erik, and he hadn't cared to elaborate. I told Dee on the bus, and she rolled her eyes.

"I'm a vegetarian now," she said smartly. Milwaukee washed by behind her done-up eyes, and I had a hard time focusing on either view: her purpled eye shadow and the sidewalks, her rose-petal cheekbones and the bus shelters, her oily mascara and the cream-brick buildings.

"Jesus, really?" I murmured. "You can get plain cheese. Just like we used to make at home, then." She huffed and put her headphones on. I thought Frank had given her the Walkman, though she'd never confirmed that. I didn't think she could have afforded it on her wage at the salon. Frank was big into gifts like that. I was suspicious of them, and I wondered if they were meant as distractions, though from what I didn't know. But I also couldn't remember the last time Leif had bought me something besides drugs or takeout, so maybe I was just jealous.

The bus started to empty out near the downtown, and it didn't pick up any new passengers. By the time we got to Walker's Point, Dee and I were the only people on the bus. It was late, and Dee had slipped into a half sleep, resting her head slightly on my shoulder. At our stop, I nudged her, and she sprang up and grabbed my hand so tightly it hurt.

"Relax," I said. "We're here." She got embarrassed and busied herself with tucking away the Walkman. I wished she hadn't brought it. It was a thief magnet.

The bar was much shabbier than the one we'd been to with Erik. Its most redeeming qualities were the permanent multicolored Christmas lights strung up behind the bar and the overwhelming smells of hot butter and meat. Dee wrinkled her nose up, but I knew she thought it smelled good. We sat at the bar, which was fairly empty, and I ordered us two beers and two cheeseburgers, one without meat. The bartender, a young woman in a crop top and a choker, stared at me. "No meat?" she yelled over the music.

"No meat," I yelled back. She laughed, and I nodded, and I saw her run to tell the other bartender, who was running the grill (a generous noun for the contraption he was cooking on), and he threw his hands up, and she gestured toward us, and they laughed conspiratorially.

"Happy?" I asked Dee.

She licked foam from the head of her beer. "Hell no," she said. "Great plan. Brilliant."

"Just drink your damn beer."

The burgers arrived in waxed paper and dripping in grease, which spread in large wet spots on the paper and covered our hands when we opened them. The most satisfying part was the waxed paper. The burger did not change my life, unless clogged arteries counts. Dee hated hers; it was clearly an unevenly sliced piece of Velveeta cut from those processed cheese-like blocks they sell in aluminum foil.

"Gross, Dee," I said. "Stop eating that."

"Well, give me a bite of yours, then," she said. She reached over to grab my burger and I slapped her hand away.

"I thought you were a vegetarian," I said. "*Now*." I stuck my tongue out at her.

Dee shrugged. "I changed my mind again."

I nodded and slid my half-eaten burger toward her. She kissed my cheek. I leaned in to the kiss.

When the bartender came to refresh our drinks, I leaned across the bar; I motioned for her to lean in too, and she was annoyed. Sweat collected on her choker and I watched it run down her neck. "Can I ask you a couple of questions?"

"That depends," she said.

"Do you know Erik Gunnarson?"

"Honey, lots of men come into this bar. I don't develop a relationship with every single one of them."

"Young, skinny, tall, reddish-blond hair, huge green eyes . . ."

"Yeah, I've seen him."

"You see him recently?"

"You a cop or something?"

"No, just his . . . friend." I choked on that word.

"Well, I haven't seen him in a month or maybe more, but I can't be sure. We've been having some real weird shit happen around here." She motioned to the back of the bar door, which, like the other bar I'd visited, had a corkboard filled with pictures and descriptions of men gone missing. "People just disappearing left and right, and the cops don't seem to give a damn about it." There was a guy waving her down at the other end of the bar, and she tossed her head in his direction.

"Thanks," I shouted after her.

"Look at you," Dee said. "Playing detective."

"You've got a bit of cheese just there." I tried to touch the corner of her mouth, but she batted me away.

"No, I don't." She laughed.

"I'm not kidding, it's right there, here, just let me." She pushed my arm away, and I shrugged.

She wiped her face, but there wasn't any cheese there. She pinched my arm. "Funny," she said. "What now?"

I got out my notebook and wrote down Erik's description. I didn't have a picture, but I told Dee we'd come back with one, and then I posted the write-up to the back of the door. It was a sad door, and I couldn't stand to look at it for very long.

"We can wait around and ask some other people too." I ordered us another round. Dee shrugged.

The bar stayed relatively empty, and we never did ask anyone else about Erik. Instead, the music got louder and louder, and Dee and I got drunk. My memories from this night are both rose-tinted and PBR-tinted. Our conversation meandered. We talked about Dee's plans for her next set of paintings, and my plans to save enough money for a plane ticket to Europe next summer. We worried aloud about Ma's loneliness and wondered when Suze would quit waitressing and "do something with her life," and we gossiped about whom Peter was dating. I loved spending long hours like this with Dee. There was no one else I felt as comfortable with. We shared the kinds of things that other people might scoff off—aspirations, fears, hopes—the kind of Hallmark shit you're not supposed to talk about out loud. But that night, even as we got drunk, and the music got louder, and the night got later, I could tell something was broken between us. We were skirting Frank, but he ghosted our conversation the whole night. I waited until I was very drunk, and Dee was mid-sip, and then I asked her.

"Have you heard from him?" I knew I was a coward for not saying his name. Her face went blank, like she was suddenly leaning very hard into the beer-induced numbness. I thought maybe she wouldn't respond, because she began picking at her cocktail napkin. I took two big swallows.

"No," she said.

I knew immediately she was lying. "I'm sorry." I didn't risk pressing her, but I wanted so badly to ask if she blamed me.

"I just miss the sex," she said. Her cocktail napkin was shredded now. This was a clever move, aimed to distract me.

I took the bait. "He didn't even make you come."

"It's not all about that."

"Did you fake it with him?"

"Do you fake it with Leif?"

I paused to consider the question. Leif had a real fear that I lied about my orgasms. I thought I did a good job of keeping it honest. I never faked it, but I left the situation open to interpretation sometimes. And if he asked, I always told him the truth.

"Nope," I said, but the pause had undermined the confidence of the response, and Dee rolled her eyes.

"Sure," she said.

I felt the conversation getting away from me. "I'm sorry." I suspected neither of us knew exactly what I was apologizing for; I hoped it would cover something I'd done or said that had hurt her over the past couple of weeks, months, years. Dee leaned in to me, and her face seemed much older suddenly. I noticed faint lines between her eyebrows and tracing her eye sockets. Ma had the same ones. Did I? She whispered in my ear. I shivered.

"You're so full of shit. You think you know everything about what you like, and why you like it, but the only difference between us is I'm honest with myself." She burped, and I couldn't help but laugh. I patted her on the back, and she drained the last of her beer and went to find the bathroom.

While Dee was in the bathroom, I used the pay phone outside to call Leif. He'd skipped work on account of a bad hangover, and I knew he was home because he always ordered shitty Chinese food and watched pay-per-view porn when he was in bad shape. He was surprised to hear my voice. "Everything good?"

"I just . . . We . . . need a ride, okay?"

I wondered if the TV screen was frozen on something nasty, some improbably large-chested woman getting slapped around by the pizza guy or whatever.

"Of course. Where are you?"

I hesitated because I knew Leif wouldn't like the answer, but I was too drunk to lie. "Walker's Point," I said.

"Fuck," he said. "Fine."

Fifteen minutes later, we were packed into the Spitfire, and Dee's head was lolling around on account of Leif's vigorous driving. Every little bump threw her head back into the headrest.

"Easy," I said. He eyed me and shook his head. I put my hand on his thigh, which he allowed. "Please."

Leif carried Dee into the house and put her, not entirely gently, on our couch. I had an image of Erik's gangly body stretched out there earlier in the summer, and felt my knees go a little weak. I stumbled and Leif reached for me.

"You too?" He scooped me up like a baby and used his mouth to brush the hair away from my ear. "What were you two doing?" At this point, I did play. I pretended to get very sleepy, and I blinked several times slowly. I nuzzled his neck and took a bit of the soft skin there between my lips. I felt his body come awake.

Leif said, "Let's go to bed, okay?"

He carried me into the bedroom and shut the door with his foot. Then he laid me down on the bed. It was an awkward pose, with my legs bent at an uncomfortable angle and my hands curled up near my face. I could feel my clothes were askew. I felt the night breeze from the open window on my bare stomach. I let my breath get deeper, and I kept my eyes closed. I could hear Leif shuffling around, and then I heard the click and swish of his camera's shutter. I stayed so still. I felt him move toward me, and he started taking off my clothes. He did everything for me. He unbuttoned my jeans and slipped my shirt over my head. He tugged my pants from my hips and gently undid the clasp of my bra. He ran his hands over everything, and I stayed limp, like a rag doll. I wanted to know what he would do when he thought I was not awake. He pulled my panties down, and opened my legs for me, and stopped. I lay as still as I could. Did he think I was asleep? Or passed out? He moved my legs, and I liked the way he put me in the position I knew he liked. He kissed me between the legs, and then, before I was ready, he was inside me. He was so hard, and I was so dry, I thought I would scream, but I kept my eyes shut, and eventually, he rolled me over and starting fucking me from behind with his hand on the back of my neck and my arms lying limp over the side of the bed. When he was done and I could feel the cum dripping out of me, he rearranged me. He rolled me over and threw our sheet on top of me, and then he straddled me, I could feel his knees pressing my hips. He kissed me on the lips, and I tasted his sweat and his breath, which smelled slightly of five spice. And then I fell asleep for real.

Leif woke me when he came to bed. He flopped down heavily beside me and tried to pull me in to him. My mouth was dry, and my body was plastered to the sheets with sweat. I tossed Leif's arms off me and padded into the kitchen. After I'd drunk three glasses of water and taken three ibuprofen, I went into the living room, where Dee was sleeping awkwardly on the couch. Through the doorway, I could see Leif's large body splayed out on our bed. I pulled the cushions off the back of the couch and took a blanket from the bedroom. Then I pulled Dee down off the couch and curled up next to her on the floor. She reached out to me and offered her hand, which I held, even though I could tell it was sweating out the alcohol in her body.

When I woke up, I couldn't feel my right shoulder anymore. I sat up and reached for Dee, but she was gone. She'd left a messy note on our coffee table. *Have to work at 10:00. We need to find Erik. I love you.* I eased myself onto the couch and held my head in my hands. I felt the blood rushing back into my shoulder, and it burned. Leif stumbled into our living room completely naked, and he wiped crusty sleep gunk from his beautiful eyes. He hopped into his sweats and flopped down next to me on the sofa. I reached for the note, because I didn't want to talk about it, but Leif had shed his sleepiness quickly and grabbed it before I did, then tossed it back on the coffee table. There was weed all over the table, empty Coke cans, a Kenneth Koch anthology opened to some poem Leif was memorizing. Leif shook tiny buds of weed from the note. "You two should give this up," he said.

"Dee's worried about him. Why aren't you?"

Leif ignored this.

"You should be," I said.

"Did you sleep out here?" he asked.

"No," I lied. "I've been up for a while now."

"I carried you to bed," Leif said. "I remember."

I shrugged. "I was drunk," I said. I closed my eyes and saw myself splayed out on our bed. I watched Leif rearrange my legs. I was a puppet. I had an urge to hurt him, and I forced myself to stare at my hands.

"I know," he said gently. He brushed some sticky hair from the nape of my neck and leaned in to smell me there. He kissed each vertebra in my neck softly. "God, you looked sexy."

I wanted to tell him I'd been awake. I wanted to tell him he'd hurt me. He reached under my shirt and teased my nipples taut. He slipped his hand in my underwear, where, this time, I was wet. He moaned when he felt the slipperiness between his fingers. I lifted my hips up and he pulled my underwear down over my hips. He knelt next to the couch and nuzzled the inside of my thighs with his lips. He kissed me. I let him. I always let him.

I was fifteen when I discovered I could make myself come by holding my hips just right and my legs open underneath the heavy stream of the bathtub faucet. I was thrilled to find I wasn't defective after all, but I was disappointed and shocked by the feeling itself. It was like someone had taken control of me from the outside and contracted my body so tightly that it only felt good because the moment of orgasm was a release from that contraction.

I felt I had to tell Dee, though as soon as I'd told her, a deep shame coursed through me, because she retreated from me slightly. Her cheeks went pink. Her eyes drilled into the center of my forehead.

"Oh my God, Pegasus," she said. She had a mindless habit of brushing her lips and tracing their outline with the ends of her hair. "That is . . . really weird." That was about all she said on the subject. I wanted to ask her how it was different than her friend Nicole on her bike. But I just shrugged and acted like no big deal, even though I was stung.

A couple of weeks later, I asked if she'd tried it yet, and she seemed annoyed. She was doing her homework on the couch in the living room. She shook her head and buried herself in her notebook, but her cheeks blazed. I knew she was lying.

"What?" I prodded her. "Are you too scared?"

"No, I'm just not a weirdo." There was a certain grit, a seriousness, in her voice that hurt me and made me want to hurt her back.

"You are," I told her. She glared at me. In a dramatic flourish, she threw her notebook on the ground at my feet. It was a cheap bright yellow composition book. It fell open on the carpet so I could see class notes written in her messy, looping handwriting, and doodles in the margins, which had become more intricate and sophisticated in the last year—profiles of classmates, landscape sketches, petals of complicated flowers. I stared at them while Dee ran up to our bedroom and slammed the door. Ma came out of the kitchen and stood in the doorway watching me stare at Dee's drawings. She picked up the notebook and gently closed it. I opened my mouth to defend myself, and Ma put her hand up as if to say, *I don't want to hear it.*

At the next session with Thomas Alexander, I handed him the Walkman. I was sorry to see this object in his hands, this thing Dee had loved.

Thank you, Thomas Alexander mouthed at me. I scanned the room. Charlie Makon, the reporter Pete had requested from the *Journal Sentinel,* was making small talk with my aunt. He was in his mid-to-late twenties, with a mop of curls and a rather furtive, concerned look about him, as if he sensed someone somewhere was always talking about him.

One of the psychic's assistants clapped her hands. I watched the journalist's head wrench toward the noise. His curls flounced on his head. The assistant ushered all of us outside to the courtyard, where Thomas Alexander and Ma were seated across from each other in identical wooden rockers. The rest of us leaned against the walls of the courtyard and waited. Thomas Alexander's bodyguards cast long shadows like sundials onto the gravel. I wished I could hide in those shadows. Wolski stood beside me. He gave my shoulder a squeeze and I put several crucial inches between us. Thick midwestern clouds crowded the sun. I shivered.

Thomas Alexander crossed one ankle over his knee. He held

Dee's Walkman in one hand and he balanced his drawing pad on his shin. He began drawing his dark looping circles. He muttered. His lips moved ever so slightly. I wrapped my coat tighter around me. Wolski reached for my hand, but I brushed him off. What was with him?

"Is she there?" Ma croaked out. Thomas Alexander didn't say anything. The circles on the pad grew larger and larger. I imagined the ink leaking through all those crisp white pages and staining the psychic's pants leg.

"We have to be patient," he said. Ma's right eyebrow shot up. There was no one in the world who could possibly tell my mother about patience. "There's something here, though." Her spine straightened infinitesimally. Probably only Pete and I noticed. What did it mean that small, even inane amounts of hope still had the power to electrify us?

"Hurry up," Ma told Thomas Alexander. "Don't dick around here, okay? You need to tell her that we just want to bring her home. That's all. We want to bring her home. We're ready for her. I'm ready."

"She's . . . Okay . . . I'm not sure it's her. There's a force. There's a spirit here. It's not clear if it's her. It might be her. It's willing to engage, though. Okay . . . it's . . . huh . . . okay, I'm confirming it is Candace."

Ma inched the working part of her body toward the edge of her seat, which twisted her torso in the rocker. I worried she might fall. Pete leaned toward Ma and Thomas Alexander on the balls of his feet like he was ready to jump between them. Wolski's body was poised too; his animal brain hadn't decided whether the moment required a fight or a flight response. My own mouth was dry and sour. I couldn't swallow. I focused my eyes on the drawing pad, which was almost all black ink now except for the corners. I thought of the photo; almost anything, I realized, could remind me of the image. It remained disturbingly, permanently at the surface of my thoughts.

"Hang on. Okay. She's telling me she knows this is hard for you. She knows you've been waiting such a long time. But she wants you to know. Hang on." Thomas Alexander kept drawing and drawing. I wanted to fall into the black mess of ink and stay there. "The spirit says it's important that you know this. Even though some of the family won't believe it."

"Can you keep her here?" Ma asked him. Her spine was a collapsed spring. All the give had gone out of it. "Please? Dee!" She was frantic and moving the right side of her body convulsively. "Dee, baby. Please, we need to know where you are. I don't have much time, baby."

"There's something else," Thomas Alexander said. His voice was monotone. Light. Like he was impersonating someone in a kind of trance. I had an image of a Baptist minister flailing on the sidewalk outside the serial killer's apartment. Did the minister believe he had cast out the evil in the city that night? Where, then, had the evil gone?

"She wants you to know. It wants you to know. It wasn't Frank. Frank didn't do it." I could hear Wolski grinding his teeth. I imagined soft shavings of his teeth falling out of his mouth when he opened it. I've heard that dreams of one's teeth falling out are very common. I forgot what they were supposed to mean, though. Sexual frustration? The sun had disappeared, and the wind was picking up. The bodyguards shifted their weight from foot to foot, and their shadows quivered. I was still biting my lip.

"It was . . . It was Erik. She wants you to know it was him. He killed her. She called him after Frank pulled a gun on her during their last argument. So Erik went to the apartment. Frank had a big dog. There was a scuffle. Erik got Frank's gun. He tried to shoot

Frank, but she leaped in front at the last minute. Erik killed her. She wants everyone to know that she knows he's sorry. She knows he never meant to hurt her. He loved her."

"I don't care about any of this!" Ma screamed. Half laugh, half exasperation. I saw Pete's eyes widen at this admission. "I need to know where she is."

"Ma'am, all due respect." Thomas Alexander's voice was smooth, like deep breaths. "I don't . . . I can't choose what is relayed."

"But can you keep her? Can you do anything at all? Jesus!" Ma cried. "Can you ask her where she is? We need to—"

In a terrible moment, Ma fell onto her knees from the chair. I heard a crunch, which might have been her patellae. She hinged forward like she'd been stabbed in the back. The fits of laughter started up. Peter rushed forward and grabbed her. Half of her body laughed and laughed into his shoulder. Thomas Alexander stood up and threw the Walkman and the notepad on the ground. Why was he always throwing things?

"Stop," Thomas Alexander yelled to no one in particular. He rushed over to his assistant to look at the photos she'd gotten. There was a bead of sweat about to fall out of a tiny dent in his forehead. Dee and I had identical dents in our forehead from when we'd scratched open our chicken pox and the wounds had scarred. Ma was ruined over these spots for weeks, but our father laughed them off. *Character,* he said, *it gives them character.* I heard Thomas Alexander ask his assistant if she'd captured Ma's fall from her chair. Peter got Ma into her wheelchair, said nothing to Thomas Alexander, or anyone else, for that matter, and wheeled her back inside toward her room. Suze nodded at me and Wolski, and she hobbled after them.

Wolski turned to me and reached toward my face. I flinched. He steadied me and kept reaching. He wiped my chin with his thumb and showed it to me. I'd bitten through my lip so it bled. He licked his thumb and rubbed his spit into my chin so the blood disappeared.

The *Journal Sentinel* reporter rushed after me as I made my way back to the car.

"Excuse me," he yelled. "I was wondering if you'd be willing to answer a couple of questions for my piece."

I shook my head. "What piece?"

"My piece about corruption at the MPD."

"My brother, Peter, is doing all of that."

"Just a few questions?" he asked. "About Wolski?"

I wanted to hurt this man. I went close to him. "I don't know what Pete told you, but we're trying to find my sister's body. That's it. What are you trying to do?"

"This was a courtesy call . . . Your brother . . . he asked," he said.

"My brother thinks you're doing a piece about Dee."

His cheeks flushed. "It is . . . it is," he stammered.

"Sure, then talk to Pete."

I got in my car and slammed the door. No one at the newspapers could be trusted. I'd learned that a long time ago.

It was July 3 when Dee called to tell me she suspected Frank had been cheating. I tried to sound shocked, but I wasn't. I think I believed at the time that all men hated all women on some primal level, but some men were just better equipped to resist the temptations of misogyny. Frank seemed especially poorly equipped.

"I found another woman's thong." She was whispering like saying the words too loud would make them truer. "In his bathroom."

"Son of a bitch," I said.

"Fucking scum," she said, but it wasn't believable.

"What did you do?"

"I ran out," she said. "I didn't even tell him I found it. I just left."

"I'll kill him," I said. "Or Peter will kill him. We can tell Ma and Peter together."

Dee gulped air. "Don't tell Peter or Ma," she pleaded. "Please. I don't want them to know."

"I won't tell," I promised.

"It's over."

"I know."

"I should go back and tell him tonight; I have to."

"Why don't you wait on it, babe? I'll come get you, and we'll catch the fireworks together."

I held my breath while she mulled this over. "Sure."

She hadn't said what I knew she wanted to say, though. She blamed me for the impending breakup. Frank had cheated because he thought she'd been unfaithful too, and the only reason he'd thought that was because I'd asked Dee to look after Erik. It's hard to tell if I'm connecting these dots only now, or if there were even any dots to connect. Her words were tinged with blame, though. I wanted to make it better.

I borrowed Leif's car and drove to Mount Mary. Dee was sitting on the steps of her dorm, wearing high-waisted denim shorts, her mess of curls already wilting in the heat, goopy eyelashes; her face was puffy and wet. I idled the car and went to her, took her in my arms, the slenderness of her body easy to hold, and she leaned in to me hard.

"I love you," I told her.

She nodded, nodded like it barely mattered, which I'm not sure that it did.

"Get in," I said.

I bent the car back east. We smelled the breweries first and the algae second. Dee pinched her nose dramatically, like we were little girls again. I hated the way the city smelled that summer. During the days, especially hot ones, the air was like an infection when you breathed it, full of yeast from the riverside breweries; it was full of sugar at night, when the confectionaries churned out chocolate all through third shift, and the smell from the giant vats that pooled inside the factories coated the city too.

At Kopp's, I bought us cheeseburgers as big as our faces, with extra pickles, ketchup and mustard, and onion rings that could have fit around Dee's wrists. We ate them on a picnic table near the marina. Families were already picking spots for the fireworks. Children screamed and laughed and ran circles around the tables. Seagulls cried above us.

I devoured my burger while Dee picked at her pickles. "Eat," I pleaded.

She shrugged. Her eyes were jumpy, darting from side to side. The low cut of her shirt showed sharp collarbones; the bones made hollow spaces big enough for tide pools.

"This city smells awful," Dee said.

They'd closed the beach because the E. coli levels along Lake Michigan's shoreline were so high and the algae blooms so thick that entire schools of dead fish washed up each day.

"I've got to have it out with him."

"What good will it do?" I took a plastic knife from the white paper bag and began cutting Dee's burger into quarters; I thought she might be more willing to eat it this way, or at least to begin.

"I want to know the truth."

"The truth is he's a lying fuck," I said. Dee's shoulders went rigid, as if I'd shocked her with an electrical pulse. "I just mean. Look. Another woman's thong?"

Dee turned toward the marina; a slice of the sun setting over the water caught the side of her face and lit it on fire for a moment before she turned back.

"That's not all." She leaned on the picnic table so the wood cut into her stomach. "I also found an ID with his face on it, except it wasn't his name; it was a driver's license issued in Ohio."

I frowned. Tried to make sense of what she was saying, but realized, above all else, I just wanted her to eat something, dammit. I picked up a quarter of the burger and moved it toward her lips. They were the same color as Leif's Spitfire. She huffed and then opened her mouth and took a messy bite so the ketchup and the brown mustard spilled down her chin and she leaned back and wiped it away with the back of her hand.

Dee and I made our way through the little camps that people had set up to watch the fireworks—quilts and lawn chairs and canopies and coolers spread out over scruffy grass. Some men whistled at Dee, *There's room on my blanket, baby,* or *Come watch the show with us, honey.* Dee made like she was deaf.

A pair of sailors in stiff crackerjacks approached us. When they were within earshot, the tall one leaned over to his buddy and said, "Too young."

We passed them, and Dee turned around and crossed her arms over her chest, a fist to her chin in mock appraisal. "Too fat, and too old," she said.

I felt my eyes grow wide. *"Dee,"* I gritted through my teeth. They started back toward us.

"Excuse me?" said the short one, the one Dee had labeled too fat.

"Run," I said.

We turned and took off through the marina, dodging people's picnics at every turn. Dee hurdled a set of lawn chairs and some people clapped. We ran up Lafayette Hill, leaving behind the marina and the whistling men, the algae and the sulfur. At the top of the hill, we threw ourselves down, breathless and laughing. It was quiet at the top of the bluff—the whole city had funneled into the lakefront. Below, the tiny camps looked like a Civil War reenactment, an army at rest. Dee lay down in the grass. I thought she was still laughing, but when I turned to her, I saw she was sobbing.

The first firework was a ghoulish green that turned us both fluorescent. I imagined we were divers swimming in a bioluminescent bay. The night felt heavy anyway, like water pressure bearing down on us. I imagined we were anywhere but Milwaukee. I didn't know what to say to Dee, so I started making promises.

"We can get out of town," I told her, touching her kneecap and moving the bone around in her skin. "We'll steal the Spitfire and drive to the Badlands. We'll get a loan from Peter and backpack through Spain. We'll move to Mexico or Thailand."

"I thought we would get married," she said.

This seemed like a stretch to me. But I had a vision then—Dee as a little girl, folding recently purchased tablecloths into her hope chest. Our mother had shown Dee and me her own hope chest, and while the thought of it had delighted Dee, it had disgusted me. At the 7-Mile fair, while I rifled through jewelry and records, Dee shopped for domestic items that had bored me—bed skirts and linens and bone-china sets. At the time, the assuredness with which thirteen-year-old Dee had prepared for her married life, a life I wasn't sure I ever wanted, had impressed me. But later, I supposed, it only depressed me.

I ignored her and kept up with the proposals. "Or Canada. Let's move to Canada. Or Oregon. Or Alaska."

Dee said something, but a set of bright white rockets exploded over the marina and I couldn't hear her. The entire show felt like an assault instead of a celebration. Dee cried all the way through it, and the air was sharp with smoke and sulfur.

A man came by selling rainbow glow sticks. I bought twenty of them because my favorite part was cracking the liquid alive and watching the neon flood the plastic and you can only do that once. Dee and I sat there cracking those sticks, one after the other, until there was a plastic pile of neon between us. Then we put them on, around our necks and our wrists and our ankles. Dee twisted a few together to make a crown. My God, she was beautiful, maybe the most beautiful thing I'd ever seen. The fireworks kept up; I wanted suddenly to leave for real, maybe for Canada or maybe just for home, the house where Dee and I had grown up, had shared a bedroom, two twin beds, a nightstand between them, where in the night, even when we were teenagers, we used to reach our arms across the space between the beds and squeeze hands, because it felt good to hold someone you loved, even if just for a minute, before falling asleep. My bed was against the window, because Dee was afraid of someone climbing up the trellis on the side of the house and taking us in the night. I promised her I would always make the kidnapper take me before her.

The grand finale started up, and the city seemed frenetic at the bottom of the bluff, so I jumped up, pulled Dee to her feet.

"Let's go," I said. Below, the lake was a looking glass of purple fire, and we left before all the other people began to make their way back up the hill and into the city night.

I drove Leif's Spitfire back to Riverwest and parked it on the street. Dee and I got high on a bench in front of the river and kicked pebbles into the murk of the water at our feet. Even in bright day, you could not see through the black water of the Milwaukee River. People said there were cow carcasses down there and a three-foot-thick sludge of tannery chemicals. Everywhere in Milwaukee, water was hemmed in by cement.

"Leif's bringing us acid," I told Dee.

She shrugged. "Sure," she said.

She was catatonic, but I didn't trust the mood. I knew it could shift at any minute, and she'd be furious and possibly inconsolable. We smoked until the smell of sulfur faded and was replaced by the smell of hot chocolate from the factory where Leif worked. I took Dee back to our apartment and put her to bed.

Dee said, "I love you, Pegasus."

And I said, "I love you, Dee."

Dee fell asleep fast. I set my alarm, so I'd be awake in time to pick Leif up from third shift. Then I climbed in beside Dee and pulled her in to my stomach and breathed onto her neck. There were tiny hairs all along the length of her neck. They looked sharp like razor blades but were soft like a newborn's scalp. She was already asleep, but I leaned over her and squeezed her hand, and she squeezed it back and pulled me in to her.

I woke before the alarm because I felt something wet in the bed. Dee and I had fallen asleep still wearing our glow sticks, and we'd broken a few of them open in the night. Dee often slept with her hands between her legs, and there was a small neon handprint on the inside of her thigh. I surveyed my own body. My arms and legs were covered with the liquid, as was the bed, and my skin burned a little bit. I shook Dee and she itched her scalp. Blinked awake. Her eyes were dust bowls of sleep.

"Let's go, baby." I didn't dare leave her alone. Outside, the sky was just beginning to lighten, purple clouds rolled over the city, sulfur lingered in the air, and the streets were covered with the carcasses of fireworks. Dee dozed in the car.

By the time we got to the factory, it was full-on morning. People flooded out of the front doors, eyes shielded, shoulders slumped, chocolate under their nails and on the bottoms of their shoes; I knew because of Leif. He opened the passenger door and kissed Dee on the cheek. "Hey, Dee," he said to her. He scanned us. "Jesus, what did I miss?"

He reached across Dee and thumbed the side of my neck, rubbing at the residue of my neon necklace. He smelled like chocolate but chemicals too. I shrugged. Dee slid to the middle of the car to make room for Leif, and she pulled her knees up to her chest, her feet on the seat. Leif looked like he might reprimand her for this, so I said, "Frank's been cheating on Dee."

"Dammit," Dee said. "Thanks."

Leif said, "I see." He patted Dee's shoulder awkwardly and she shrank from his touch.

"Nothing's for sure," she said. She was slipping back into the denial phase.

"Like hell," I said.

"Can we go?" Leif put his head in his hands, his upper body leaning against the dash. The car was too small for the three of us. I nodded and reached across Dee to put my hand on his cheek and pinch it. He flinched.

Leif contended that acid was the most patriotic thing we could do on the Fourth of July. Dee's news didn't seem to affect his plans; he said Dee and I could split my dose. There are so many nights I dream of this day, of this decision, of the millions of different outcomes, all of them preferable to the actual outcome, had we not taken the acid.

The three of us sat cross-legged on the bedroom floor while we waited. The shades were drawn, but outside, sparklers fizzled, children laughed and screamed at cheap fireworks that sounded like gunshots. The thick smell of propane, and grilled meat, and sulfur wafted through the open windows. By noon, the neon of the glow sticks had taken on a new and darkly significant meaning; we were marked, all three of us, though for what, it wasn't entirely clear. Leif said, *We've been poisoned.* I said, *We've been blessed.* Dee said, *You guys are toast.* The rainbows on Dee's cheekbones were unbearably beautiful, and her clavicles began whispering to me about Frank and feminism, and also blow jobs and bowling balls, and I said all this to Dee. I said, *Can we trust a man who owns his own bowling ball?* And Dee said, *Fuck you, Peg.* And the rainbows bloomed across her body again, so I put my hands over my eyes to shield myself from her light, which was warning us about the apocalypse in one year, or two years, or one hundred thousand years from now, when the sun would explode and the whole of our solar system would be wiped by collapsing light. I said this out loud, maybe, because Leif said, *I know, baby, baby, baby.* I thought we were all on fire. The bioluminescent bay burned on the back of my eyelids. Where had I seen the pictures of this place? Or had I invented it? A small dark bay, a cobalt sky, the ocean alight with a green pulse. I loved the pictures where the photographer left the shutter open for ages but kept the camera very still so all the captured light was viscous, like lava. I wanted my own set of sparklers. I wanted to watch the light as I turned it in circles around our bodies. I asked Leif if we had any and I opened my eyes and he was nodding and moving toward me. Dee was gone from the room and I asked after her, but Leif said, *She's okay, she's okay, we're all keeping it together.* He kept moving toward me, my legs were still crossed, I burned after those sparklers. I wanted a set of them in my own hands. Leif was in front of me. I studied his face as if I'd never met him before. The sharp nose, the reddish blond of his hair and beard, the eyes green like that bioluminescent bay, all alive with light. I wanted him to stay away so I could keep looking and looking, but he kept moving closer, until his face was pressed against mine and the light was blurry like the red and white flood of headlights on a busy freeway at night. He opened my lips with his own and put his tongue in my mouth, running the muscle across my teeth, and I shivered. He put his hands under my armpits and pulled me to my knees, where I knelt and he stood. He was naked. I thought I heard gunshots and laughter and I shivered again though it was hot and I sweated beneath my arms and between my legs. Leif cupped my chin, his hands were on fire with neon and light. He was moving me like a puppet. I didn't feel anything. I wondered if he'd sucked all of my feeling into his own body—was that the meaning of possession? He opened my mouth again, this time with his hands, and he tested my throat with his fingers. I imagined the inside of my mouth swallowing all of the neon on his hands, a gaping black hole capable of eating and holding all light. He put himself inside my mouth and pressed his navel against my nose and I thought hard about how hard I wanted him, and wasn't this what I wanted? I felt it after it happened. He had slapped me across the face while he was still in my mouth and I didn't feel it so much as I saw the color of it, which was a sharp red rocking the waters of the bay on the back of my eyelids. He pressed himself harder into me and slapped the other side of my face, so my neck twisted against him and my body began to float from me. And this is what we did: He hit me and pushed himself deeper down my throat, and then he hit me again, and I felt myself pulling him down into me, like I could swallow the whole of his body, because I was invincible, I was large, larger than he was, even, and he tossed my face from side to side, harder and harder, until I felt him collapse under the weight of his own coming and he fell onto me and I spit everything in my mouth onto his chest. There was a noise from the doorway of the bedroom and I turned my head, which spun on its swivel, and Dee was sitting there in the doorway on her ankles, shins tucked beneath her, eyes open too wide, and she reached her arm toward me and opened her palm flat toward the ceiling so Leif and I could see her dose, which she had not taken, crumbled in her hand. She said, *Can we trust a man who beats his girl?* She had one of Leif's thirty-five-millimeter cameras up against her face, and she adjusted everything slow, with enough time for me to stop her, or to protest, but I didn't. She took the picture and the noise of the shutter was like a bomb exploding in my head.

After the second consultation with Thomas Alexander, another even greater wave of destabilizing uncertainty shook me. It was much worse than what I'd felt after realizing the necklace was not Dee's. This time I sensed I was waking from a spell of unconsciousness. The memories I'd curated so carefully for the previous thirty years became, inexplicably, irredeemably strange to me. I'd spent the decades since we'd lost Dee taking care of my memories the way other people take care of their families, their homes, their bodies. I had sunk all of my energy into remembering the months before Dee went missing. And for the first time since she disappeared, I began to wonder if I had done a bad job. I saw their fabricated nature more clearly. I understood then what Dana had been trying to tell me: She had wanted me to be ready, to be so confident in my story, in my case against Frank, that I could not be destabilized. But, I had not been ready for this version of events. Or for any version that differed from my own.

Because this possibility, that Erik had killed Dee, though it seemed absolutely improbable, had in one morning made clear to me the fickleness and the fragility of all my memories. I felt a different kind of fear then. Certainty is like a drug: a great comfort. When it's lost, the effect is that of withdrawal: fever, nausea, sweating, headaches, intense, unending pain, and above all else, an ocean's worth of desire to regain that which will make the pain stop.

I thought about the family from the video I'd watched. How the psychic had disappeared the deadness in those people's eyes, even though what he had said to make this deadness disappear had probably been wrong. Still, in the moment, it had worked. I went into the bathroom and stared into the mirror. The deadness was still there. It ate light. Maybe mine was more intractable. Maybe mine was permanent. I didn't know. I wished it would go. I stared at myself for six long minutes, and the hugeness of my pupils brought the photo to mind again.

For the first time in thirty years, I had the urge to call Leif, who, after he left me in Milwaukee, had called me regularly, though I'd often shirked his calls or said nothing on the phone while he talked. When he first left the city, he called once a day, then it became once a week, then once a month, and finally, once a year. I'd answer and let him talk. Let him tell me every little detail about his life that he cared to share. Sometimes I'd hang up if he started in on a topic I couldn't bear to hear. Other times I'd let him run on and on about his new life: a son (who looked like Erik), a wife he saw every few months in Idaho, the house they were refinishing, the book he was writing (and had always been writing), his inability to find his brother anywhere along his trucking routes. And much later, the admission that Erik had died of cancer. Leif had been invited to his brother's funeral by Erik's husband, Lance, a small bustling man who was a professor of botany at the University of California–Davis. They'd lived a quiet life together off campus with two dogs and several overworked bookshelves. Erik had an art studio behind the house, and he'd sold his ceramics at the local farmers' market. I drank for days after hearing this news. I was overrun with jealousy, and something a notch sharper than grief. I wanted so badly to one day discover that Dee, somehow, had lived this kind of life too—full of wide-open vistas and safe, easy love.

But I never said a word back to Leif, not even when he'd revealed the news of Erik's life or death. After hanging up the phone, I'd feel as if I were waking from a bender. There was always a thick greasy splotch on my phone's screen, which made me sick to see. For a long time I believed that withholding my voice from him was a kind of punishment, though it may have hurt only me. I became an open, empty container into which Leif poured all his muck. Maybe I liked it.

I wanted suddenly, though, to tell him what the psychic had said about Erik, or what the psychic claimed Dee had said. I also hoped that Leif might have some kind of evidence that would prove, beyond a doubt, that Erik could not have possibly done this. I needed him to corroborate my case against Frank too.

I called him and the phone rang and rang, and finally, I left a long, barely intelligible message describing the few weeks since the psychic had arrived. When his voicemail cut me off with a long, harsh beep, I couldn't be sure what had made it in the message and what had been left out. After I put the phone down, I went to the bathroom to throw up.

t took two days for Leif and me to come down. He said maybe the acid was laced with something else; he said he was sorry. My face was split wide open. He'd hit me harder than he remembered, and I was black and blue and swollen for a week afterward. When the drugs left my system, I knew something had gone rotten between us. I didn't know if it would stay rotten.

Leif tried to touch me, and I hissed or spit or clenched my teeth at him. I said, *I hate you, I hate you, I hate you,* though I meant it for myself. He slept on the floor next to the bed in a tangle of blankets, and I saw bruises on his thin, bony hips when he changed. Once, as I was falling asleep, Leif whispered to me from the floor. "You liked it," he said. It was not a question. Dee's voice echoed in my head, *I like it.*

I rolled to the wall and put my forehead against the stucco. I didn't leave the apartment. I didn't go to work. I didn't write. For almost two weeks after the Fourth, I lay in bed for entire days and nights and held my own face. I didn't try to reach Dee, though my missing her was like a wide-open wound. I was afraid of what she might say. It hurts to think now that I spent this time embarrassed and afraid for myself when I should have been afraid for her.

One morning near the end of July, Leif came home early from third shift, around 1am, and turned on the news. Dried milk chocolate flaked from his forearms. A reporter stood in front of the Ambrosia chocolate factory. The police had arrested a former Ambrosia employee they believed was responsible for the murder of more than fifteen young men. Leif and I watched the reports like they were one long, bad movie; we couldn't stop. Our phone rang and rang. We ordered Chinese food and slipped the money under the door and retrieved the food after the man had left so we didn't have to see any real human faces except our own.

Here is what they said they found in the serial killer's apartment: four severed heads, seven skulls, two hearts, arm muscles wrapped in plastic, an entire torso, three bags of human organs, four entire skeletons, a pair of severed hands, two severed and preserved penises, a mummified scalp, and two dismembered torsos dissolving in a fifty-seven-gallon drum of acid. The reporters kept vans and cameras outside every place this man had ever been in Milwaukee—the chocolate factory, his grandmother's house, his own apartment building, the bars he'd frequented. Some of these bars were the same bars we'd been to with Erik. Leif and I watched these places on the screen. I still don't know what we were hoping to see or not see. I worried Erik's photo would flash on the nightly news, and I sensed Leif worried too, though he never would have acknowledged our shared fear. Our phone rang and rang. I had competing urges to call Dee, because I wanted to know if she'd heard from Erik, but I also wanted desperately to unplug our phone. I was afraid of what she might say about Erik, about the Fourth, about me. I did neither, and Leif and I kept watching and waiting and I was certain, and I was right, that the world had ended.

Whenever something really spooked Leif, he took to sleeping with the gun on the floor next to our bed. After I banished him to the floor, he slept next to his gun. I hated this habit, and I knew a gun wouldn't have saved us from the serial killer anyway, or from the kind of evil that had produced him, or the kind of evil apathy that had let him flourish, but I couldn't blame Leif either. He needed the Band-Aid, and who was I to point out the ridiculousness of his solution. The fear was always real. A couple hours after Leif had gotten home, and after we'd turned off the news, and let the stillness soak the apartment, someone banged on our door. Leif took his gun to the peephole and peered through. He opened the door, and Erik was standing there, skinny as hell. He looked a little wet, like he'd been in a rainstorm and his clothes had never dried. There was a sweaty sickness on his face; his lips were cracked and dry. I could see he'd been biting them raw. His chin had a bloodstained tint to it. I touched my own sore face.

Leif doubled over and began to sob. I had never seen him cry. I wished he would put the gun down, but he kept it in his right hand. It dragged against the floor as he cried. Then he held Erik, and I remembered the story he used to tell about the day they brought his baby brother home from the hospital—how he'd carried him all around his own tiny world of that flat and given him a tour of his new home. He held Erik's shaky frame so tightly I was afraid he'd break one of his brother's bones. Erik sagged into him.

"I'm sorry," Leif sobbed. "I'm so sorry."

"Leif," I cried. "Enough." I couldn't bear to watch the scene any longer. (Or maybe now, in my memory, I can barely stand to recollect the moment—this, if I had ever seen Dee again, is what I would have said.) Leif punched his brother in the shoulder, and Erik rocked back on the threshold of the apartment. I shivered at the sight of Leif's fists. I was like an animal afraid of the place where I'd been hurt.

"Get in here and shut the damn door," I said. They were rattled by the edge in my voice. Erik threw his large, thin body down on our sofa, and he ran his hands up and down his face. A debilitating sense of relief rushed over me—I felt as if I were watching the scene from underwater. I am ashamed to say that the source of the relief was not just that Erik was safe and alive, though of course I was thankful for that. But I was also relieved that I wouldn't have to call Dee to ask if she'd seen Erik. Now I see this was a selfish mistake. An easy way out. I don't know for certain if it cost me Dee, but it could have.

"Where in the hell have you been?" Leif asked Erik.

Erik's right knee shook rhythmically. I wanted to put my hands on it, but touching Erik felt almost like touching Leif, so I kept my arms crossed tightly across my chest.

"Shit is crazy, right?" Erik said. "I mean, Jesus. I can't believe any of it. I just can't believe it."

"What do you need?" I asked. He looked hurt. I had a memory of huge waves crashing on Bradford Beach. The lake was always threatening to wash the whole man-made shore away. One day maybe the lake would shrink or disappear completely, and we'd be left with a barren lake bed full of the fossilized remains of monstrous animals. *You're making it worse.*

"I thought you'd be worried," Erik said to Leif. "I came back."

"I know, buddy," Leif said. "I know. I'm sorry I kicked you out."

"Are you going to lose your job now?" Erik said.

Leif knitted his brows. "Why the hell would I lose my job?"

"Everyone's saying this guy hid bodies in the big vats at Ambrosia. A business can't come back from something like that."

"That's nonsense," I said, though I supposed, given the news accounts, it was probable.

Erik turned to me and saw my face for the first time. "What

the hell happened?" he asked. Leif's face reddened, and I hated him for it. He'd done this to me. The least he could do now was keep it a goddamn secret.

"I got mugged," I said. This was my new official story.

"Jesus," Erik said. "I'm sorry. This fucking city, man. Unbelievable. I told you it's not safe around here."

Leif's face began to pale, and the redness faded. It pained me to see how relieved Leif was to know his brother did not believe him capable of beating me. Erik came to me and opened his arms. We'd hugged many times before, but I was skittish now. I stepped back and got embarrassed.

"It's late," I added and stomped to the bedroom and slammed the door.

"She okay?" Erik half whispered. I put a pillow over my head and tried to burrow into the dirty nest of blankets on our bed, but the walls were too thin.

"I don't know," Leif admitted, and for some reason, this admission made my heart grow for him. I hated myself for that. I hated that I still had room for him. I was beginning to understand that I'd always have room for him.

"I'm taking you to Ma's tomorrow. She's probably worried herself into a heart attack about you by now."

"Fuck."

I wondered how long it had been since either of them had seen their parents. Leif didn't get along with his mother, but Erik had been close with her before he'd come out. I'd never met her; Leif said he didn't like his mother mucking around in his relationships. I always pictured her with long blond-gray hair, fine features, strong hands.

"I won't see him, though," Erik said. Neither of them got along with their father, who, from what I'd gleaned, was a large, mostly quiet man who was prone to violent outbursts.

"Understood," Leif said.

"I've got to get out of this fucking city," Erik said. Leif was quiet.

When Leif finally came to bed that night, he set the gun gingerly on the floor and tried to get in next to me. I was wide awake, and I rolled over and put my hand in the middle of his chest. I pushed him to the edge of the bed, where he sat with his back to me. He sat there for a full minute, all hunched over like he'd been kicked in the stomach.

"Don't," I said. He nodded into his hands and slipped off the bed. He toyed with his gun until he fell asleep. I listened to the swift swish and click of him loading and reloading the clip.

Dana showed up unannounced at my apartment after the second session with the psychic. The place was a mess and I'd already started drinking, but I felt I had to let her in. When I unlocked the door, she stood in the doorway and surveyed the apartment behind me.

"You're getting worse," she said.

"Thanks, Doc," I said. "You hungry?"

I had nothing to offer her, but this seemed like the right question. She shook her head. Her eyes were a little runny with makeup. I wasn't sure if it had worn off over the course of the day or if she had been crying earlier. She sat on my love seat and put her composition books and her phone on the coffee table. Her phone did not stop buzzing. She tucked her feet underneath her. "This is about what the psychic said."

"Oh, baby," I said. "Please. Not tonight."

She opened her notebook. Her phone buzzed again. She ignored it. "Just hear me out." I said nothing, so she continued. I itched for my wineglass, but I'd left it in the kitchen. "Before Aunt Dee went missing, Erik was missing first. Isn't that right?" I nodded. Her voice affected a distinctly adult tone that pained me to hear. "But according to your records and the interviews"—she tapped her pen on a starred bullet point in her notebook—"Erik showed up at your apartment near the end of July. My dad and Grandma reported Aunt Dee missing on July ninth." I thought on this. I nodded. "Didn't you ask him if he'd seen Dee?" she asked me. "You saw him after Dee disappeared, right? Didn't you ask him if he'd seen her?"

"No," I told her. "I didn't."

"Why not?"

"I wasn't in the best place at the time . . . I didn't think . . . I didn't know I needed to ask." I was embarrassed to admit this. I swallowed. My saliva tasted sour. "I didn't know she was missing yet."

"Right," Dana said matter-of-factly. That she did not judge me for this admission surprised me. She continued, "So. If Erik knew something, anything, about Dee being missing, don't you think he would have said something to you?"

I nodded slowly.

"He didn't know," she said. "It couldn't have happened the way the psychic said."

In spite of myself, I clenched my jaw. I suddenly understood my mother's admission at the last session: *I don't care about any of this.* We just wanted to find Dee's body. And we no longer cared what the psychic said about what happened as long as he found her, and as long as I could finally prove to the police that I wasn't just a traumatized hoarder. Or that's what I told myself. I guessed my mother had a similar rationalization. I shook my head. "I didn't think it did happen like that," I told Dana. "It's ridiculous."

She eyed me and frowned. "You seemed upset, though."

"I did?" I believed I'd mastered the art of stoic reactions. Maybe Dana knew me better than I thought.

She nodded. "Most of these files"—she gestured toward my study and pointed at her own notebook—"they're about Frank." I didn't like hearing this name out loud, and I especially didn't like to hear my niece say it. "You've basically been stalking him."

"Dana," I warned her. "I have not been stalking him."

"All of your evidence—it's all about Frank, though."

I paused. It was true. When Dee first disappeared, the police had not taken Frank seriously as a suspect, and even after Wolski finally spoke with him, they still decided to chase down a series of alternative and ultimately unfruitful leads. Meanwhile, I'd done the opposite. I'd spent the past thirty years focused solely on documenting Frank's behavior before, during, and after Dee's disappearance. I had rarely considered other possibilities than the one that involved Frank.

"Your father will be upset with me if we discuss any more of this."

She shrugged. "He doesn't care. And besides, I'm afraid if I don't tell you, no one will."

"Tell me what?"

She bit her lower lip. "You really don't have that much on him."

"You sound like Wolski," I said.

She shook her head. "No. I mean, I *believe* you. I do. But what you've got is mostly circumstantial."

"I know," I told her. "That's why we need to find Dee." Dana frowned. For a moment I thought she was about to cry, and I felt trapped, panicked. I chastised myself for speaking so freely with her about my sister. Dana was still only fourteen, even if she often acted much older.

Her phone buzzed again. I peered down to look at the caller: *Cal.*

"Who's that?" I asked her. I wanted to take control of the conversation.

"My ex-boyfriend. I broke up with him yesterday," she said. This divulgence made her blush. "He wants another shot."

"I'm sorry," I said. She shrugged. I hadn't even known she was dating. I thought of her soggy clothes hung over the backs of my kitchen chairs. Her voice trembling: *I kept thinking about floating down to the bottom. How long it would take to sink.* She looked at me seriously and then, in a way so reminiscent of Dee it made me shiver, she said dismissively, "I didn't love him."

hadn't answered the phone in over two weeks, afraid it would be Dee wanting to talk about what she'd seen on the Fourth of July. I suspected, in those weeks after the Fourth, that she'd long since made up with Frank. I envisioned her enjoying languid and extravagant *I'm so sorry* dates followed by careful, devoted makeup sex. The thoughts sickened me. But also, I sickened me. What would I tell her about myself? How could I tell her to leave Frank when she'd seen the way I let Leif treat me? And how *had* I let Leif treat me? What did Dee think it meant? I don't think I knew what it meant. Each day, I told myself I would be ready to pick up the phone, to have these conversations, to figure it out with her, because I needed her, and she was the only person in the world I loved without reservation.

When I finally did answer the phone, a day after the news about the serial killer broke, I was surprised to find that it was not Dee but my mother. Suddenly, it was clear that she was the one who had been dialing our landline for days on end, not Dee, and also that she was frantic.

"Where have you two been?" she yelled at me. I had to move the receiver away from my ear. *You two.*

"Who?" I asked her.

"Where have you and Dee been, and why haven't you answered my calls? Have you seen the news? This city is out of its goddamn mind."

"I haven't felt good. I had the flu," I lied quickly and without much thought.

"What about Dee?"

I shook my head, confused. "I don't know. I don't know what you're talking about."

"Margaret," she said. Her voice took on a frightening robotic quality. I realized she hoped we'd been together. "When did you see her last?"

"July Fourth," I said. And then my mother lost it.

I'm so ashamed now to say I didn't really believe her. (I carry the weight of this disbelief with me every day.) I thought the news of the serial killer's crimes had thrown my mother into a fit of hysteria. I figured Dee and I were playing a dumb game of chicken, though truthfully, it's hard to remember what the hell I was thinking. I think about what I was thinking all the time now. We'd done this kind of thing before, after a big fight; whoever called first lost. Once it was over, we didn't keep score, but the bouts of silence could last weeks.

My mother told me she was sending Pete to get me. I agreed, but I didn't have the strength to tell her Pete didn't know where I lived.

Leif was getting ready to take Erik over to their parents' house, but he paused, hunched over his bootlaces. "What's all that?" he asked.

"She thinks Dee's missing," I said.

"Is she?"

I paused. "I don't know," I admitted. "She's probably just with Frank."

Leif shook his head. "Yeah, your ma's crazy," he said.

I bristled at this. "Watch your mouth," I said.

He was right, she was crazy, but only I was allowed to say it. Leif shrugged.

Erik came out of the kitchen with a milk mustache. I remembered Erik and Dee sipping out of the SlimFast cans with their limbs all tangled up in her bed.

"What's wrong?" Erik asked.

"Let's go, buddy," Leif said. He ushered his brother to the door.

I suddenly had an urge to tell Erik about my mother's phone call. To hear what he would say.

"Wait," I said. Leif undid all the locks on our door. Erik looked like a baby boy, with his sleepy eyes and his messy milk face. I sensed I was missing an opportunity, although I probably can see the chance only now that I know. I had no words for the thing I wanted to say to Erik then or the one thing I should have asked. I only had a feeling I could not voice. Leif took his brother's shoulder and nudged him out the door. He locked the door behind them.

I imagined them pulling up to their parents' house. I bet they lived in one of those tiny shotgun houses on the South Side. There were probably geraniums hanging in green plastic baskets from the front porch and a leaning arbor coated in climbing vines that was a gateway to nothing except the alleyway behind the house. I imagined the boys pulling up in Leif's flashy car, and their ma puttering around in the kitchen, hearing the noisy engine, and running to the screen door.

My baby, she'd yell. *My beautiful, beautiful baby.* (It's a well-known fact that mothers reserve the softest, sweetest parts of their love for their youngest children.) She'd run her tiny hands all over Erik's face, and she'd thank God for bringing him back to her, and she'd thank God for giving her two beautiful sons, and for saving them from that terrible, terrible man.

After Dana left, I drove drunk to see the old place Leif and I had shared so briefly in Riverwest. Isn't it amazing the way time works? How our memories can stretch the shortest moments into long, infinitely unwinding wires of feeling. The year I spent with Leif in Riverwest looms so large in my life that it is easy for me to believe we lived there for decades, but it was, in fact, no time at all.

After I turned onto the street and pulled the car to the curb, I was surprised to see that the house was missing. The houses in Riverwest are tightly packed. The long, empty lot was like a missing tooth. A police car, lights flashing, screamed down the street. I parked my car and got out. The concrete steps up the short steep part of the lot and the attached railing were intact. I climbed them slowly, like maybe a thousand more steps would follow. Like I knew I still had a long way to go. In the lot, I walked through some scrubby grass peeking out of fresh snow. When and why had they knocked it down? I went from room to room. I paused in the living room where I fell down onto my hands and knees. A floodlight from one of the houses next door registered my movement and shone a bright cone of light onto me. I looked up. I thought, in only a heartbeat's worth of time, that I would see Dee. (Sometimes this sort of thing still happens to me.) In the second floor of the house next door, the dark shadow of a human body moved. A face looking down. I stayed there, letting the snow soak into the knees of my jeans until my kneecaps froze. Two more cop cars rushed down the street. I stayed on my knees there in my old house for so long that the floodlight went off and I fell back into the dark.

When my phone rang, I felt like I was waking from a deep sleep. I had a memory of a period in my life when I didn't eat for a matter of weeks: I stayed in bed and used all my energy on memories. Memories of Dee as a girl, of me and Pete and Ma and Suze and Dad when he was alive. Anything from before. Everything from before. I tried to remember and remember. I tried to keep anything I could. It was a long time before I became aware that no matter what I did, no matter how hard I tried or how little I ate, I could not remember the only days that mattered. And then maybe I tried to forget that fact.

"Do you know where I am?" I said to Leif.

I heard a sharp intake of breath.

"Where?" he asked.

"I'm inside our old place."

"Yeah? How's it look?" he asked me. He spoke as if he thought I was unwell, as if I were a crazy person in a movie about crazy people. He was playing the sane person talking in that way the sane people talk to the crazy people in the movies about crazy people.

"It's gone."

"Gone how?"

"They knocked it down," I told him.

"I'm sorry to hear that."

"What's wrong with your voice?" I asked him. "Why are you talking like that?"

"How am I supposed to talk? Huh? I don't hear a word, not

a single word, from you for thirty fucking years, and you want to critique how I'm talking?"

I breathed. I moved. The motion detector went off again, and the cone of light shone in my face. I went to sit on the steps of the building. We hadn't spoken in so long, but it still felt easy with him, like we were always caught up, always right where we needed to be in relation to each other. That's how it used to be, anyway; maybe I was just remembering the way it used to be.

"Do you think that's what happened?" I asked him. He knew what I meant.

"No," he said. There was a long pause. I thought I heard the click of a cigarette lighter on the other line. The deep inhale. "I don't know. I suppose it's possible."

"It doesn't make sense. The night Erik came to our place. He would have told us if he'd seen Dee . . . if he knew anything." I was, I realized, mostly repeating what Dana had said to me.

"Erik didn't tell me shit. He didn't trust me. You know that."

I was quiet. I knew that from the long conversations Leif had with himself while I listened. Erik had died without ever speaking to Leif again. It had been Lance, Erik's husband, who had reached out to find Leif, after Erik had passed.

"I know," I said.

"I will tell you this. I'm going to get my shit together. This quack you all have working for you is famous. Actually famous. If any of this comes out about my brother, I will be ready. I owe him that, at least."

"What does that mean?"

"It means I'm changing directions with the book," he said. He'd referenced this book he was writing many times over the years. I was never sure if he was actually writing it or just talking about it.

"No one wants to read your dumb little book," I said, and I

felt very old and very childish and extraordinarily embarrassed. My cheeks were hot. I turned back toward the empty lot where our house had been. Someone in the house next door had opened the screen door and was staring at me. "I'm sorry," I said, not to Leif but to the person whose property I was infringing upon.

Leif accepted the apology nonetheless. "I know," he told me. His voice took on that dull, affected wispiness again. I cringed.

"Maybe you could come back." I tried out these words and instantly regretted them. "Now." There was a long pause, and I listened to Leif's breathing the way he had listened to my breathing once every year for the last thirty years.

"I don't think so," he said finally. I nodded into the phone. The person from the house next door yelled, *Hey,* and I shouted back, "Okay, okay, I said I was sorry." And I hung up on Leif.

GIVE THE PEOPLE LIGHT AND THEY WILL FIND THEIR OWN WAY.

THE WISCONSIN LIGHT

Community Stunned by Murders, Angered by Press Coverage

VOLUME FOUR, NO. 15—JULY 25, 1991—AUGUST 7, 1991

BY JAMAKAYA AND TERRY BOUGHNER

[Milwaukee] – Allegations of "homosexual overkill," which first emerged at a murder trial in Racine County on July 19, have been reiterated by authorities and the media in reference to the separate more recent mass murder discovered in Milwaukee on July 22. The multiple murders uncovered that night are the worst such crimes ever recorded in the history of Milwaukee.

Jeffrey L. Dahmer, 31, is being held by Milwaukee police as the primary suspect in at least eleven grisly homicides. The skulls and severed heads of eleven people, along with numerous organs and limbs in varying states of decomposition were discovered in Dahmer's apartment at 924 N. 25th street late in the evening of July 22.

Police were alerted to the murders by a man who had apparently fled Dahmer's apartment that night. The man, who had a handcuff locked around one of his hands, hailed a police car and led officers back to the scene of the alleged crimes.

After a July 24 hearing before Judge T. Crivello determined that there was probable cause to hold and charge Dahmer, bail was set at $1 million. Formal charges were expected to be filed on Thursday, July 25. (The *Light*'s press deadline for this issue was 6 p.m. on July 24.) Gerald Boyle, Dahmer's attorney, stated that his client was cooperating with police and helping to identify the victims.

Police and medical authorities believe all of the victims were men and it is likely that all were African-Americans or men of color. Dahmer is white. The first victim to be identified was Oliver Lacey, 23, of Chicago.

According to an affidavit filed in Milwaukee County Circuit Court, Dahmer met individuals at taverns and shopping malls and induced them to return to his home by offering them money so he could take photos of them. Patrons in several of Milwaukee's Gay bars claim to have seen him in these establishments.

The relatives of Tony Hughes, 21, who disappeared in Milwaukee on May 24, fear that he may be one of the victims. Hughes was last seen leaving Club 219, a Gay dance bar on Milwaukee's south side.

Police reported that along with the human remains confiscated at Dahmer's apartment were photos of mutilated bodies, body parts, and homosexual acts. Police were quick to label the murders "homosexual overkill," and that phrase was again reported throughout the local print and broadcast media.

[Milwaukee] – Members of Milwaukee's Gay and Lesbian community, both political leaders and average bar patrons interviewed by the *Light*, have reacted with wide-spread shock, sorrow, and dismay at the news of the grisly murders/dismemberments discovered on Monday, July 22, 1991. The mass killings are believed to be the worst such crimes ever perpetrated in the city of Milwaukee.

Anger was also expressed over the fact that the media was seen by most as labeling the crime as being brought about, in part, by homosexuality.

"I'm disappointed with the press for the 'homosexual' angle," said Stan Straka. "They were so quick to take off with it. There's been over 90 murders in our city this year and none of them was labeled 'heterosexual.' This type of reporting just brings more hatred towards our community."

Tim Grair, a member of Queer Nation/Milwaukee, commented that to him it was "a horrifying and frightening experience." Grair went on to add: "To me this whole situation makes grotesquely clear the importance of self-awareness training and I hope this spurs more people into action with the street patrol."

Scott Gunkel, President of the Lambda Rights Network, expressed stunned shock over news reports and added, "there can be no excuse for blaming the whole Gay community for this deranged act."

Karl Olson condemned the "accusations that the murders are examples of 'homosexual overkill' which seems to imply that all Gay men are culpable. As a community we need to rise up in pride and counter the insinuations that underlie this act." Olson urged Gay men to "affirm the power of coming out" so that Lesbians and Gay men can free themselves as well as teach others that Gays and Lesbians are "not the monsters some fear us to be."

Olson went on to say he believed that if "this man, the suspect in the crimes, had been a self-affirming openly Gay man who loved himself and others, Milwaukee would very likely have been spared this tragedy."

The same day I spoke to my mother, I was reading the serial killer coverage in bed, with my eyes barely open and drifting off to a bad sleep, when someone knocked on the door. We rarely had visitors to our place, and I tried to pretend like I wasn't there. I hadn't the slightest intention of answering the door or speaking to anyone. I rolled my face into my pillows, which smelled musty and wet because I hadn't washed them in a long time. I pulled the covers over my head. The knocking intensified, so I reached to the floor where Leif had left his gun the night before. I picked it up and padded to the door.

"Margaret," Peter yelled through the locks. "You better open this goddamn door." I fumbled with the locks, and Peter swung the door open. He was tired, and his hair was in need of a wash. I had forgotten my mother said she was sending Pete, and I was surprised he found me so quickly.

"How did you find me?"

"What? Like you're some kind of Houdini. I got the address from Leif." He eyed the gun in my right hand. "Jesus H. Christ. Put that fucking thing down and get your things. We're going to the station so you can give your statement, and then I'm taking you home."

I couldn't move. He grabbed the gun from me, and I spooked and jumped away. And that was when he finally saw me.

"What the fuck is this?" Peter asked. The large soft pads of his thumbs traced both of my cheekbones where my bruises were now fading. I shivered; it was the gentlest thing I'd felt in weeks, since I'd curled up to sleep that neon nap with Dee before the Fourth.

Then Peter took in the apartment with a wide-eyed swoop, rotating his head on his shoulders like I've seen cartoon owls do, and I saw the place through his eyes. The dirty floors, the grime on the baseboards, the dust collecting in the spaces where the ceiling met the walls, the takeout containers and half-smoked joints and ashtrays, empty whiskey and wine bottles, books with pages torn out and littered like heaps of half-alive beings near the bed.

"Do you . . . live here?"

I nodded weakly. His eyes were wide. Under different circumstances he would have reveled in the idea that he'd found me out and that he would have the opportunity to rat me out to Ma.

"What happened to you?"

"I got mugged," I said.

"Mugged," Pete repeated. His eyes narrowed to slits.

"Let's go. I'm ready."

I went into the bedroom where I started throwing dirty clothes into a duffel bag, into which I also threw *Fear of Flying* and my birth control pills. There was a great crash from the other room. When I went into the living room, Peter had punched a hole in our wall.

"I'll be outside," he said.

Peter was smoking on the stoop, and when I came out, he flicked his cigarette butt into an old gallon-size pickle jar that Leif used as an ashtray. Peter took my duffel from me, which was annoying but I wasn't about to say, and he threw it into the trunk, opened the passenger door for me, then started the engine. I got into the car and looked at the apartment: the peeling paint, the ill-fitted windows, the scruffy grass in what passed for the front lawn.

Before we drove away, Peter said, "Goddamn. When Ma finds out about this. She's already catatonic on account of Candace. If you hadn't answered the damn phone, I swear. She was a day away from filing a report for you too. But we also know how you can be . . ." He eyed me. "Sometimes you fall off the grid. But Dee . . . Dee never misses her dates with Ma."

I turned to the window. I pulled the mirror down from the visor and set to powdering away the fading scars.

"She's really missing?" I asked Peter. He gave one tight nod. My stomach clenched, and I felt instantly carsick. I tried to process the information, but it seemed like it was happening to another version of myself in another world.

"How come you didn't know?" He eyed me. "You two have one of your fights?"

Images from the Fourth flashed hot on the back of my eyelids when I blinked.

"Something like that," I said. I was afraid to ask, but I needed to know: "How long has it been?"

"I don't know, Peg," he said grimly. "You tell me. Officially or unofficially? Ma filed the report on the ninth. Dee had promised to do Ma's hair that morning, nine a.m., and you know Ma. You gotta be on time. Dee didn't show. Ma drove to her dorm. Her roommate said she'd seen Dee pack a bag on the third. All of which you would have fucking known if you'd answered the god-damn phone." He paused. He breathed. "What the hell happened between you two?"

I swallowed. Tried to get the days straight. "The day before the Fourth, Dee called me to say that she'd found Frank out."

"Who the hell is Frank?"

"She's been seeing him . . . since March, at least, I think."

"You think?"

I nodded. Peter's hands on the wheel were white. His fingernails were tattered and bloody. They looked like they hurt. "This is the first we're fucking hearing about him."

"Well, he's a piece of shit. She doesn't want you two to know about him. I honestly didn't think he would be around as long as he was." I threw my hands up. He motioned for me to just go on. "Anyway, on the third, she called to tell me that she found another woman's thong at his place and a driver's license with another name, issued from Ohio, right? She said she was going to have it out with him, and I convinced her to wait on it and come spend the Fourth with me and Leif." Peter huffed, but I kept on. "So the night got away from us, and when I woke up, Dee had left without a word."

"Hell of a story, Peg," he said.

"We need to find Frank. We find Frank, we'll find Dee. I'm sure of it." I could hear panic rising in my voice. Pete shifted uncomfortably in his seat. "We should start looking for him now. We don't need the police. Come on. I know some places we can start." The bowling alley came to mind. I clawed at my seat belt.

Pete put his hand on the flat part of my chest. I threw his hand off. "You need to tell the detective."

I began to sob then. Long, exhausting wails over which I felt I had no control at all. "Please stop the car," I cried. "Please. This is crazy. I can find her."

"You're not listening," Pete said. There was a certain automation to his voice; had he learned this in law school? "We've already tried. When we couldn't reach you. We've already tried all that stuff."

"You didn't . . ." I struggled to think clearly. "You couldn't have . . . You didn't know about Frank. I have some ideas. We can go now."

"You have to tell the detective," Pete said. "That's where we're at with this now. Okay? You're not getting it, Peg. She has already been gone for at least fourteen days. We need real help now."

Fourteen days. Did I even believe that number? I didn't know what they'd already tried, where they'd already looked, so maybe I still wasn't convinced. I thought maybe Frank had tried to make up for his bad behavior by taking Dee on some gaudy trip to the Dells or Door County. Or maybe she was holed up with Erik in a high-ceilinged Walker's Point loft belonging to one of Erik's flavors of the moment. I didn't dare voice these hypotheses to Pete, who I could tell was losing patience with my incredulity. Fourteen days? It wasn't possible.

I clutched at my seat belt. Milwaukee gushed by me in my peripherals; I felt I was being swallowed by its pathetic skyline. Peter drove white-knuckled and hunched over the steering wheel like we were about to hit heavy rain, though the sky was blue enough to see through.

Article VI. Witnesses

RULE 601. COMPETENCY TO TESTIFY IN GENERAL

Every person is competent to be a witness unless these rules provide otherwise.

B efore the third, and what would turn out to be the final, session with Thomas Alexander, I went to meet with my mother privately. It would be a lie to say that I wasn't somewhat disturbed by the conversation I'd had with Dana about my files. I wanted to know what my mother thought of the psychic's version of events, or maybe I wanted her to refute what Dana had said. I wanted her to tell me that what I had, what I had spent decades building, would be enough, especially once we found Dee.

My mother was surprised to see me. When I walked in her room, her eyes were closed, and when she tried to flutter them open, only the right eye came awake. She pushed her left eyelid open with her right index finger. I sat on her bed. She looked smaller than I ever remembered, and her skin was translucent and stretched tight over her bones.

"I'm so tired, baby," she said.

I nodded. "Me too," I admitted.

"Would you read to me?" She motioned toward a copy of *My Ántonia*.

"Okay, Mama," I said. "But I want to ask you something first."

She frowned slightly. She knew what it meant when our conversations began this way. It also occurred to me that she thought

I'd come only to visit: to be with her. I cursed myself for not doing that more often, especially since the prognosis.

"Is it true what you said?" I asked her. "You don't care what happened anymore?"

"Of course I care," she said. She broke eye contact. "But knowing won't change anything for me one way or the other."

I thought on this. That was how we were different. I believed it would change everything for me. I felt sometimes that I would be consumed by the unknowable. This was why I'd worked so hard to build my own case against Frank, because it's always easier to believe in something, no matter how flawed, than to believe in nothing and to admit you know nothing. Hardly anyone ever admits this. It was only at the end of her life that my mother was able to do so.

"So if Frank—if the person who did this to Dee—gets away with it forever, you think you'll feel the same way, the exact same way, as if he is arrested, tried, and sent to jail?"

She shook her head. "I just want her next to me. Finding her is enough. It has to be."

"It's not enough." I felt myself becoming frustrated, which often made me feel like a child again, especially in front of my mother.

She softened her tone. "Peg, baby, we've had this discussion. Why are you pressing it again?"

"Because I think this time is different." My mother looked at me, eyes narrowing, her jaw beginning to tense. "I think this time I'm going to get him," I kept on. I began to tell her a little bit about the files I had and how Dana was helping me. I tried to explain to her why this time felt different. When I'd exhausted myself, she gasped, drawing in air as if she were breathing through a straw and couldn't get enough. She was aware that if she told me what she really thought, it would break me, so she did what we do when we cannot bear to be honest with our loved ones: She said nothing. She motioned at her book again. This time I opened it.

My mother was drifting off to sleep when Suze arrived. My aunt seemed surprised to see me there, which I took very personally. As if I never visited my mother. When Suze saw her sister sleeping, she gestured for me to step into the hallway so we could chat. Outside Ma's room, she wrapped me in a tight hug. I leaned in to it for a second.

"I wanted to ask," she said. A nurse smiled at us as she hurried past. Suze produced a forced half smile, then turned back to me. "What's your feeling on these sessions—do you think we have a shot?"

I wondered if she'd come to Ma's for the same reason I had—to gauge Ma's hope. Suze needed to know how she should prepare. It occurred to me then that we were all pretending at something for one another's benefit. It's hard enough to gauge your own capacity for faith, let alone someone else's.

"I think—" I paused. I wanted to be careful. I wanted to be honest. "I think we're going to find her this time." I saw a twinge of disappointment on my aunt's face, or maybe it was something else. A feeling we had no name for: hope, but sicker and murkier. A kind of troglobite.

She nodded. "Me too." She looked past me into the dark cave of a room where her sister was dying. "Me too," she repeated. It frightened me to admit that I had no idea if this was what she really felt.

Our detective, Pete told me, was Gary Wolski, Jr. No relation, apparently, to the bar, whose bumper stickers were plastered all over the city of Milwaukee: *I Closed Wolski's.* I had once closed Wolski's too, with Dee no less, but we were underage, so we didn't think we should wait around for the sticker. I also didn't have a car at the time. Peter and I met Wolski Jr. at the Milwaukee Police Department, which was in an odd part of the city, home also to the coroner's office, the morgue, the courthouse, and several very old, very grand churches whose stained glass windows had been removed or boarded up to prevent looting. The freeway interchange hovered above the surface streets and cast long, permanent shadows on the buildings beneath. In 1997 a muralist painted the walls of the on-ramps with three full-size blue whales and two calves swimming through deep blue ocean and thick kelp forests. The whales' eyes were trained on the Grecian columns of the Milwaukee County Courthouse. It became the only beautiful part of that section of the city. Not long after they'd dedicated the mural, Milwaukee redirected the highway and demolished the mural in the process. Dee never saw it, but I knew she would have loved the painting.

Because of the wind off the lake, this was also the part of the city where all of the floating garbage collected and stayed—stray newspapers, egg cartons, plastic bags, condom wrappers, cigarette butts. Heaps of garbage piled up in the street corners, wound around lampposts and electrical poles, and got caught in fences and underneath car tires. The city didn't seem to mind that their political headquarters were situated in the filthiest part of the city, which is to say I never saw anyone trying to clean any of it up.

MPD HQ was housed in a tall, skinny building with very few windows. As soon as Peter and I pulled up, I wanted to leave. The perimeter of the property was ringed by news vans. The spirals of their satellites made the city block look like a Dr. Seuss book. Reporters had flocked from across the nation to cover the Milwaukee Cannibal.

Newscasters milled about on the sidewalk and in the street. One man was eating a hot dog, the yellow mustard dripping down his chin. He wore a fedora and was clutching a microphone in his hot dog–free hand. He caught my eye and headed in our direction. Instinctively, I touched Peter's wrist, and he turned toward the reporter. Maybe Peter's face deterred the man, because he stopped short and busied himself with the remainder of his hot dog.

"What are they waiting here for?" I asked Peter.

He shrugged. "Fucking vultures," he said.

In what dark corner of the city were they keeping the serial killer? They'd started warning parents about letting their kids watch the news because the coverage was so gruesome. Pictures, he'd kept hundreds of pictures of the men he'd murdered, and pictures of the procedures of these murders, in a drawer in his bedroom. He had wanted to be caught.

Tracy Edwards, the man who'd led the police to the serial killer's home, and thus precipitated his arrest, began an extensive national TV circuit. He was on all the talk shows, and we could trace the sensational crescendo of these interviews from network to network. Of course, he didn't need to do much to sensationalize; the whole story was about as sensational as it gets. This man, like Konerak Sinthasomphone before him, had escaped in handcuffs from the apartment. He'd flagged down a pair of cops on their beat and led them back to the serial killer's apartment, where a struggle ensued, and where the cops found pictures of mutilated victims and, eventually, the bodies of some of the victims too. On TV, Edwards liked to describe the sound of the serial killer's scream when he understood he was about to be arrested: a primal scream, a death scream.

Inside, we took the elevator up to the fifteenth floor. It's true what they say about some buildings: There was no button for the thirteenth floor. It unnerved me that the police were a superstitious bunch too. Peter and I held our breath, and I refused to make eye contact with him, even though I could feel him trying. His face was fluorescent under the elevator lights.

Wolski Jr. met us at the elevator. He shook our hands and, to my annoyance, called Peter "Pete" like he was already a part of the family. He was a short man and, at that time, just on the precipice of graying. He seemed to me then the kind of man who took aging very personally and went to great lengths to delay it. I imagined him rising very early and doing push-ups straight out of bed; he seemed like the kind of man who had a punching bag hanging from a hook in his bedroom. He nodded toward a door at the back of a large, open room.

We wound our way around desks that were mostly empty; phones rang and no one picked them up. I was reminded of those days after Dee had left when Leif and I were coming down and it seemed the phone might never stop ringing, and my stomach ached when I thought I might have missed a call from her.

Wolski ushered Peter and me in, but Peter shook his head and took a seat near the door. Wolski nodded at him like they had some kind of understanding. This annoyed me too, but I made an effort not to show it.

"Your mother has already filed the report, so we've got most of what we need," Wolski said.

"Need for what?" I asked.

"For the report."

I frowned, and Wolski began to eye me like I was slow. Many men believe they are smarter than most women.

"However, you might be able to fill in some gaps in the days before she went missing, so I'm going to ask you a few questions, and you just answer to the best of your ability."

I nodded for him to go ahead.

"When did you last see Dee?"

The noise of the shutter echoed in my head. It rattled me to think that image existed somewhere in the world, even if it was only burned backward onto film by light.

"July Fourth," I said.

He shuffled his papers and added something to one of them. The end of his pen was riddled with bite marks. "What did you guys do?"

"The day before the Fourth, she'd found out her boyfriend—"

"Hold on," Wolski said. He put his hand up but continued to write. He did not look at me. "Both your mother and Pete said she isn't seeing anyone."

"Well, she is. Or was. She doesn't want my mom or Pete to know because Frank is . . . older."

"How much older?"

"Thirty-five," I said. "Or that's what he told Dee."

Wolski scribbled and scribbled. "Okay, so she was seeing this . . . Frank? Does Frank have a last name?"

"I don't know," I admitted.

"What about an address or a telephone number?"

I blinked. I realized I had no idea where he lived. I shook my head.

Wolski frowned. "Okay," he said. "So what happened on the Fourth?"

"The day before the Fourth, she called to tell me he was cheating on her. She said she was going to confront him about it, and I told her to wait. She agreed, so I went to pick her up at her dorm. She was a mess, real upset, so we went to get a burger and catch the fireworks together. After the show, we went to bed at my place, and then we went to pick my boyfriend up at Ambrosia at the end of third shift. The three of us spent the Fourth drinking, and Leif and I passed out, and when we woke up, she was gone."

Wolski hadn't raised his head, but he moved the chewed pen furiously. When he did look up, he leaned across the desk toward me. I didn't like the feeling of his eyes scanning my face.

"Isn't it possible she's left with this . . . Frank and didn't tell anyone?"

I shook my head, and bubbles of white light burst in front of me. I was suddenly dizzy, so I put my hands on Wolski's desk to steady myself. The desk was sticky.

"I mean . . . I'm not sure. Maybe. Either way, you should find him."

"She didn't tell your mother or Pete about Frank. Seems like she might leave without telling them that. Maybe without even telling you."

"Maybe. But I think she would have told me."

"Pete said it was hard to reach you. Maybe she did try to tell you."

I thought on that briefly. I could feel him taking control of the interview. He was telling me what happened when it should have been the other way around. I shook my head. "She would have left a message or something . . ."

He consulted his report again. "Dee's roommate, Felicity, told your mother that Dee had packed a bag on the third."

I shook my head. "Dee always packs a bag when she comes to stay with me."

"But she didn't stay on the night of the Fourth, did she?"

My heart was beginning to pound through my T-shirt. "No," I said.

Wolski returned this with a curt nod. He consulted his notes. "So you guys didn't talk for almost two weeks, right? That's what Pete said. Why not?"

I clutched myself. I glanced at the door and wished Peter had come in with me. "We . . . we had an argument," I whispered.

"Was it about Frank? Maybe she left but didn't want to tell you because you'd just had a fight?"

I shook my head. "We didn't argue about Frank."

"What happened to your face?"

I knew I answered a beat too late, and Wolski registered it, even if he didn't write anything down. "I got mugged."

"Did you report it?"

"It seemed like you guys had your hands full," I said.

Wolski stood up and rifled around his desk, looking under papers and paperweights, moving pictures of men in military garb and binders empty of their paper guts, and he eventually found an official-looking folder. He slid his notes into the folder but not before I saw a stamp of red ink. I was shot through with despair. At the top of Dee's missing-persons report were the words: *Noncritical Missing.*

"What does that mean?" I asked him. He ignored me.

What it meant, I learned later, was that Wolski did not think Dee's disappearance was very suspicious. What he did think was suspicious was my split face. I picked up my bag to leave, but Wolski stopped me.

"One of her friends at school said she was also sleeping with an . . ." He rifled through his dumb report again. "Erik?"

My heart fell. "Erik is just a friend," I said.

Wolski stared at me. "We'll need to speak with him as well," he said.

"Fine. So what do we do next?"

"I've entered all her information in the system, but unfortunately, that's about as much as I'm authorized to do unless there's evidence of foul play. It's not a crime to leave the city without telling your family."

"There is evidence."

Wolski leaned toward me again, and a vein bulged in his temple. "The only evidence of foul play is your split cheekbone there, and I don't think you want it in here." He shook the report at me.

"I'll need a copy of that," I said.

He handed me the one he'd just stamped.

I snatched it, and I didn't wait for him to let me out. I swung the door open and Peter jumped to his feet. I almost hit one of them when Wolski gave Peter that knowing look, the one that said, *Fucking women,* and then held his hand out and said "Pete" again.

"I hate him," I said to Peter when we were back in the car.

Peter put his forehead to the steering wheel, and the car horn blared for several seconds. The reporters cast interested looks in our direction. They were stalking the city block waiting for someone to say something—a policeman with his guard down or even a family member of one of the victims. Jackpot. As the police released the victims' identities, news vans began to take shifts outside the families' homes: on the South Side of Milwaukee, in Wauwatosa, Racine, Chicago, Coventry, Ohio, the birthplace of the serial killer's first victim. Police details were dispatched to keep reporters from the victims' families. There was a photo in *Time* magazine of a little girl who'd set up a lemonade stand near the media camp in the serial killer's hometown of Bath, Ohio; she sold Cannibal Lemonade to the reporters and whoever else for a buck a cup.

I tugged on Peter's arm and he lifted his head.

"He's not terrible," Peter said. "I think he's very professional."

"They gave us the dregs," I said.

He drove us back to Ma's, and on the highway ramps, we passed over the police department and over the serial killer in his cell too. The downtown fell away from the highway as we headed west, away from the breweries and the factories churning out chocolate, and cheese, and sad, sad lives. Peter kept his eyes on the road.

"Don't expect Ma not to notice your face," he warned.

I pulled down the passenger visor and flipped open the mirror. Though the swelling had gone down, I had two long thin marks, one on each side, tracing the curves of my cheekbones; the skin underneath my eyes was puffy and red; and my lips looked larger than normal, chapped and red. Wolski's voice rang in my head. I rifled around in my purse and came out with a makeup bag, which I hardly ever used. I set to applying a thick layer of foundation, eye shadow, some white liquid Dee had given me that was supposed to reduce bags, a smear of lipstick. I turned to Peter. "Better?" I asked.

He eyed me. "You never wear makeup."

I wiped off the lipstick on the back of my hand.

My parents used to own one of the oldest houses in our neighborhood in Wauwatosa. It was a cream-brick farmhouse, built in the 1860s and awkwardly annexed with beige prefab additions ever since. It was a low, sprawling structure with thick wooden beams and floors that sloped badly. By the time Peter was fifteen, he could not stand up straight in his bedroom on the second floor. After our parents had redone the kitchen, after they'd ripped out the sink and pulled up the stove and the dishwasher and the rotten wooden floors, we'd found the wooden support beams were riddled with bullets. Upstairs, in our parents' bedroom there was a small, rectangular window that our father said was for shooting your shotgun outta. The house was full of ghosts too, though only Dee and I were aware, and only Dee could communicate with them. When we saw the bullets in the beams, we knew this house had seen it all—births and deaths, weddings and funerals—and there was a certain reverence that came from the knowledge. The shock would have been to discover the house contained no ghosts at all. When they'd wanted to build the railroad right through the center of the house, the company had paid for the house's transfer to a lot a few acres to the south, and that's where it stands now. Ghosts and all. When the train came through, the house rattled inside its old wooden frame. Dee and I began to consider it a kind of rocking of our childhood beds, and it would have been if the horn the conductors used had not been so loud.

Even when we'd both moved out, Dee and I still longed for the house, and its creaks, and ticks, and sloping floors, and the bedroom we shared in the tiniest room on the second floor. How many nights had we stayed up too late talking and slowly let the ghosts fill in the spaces between these conversations, which, as the night wore on, grew longer and longer until we were listening to just the ghosts moving through the house and then to our own shallow sleepy breaths.

During her first year at Mount Mary, Dee would often call me and say she was going to spend the night at Ma's. Inevitably, I'd end up there too, drinking wine with Ma and Dee and sometimes Suze, then squeezing Dee's hand in the dark before passing out in my twin bed. I know no greater feeling of safety than falling asleep next to Dee in my childhood bed. I used to think I'd achieved the same feeling while falling asleep tucked into Leif night after night, but I suppose I'd been fooling myself.

Dee and I were in elementary school when, within a year, two things happened that made our parents want to sell that house. First the kitchen caught on fire. Dee and I were too young to completely understand how it had happened, and neither our parents nor Peter seemed willing to fill us in properly. As far as we could see, someone, probably our father, had left something plastic in the oven, forgotten about it, and then punched the preheat button. Our father was supposed to be watching us while Ma was at the store. He was tinkering with an old car in the driveway when he realized he needed some crucial part from his shop. He left us on our stomachs watching *Sesame Street* in the living room. He looked at me and said, *Don't move.* He threw some cookies at us. Dee grinned at me. She suggested jumping on our parents' bed while they were gone. We were still arguing about what forbidden game we'd play while we had the house to ourselves when I smelled the smoke.

In school, we'd gone to an office building that they'd converted to a fake house for the purpose of teaching children how to handle emergencies in the home—fires, tornadoes, break-ins, and the like. I felt prepared. I told Dee we had to stay on our stomachs and crawl to the kitchen door. She thought the whole thing was a lot of fun. I put my hand on the door that separated the kitchen and the living room, and it was hot. I knew we had to keep the door closed. We crawled to the front of the house and slid on our bellies through the front door and onto the concrete porch. I scanned the driveway and the small yard for our father, but he wasn't there. Dee and I held hands and walked to the neighbor's house. A single woman lived there with four or five pugs. They were sad-looking animals, always huffing and puffing on walks, but she loved them. They were a fixture of our neighborhood. The pugs barked when I knocked. She answered the door in a pale pink robe with cartoon pugs stitched on the pockets. Her hands disappeared into them.

I used her phone to call 911. When our mother arrived home from the store, and our father got back from the shop, they were terrified to see two Wauwatosa Fire Department trucks parked outside our house, and smoke billowing from the chimney and kitchen windows. Our mother picked up the bag of groceries she'd just bought and threw the whole thing at our father. *Where the fuck have you been?* A carton of eggs tumbled out of the bag and smashed on the sidewalk. The yolks were bright yellow against the grainy concrete. It made me sick to look at. Luckily for our father, he was spared the worst of her wrath because everyone was so impressed with the calm, confident, and efficient way I'd handled the situation. Everyone was so pleased with me. Everyone except Dee.

"Where'd you learn all that?" Dee asked me a day or two later, after the fire was fully out and we stood in the kitchen looking at the smoke-scarred walls: They had turned a disgusting ash.

"At school," I told her. "Emergency preparded . . . prepar-adedn . . . being prepared for an emergency."

"Wow," she said. She frowned at me.

"What's wrong?" I asked her.

"Well, I just feel like you used up our one emergency. Now, even once I learn that stuff, I'll never be able to test my skills, you know?"

"I don't think you're supposed to *hope* to use them. That's the whole point of an emergency—you want to be ready, but you don't want one to happen."

She shrugged. She was jealous. I could always tell with her. Sometimes I wondered if I was the only one who could see it. I know our father never did. The way he doted on her.

"Still," she said. "I wish I could have taken a crack at that."

I rolled my eyes. "Maybe we'll have a tornado soon, Dee." I stuck my tongue out at her.

"Whatever, that's dumb. Too easy." She threw her hands up. "Everybody knows you just have to hide in a ditch and wait."

After the fire, there was a drug bust at the house across the street. As it happened, Dee and I were friends with the little girl who lived in that house. Her name was Tina. Dee was closer with her than I was. Honestly, I found her a bit strange, and not in an interesting way but in an unnerving way. For example, she said she could talk to the dead; she said she had a twin sister who died when they were babies but who spoke to her from the other side. She scared me, but that's probably *why* Dee liked her. The two of them spent a lot of time playing fortune-telling games—using cootie catchers to guess their future husband's name, their profession, whether they'd be rich or poor, if they'd live in the city or the country. I didn't like these games, so I refused to participate, though I would sit and listen from time to time. They had a calm, lullaby-like quality.

Anyway, one day after school, Dee and I were playing in the living room, in front of the modest bay window through which you could see the house across the street. The lots in that part of Tosa were pretty small. Even with the street and our small front yard, there was probably only two hundred feet between our front window and theirs.

When eight police cars came roaring down our block, Dee, Ma, Pete, and I stood in front of the window and watched men in black vests and helmets pour out of emergency vehicles like ants from a disturbed colony. Dee looked at me, her eyebrows raised and her chin pointed slightly down, which was her way of indicating she was very interested. For my part, I was afraid. So was our mother. We don't know who started shooting first. Probably it was the cops. Our mother shoved us to the ground and put her hands on the back of our necks so we went facedown into the carpet. Peter lingered, trying to see what was happening, and my mother swiped at his ankles to get him down to the ground.

The four of us were there long after the shooting stopped and Tina's father had been loaded into the back of a wagon. We heard from the neighbors brave enough to peek at the scene. We were still on the ground when our father arrived home with a bucket of Kentucky Fried Chicken. We never saw Tina again.

The combination of these two events threw my parents into a frenzy; they wanted to find a "safer" neighborhood and a house that hadn't burned half to the ground. In retrospect, I'm not sure they ever had the money to actually move, especially consid-

ering the house had depreciated since the fire. I'm also not sure a
"safer" neighborhood existed; Tosa *was* safe. But either way, for a
few months, my parents spent most of their free time canvassing
some of the wealthier neighborhoods, collecting brochures and,
from time to time, touring properties for sale. Maybe just the act
of searching made them feel better.

Anyway, of all the houses we toured, I remember only one. It
was a large white house in the Washington Highlands. This property was well outside what my parents could afford, but of course,
we understood that only later. The Washington Highlands had
been built on a tract of land once owned by Frederick Pabst. After
he died, the land was subdivided, and some fancy city planners,
influenced by the then-popular city garden movement, came in to
design the neighborhood, with large lots full of stately trees, gentle
hills, and creeks that ran through people's backyards. This house
too had a big, beautiful sloping backyard through which a shallow
but wide creek ran. It had four bedrooms, which meant we could
each have our own. It had a glass sunporch with built-in benches,
where I imagined lying on my stomach for hours, reading. The
best part about the house was the yard. We all begged our parents
to move there. Even Peter. We cried. We yelled.

As usual, Dee was the most animated. She ran through the
backyard, kicked off her shoes, and stood in the creek splashing
in the water. *Get out of there, Candace, you're destroying your clothes,*
our mother yelled. Our father laughed. I frowned. I knew if I'd
been the one to do that, he'd have scolded me. Everything Dee did
was precious to him.

That day Dee said she wouldn't get out of the creek until our
parents agreed to buy the house. Our mother said we were getting
in the car, and Dee better be in there in two minutes or else. The
four of us went to sit in the car and we waited, and we waited, and
we waited. It started to get dark. No Dee. Eventually, our mother

punched our father in the arm. And shoved him out the driver's side. When he returned, he was carrying a drenched, shivering Dee in his arms. She'd been sitting in the creek for at least thirty minutes. He'd thrown his old Carhartt over her so it swallowed her body. He asked my mother to drive and then he held Dee in his lap the whole way home. She tucked her face into his neck. Once she turned around to see me, and I caught her eye from the backseat. She made a prideful face, with the corners of her mouth turned up slightly and her eyes wide, that would have been impossible for anyone but me to read. It meant *I won*.

But, of course, she had not won. We stayed in our small cream-brick house for the rest of our childhood. Some days it's hard to imagine the alternative. Other days the alternative is what makes me spiral. I like to drive by the big white house in the Highlands and park my car across the street from its grand sloping driveway. (I never drive by our actual childhood house.) I'll walk through the Highlands imagining how our lives might have been different if Dee had gotten her way. Sometimes I indulge in the idea that perhaps if we had moved, because the course of our lives would have been so altered, she'd still be with us. I imagine her protest in the creek as an unconscious fight for her life. Other times I can see how ridiculous this line of thinking is, and then I wonder if moving would have changed anything at all. So often, more and more, I'm struck by the debilitating feeling of having no idea how I got here, or anywhere. In practice, it seems easy to trace my movements from this present moment to those past moments that led me here or there. But once I begin, the sense of forks along the way feels unmanageably oppressive. *If I hadn't done this, then I wouldn't have done this, or this* . . . The origins of consequences, like the beginnings of cracks in concrete, become too difficult to track.

After Pete and I left the police department, we drove to Ma's. The closer we got to our childhood home, the more nervous I became. This was the first time I'd seen Ma since Dee had gone missing. At first my mother seemed relieved to see me and grateful to Pete for dragging me from my apartment in Riverwest. She held my face between her papery, sun-spotted hands and cried with no noise. She gave me a wet kiss right on the mouth, like she used to do all the time when we were babies, and she pressed hard against my lips. I was reminded of the night in Riverwest when I'd thought about kissing Dee. I wished then I had kissed her. I wished I'd kissed her more and more. When my mother pulled away, my face was wet with her—her salt and spit ran down my chin. I wiped it away with the back of my hand.

"Hi, Mama," I said.

Then she slapped me hard.

My head stung, and Leif burned on my eyelids too. His hardness getting harder, the bloodier I got.

"What the hell is wrong with you?" she asked. "Your sister is missing, Margaret."

The word *missing* hit me as if she'd slapped me again. It's odd now to think that it took so long for the seriousness of the situation to sink in with me. Was it the fact that I was wrapped up in my own tailspin? Was it the fact that I didn't want it to be true? Either way, the weight of the word *missing,* the state of it, seemed to hover above me, just out of reach, in the weeks after I discovered that Ma had filed Dee's report.

"And Pete said you've been living in Riverwest. For Christ's sake. You're lucky to be alive." I didn't want to speak to the dramatics of this comment, so I bit my lip.

"I'm sorry I didn't tell you."

"You're going to be sorry."

I looked at Pete. He shrugged.

"I really don't know what happened, Mama. I saw Dee on the Fourth, but we had a fight . . . Not anything serious. Just the usual stuff. And she ran out. She didn't even call me once after that."

"Then you should have known."

She was right. I should have guessed something was wrong.

"I want you to stop thinking about your own damn self so much."

I nodded. She had said what I was thinking. I thought I would cry, so I scrunched my face tight.

"It's not your fault, though, baby." I put my hands to my face, afraid they would come away wet, and felt the places where my cheeks were still sore. Wasn't it, in some way, my fault? Was that why I resisted believing Dee was gone? Because if I let that fact sink in, I'd also have to admit how much of her disappearance could be my own fault?

"But we're gonna find her?" I croaked. Ma brushed my jaw with her fingers. Peter coughed. "We just need to find Frank."

"We'll find her."

Ma stepped back but held the frame of my shoulders as if she were afraid I might leave. I took in the living room, and suddenly, I did want to leave. The house had been turned into a command center. A tattered map of Milwaukee spanned the entire north-facing wall. Lake Michigan was a wide blue mouth reaching toward the window. There were tiny red dots to show where Dee had been before she went missing—home, the mall, classes, work, a restaurant on Brady Street. (There was no dot in Riverwest.) It gave the city a diseased look, all the dots spread across the map like chicken pox. I thought of a picture of us when we had chicken pox together—all three of us lined up tallest to shortest, Dee last, barely four, with our shirts off to show the speckled skin.

The coffee table was littered with legal pads and phone books, numbers and notes, and more maps. The ink made me dizzy, so I collapsed on the leather sectional and put my head in my hands. I felt my mother's eyes on the back of my neck. I realized she blamed me, in a way, for losing Dee. She couldn't know, and I hoped she never would know, the circumstances surrounding Dee's disappearance, but she knew I'd ignored her calls for weeks. She put a cup of black coffee in front of me.

"So what the hell is going on, Margaret?"

I told my mother what I'd told Peter and Wolski, how Dee had been seeing Frank, how she had found out that he was cheating on her and maybe lying about his identity, and how she was planning on confronting him. I could tell Ma was stung that Dee and I had kept her relationship with Frank a secret, and that she wanted to have words with me about this, but there were too many logistics to discuss. Instead, they filled me in on everything they'd been doing so far—the interviews, the phone calls, the posters, the hotlines.

Later, Suze arrived to help us make pie and to busy the house, which was empty, and quiet, and full of worry and other things my mother wouldn't name. Even the ghosts seemed reluctant to go about their usual ghostly business—slamming doors, and clanging pots, and rattling paintings in their frames. My aunt arrived in a flurry of perfume and incense. She carried grocery bags stuffed with red wine and Crisco and rhubarb, and she marched to the kitchen like it was Thanksgiving in July. Peter was asleep when she arrived, but my aunt roused him, and we all went into the kitchen. Ma opened a bottle of green chartreuse and poured shots for everyone. Then we made pies. I remembered this from my father's death too. My mother and my aunt had dusted the whole kitchen in flour, and the ceramic tiles were slippery with wayward Crisco for weeks after his funeral. My mother hated idle hands.

We mixed the dough in big blue glass bowls, and then my mother spread waxed paper over the whole kitchen table, and we stood on the chairs and dusted the paper with a thick coat of flour, and then we rolled the crust. I had no idea what we were going to do with all of those pies—meat pies with carrots and onions and potatoes and cheese, fruit pies with strawberry and rhubarb and apple and blueberry, and sweet pies with pecans and key lime and chocolate. We baked them in rounds, and the kitchen got so hot we all had to go sit out in the backyard. We finished the green chartreuse and watched the fireflies flit through the tall grass. When the pies were done, my mother was exhausted, so Suze put her to bed.

The kitchen was still too hot to breathe in, so we sat outside. Suze chain-smoked and I sat on the stoop beneath her so she could brush my hair, which she said looked like a rat's nest. I closed my eyes and leaned against her shins. The night was humid and quiet, except for the rush of the traffic toward the city that echoed behind our fence. It was a night Dee and I probably would have gone out drinking. She would have tried to get me to wear a dress; I would have asked her to pick a top that covered her belly button and her stunning hips. (It mattered not at all; men hounded her in her track sweats and her dresses.)

"I'm going to tell you something no one else will," Suze said.

I turned to face her, and she tucked some stray strands of hair behind my ear. I shivered. *The human ear is a very delicate thing*, I thought.

"What's that?"

"You're going to have to tell the truth eventually," she said.

"I am telling the truth," I said.

"Then tell it better."

Suze stroked my head.

Suze left after midnight, and I didn't have the courage to go into my old bedroom, the one I'd always shared with Dee, so I curled up on the couch and read and reread the missing-persons report. Each time I read it, Dee became more and more of an abstraction, a character, a sketch of a human, and it scared me but not enough to stop reading it. The thing was, I was looking for something. Now I can see that I was trying to understand if *I* really believed she was missing. I think I still believed (or was it just a hope?) that Dee was laid up somewhere with Frank, hiding from me, and Ma, and Pete, from the repercussions of the Fourth. Or maybe she was scared to hear what I might say when I found out she was back with Frank? This prospect hurt most of all.

I woke up in the night and forgot where I was. I reached down to the floor to find Leif and his gun, but my fingertips brushed the worn carpet instead. We were not allowed to eat in this room when we were younger, but we used to do it anyway, when Ma wasn't home. There was often a thick, crumby line of food left between the couch and the coffee table. Ma cursed us for this. I ran my fingers there, but the carpet was clean. I called Leif from the living room phone with my eyes closed. He did not pick up.

The psychic, overwhelmed by the enormous popularity of his tours, canceled and rescheduled our last session three separate times. I could tell, during those weeks, that we were losing Ma. Sometimes when I visited her, she was disoriented; *Where the hell am I, baby?* she would ask me. She would laugh and cry within the same sentence. Sometimes she didn't speak at all and just stared at the pictures of Dee that she piled up next to her bed in a sad heap of toppled frames. So when Pete called me after the latest cancellation, I assumed it was about Ma.

"Do you have a minute?" Pete asked me on the phone.

"Of course."

"Great," he said. He exhaled heavily. "Can you come over?"

"Oh, Pete," I said. "It's late. I'm—"

"It's about Dana."

"Okay," I said.

Though my brother's house was lit up, and from the street the windows shone with warm yellow light, inside the house had the cold air of punishment. Peter let me in through the garage without a word. The house was too quiet. In the kitchen Helena sat at the table in front of a plastic tub containing two bedazzled cell phones and associated accessories. A pit of wire snakes. Alive. Pete tossed a thin manila folder on the table. Helena slid it toward me. A sticker on the folder's tab said: *Property of Wauwatosa Police Department.* I opened it, though I did not want to.

Inside there was a grainy cell phone photo, a screenshot of a Snapchat frame, that the police had blown up and printed on glossy paper. Most of it was blurred, but this was what I could see: a girl on her back in bed, her top off, her hand reaching down into her underwear. There was a stuffed dog with glassy eyes on one of the pillows. A cereal bowl with a few sad Cheerios encrusted in dried milk on the bedside table. A girl's room. A baby's room. I looked at the photo too long. I turned it over and slid it back toward Helena. Though what was visible of her face was obscured, the girl, I knew, was Dana.

In a poorly devised revenge plot, Cal, the boy Dana had been seeing, had distributed this screenshot to all his friends, who had then begun to distribute it to boys beyond her high school. A mother of one of the boys had found the photo and reported it to the police. Cal was being investigated for possession and distribution of child pornography. Pete and Helena decided to take away the girls' phones because it seemed the vitriol would not stop. This only angered Dana's sister, Sophie, who felt it was unfair to punish her for what was happening to Dana. Pete and Helena asked me to speak to Dana, who had locked herself in her room and refused to come out. I said I would try. I sat in front of her bedroom door and I said, *I love you, baby,* and *Why don't you let me in?* But she made no noises behind the door, and eventually, I just began banging my forehead against the wood. Sophie came out to watch me: I saw that familiar look of pity tinged with fear. I was accustomed to people looking at me this way. I was numb to it. After I'd become nauseated and disoriented on account of hitting my head against the door, Sophie went to get Pete, who pulled me away. As my brother was guiding me down the stairs, Sophie kicked at the bottom of the Dana's door and produced a thin crack in the wood. I stared at it. *You slut,* Sophie yelled at the door, *you ruined everything.*

Pete called me a few days later to say that Dana's pediatrician had suggested she be put on suicide watch. He'd prescribed her some antidepressants and said they might want to look at other schools.

"And she's asking for you now," he told me.

I swallowed a gulp of wine that dried my mouth out. "For me? Are you sure?"

"You should come by," he said.

The morning after Pete picked me up from my place and I met Detective Wolski for this first time, Ma doled out tasks. Some of our extended family, with a few from my father's side who didn't have work or were able to take off, came over and we strategized. The day was sunny, and the walls of the kitchen shone hot yellow; I'd drunk too much of that nasty chartreuse.

Ma assigned us tasks that, if Dee had been labeled *critical missing,* the police department would have been required to undertake. Because her case hadn't warranted sufficient suspicion, according to Wolski, we were supposed to exhaust our own investigations. These included, per the Milwaukee Police Department Missing Persons SOP: Conduct a search of the home and grounds from which the person went missing, conduct a search of the last location the missing person was seen and conduct an interview of those who last saw the missing person, fully identify and separately interview anyone at the scene of the disappearance of the missing person and treat the location as a possible crime scene, identify any areas at the incident scene that have been disrupted or may have the potential for the presence of evidence and safeguard those areas, broadcast a description of the missing person and vehicle, and conduct a canvass of the neighborhood. Ma, Pete, and Suze had already exhausted a number of these items by the time they brought me home to help.

Ma asked me to call the *Milwaukee Journal;* she said we needed an announcement in the paper. I spent the morning listening to a bad recording of Beethoven's Fifth, and I never got through to a human. I borrowed Suze's car and drove back downtown. No one profited more from the murders than the newspapers; the week after the serial killer was arrested, circulation and sales hit record highs. Milwaukee, and the rest of the nation, had a dark, insatiable appetite for this story.

The first of the victims to be identified was a twenty-three-year-old man named Oliver Lacy. He was engaged to the mother of his two-year-old son at the time of his death. Lacy's mother identified her son from a photo of his severed head. Minutes after she'd returned from the Police Administration Building downtown, her house was swarmed with reporters. On the evening news, she sat in her recliner with her granddaughter on her lap and blinked into dozens of flashes. The fuzzy ends of microphones brushed her lips. When one cameraman turned his lens on the scene behind him, we saw reporters standing on her coffee table, framed family photos smashed on the ground, mud and grass from the reporters' boots on her carpet.

Inside, the *Journal* offices were packed with people in motion, weaving around desks, typing furiously on massive IBMs, dropping paper, picking up paper, passing out coffee and sandwiches, shouting to one another from across the room or into phones. It sounded like everyone in the room was being paged, but no one seemed to mind the cacophony of fifty pagers going off at once. No one noticed me. I approached the desk closest to the office doors, where a young woman was holding a phone to her ear with her shoulder and writing furiously on a legal pad. I waited, and she flitted her eyes up at me, once and then twice, annoyed. She put the phone down, kept writing, and asked, "Can I help you?"

"I hope so," I said.

She glared. I supposed if I said the serial killer's name, they'd roll out the red carpet. Peter said some of his lawyer friends had heard other media outlets, particularly national ones, were giving limousine rides and steak dinners to the killer's relatives or neighbors, even his prom date from high school, in exchange for exclusives.

"We're very busy," the woman said.

"Who can I see about getting a missing-persons announcement and photo in the paper?"

"Is he gay?"

"Excuse me?"

"Is the missing person gay?"

They had yet to identify all the victims.

"It's my sister," I croaked, not sure what to say.

"Oh," the woman said, obviously disappointed. She pointed across the room at a cubicle fitted into a corner. "He might be able to help you."

I knocked awkwardly on the wall and poked my head into the makeshift office. A young man, a boy, really, whipped around in his swivel chair. His eyes were wide, rimmed red with fatigue and chemical alertness.

The walls of his cubicle were lined with photos. One wall was just children, and they were mostly stiff school photos—cheesy smiles against purple and green backgrounds, pressed collars and combed hair. Others were candid—a girl at her dance recital, another at a picnic; one boy grinned at the bottom of a Christmas tree, the presents like a fort around him. One wall was covered in photos of young men.

"We're a little behind," the boy said. I scanned the photos:

Milwaukee's missing. Where were all of these people? "We've been flooded with requests, mostly by families of young missing men. Now everyone thinks maybe their son was one of the serial killer's victims. Can you imagine?"

There was a face I recognized: the jazz prodigy from Chicago whom I'd seen on the news a few weeks back. I stared at this man; I wondered if he was dead.

"Can I help you?" The boy fidgeted. The small, tired look of him made me want to take him into my arms and rock him to sleep.

I nodded. "My sister's missing. We need an announcement in the paper."

"Okay," he said. And it was that simple. He asked for a copy of the missing-persons report, as well as a photo. He ran the report through the copy machine without looking at it.

"Do they always make the family do this?" I asked him.

He shrugged. "*Journal* and PD relations are at an all-time low, but usually, the detective passes along the information, or whoever filed the report. Who's your assigned detective?" He flipped to the front of the report he'd just copied. His face reddened.

"What's wrong with Wolski?" I asked.

The boy was embarrassed, and he hesitated. "He's not a bad guy," he offered.

"But . . ." I waited.

"He's got bad stats," the kid said.

I wasn't following. "Meaning?"

"Meaning he doesn't usually find the people he's looking for."

I frowned, and I could tell the kid felt like he'd said too much.

"But that's not always a reflection of the detective," he said. "Obviously, some cases are more easily resolved than others," he added.

"Wolski thinks she ran away with her boyfriend."

He shrugged. "So you know what I mean."

The *Journal* didn't print the damn thing for a week, and when they did, it was hidden in the lower corner of page eleven: a two-inch-square box below a shrunken, grainy version of Dee's face. The notice was printed in the same issue that called 1991 Milwaukee's "deadliest year ever," citing not only the gruesome murders of that summer (eleven and counting) but also the murder of a nine-year-old boy by a group of teenagers who'd allegedly killed the boy on account of the Chicago Bulls jacket he was wearing.

Leif called that week to tell me Erik had run away again. Leif was out of breath, and his voice was strained, as if he were choking. He said Erik had seen the tiny report about Dee in the newspaper and had spooked. Was he afraid of Frank? I was afraid of Frank. Maybe we were the only ones. Leif said he had no idea where Erik had gone. He had left in the middle of the night with a backpack and fifty-two dollars in cash that he'd stolen from Leif's wallet. He hadn't left a note or a forwarding address.

"So he's not with you?" Leif stammered.

"Why didn't you call me sooner?"

"I can't be responsible for everyone, goddammit."

"I tried to call you," I repeated. I'd called our apartment and his parents' house every night to talk to him about Dee's disappearance, but the phones had rung and rung. Once his mother had picked up their landline and shouted, *We're not interested!*

"I bet Erik and Dee are together somewhere," he said. "They probably decided to take a trip. Get some air, get out of the city." I thought of all the empty, airy promises I'd made Dee on the night of the third—Canada and Thailand, a house in the woods or the jungle. A place where we'd be safe.

"You're dumber than Wolski," I told Leif.

"Fuck you," he said.

I hung up. I put my head against the wall and rolled my forehead across the stucco. The wall felt almost like a cool ice pack. Pete put his hand on my shoulder and I jumped.

"Any news?" Peter asked me. He wrung his hands.

"Erik's run away," I told him, and he threw his hands up, frustrated by any news that didn't seem Dee related. "Again."

"Who the hell is that?"

"Leif's brother," I said. Pete squinted. I explained, "Dee and Erik were friends. Became friends."

"I see," Pete said. "Peg? I need to know from you." He paused.

Pete and I had never been all that close. I'd always thought he was hard on me, unnecessarily so. I never understood why. "What?" I gulped.

"What do you think is going on here? What's happened to her? Is she with this kid? Is she . . ." Neither of us wanted him to finish asking that question. I nodded, though.

"She isn't with him. I don't know, Pete. It's bad . . . You know she wouldn't . . . We don't go this long. Ever. You know that."

He clenched his jaw. Rifled around in his pants pocket for his cigarettes. Though Pete had once told me he abhorred the habit of smoking, after Dee went missing, he started smoking almost as heavily as Suze. He plugged a cigarette in his mouth and spoke with it clamped tightly between his teeth. "That's what I thought. Now you need to start acting accordingly."

"What's that supposed to mean?" I asked him.

He went toward the door. "You're taking this all a little lightly, no?"

"And you're a real asshole, you know that?"

Ma heard us and stormed into the room. "What is this?" she yelled.

Pete hid his cigarette but inched toward the door. "Nothing, Ma, nothing."

I stared at the carpet.

Article VI. Witnesses

RULE 608. A WITNESS'S CHARACTER FOR TRUTHFULNESS OR UNTRUTHFULNESS

Reputation or Opinion Evidence. A witness's credibility may be attacked or supported by testimony about the witness's reputation for having a character for truthfulness or untruthfulness, or by testimony in the form of an opinion about that character.

Before I went back to Pete's to see Dana, I tore up my apartment looking for the photo. It had occurred to me that it was the only thing I had to offer her. I thought it might represent a way forward. Or that it might make her listen to me. Or that it might help her imagine a life after the photo of her that Cal had circulated. I'm sure my method was not sound. I'm sure with any other fourteen-year-old, it would have been abhorrent. Maybe it was abhorrent even with Dana. I knew Pete and Helena certainly would not approve. But it was all I could think. Sometimes understanding the ubiquity of your pain can soothe that pain, but perhaps that was too cruel a lesson for a child.

These thoughts were as depressing to me as the existence of the photo itself. I couldn't remember what I'd done with it since the day I'd wanted to hide it from Dana, and I made a mess of my place looking for it—I opened the boxes and rifled through the papers, tore down stacks of books, kicked up dust. Eventually, I found the damn thing in the top drawer of my dresser. I slipped the photo into my purse and drove back to Pete's.

At first I was afraid she was going to refuse to let me in again. I knocked three times and heard nothing behind the door. I reached into my purse and felt the photo there. I wished suddenly I hadn't brought it, or that I had brought something else—flowers or a book. Something normal. The photo felt like a hot, heavy coal.

"Come in," she said. I opened the door. Dana was sitting on her bed in her pajamas. They had polar bears on them. I was reminded of a time when she had looked at me very grimly and said: *Did you know if greenhouse gas emissions remain on their current trajectory, polar bears will be extinct in my lifetime?* She had always been a practical but lugubrious child. She hugged her knees into her chest, which made her look very small. Her hair was greasy and stuck to the sides of her face.

"I love you," I told her.

"I love you too, Auntie Peg," she said. "I'm glad you're here." Her words were robotic. I wondered what kind of drugs they had her on. I tried to see beyond the dopiness of those chemicals and into *her*. I sat on the bed with her. She moved away from me.

"How are you?" I asked.

She nodded. I didn't dare touch her.

"I came to tell you something," I said. "About me."

Dana frowned. "Yeah?"

"Something, well, some things have happened in my life." I felt my throat closing. I wondered if this wasn't a terrible idea, and then I knew it was, but I didn't think I could turn back. "I've wanted to die before. Because of these things." Maybe I was admitting this to myself for the first time. Dana's face was blank. The type of blankness that could easily explode into rage. I was scared of her. I reached into the bag for the photo and laid it on her lap. I felt, for a moment, that the photo might singe the polar bears on her pajamas. Even medicated, Dana blushed brightly upon seeing the photo. She picked it up and put it close to her face. "This is . . ."

"That's me, yeah," I told her. "And my sister . . . Dee . . . your auntie Dee took that. She saw this."

Dana stared for a few seconds longer and then handed the photo facedown back to me.

"What is that?" she asked. In the hallway, we heard a door slam. "It's disgusting." She wanted to wound me. I didn't mind. So little could hurt me the way I'd already been hurt.

"I know," I said.

"Why did you show it to me, then? What is it?"

"It's a mistake I made," I said. "The biggest mistake I ever made."

Dana's face was still red, and her eyes were watery and sick.

"And I'm still here," I said. "Even . . . after this."

I put the photo back in my purse. We were quiet. Dana stared out her window.

After a long time, she looked at me and said, "But you're so sad."

After the *Journal* article ran, Wolski called to say he'd gotten an anonymous tip from a caller who'd seen Dee in the Menomonee Falls cemetery the day she left Leif and me in Riverwest.

"Wolski wants to know if we want to go out and canvass the cemetery," Peter said. He was holding the phone against his chest and winding the cord around his forearm. By this point, we had begun to sink into a very specific, very desperate kind of existence.

"We?" I asked. "Jesus, isn't that his fucking job?"

Ma and I were eating strawberry rhubarb pie at the kitchen table. She pushed crumbs around with the tines of her fork. Lately, it had been difficult to get her to eat anything except pie. Peter eyed Ma with her half-eaten plate. He shrugged.

"Let's go today," Ma said. "This is our first real lead since—" She paused. They both turned to me, and I realized what a disappointment I'd been to them. They'd hoped to find Dee holed away with me in Riverwest, or they'd hoped I'd know more about the night she disappeared, the days and the weeks after. I was crushed that I knew only slightly more than they did.

"We can be there in an hour," Peter said into the phone. "Any chance of getting a second detective out there?" He nodded grimly;

I knew Wolski had told him there wasn't a snowball's chance in hell of it.

Ma tossed the rest of her pie in the trash can.

The cemetery was well kept, thoroughly manicured, and even in late July, very green. There wasn't a fallen tombstone, or a brown patch of grass, or a wayward plastic bag in the whole sprawling place. The tombstones sprouted from the ground in straight even rows. Ma and Suze and Peter and I walked the winding footpaths and sweated in the afternoon heat. Peter said to look for anything suspicious, but there wasn't a single leaf of grass out of place. This was the kind of cemetery where visitors were encouraged to plant flowers at the foot of a grave rather than bringing their own, because cut flowers browned and needed to be collected as trash. But what then could people bring when they went to visit a grave? I always found it comforting to have something in my hands when we went to visit Dad's grave. I liked to bring a worry stone that I'd worn smooth over the course of the year. Here, I didn't see mementos at any of the graves. If there was something out of place, we would see it. At the top of a gentle hill, we saw a funeral underneath two big oaks. A man, a woman, and a child stood graveside while the undertakers lowered a heavy metal casket into the ground with a crank. The man held a shovel like he'd never had cause to use one. There was a priest reading from some papers, but we were too far away to hear the words.

Wolski came late and he came alone. We'd covered almost the entire area when he found us peering down on the burial below. He half jogged over to us, I suppose to give an air of urgency, or because he felt awkward walking while we all watched his approach. Suze lit a cigarette and blew smoke in his direction.

"I don't think we can smoke here," Wolski said.

Suze inhaled deeply.

"We're done," Peter said.

Wolski shook his head. "I was just speaking to a few of the groundskeepers—do you know who runs this place?" Wolski was often nauseatingly rhetorical. "This guy's parents." He held up the terrible sketch of Frank I'd helped the police artist, a buddy of Wolski's, draw a few weeks back. I didn't know if it was my memory or the artist's lack of skill, but the sketch was . . . disturbing. It was accurate enough, but he looked a lot less sleazy in the sketch than he had in person. Wolski was smug; he bobbed his head. "I was just speaking with them. They said his name isn't Frank, it's Anthony, but they call him Tony. And as far as they know, he lives in Ohio now."

At the bottom of the hill, the man tossed a shovelful of dirt over the top of the casket, then accidentally dropped the shovel into the grave. The shovel clattered against the casket, and the noise shook a few birds from the oak trees. The child screamed, and the woman clamped her hand tightly over the child's mouth; she rubbed his upper arm vigorqusly but would not hug him. The child screamed louder and shook the rest of the birds from the trees. He kept on until the man hit the child and he stopped. I thought suddenly of Leif. We hadn't spoken for a week or more. The birds flew from the trees and toward the undertakers' house. There was a thin gray line of ashy smoke funneling from a brick building and into the sky.

"What's that building over there?" I asked.

Wolski followed my gaze. "The crematorium."

The day of the last session was a Sunday. I felt that Sunday as if we'd been at it all for centuries: not just missing Dee and hoping she was alive and, when so much time had passed that we knew she wasn't, hoping that we would find out what had happened to her and, when even more time had passed and we figured we'd never know for sure, hoping still that we'd find her body somewhere in the city of Milwaukee. It wasn't just all that, though this progression by itself entailed a certain wrenching fatigue.

But the weeks since the psychic had come to town had felt longer than the last ten years combined, and they produced a different kind of exhaustion. At least for me. Maybe it was the pretending, or the way in which I felt I had to pretend I wasn't fooled by this kid, while at the same time I desperately hoped and at some point had begun to believe that maybe, somehow, he'd work a miracle for us. I remembered spinning slowly through Milwaukee's sky with him at the bar at the Hyatt. His insistence on the photo. It was this kind of nonsense, these "embarrassing" feelings, as Henry would have called them, that I had to fight. But as the weeks wore on, I found myself less and less capable of drumming up incredulity and more and more alive at the prospect of finding Dee's body. Some people think faithlessness is an easy way out, because they know sustained belief takes mountainous effort. But a commitment to incredulity, disbelief, hopelessness is its own kind of exhausting faith. The difference between them is one fills you up, the other drains you dry.

Pete's pet journalist, Charlie, was there again that day. He was fresh-faced and full of jittery energy; he clicked and unclicked his pen on repeat. He refused to make eye contact with me. Otherwise the group was relatively small—Ma, me, Pete, Suze, Wolski, and of course, Thomas Alexander's entourage. Dana had wanted to come, but Helena didn't think it was a good idea. I promised I'd fill Dana in on everything. Since I'd shown her the photo, she'd renewed her efforts with my files. I told myself this meant it hadn't been a terrible mistake. At the very least, it had gotten her out of her room. It was as if now she believed she had a piece of the puzzle that mattered. But I was afraid of what she was looking for.

While we were all taking our places, the lights began to flicker. Thomas Alexander was seated at the community room piano, idly tapping at the keys. Dee's Walkman was on the bench next to him just barely touching his thigh. When the lights went out he became very still. Then Thomas Alexander began to scream.

It was an odd noise, something like the way I assume an animal might sound when it's being eaten alive. A hair short of human. The room went quiet, and I expected that Thomas would stop once he had everyone's attention, but he didn't. He just kept screaming; the pitch of the noise was infuriating. The lights flickered. Pete's journalist whimpered. Outside, it began to snow in heavy wet clumps. Late May. The sky was dark and full of snow. The lights glared on again and Thomas Alexander kept screaming. I wondered where the nurses were—why hadn't they come to see who was screaming? A girl on Thomas Alexander's team, whose job I'd never really understood, ran over to Thomas and put her hands on either side of his flawless face. His eyes roamed wildly in the sockets. We waited. Thomas Alexander screamed. I caught Wolski's eyes. He blushed. The girl was rubbing her hands over and over Thomas Alexander's cheeks. She leaned in to him and brushed her lips ever so slightly against his, leaving a millimeter of space between their lips. It was not a kiss. The screaming stopped. The lights flickered off again. And then on again. I looked around the room and felt for a moment as if I'd slipped out of time. Who were all these people? Why were they here? Who was this child screaming at the top of his lungs?

The psychic leapt up from the piano and rushed to Ma. He held Dee's Walkman in one hand and my mother's hand in the other. He pushed his Ray-Bans to the top of his head, revealing a sweaty, unwashed face and sunken eyes.

"She wants to tell you where she is," he said. His makeup from the night before clung messily to his eyelashes and stained his face black. Had he slept yet? Had he been crying earlier? What was wrong with him?

"Where?" Ma whispered. The snow was getting heavier outside, and it was almost dark. In the west, the sky was turning the dark purple of a plum skin, but snow fell and fell.

An assistant spread a map across Thomas Alexander's lap and handed him a Sharpie. He bent down close to it. His spine made the shape of a C. He drew a big mark over the County Grounds. "She'll be here," he said. Ma leaned over. She groaned. "Underneath a dog."

Ma took the map from him and motioned at Peter to come take a look. I went over too. Pete held it out and we peered into Milwaukee's sad grids. The X marked an old, unkempt cemetery. I had a memory of Dee telling me Frank had taken her on a date there. Thomas Alexander tapped this X over and over again with the Sharpie.

"Here," he said. "Here, here, here . . . There is a cemetery here that everyone has forgotten about. Is that right? That's where she is. She told me. In the woods, there is a shrine. Not to her. The shrine is for the dog. But she'll be there."

Wolski came up and peered over Thomas Alexander's shoulder at the map. He pinched the bridge of his nose and shook his head. "Milwaukee County owns all that. I think they lease it to the medical college? Either way, totally blocked off. Private. Has been for a while now."

Ma didn't hear him, and if Thomas Alexander did, he took no notice. Charlie Makon was scribbling notes on an old-fashioned reporter's pad. I wanted to burn the damn thing.

"This is it," Thomas Alexander whispered. The room was closing in. All of us were getting closer and closer to Ma and Thomas Alexander. The bodyguards were moving toward the center of the room too. Thomas Alexander turned to look at me. "And Dee said to tell you, he's coming back."

The next time Leif called Ma's for me, I could tell he was in a bad way. I drove to Riverwest in Pete's car to bring him pie, because that was all I had. The apartment was a shit hole, and this had never been more apparent to me than that night. Leif was collapsed over the kitchen table, which was littered with ramen noodle wrappers and beer bottles. The apartment had the sad smell of stale cereal. My spider plant was on the kitchen floor, half of it spilled out of the pot, its white roots reaching toward the window.

"You killed my plant," I said.

Leif raised his head. His eyes were slow in the sockets, but I could almost see his heartbeat through his thin white shirt. He was drunk and speeding. I knew about this mixture: It was a toxic combination that allowed him to keep drinking long after he poisoned himself.

"You left," he said. Leif was a child; he lived in a tit-for-tat world.

"Dee's gone."

"I'm going to lose my job."

"Jesus, you're self-centered."

Without taking his eyes off me, he groped around on the kitchen table for his whiskey. He finished what was left in the glass and beckoned for me to come to him.

"Did you hear me?"

He stretched his arms out toward me.

"Dee's gone."

He said nothing, but the lovely length of his arms pleaded for me. I yelled, "What if she's dead." It was the first time I had allowed myself to voice this possibility, which had begun to seem probable, after we'd learned of Frank's real identity and seen the long, winding funnels of smoke rising from his parents' crematorium. I had begun, at that point, to take Frank's involvement in Dee's disappearance for granted.

I began to sob. Leif blinked with wet and bleary eyes, and still he held his arms up for me to come to him. I stared at the shriveled plant on the ground. I went to him. I climbed into his lap, straddling him in the chair, and he pulled me into him hard and fast. I buried my face in his neck, where his pores sweated out whiskey. The smell made me a little sick, so I pulled away, but he held me tight against him. Was the Fourth the last time we'd touched like this?

"Would you kill me?" I asked, forming the words like dark shapes pressed into the skin of his neck. *Kill me.* When I was a little girl, Ma used to say she was going to kill my father all the time: *If your father doesn't come home soon, I'm going to kill him.*

"Baby," he said. He held my face in his hands. "Oh, baby. What the fuck is wrong with me?" He kissed my face gently with tight, pursed lips; he kissed my eyelids and both my nostrils, the tip of my nose, my cheeks, the corners of my lips, he opened my mouth and kissed my teeth and my gums, he kissed both earlobes. "I can't believe I hurt you." I didn't say what I was thinking, which was: *I can.*

I spent the rest of the night coaxing him to drink water and trying to put him to bed, but his heart raced like an infant's at birth. And so he wrote and wrote, filling his tattered notebook with illegible script. Eventually, I collapsed in a tangle of dirty sheets in the bedroom. The mattress was half exposed and filthy beneath the sheets—sweat stains and cum stains and wine stains were brown continents spilling across the sagging mattress. I slept in my clothes.

Leif woke me at six a.m., took off all my clothes, and while I was still half asleep, and the city outside was night-dusted and groggy too, he licked me so gently, and with such a singularity of mind, such an intense focus and fervor, I must have come five times. I put my fingers deep into his ears each time.

He crawled up me and collapsed on my chest. He laid his head on that flat part of me, kissing the place between my breasts and burying his face there. *I love you, I love you, I love you.* I felt his mouth moving. I kissed the sweetest part of his body, that lovely, oily place on his neck, but it still reeked of whiskey.

After Leif fell into an agitated sleep (his eyes moved fast beneath their lids), I walked around the apartment with intentions of tidying up. The rooms felt strange and dangerous; Leif's life without me was one of uninhibited consumption. I poured myself a finger of whiskey and sat at the kitchen table. I wanted to talk to Dee so badly, the need felt like a large, heavy hand pressing down on my chest. In the bedroom, Leif groaned, and I finished the whiskey.

A fist on the apartment door roused me in the morning. Hard white sunshine lit the kitchen like the inside of a bulb. I forgot about the peephole. Leif said to always look first and open second, and I wished I'd remembered this when I swung open the door and found Wolski's grim face on the other side. His fist was half raised, poised to pound on the door a second time; with him was a young man, a boy almost, in a crisp police uniform.

"Backup?" I asked. The boy blushed and lifted his chin a millimeter higher.

Wolski frowned and scanned the apartment behind me. The living room was in shambles. The overturned bookshelf spilled dusty paperbacks into a heap on the floor. The turntable was upside down. There were takeout containers strewn across the coffee table and leaking onto the brown carpet.

Wolski turned to the boy. "Get him."

Leif became the primary suspect in Dee's case. Wolski liked him for a perp. And there's no denying he fit the bill rather well—a drunk, a poet, a foreign name. I'm not sure they had a sound legal case for his arrest, but I don't think Wolski needed one. There wasn't a police officer or higher-up in that building who gave a damn about what Wolski was up to on the fifteenth floor. I followed the cop car to the station, and Leif's face was ruddy with whiskey, either speed or fear twitching the muscles at the corners of his eyes, and I waved as they took him through booking because I didn't know what to do with my hands. As soon as my hand was in the air, I knew it was the wrong gesture.

Wolski took me to his office and handed me a manila folder.

"You people are so fucking stupid," I said. "Why haven't you found Frank yet?"

He shook the folder at me. I took it and had the urge to shake it in his face. His breath smelled of coffee and grease.

"What the hell is this?" Wolski asked.

It was the picture: I'm kneeling on Leif's bedroom floor; the floorboards have a harsh, knotty grain to them, whorls of wood beneath my knees. Leif stands in front of me with one hand on his dick and another on the back of my neck, where he has a tight fistful of my hair. My body is twisted grotesquely away from him and toward the camera. (Toward Dee.) My face is messy—swollen, and sticky with my own spit and tears, and puffing in anticipation of bruising. Leif's fist is at the back of my head, up his long, taut arm. He is naked. (And even then, in that photo, the pull of his body on my own was strong. Was it shameful that this photo awoke a want in me?) Leif doesn't look surprised, he's so alive in the moment, a picture couldn't have seemed more natural to him. How was it that nothing about him looked out of place in this picture, not his nakedness or his sure expression, not his hand on his cock or his heavy fist at the back of my neck. Meanwhile, I couldn't have looked more out of place or more afraid. My pupils are large, black holes. They eat all of the light in the room. I felt, looking at my own eyes, as if I were falling into a black hole. I've read that it's not entirely clear how we would die if we fell into a black hole. When I'd had my fill of my own dark gaze, I held the folder close to me.

"Where did you get this?" I asked.

"Anonymous mailer. Return address in Illinois. When was this photo taken, Peg?"

I paused. "The Fourth," I said. Wolski began annotating the back of the photo furiously. "But Frank, he sent it. Are you even looking for him?" (Though we understood, after Wolski had met the guy's parents, that he had been lying about his name, I was unable, ever, to call him anything except Frank.)

"How do you know Candace didn't send it?"

Candace. I felt my face get hot; I was getting angry, which usually had two effects on my ability to converse. Option one: shockingly articulate. Option two: shockingly inarticulate.

"Jesus. Christ. Dee . . . She wouldn't have sent that to you."
(Option two.)

"She took the picture, didn't she?"

"What's Leif arrested for?"

"Illegal possession of amphetamine. Illegal possession of a fire-arm. Evading arrest. But look, Peg, I'm going to level with you. He's the best suspect we've got. You show up here more or less black and blue two weeks after Dee goes missing; meanwhile, Frank's nowhere to be seen. We get this picture, which presum-ably Dee took, because you said it was only you three together on the Fourth, and that means she saw Leif beating the living hell out of you. Maybe Leif didn't want Dee to tell the world about all this; maybe he knew she'd go to your family." Wolski leaned back in his chair, satisfied with the story he'd just spun.

"Leif's got nothing to do with Dee," I said. "We drank too much. I already told you that, but it doesn't have anything to do with Dee's disappearance."

Wolski shrugged skeptically. "It's going to be a lot easier to find your sister when you start telling the truth. That's one thing I'm certain of," he said. What passed for Wolski's police work was unbelievable to me.

"You've got to understand, Leif didn't do this. He's got alibis and he won't stay locked up, I know that. But you have to under-stand, he would never do this."

Even as I said it, I knew. Wolski didn't *have* to understand any-thing.

"He hit you, didn't he?" Wolski knitted his hands behind his head, and his breath left a thick scent of bacon grease hanging in the air between us. I could not deny this, not only because Wolski had the picture but also because the connection hadn't been en-tirely clear to me before now.

"Fuck you," I said.

Wolski bowed his head. He gestured at the closed door.

I left Wolski's office, clutching the manila folder against my chest. I knew he'd made copies, probably many copies, and that he wouldn't miss this one. I wondered if Wolksi had shown the photo to Leif. If Leif had seen it, he was, right now, I suspected, writing a long poem about the photo. I imagined him somewhere in the building, coming down harder than ever, steadying his hands on the bars so no one would see him shake. Were they still holding the serial killer here too?

The media camp outside the police department had withered since I'd been there last with Peter. I supposed they were following the proceedings at the courthouse, or harassing families, or canvassing the serial killer's old neighborhood. On North Twenty-fifth Street, national gossip rags were paying the locals five hundred a piece for exclusives.

The serial killer had offered many of the men he murdered money, fifty or a hundred bucks, if they'd come back to his apartment with him and pose for a few pictures. In the newspapers, the detectives called the victims *facilitating victims* because they'd lived lives of poverty, and risk, and sexual deviance. The police union lobbyist said, "These men all chose the lifestyle that got them killed." And one *Milwaukee Journal* reporter, Anne Schwartz, wrote that of course these men didn't deserve to die, but that their lifestyles and unnecessary risk-taking contributed to their deaths. She prided herself not only for being the reporter who broke the case, but also for being the first in the media to publish the victims' criminal records.

On the news, State Representative Polly Williams defended the men, saying, "Because of the conditions here, we have our Black men now that will fall prey to this kind of stuff because they don't have jobs, they don't have money. So if somebody comes and offers them a hundred bucks to pose for a picture, they'll take it, because they need to live."

I'd expected Peter and Ma to be in hysterics at home, but when I got back, the house was empty. The living room was covered in notes and newspapers and pie plates and crumby maps. The house smelled like it needed to be cleaned—stale crust and damp dishrags and stewing garbage. I paced the house, nervously waiting for Peter or Ma to come home. When it started to get late, I called Suze at her house, but I got the machine. Where the fuck was everyone?

Night shadows had begun to spread in the house, throwing the mess of the living room into darkness. I left the lights off but turned on the TV. Fox 6 News was doing a segment on a local Baptist minister and his wife who had taken it upon themselves to exorcise the evil from the serial killer's apartment building. Maybe they could exorcise the chocolate factory too, so people wouldn't lose their jobs. The couple was standing in front of the lot with their arms raised. They weren't speaking English or any other language I recognized. The sidewalk was dusty with dry summer heat, and the wind off the lake whipped the dust around their ankles. A little boy was playing in the corner of the camera's frame with a plastic fire truck. He didn't seem fazed by the Baptist minister and his wife, who'd begun jerking their arms above their heads and stamping their feet. The boy didn't seem to notice the cameras trained on the minister. The exorcism was without commercial break, so I watched and I watched and I watched. I realized I wasn't watching to see the lot relieved of its evil (I was convinced this was an impossible endeavor); I was watching for the little boy in the corner to look up, to notice the cameras, to notice I was watching. I watched and I waited and he never looked, and I thought I would cry.

The minister's wife was now flailing in the dust. Some of the church volunteers held her so she didn't bite her own tongue or smash her head open on the curb. The minister was still at it on his feet. I didn't think it could end. The camera cut back to the news station, and I jumped because Peter coughed beside me. I whipped around, and Ma and Peter were standing on either side of me. The gray light of the TV shone on their faces and made them look sick. It was deep night now, and the lights of the house were still off. I'd let the night take the house completely.

"How long have you been there?" I asked. I croaked on the words, and Peter held my shoulder.

"Ten minutes," he said.

Ma went from room to room, turning on lights and closing blinds. I thought I heard her in the kitchen reheating leftovers— the opening and closing of the fridge door, the microwave humming awake.

"They took Leif," I told Peter.

He sank to the living room carpet with me, crossed his legs, and faced me. Without turning from me, he switched off the TV. "We know," he said. "We talked to Wolski."

"Where have you been?"

Peter sucked on his bottom lip, which made his chin look weak and vulnerable. "We went to your place."

I felt like I'd swallowed an ice cube. "You've got to be fucking kidding me." I rubbed my temples. "Is there no one I can trust?"

"Peg." He paused. He inched closer to me. "We just want to know."

I inched back. "You think he did it?"

Before I could hold them in, I felt thick hot tears on my cheeks, pooling at the tip of my nose, and dripping into my lips, where I licked them off. I started to shake, but I made a point to stay silent. I'd conceded something with the word *it*. I wanted suddenly to be exorcised as well, to be cleansed of the parts of me that were always fucking up, the part of me that had been lost to Leif, to bad wants, and which had cost me Dee.

"Please." I spit tears at Peter. He didn't wipe them from his cheeks. "You know it's Frank, Ma knows it's Frank, please help me fix this with Leif. I know you can fix it."

Peter shook his head. "But what happened?"

"We had a fight. Like I said." My cheeks were hot. "Please, Leif would never hurt Dee."

"Did he hurt you?" Peter reached out to graze the fresh scar on my cheekbone with his fingertips, and I recoiled.

"Never," I lied.

Peter's hand was suspended in the space between us, and he let it drop down onto my knee. He tugged at my knee and pulled me toward him, and I let him. He wrapped me up, holding me tighter than I ever remembered him holding me. He rocked me, and I went limp.

Peter carried me to bed, the one next to Dee's, and tucked me in tight. I fell asleep fast and dreamed of Leif speeding and licking my clit and I came in my sleep, which woke me up. I cried because I felt guilty about the dream and because I hadn't dreamed of Dee, and in the dark I grew afraid I'd forgotten her face already. I went downstairs to stare at our high school portraits. Ma had all of our pictures lined up in age progressions on the walls of the foyer. Dee's high school portrait was like a punch in the gut. I couldn't look long at all.

I wandered into the living room and turned the news back on; it was still showing the footage of the minister exorcising the building. The next day the newspapers reported he'd been there all night long. His wife had grown tired and gone to sleep in the car, but he'd stayed on that dusty sidewalk through the night, demanding that the devil release this lot, release this neighborhood, release Milwaukee. He'd collapsed at sunrise, is what they'd said. I imagined the little boy with the fire truck had been called in for supper while the minister was still at it, had been bathed, and read to, and put to bed, while the minister was still at it. *Something evil has gripped our city.*

LEIF: Where's Peg?

PETER: I'm asking the questions. When was the last time you saw Dee?

LEIF: July Fourth.

PETER: What did you do on the Fourth?

LEIF: Dee called Peg crying the day before because Frank was cheating on her. So Peg invited her to spend the Fourth with us. I worked third shift that night, as usual, but we stayed up and celebrated the Fourth together.

PETER: Celebrated how?

[PAUSE]

LEIF: Sparklers and apple pie and shit. You know.

PETER: Why did Dee leave?

LEIF: She walked in on Peg and me having sex. They got into a fight. Dee left.

PETER: Did she say where she was going?

LEIF: No.

PETER: Look, cut the crap, Leif. I know you guys dropped acid. Did Dee do it too?

LEIF: I don't know. I think so.

PETER: You think so.

LEIF: I was tripping.

PETER: What about your brother?

LEIF: What about him?

PETER: Peg says he's missing?

LEIF: Seems that way.

PETER: And? Dee too? Doesn't that seem odd to you? Were they spending a lot of time together?

LEIF: Look. The shit Erik's going through . . . It's got nothing to do with Dee.

PETER: Why do you say that?

LEIF: Erik's . . . a troubled kid, okay? Dee's got none of those kind of problems.

PETER: Where is he?

LEIF: Like I said, I don't know. I wish I did. But I'm telling you. This is normal behavior for him. He runs away. Disappears all the time. He always shows up again.

PETER: When he does, you let him know we need to talk to him.

LEIF: Sure. He doesn't know anything about this stuff with Dee, though. I guarantee you.

PETER: Who, in your best estimation, might know?

LEIF: I'd be knocking down Frank's door if I were you guys. I met the guy, and he is a real piece of work.

PETER: We can't find him either.

LEIF: Jesus, everybody's got the idea to disappear except me, I guess.

Article VII. Opinions and Expert Testimony

RULE 702. TESTIMONY BY EXPERT WITNESSES

A witness who is qualified as an expert by knowledge, skill, experience, training, or education may testify in the form of an opinion or otherwise if: (a) the expert's scientific, technical, or other specialized knowledge will help the trier of fact to understand the evidence or to determine a fact in issue.

Wolski said that according to state law, if we wanted to excavate the spot the psychic had identified, we'd need to hire an archaeologist. He found a woman who had led the excavation of the largest cemetery on the county grounds. The Wisconsin Historical Society confirmed: There was no other archaeologist in the state who knew these cemeteries better. Wolski contacted her, gave her a brief overview of our situation, and she wrote back immediately and asked us to come in.

Pete asked if I'd go with Wolski to meet this archaeologist at UWM. I don't know what I expected—someone in a pith helmet and a khaki vest?—but the woman we met was fashionably dressed in knee-high leather boots, leggings, and a floral-print dress. She had a streak of blue in her curly black hair. I stared at it and she smiled. She said we could call her Dr. P.

She ushered us into her office, a bright, sunny room with potted plants cluttered on the windowsills, dusty books, and pictures of children. There was an odd sculpture on one of her bookshelves: a brass pelvis through which a tiny brass human head was peeking out. The head was attached to a metal chain so one could pull the head all the way through the pelvis. Outside her office, young people stood on rubber mats, bending over skeletons—people, actual people—and taking tiny notes on pieces of paper.

She sat down and motioned for us to do the same.

"What can I do for you folks?" she asked us.

Wolski pulled out a map of the county grounds. He handed it to her. "We have reason to believe that Candace McBride might be buried here," he told her. "I understand this land is in development."

She nodded. "The Medical College of Wisconsin leases it from Milwaukee County. They have plans to build a cardiac hospital. But they knew what they were getting into." She pointed at the map behind her, which had the outlines of hundreds of coffins spread in acres across the Milwaukee County Grounds. There was an empty white space, and she took the map from Wolski and pointed from the place where he'd showed her the X on his map to the empty place on her map. "See this?" she asked us. "Graves. Known graves all around this swatch. Every indication would suggest there are people buried there too."

"So what will the Medical College do?" Wolski asked her.

"We're going to excavate some of these graves so they can build their hospital. But they're not breaking ground for another couple of months."

Wolski shook his head. "We want to dig here," he said. "Can you help us?"

She paused. I looked at her desk, where there was a Ball jar filled with dust. When I looked closer, I thought I saw the glint of bone fragments floating in the dust.

"Can I ask why you have reason to believe she's there?"

I felt my face flush. "A psychic," I told her. At first she thought I was joking, and then when she realized I wasn't, she straightened her face. I immediately respected her.

"Okay," she said. "Let's do it."

When I got back to my apartment, Leif was waiting outside. When you don't see someone for a long time, it's easy for them to become frozen in your memory. When I remembered Dee, or Leif, or Erik, I thought of the way they were that summer, young and beautiful, sure, but also smug. I had been like that too once, wasting days carelessly, because I believed I had an endless supply of them ahead. But Leif had shed his smugness and taken on a humility in his carriage, which was almost as shocking to see as his gray hair or his green eyes faded to pale moss.

"I thought you said you weren't coming back," I said to him.

"I changed my mind," he said. "I didn't want you to be alone."

"I've been alone. How did you find me?"

"Are you going to let me up or no?"

I unlocked the door and he followed me inside.

After Dee disappeared, something odd happened to my relationship with the city of Milwaukee. As a young woman, I believed I knew the city quite well—all its east-west arteries, and the borders of the neighborhoods through which these arteries ran, each neighborhood's quirks, and, importantly, all of the underage bars. But after my family had pored over many maps of Milwaukee in an attempt to plot Dee's disappearance, the city became strange and ugly to me. After I'd looked at the city on the maps, the place took on an odd, unfamiliar persona in which every shape carried some previously unforeseen potential for danger: the jaggedness of the shoreline along Lake Michigan, the crooked rectangles of the neighborhoods, the tannic rivers bleeding their way through the city to the swamps in the suburbs, the highways built up like militaristic border walls between the rich and the poor.

And upon seeing Leif for the first time in thirty years, I was reminded of this unsettling experience: the way something or someone you once loved can become frightening and strange to you. It can happen faster than you think.

Leif walked around my apartment like it was a museum. He kept a respectful distance between his body and my belongings as he wound his way around the stacks of shit spread across my living room floor. The stacks reminded me suddenly of the pictures I'd seen of those sad islands of plastic floating in the ocean: People said they grow larger every day. I had no doubt it was true. He considered the place much as Dana had the first time she visited; I could tell he didn't want to appear too disturbed for fear of spooking me or for fear of being thrown out. But I didn't really mind; I knew how the place looked. I understood that over the year (probably since I'd split with Henry for the final time), my living conditions had tipped perhaps irrevocably into the realm of the insane. Leif stared at a stack of library books reaching toward the ceiling; their plastic covers shone down incriminatingly at me.

"Why are you here?" I asked him.

"You asked me to come back," he said.

"I didn't mean it."

"You did."

"You can't stay," I said.

"I see that." He eyed the apartment crammed with junk. "Look, we want the same thing, right? We don't want *that* story to be *the* story."

"I don't think I even care anymore." I tried out my mother's language, but it felt wrong in my mouth, in my body.

Leif could sense that. "You know I don't believe that," he said.

He tried at a laugh, but it came out as a grunt. I thought of my mother. Were none of us, anymore, capable of expressing the appropriate emotion? Perhaps we had all been inflicted with a kind of emotional lability. It occurred to me that of course we had. I shrugged at him and then I became irate. I didn't like people using my own pathetic capacity for hope against me. Not even my family was allowed this transgression. There was too much at stake. There was always so much at stake.

"He's dead, you know," Leif said. "Erik."

"I know," I said.

"I wasn't sure you'd heard me," he said. "I tried to call . . ."

"I . . . had a hard time with those calls."

"Yeah. Anyway, I did enough damage when he was a kid. So this is the least I can do—I'm not gonna let this fraud tell a bunch of lies about my brother."

Leif reached for my stolen copy of Edith Hamilton's book (perhaps it reminded him too of Erik or of Dee), which was wedged at the bottom of a precarious stack. I turned away before the entire thing toppled to the floor. I only heard the thud of the books as they hit the hardwood.

After they arrested Leif, Peter called in a favor with one of his law school buddies at Marquette. He said with all the bad press, and the serial killer coverage, the last thing the Milwaukee PD would want was some press-hungry law student sniffing around the missing-persons unit. He was almost right.

Over breakfast, Peter told Ma and me he had begun to take the matter of Frank into his own hands. He'd gone to the bowling alley where Leif and I had hung out with Frank and Dee. He'd shown the police sketch of Frank's face to the owner, and mentioned something about the cops, and the guy had given up an address he thought was Frank's. Apparently, they hadn't been that good of buddies.

"I think we should go over there and check it out," Pete said.

Ma shook her head. "That's a job for a cop," she said.

"The cops are too busy for us," he said. "In case you haven't noticed. Wolski is barely helping as it is. *I* did this all on my own."

"Yeah, I don't know, Pete," I said. "I don't know if it's safe. Or legal?" I was torn. I wanted the chance to find something that might incriminate Frank, but the idea of going to his apartment frightened me.

"I thought you, of all people, would be on board. Where is this damn guy, anyway? It's getting ridiculous."

Peter shook with nervous caffeinated energy. None of us slept very well at night, and we all required an unhealthy amount of coffee just to stay upright during the days.

"What did Wolski say?" Ma asked.

"He said absolutely we should not go over there without him. If he has time later today, he'll check it out."

I became defiant then. "Fuck that," I said. "Let's go."

Pete looked pleased.

Frank's apartment was in the Menomonee River Valley, a low-lying post-industrial desert full of abandoned factory buildings, some of which had been converted into posh apartment buildings and some of which had been left to rot. Frank's building had been converted from an old light fixture factory. I had a memory of the place from when I was a little girl. The building had large, high windows, and from the highway overpass, you could see through these windows to the thousands of lamps strung up to the factory ceiling. They'd kept the lights on so often, and there were so many of them, I wondered if that was part of the reason they'd gone out of business. On one side of Frank's building was an abandoned lot; I couldn't remember what, if anything, had been there before. On the other side was a dilapidated warehouse that looked perilously close to falling into the river.

When we got there, Peter and I stayed in his car for a minute, surveying the property. We didn't talk. I wanted to know if he had a premonition too, if he felt what I was feeling, but I didn't even know how to say what I was feeling. *Is this the last place Dee was alive? Is this my fault? Is Frank in there? Is Dee?* And you know how it goes with premonitions: People never believe you anyway.

We were just about to go in when Wolski showed up. I looked at Pete, who frowned.

"Did you tell him we were coming?" I asked him.

"Hell no," Pete said. A swell of suspicion rose up inside me. We watched Wolski approach our car. I felt compelled to punish him for his incompetency, for his duplicitousness.

"You look like shit," I said while he shook Peter's hand. Wolski's hair was long and uncombed and fell in greasy strips across his unshaven face. His clothes were wrinkled. He needed a shower.

"Long night, kid," he said to me. He added to Peter, "I told you to wait for me."

Peter's face went red. "We've been waiting, Gary."

"Fine," Wolski said. He tried to soften his tone. "We're here now, so let's get this done."

Wolski outlined our procedure. He handed us gloves. We weren't supposed to touch anything. And we'd stay behind him as we entered the apartment. If Frank was there, Wolski had a list of questions (as did we), and we'd talk for a bit, survey the apartment to the best of our ability, and leave. If Frank wasn't there, we'd leave a note on his door relaying our information and our need to speak with him as soon as possible. Wolski's plan seemed very rational, but even so, I felt nervous as we went inside. Someone had left a jamb under the front door to keep it open: a construction crew, maybe. There was a long list of buzzers but no names next to them. The building was quiet and smelled of fresh paint. It didn't have a lived-in feel about it. We took an old elevator up to the sixth floor.

Wolski knocked, as he had on Leif's apartment door, and we waited. There was a faint noise inside the apartment, but it didn't sound like someone coming to the door. Wolski knocked again, and again, and when the noise on the other side kept up but no one came, he shouted, "Milwaukee PD. Open up." I smelled something like shit wafting from under the apartment door. Wolski knocked again, but still there was nothing. Peter had a frightened, desperate look on his face; it was like looking into a mirror. Before Wolski could stop him, Peter grabbed the doorknob and then kicked the door, which was unlocked, wide open on its hinges. The smell of shit hit all three of us, and Wolski put a wrinkled sleeve up against his nose. "Dammit," he shouted. "Not part of the plan."

Inside, there was dog shit everywhere. The apartment was relatively bare, but the few pieces of furniture left had been destroyed, chewed to bits, covered in fur, and saturated with dog piss. There was a noise from the bedroom, a throaty bark, and then a massive blur of fur lunged at all three of us. But before the dog was halfway to us, Wolski had shot it twice in the head. The animal fell in a starved, writhing heap of fur on the floor.

"Jesus," Peter said. "Why didn't you just close the door?"

"Why the hell did you open the door?" Wolski asked. "You're welcome, by the way."

The dog was still twitching. I almost wished Wolski would shoot it again, but I didn't know if I could stomach the sight of another shot. The blood leaking from its head was beginning to spread across the floorboards. The smell of the place was awful. Why hadn't anyone called about the animal? About the smell? Did no one else live in the building?

Wolski was breathing heavy. His gun resting against his kneecap, he was doubled over, trying to catch his breath. "Dammit," he said. "Last night," he offered cryptically.

This seemed like an invitation to ask, but neither Peter nor I wanted to know anything about his night.

"We're here now, so we might as well look around," Wolski said after he'd finally caught his breath. "Like I said, just don't fucking touch anything."

I wanted to leave. I couldn't take my eyes off the dead dog, whose muscles had finally stopped but whose eyes were open and rolling up and down. Its thick pink tongue lolled. It had on a choke collar that had become embedded. I tried to think of the dog as a puppy, but this thought paralyzed me. Peter had begun his search, and I tried to move but found that the prospect nauseated me.

Wolski came up beside me. "In the city, they train the dogs to attack men in uniforms—it's targeted toward police officers, obviously, but it gives everyone hell. Mailmen, firefighters, paramedics, mechanics in jumpsuits," he offered.

"We're not wearing uniforms," I said.

"We're used to them charging, I guess, is what I'm saying. Come on, let's get to work."

I followed Pete and Wolski around the apartment, eyeing the bloodstain blooming in the center of the place, and barely seeing anything except the dog. I went through the motions, but I wouldn't have seen something important if it had hit me over the head. According to Pete and Wolski, the most interesting thing was that there was hardly anything of interest. The place looked like it had been swept of personal effects. Frank's things (beside his mad dog) were gone, and it wasn't like he'd left in a rush and grabbed only a few things, he'd taken everything. It looked calmly, methodically cleansed of his belongings. It was like he'd been warned.

In the car on the way home, I smelled Peter; sweat stains were spreading beneath his armpits like large, dark bodies of water. He clenched and unclenched his jaw, and I worried he'd file his teeth to grit. He slammed his fist into the steering wheel, the horn blared, and people changed out of our lane, sped past us, or held way back.

"We'll get a ticket if you keep this speed up," I said.

Peter eyed the speedometer. "In case you haven't noticed, the fucking police are hog-tied in this city."

"Still," I said. "You're scaring me."

Peter's face softened, and he eased off the accelerator. Sweat dripped from his temples. I wiped a drop from his chin with my thumb.

"I should kill him," Peter said.

I watched the city shift into suburbs behind the highway fence. Kids on bikes chased one another in the cul-de-sacs next to the freeway.

"Then you'd be him, Pete."

He shook his head, spraying the windshield with sweat, and he pounded the steering wheel again. "Will you stop being such a fucking hippie?"

"Fuck you," I said. I put my head between my knees, and Peter punched the accelerator.

B efore the excavation was scheduled to take place, I returned home to find Leif outside my apartment yet again. He grinned when he saw me and offered up a cooler full of beer and cheese and a large beach blanket. I wanted desperately to be able to see what he saw when he looked at me. I wanted more than anything to be out of my body and looking at both of us from a distance. From very, very far away. Maybe I even wanted to be in his body, or any body other than my own.

"For old times' sake, yeah?" he said. He gestured at the cooler. Together we drove to Bradford Beach, where we used to spend hot, lazy afternoons reading in the sun and cooling off in Michigan's phosphorescently blue waves.

"So what happened with the psychic?" he asked me in the cab of his truck. I tried not to look too closely at anything: fraying USB cords tangled in balls on the floor, fast food garbage shoved into the doors, kids' artwork taped to the dash. The array depressed me. I stared out the window.

"He said he found her," I told him.

He nodded. "What do you think?"

"I think I believe him." I caught his face falling out of the corner of my eye. It didn't hurt me. That much, I guess, had changed.

"Why?" he asked.

"He . . . I don't know . . . He knew you were coming back. He knew about the photo. I mean, I know it sounds crazy."

"No," he said. "You're not crazy."

"I didn't say I was crazy."

We were quiet. Seagulls cried.

"But what about Erik?" he asked me. "You don't think he did this, do you?"

"No," I said. "I don't think so. I don't know why the psychic said that. You know I've been building a case against Frank? I'm feeling certain I'll get him this time. Once we have her body." Though as I said it, it occurred to me that nothing was for certain, and so little was *known,* and we both knew that.

At Bradford Beach, we sat in the manicured sand side by side. Our hips touched. Behind us, newly built tiki huts offered faux-tropical drinks and beer in boots. Leif shook his head. A few miles away, the new trolley was offering free rides back and forth from the casino in the valley to the restaurants in the Third Ward. At the lakeshore, two new skyscrapers pitched unevenly toward the sun, and on either side of the freeways, belly scrapers leveled lots for more high-rise condominiums.

"This place," Leif said. "I never thought it would be like this."

"Like what?"

"So shiny."

I nodded.

"I mean, they just built right over all of it."

I thought of the empty lot at 924 North Twenty-fifth Street and I thought of the empty lot where our apartment used to be. The history of cities, it seems to me, is ultimately one of erasure disguised as innovation.

"Do you have anyone? Is there . . ." I didn't know for sure what I was asking.

He eyed me. "You my ma now?"

"I'm just asking if you have family. You still married?"

A pair of teenage girls walked by in shorts and sports bras, despite the early-summer chill, holding a couple of drinks. My mouth turned to acid. Leif followed their bodies with his whole head, and then when he became aware he was doing so, looked away fast. He reddened just slightly. Then he glanced back at me. "There wasn't ever anybody but you, baby," he said. "Why? You wanna come on the road with me?"

I punched him hard in the shoulder. He reached into his pants pocket, shuffled through his wallet, and produced a school photo of a handsome boy, just on the precipice of puberty, with dark red hair and green eyes. He looked so much like Erik that I felt confused for a moment: untethered from time and place. I felt as if at any moment Dee and Erik would walk up to us, holding each other around the waist and sharing some private joke Leif and I wouldn't get. I squinted out into Lake Michigan's glassy surface, where algae bloomed and bloomed. Despite local business investment into the School of Freshwater Sciences, they couldn't keep the damn place clean. In Indiana, BP dumped thousands of pounds of raw sludge into the lake every day. Was the bottom of the lake made up entirely of layer upon layer of this thick sludge? Would it rise up to the surface one day and make the lake once and for all inhospitable and poisonous?

"This is my son," Leif said. (I knew this.) "Whip-smart."

I wanted him to put the photo away. "Congratulations." The word came out like exhaust from a broken tailpipe.

"Don't do that," he said. He put a hand on my leg. I moved away from him. "You asked."

"I mean it," I said. "He's beautiful."

I can't explain it now. The reason this photo crushed me. I suppose I felt then the tragedy of this beautiful boy's life stretching out for eons in front of me. Even the happiest of stories, it seems to me now, contain the extraordinarily fruitful seeds of tragedy, of lifelong suffering.

Leif pocketed the photo and we stared into Milwaukee's nascent summer. The pair of girls who'd walked by us returned to their group, and one of them said something that made all the kids turn to stare at us and laugh. I had an image of Dee taunting sailors at the lakefront—*too old*.

"How about you?" he asked me.

"Henry." I offered up the name like Leif would know it. "He was . . . That was my last shot. I think."

"I'm sorry," Leif said. He paused. "What happened?"

"He wasn't you." I had meant it as a joke, but the delivery was off, and Leif frowned at me. He shook his head.

"I'm serious," he said.

"He wanted the whole thing, you know—the house and the kids, the Christmas-card pictures," I told him.

"Sounds nice."

I shrugged, finished my beer, and reached in Leif's cooler for another. "No," I told him. "I wasn't capable."

t was golden hour when we got back from Frank's place. The wide faces of Ma's sunflowers were turned up high but seemed about to tip with the weight of all that ripe light. When we pulled up, Ma was sitting on the porch painting her toenails. The banality of her movements pained me to see. For a moment I thought the flowers might topple on her, and I had the urge to shield her with my own body.

Instead, I brushed by her with a quiet *hi* and closed the door behind me. Outside, I heard Ma's voice rising with a question, and I could almost hear Peter's stupid shrug; that was how hard I assumed he threw his shoulders into the gesture.

I climbed the stairs to our bedroom. The room was filled with rusty light, which charged the dust in the air with frantic energy. There was a thin layer of dust on most of the furniture, our dressers, our sleigh beds, our white wooden desks, which were covered with little poems of angst, and the names of first loves, with nail polish and makeup spills. My father had made these desks for us, and we'd loved them, but their impracticality depressed me now. By the time we were teenagers, they were already much too small for us. There was something beautiful but also eerie about the white, miniature furniture in the room. My parents had never been good at giving up on things, insisting that what we'd had as small girls would work for us well into adulthood. I wondered if we'd inherited this doggedness from them. I wondered if it had produced a kind of arrested development in us.

Since I'd been back at Ma's, I'd resisted the urge to stay in our little white room on the second floor. I'd spent most of my nights on the couch or pacing the hallway between the kitchen and the living room, picking at the pies so my fingers were sticky in the morning. I sat down on Dee's bed, and the dust from her comforter rose in clouds around me. The window near my old bed was open, and I could hear Peter and Ma's voices in a sad tangle on the porch.

I felt the night coming down around me. Sunlight always lingered in unlikely places in that house: pooling in carpeted corners where the ghosts lived, sliding down the pineapple wallpaper, electrifying the dust.

I breathed deep in an effort to swallow as much of the dust in the room as possible; I imagined it clogging my throat and choking me to death. The house phone rang, and I went into the master bedroom, where there was a landline.

This is a collect call from an inmate at the Milwaukee County Jail. Press one to accept.

Leif. I heaved my body onto my parents' old four-poster bed.

"Hello?" Leif's voice was muddy with static. "Peg?"

"Yeah," I said. "I'm here."

"You've got to help me."

"We're trying."

"No. I mean. I told them I had something to do with it."

"Wolski showed you the photo?"

"I'm sorry, Peg."

"You have an alibi. Jesus. I mean—you didn't do it. What the fuck were you thinking?"

"They tricked me."

"They tricked you." I put my hands over my mouth because I was suddenly afraid of saying something awful.

"What did you say?"

"I . . . I don't remember."

"Fuck."

The line was quiet.

"I wanted it to stop."

I understood how shortsighted we all were—Leif, and me, and Dee, and Peter, and Ma, and Wolski too. Maybe Frank was playing some kind of long game. Maybe he was the only one. I pictured Dee at the picnic table in Lake Park. The wood of the table cutting into her rib cage. She said Frank had a driver's license from Ohio. I was spinning wheels, and Leif coughed on the other end of the phone.

"I don't have a lot of time. You've got to help."

"Peter's sending a buddy of his from Marquette. I don't know if he can help anymore. They should have appointed you a lawyer already if you've been . . ." I hesitated, holding the word *charged* in my mouth.

"How'd we end up in some fucking detective novel?"

"The photo."

"I never meant it. What I did."

"Stop," I said.

"I think about it all the time, Peg."

"Don't," I warned him.

"I love you."

"Yeah."

We all lived time out of mind for the rest of that summer. I didn't notice any time passing. Peter and Ma were consumed with tasks they hoped would provide some kind of answer: manning the hotlines, methodically going through Dee's things in her dorm room, reviewing her phone records, tracking the transactions on her debit card, typing and filing interviews with her friends, employers, teachers, colleagues. Ma made sure the list of tasks never ended. I couldn't believe they were doing all of the police work. Wolski was in and out of communication. We weren't always sure where he was or what he was working on. Once they had Leif in custody, Wolski stopped trying to find Frank for a while, and it seemed like he quit investigating other leads too.

I helped with some of the tasks, although looking back, I think it's safe to say Ma and Peter and Suze resented my level of effort. The problem for me was by that point, I believed I knew who'd done it. I suppose those efforts could have proved Frank's guilt in some way, but it was like searching for a needle in a haystack, and anyway, the police had decided he'd had nothing to do with it. They, meaning Wolski mostly, didn't even seem convinced Frank had known her. Instead, I focused my energy on trying, again, to harness the power of the press. But, given the circumstances, and their obsession with the serial killer, this was almost impossible.

I went to the courthouse often because I knew the street outside was always full of reporters. Usually, there was also a group of protestors who gave speeches about their attempts to notify the MPD of loved ones' disappearances. They relayed accounts of cops repeatedly telling them there was *nothing they could do*, especially when people *chose high-risk lifestyles*.

The recent coverage of the serial killer's case reflected very poorly on the police. For starters, the *Journal* and several national news outlets ran front-page stories about the police officers who had been called to the scene of fourteen-year-old Konerak Sinthasomphone's brief escape from the killer's apartment back in May.

One report published the transcripts of the radio call, in which the officers had joked about the *domestic dispute,* saying the lovers had been reunited, and the officers needed to come back to the station to get *deloused.* Another outlet published the transcripts of a phone call between an officer and a Black woman named Glenda Cleveland who called asking after the boy. The officer was dismissive and short-tempered with the woman as she repeatedly asked if Konerak was really an adult. (Back at his apartment, the serial killer had shown the officers pictures of Konerak in his underwear to prove the boy was his lover. Behind the closed bedroom door, the decomposing body of his previous victim lay on the bed.)

In some bizarre twist, reporters later discovered Konerak was the brother of a young man whom the serial killer had lured back to his apartment several years prior. This boy had escaped from the apartment after he was drugged, and his family had pressed charges. The serial killer was charged with sexual assault. The DA wanted him in prison for at least eight years. But the serial killer's lawyer argued that he needed mental health attention for his alcohol abuse and sexual orientation issues, and that he would not receive this kind of attention in prison. At the trial, the serial killer had pleaded with the judge not to send him to prison. *Don't ruin my life. Don't ruin my life.* Unbeknownst to the DA, the killer's lawyer, the judge, or his parole officer, he'd already murdered four men at the time of that sentencing. The judge sentenced him to one year in prison, during which he was allowed to keep his job at the chocolate factory.

How, the media wondered, had this man slipped through the cracks so many times? This phrase seemed to be on repeat that summer. But what exactly does it mean to *slip through the cracks*? What if what it really meant was that the system had worked perfectly for him? Why hadn't the officers entered the man's information into their computers on the night they found Konerak? If they had, they would have discovered he was a convicted child molester on probation. The Milwaukee police chief, Philip Arreola, released a statement saying that criminal background checks were discretionary; officers didn't do them every time they were called to the scene of an altercation. The Black community was outraged; their criminal records were referenced during routine traffic stops. The serial killer's record hadn't seemed important to those officers because he was white, even though a naked, bleeding boy had run from his apartment into the street.

For cops in the city of Milwaukee, including Wolski, it seemed that almost overnight, the serial killer case had turned into a "race issue." But for the families of the victims, those who'd asked the PD repeatedly to look into the disappearance of their sons and brothers and friends, it had always been a race issue. The police began to be heckled on the street; it was not a proud time to be a Milwaukee police officer. Often Wolski would say things to Pete and me like "Jesus H. Christ, it's like these people forget who the actual criminal was. Dahmer killed those men, not the police."

The sister of one of the victims was very vocal about her contempt for the Milwaukee PD and the *Journal*. She often protested with a large group outside the Milwaukee Police Department and outside the Milwaukee County Courthouse. She was part of a coalition of victims' families who were demanding, among other things, that the police officers be fired. On the steps once, I listened to her as she ignored a reporter's questions altogether and gave a speech about the police department's inability to protect her brother during his life, and after his death too.

"I went to the PD six times over the last two months, and I asked them to figure out what happened to my brother. You know what they told me? They said get in line. I don't even know if he had a missing-persons report. They said lots of people with his *lifestyle* go missing. They aren't responsible for those people. That's what they said. *Lifestyle.* They were careless. They were worse than careless. They were malicious, and now my brother's dead, and they've splashed his dead body across the national news too. What about respect for my family? We've gotten no respect from the police, or the media, or the community. Candlelight vigil doesn't mean a damn thing to me. I want these men removed."

After she had finished her speech, and as she was turning to leave, without thinking, I tugged at her arm. She ripped her arm away and turned to me with angry eyes, clearly figuring me for a particularly aggressive journalist. But then she took me in: ripped jeans, dirty fingernails, muddy sneakers, messy bun, sunken eyes, and I realized, with a sharp pang of regret, the scars on my cheekbones. What did they mean to her? She took pity on me, maybe. A reaction I was learning to get used to.

"What?" she asked.

I hadn't prepared anything to say. I couldn't remember why I'd wanted to talk with this woman. I was embarrassed to be bothering her the way I saw the journalists on TV often did. I guess now I think I wanted to be her, not only because she knew what had happened to her brother but because she was so composed in the face of it all.

"I need help."

"Well, you're at the damn police station," she said, like it was a joke. Which I understood.

"Do you know Wolski?"

"Are you asking me to get a drink?"

"The detective, not the bars, up in the missing-persons unit."

Her face softened, and she looked fifteen years older than she had seconds before. "Never heard of him," she said softly. "Are you okay?"

The question had a bad effect on me. I couldn't remember anyone asking me this since Dee's disappearance: not Peter, or Leif, or

Ma, or even Suze. I startled her with a sob that I tried to disguise as a cough. She stepped away from me. Humans think many social conditions are contagious. Wasn't that our greatest fear, that the serial killer's "condition" was contagious? They said he was controlled by his fantasies. We are all, each one of us, terrified of losing control, or terrified that the person sitting next to us on the bus will lose control. The district attorney himself would ask later, at the serial killer's trial in February, "Wouldn't we all be in trouble if we followed all our sexual desires, regardless of what those desires were?"

"My sister," I started. The woman nodded like she knew the whole story already. "They say . . . They say the longer someone's missing, the less likely it is they'll be found alive, or at all."

"How long has it been?" She started looking around for her family. I could see she wanted away from me. Tragedy multiplied by tragedy does not seem to make more potent tragedy. People are lying when they say they're heartbroken for the families of the serial killer's victims; only the families are heartbroken. Only my family is heartbroken. We can only attend to our own, and sometimes we can barcly do that.

"Four weeks." The weight of those four weeks hung in the air between us. She breathed them in and coughed them back out, and she touched my shoulder.

"Keep waiting, baby," she said. She looked me up and down again. Her eyes lingered on my throat. "Look, I'm guessing your sister is as pretty and as white as you are. They'll find her, but you gotta stir up some stink first so people know."

"How?" I asked her.

"Her pictures. And a story," she said. "You've got to have a story." She left me standing alone. I didn't know what the hell she meant. We did have a story. Though at that very moment, I realized, I couldn't think of what it was: How did it start? How did it end? What had happened? How did it fit into the only story people wanted to hear that summer? Was that the problem? That Dee's disappearance didn't fit into the serial killer coverage? It couldn't.

On the bottom step of the courthouse, there was a layer of trash so thick that I couldn't see the sidewalk below. While the journalists congregated around the families and near the door (they hoped for shots of the serial killer in his orange jumpsuit, the top three buttons undone so his chest hair poked out baby-fine), I kicked at the garbage like it was fall leaves. The wind off the lake picked it up in great spiraling waves and heaved it up the courthouse steps. Empty Doritos bags, hot dog wrappers, PBR cans, gum wrappers, newspapers all rose as I kicked them, and they coiled around the journalists' legs. I could not make this up. There are videos of it: A wayward cameraman interested in the wrong thing at the wrong moment taping a skinny girl kicking garbage. He missed his shot of the serial killer that way, and I missed my opportunity to speak.

The Milwaukee County Institution Grounds were part of a large swath of land west of the city. Milwaukee County had bought this land from farmers in order to house the impoverished, insane, and ill citizens of Milwaukee back in the 1800s. There was a poor farm, an orphanage, an insane asylum, and eventually, several hospitals and schools. The land was also used to bury the city's unfortunates, which included anyone who could not afford a burial, or anyone whose body was left unclaimed at the morgue. (Also, evidently, cadavers, and bodies that had been subjected to dissection by scalpel-wielding medical students, were buried in boxes of body parts and medical waste on the county grounds.) The county was in the business of burying its poorest citizens until the 1970s, when it began paying private funeral homes to do that for them. Milwaukee County claimed to have forgotten the location of a number of the cemeteries. As a result, construction in this part of the city often turned up a slew of trashed or intact coffins. Later, the county grounds would be home to the Medical College of Wisconsin, a prestigious teaching-research hospital, a state-of-the-art cardiac hospital, a children's hospital, a mental health complex with a disturbing reputation, and a lot of open, empty land. Some of this land contained remnants of the old cemeteries, many of which were no longer marked, but some of which functioned as unofficial dog parks.

The Milwaukee County Asylum Cemetery was not a beautiful spot as Dee once described it. The county hadn't exactly hidden this plot but hadn't made it accessible either. We found it at the end of a gravel road. There was an unpaved turnaround in front of the grassy field, a historical marker, three green dumpsters, and two porta-potties that smelled like they hadn't been serviced in a long time. True, the field was quiet and green, and there was a vantage point near the middle where one could look out and see the county grounds below. It wasn't possible to see Milwaukee's downtown or the lake, though. And upon closer inspection, the grass turned out to be the particularly scruffy and tough sort, and the city hadn't planted it evenly, so there were large patches of dirt and weeds. Dandelions grew thick. There was also an odd, conspicuous wooded thicket in the middle of the field. The growth didn't look very old, but it was thick and thorny.

Back in the nineties, I'd read a story in the *Journal* about people sneaking into this cemetery and digging up skulls to sell, or to use for unspecified rites around Halloween. The place had no security (the county had no budget for this cemetery), so in lieu of that, they'd done their best to make people forget that anyone had ever been buried here. The weathered brown sign was the only indicator:

The ground before you contains the mortal remains of approximately 200 souls who died at the Milwaukee County Asylum/ Hospital for the Insane. These burial grounds were open from March 1880–November 1914. Patients without financial means or family to claim them found a place of eternal peace here.
May they, at rest, find the peace and sanity they desired in life.

Ma crossed herself in front of the sign. If Milwaukeeans had been stealing skulls from the cemetery since it was abandoned, I doubted these "souls" were finding any peace or sanity in death. I didn't know if the conditions of your death or the place of your burial had any impact on the state of your soul in the afterlife. Both Ma and Dad had been raised Catholic. Our father claimed that he'd been forced to tie too many nuns' shoes, that he'd been rapped on his palms too many times, and that he'd spent far too much of his childhood confessing sins he hadn't committed, to raise his own children Catholic. Following his lead, Ma claimed to renounce her own family's Catholic traditions, although I knew she clung to more of them than she wanted to admit. I heard her prayers, at least twice a day when we were growing up, and some- times three or four times a day after Dee went missing. Her voice took on a trancelike, lyrical quality that I found very soothing. I couldn't hear what she was saying, but it didn't matter. I knew by the song of the words what they meant. (*Bring her home. Bring her home. Bring her home.*)

Peter, Dee, and I, well, we were believers during desperate times, and we were agnostics during good times. Ma's family used to chide her for letting us waffle and then for letting us go. Peter and Ma started going to St. John Vianney's together that sum- mer. I couldn't bring myself to do it, and I suppose they took it as another piece of evidence against me; I couldn't even enter such a holy place because my list of sins was so long. I guess they were right.

Twenty of us showed up to walk the county grounds, in- cluding a crew of ten archaeologists, all volunteers recruited by Dr. P. Wolski brought along a buddy who had a sniffer dog and had offered his services pro bono. Ma, Pete, Suze, the psychic, and his crew were there too. Leif, who was staying at the Hyatt and was plotting some kind of rebuttal to the psychic's story, offered to come along, but I insisted he stay away. He called me from his hotel room to make his case one last time. "I want to help," he pleaded. "Please."

"You can't," I told him. I felt some rush of pleasure at denying him what he wanted, though this feeling was tinged with a kind of dull regret. I hung up on him.

Ma handed out maps from her wheelchair and refreshed us on that grim list of things to look for: Dee's clothing (on the Fourth, she'd been in high-waist denim shorts, a white top, and sneakers), or her personal effects (she always wore a thin silver chain our dad had given her for her thirteenth birthday), or even anything belonging to Frank (he wore a gaudy graduation ring and had a rose-gold watch with a broken second hand).

Meanwhile, Dr. P walked us through the archaeological procedures. They would excavate a two-meter-by-two-meter pit in the spot Thomas Alexander had pointed out. They would screen all of the dirt from this pit through quarter-inch mesh shaker screens in order to catch anything small or fragmented. Peter had brought a bag of shovels. The summer Dee disappeared, Peter had begun to collect shovels. He frequented garage sales, thrift stores, and flea markets to buy up old shovels. He taught himself the art of hand filing them so they cut through compacted dirt, or heavy clay, and through the roots of hardy plants. At first, the archaeologists admired his collection, and then were embarrassed when they realized the sad nature of this admiration.

We split into three groups. The psychic and his crew hung back with Ma in the gravel parking lot. Dr. P ordered some of the archaeologists to walk in transects through the field outside the thicket. They kept their heads bent toward the ground. And the rest of us went to dig in the woods. Sometimes I look back on those kinds of canvasses (this was, of course, not our first), and I get the sense that even if there had been something huge (a piece of Dee's clothing or jewelry), we might have missed it just because we were looking so hard. I don't know how it's possible, but it strikes me as true that over the years, the harder and more intensely we looked for her, the less likely it became that we'd ever find her.

When we got to the thicket of woods, Peter removed a machete from his bag of tools, another thrift store purchase, and began hacking away at the vegetation, so it was easier for us to search and for the archaeologists to dig.

Inside the thicket was a small path, which led to a shrine. Peter wanted to conduct a search of the entire area, so he continued hacking away at all the vegetation. He was enjoying the sensation of destruction. The shrine was at the foot of a makeshift wooden cross that was wrapped in barbed wire and pinned to a scrawny tree. There were dozens of tiny mementos beneath the cross: rocks placed in concentric circles, fake garlands of blue flowers, a deck of playing cards, lighters, a pack of cigarettes, a pen, some bones (which we later learned were from a butchered pig), a plastic bottle of Smirnoff. It was hard to tell what was garbage and what was an offering. There was no indication of who had made the shrine, or to whom or what it was dedicated, or why it was there. Peter seemed less interested than I was. He picked through the mementos quickly and, seeing nothing that leaped out at him, kicked one of the rocks that framed the shrine. It rolled out into the field. Peter squatted in the undergrowth and looked around him. One of the archaeologists began to sketch the shrine in a weathered field notebook.

"This is bizarre," I said. My voice echoed in the woods.

"I don't believe it," Peter said.

"I feel something about this place, though," I said. I expected him to guffaw or roll his eyes at me, but he nodded.

"I know. I had the same thought as soon as we pulled up," he said. He shook his head. Sweat poured from the sides of his face.

I crouched down too, so Peter and I were at eye level. Behind him, I noticed an odd patch of freshly upturned dirt, relatively free of vegetation.

"Pete," I said. He turned his head to follow my gaze. He sprang up to his feet and began rifling around in his canvas bag. He pulled out a short, sharp shovel and began removing the loose dirt. I didn't say stop, because I knew he wouldn't listen, and because I didn't want him to stop. He tossed the dirt into the archaeologists' screen, and they sifted through it all with gloved hands. Though I didn't think he was supposed to be the one digging, the archaeologists, at Dr. P's request, let him. I recognized the look on their faces. It was the only look I ever got anymore when people learned about Dee. Pity.

Peter was still digging; his arms and hands had become caked in dirt. I went into his bag and found another shovel so I could help him. I felt we were completely alone. Ma and our aunt and the psychic were waiting outside that copse, only a few feet away, but they might as well have been a universe or a millennium away. Peter and I were stranded in that tiny spot of woods, which was a different world than the one outside. My back ached and my hands were rubbed raw by the handle of the shovel when we stopped. There was a black plastic bag at the bottom of the hole. It was then I remembered we were digging in a cemetery. It was then I remembered the stories of stolen skulls and looted graves. Dr. P put her hand up. She hopped down into the pit and used her trowel to open the bag enough to see inside. I was on the ground with my head in my hands, because I sensed I'd know by the sound Pete would make when he saw what was inside. I didn't want to see;

I couldn't see. Peter huffed, and some of the tension in his body entered the air between us. I felt it as a great breath of wind. I felt cold even in the heat.

"It's somebody's dog," Pete said. It was like Thomas Alexander had said. I believed then, I knew unequivocally, that she would be under the dog. Pete collapsed onto his back. His feet hung into the grave, and he lay down with his arms flung over his face. The shovel lay like something else dead. I wanted to go and lie with him, to fit myself into that space beneath his arm and his shoulder, and rest my head in his neck, but I stayed where I was, and I tried to regain my breath.

While Peter and I stayed still and panting, Dr. P had carefully removed the dead dog in its plastic bag shroud, and kept digging. She was much, much better and more efficient at it than we were. Every once in a while, she would use her trowel to scrape at something. We both jolted when we heard her trowel hit something metallic in the ground. We all peered into the hole and saw the outlines of a coffin appearing. The sniffer dog whined and pawed through a pile of back dirt. His handler yanked on his choke collar.

When I arrived home from the courthouse, Peter and Ma were waiting conspiratorially for me at the kitchen table. The TV was on. It seemed that summer there was always a TV on somewhere.

"What were you doing at the courthouse?" Ma asked.

The tapes. Five o'clock news.

"A hello would be nice."

"Peg." Ma put her *not fucking around* voice on. Peter was rubbing his temples.

"I went to meet someone."

"You shouldn't be on TV. Not with Leif still . . ."

"We should be on TV. Who knows about Dee besides us? Even if we had half as much coverage as the serial killer families, we'd be getting somewhere, but we can barely get her fucking picture in the newspaper."

Ma inhaled sharply. I knew what she was going to say, but I didn't stop her.

"Those people's children are *dead*, Margaret. They're not *missing*, they're *dead*."

"Dee might be too."

Ma stood up and slapped me on the back of the head so my chin fell hard onto my chest. I kept my face turned down. I begged my-self not to cry. I was such a child, then, Jesus.

"Ma," Peter started.

"Don't use your condescending voice on me, Peter." I didn't need to see Pete to know he was stung. "You're not trying hard enough," she said to me.

"Fuck you," I said.

Does it matter that I'd never said anything like this to my mother before? Once when I was thirteen, I told her I hated her; I can't even remember what we'd been arguing about. I cried and cried. I felt so guilty. I cried until my throat was sore, and when I was done and my mother came for me, she wrapped me up, and I said I was sorry and I hadn't meant it. This was different. I was someone she didn't know now; she'd made me into a suspect. She didn't know what it was, but she knew I was guilty of something.

In the weeks since Dee's disappearance, I'd begun to lose weight. In the shower, my hair fell from my scalp in long dark clumps. My hands sometimes shook without warning. I'd be writing or reading or putting a fork to my lips, and the tremors would start. I was shrinking. Ma and Peter either didn't notice these changes or they ignored them, afraid of what they might mean. *Why was I so guilty back then?* It's difficult to take stock of those first few weeks following Dee's disappearance. The days ran together like a bad dream that started over every time I fell asleep. I was waking up every day to discover she was still missing, and the weight of this rediscovery did not diminish over time. I'm sure Peter and Ma can attest to this too. I still wake up to remember I've lost her. The same is true of my father, and he's been dead for forty years now.

I understood the extent of my shrinkage only after I saw Leif for the first time since his arrest. He called to tell me that they were going to keep him and try him for illegal possession of a firearm, and amphetamine possession too. He asked if I'd come to see him at the jail, where he'd be held until his trial. Pete's buddy had told him he was facing a minimum of eight months to a year; if convicted, he'd spend his time in Prison City.

We met in the reception area of the Milwaukee County Jail. There was a long list of rules posted on the door. I had to leave most everything I'd brought in a locker in the lobby. I read the signs outside the room. *No excessive showing of cleavage. No showing of the midsection. No spaghetti string shirts allowed. No high-cut shorts or skirts/dresses. No pants/shorts hanging below or to middle of buttocks. No muscle shirts. No jackets or hoods. No headbands, head scarves, or hats. Only one layer of clothing allowed. No loud talking, excessive emotionalism, or any other disruptive behavior.* I looked down at my bare knees and was suddenly, agonizingly aware of their girlishness.

Through the metal detector and the heavy self-locking door was a cinder-block room with fifteen round tables that were chained to the floor. Leif was already seated at one of these tables. Everyone looks guilty in prison. Even if you've never so much as sworn out loud, in the right context, you'll look like a murderer. Leif was a beautiful man. His good looks were obvious to the casual observer—the thick reddish-brown hair that fell in just the right places across his face, his wide oceanic-green eyes, his height, and his hands. These were the kinds of things that drew people to Leif. But his real beauty was in the energy his body emanated. This restless momentum manifested itself in all kinds of unexpectedly beautiful ways, his appetite for making me come, his tendency to dance in the evenings while getting ready for work, his ability to make sullen people laugh.

He was still beautiful, but I could see that the past few weeks had robbed him of the energy that made him Leif. He was wearing prison blues, starched short sleeves, and dark blue pants. His hair was long, and he'd begun to grow a beard that did not look particularly well cared for. He stood up and hugged me, and it was hard to remember the last time we'd touched. Was it in his apartment when he'd been speeding so hard he'd been insistent on making me come again and again? As he hugged me, he stroked the back of my head, combing my hair gently with his fingers. I felt him get a little hard against my stomach, and I drew away from him. I squinted at him.

"What was that?" I asked.

"Jesus, Peg. I'm so horny I can't see straight. I'm losing my mind in here." His eyes did have a starved, hungry look.

"Well, that's the least of your worries right now."

Leif nodded. He looked down at his own hands, and we both saw they were full of my hair. The long dark strands were wound around his fingers and plastered to his sweating palms. I had an image of snaking hair from a drain. He wiped his hands on his pants. He took stock of me and he was shocked. How much different could I be?

"You're skinny as hell," he said.

"I hadn't noticed."

"I'm worried about you," he said. "I mean, Jesus, when's the last time you ate something?"

"I'm fine. What's going on with all of this?" I gestured at the jail. A woman seated two tables away from us was in danger of violating the excessive emotionalism rule. She was waving her arms above her head. I looked away and Leif was watching me.

"I don't know. Donald, the lawyer your brother got me, thinks an illegal search argument might work, but also since I've got the prior, I don't know, I don't understand much of it."

"Prior?" I asked.

"Your hands are shaking. You sure nothing happened to you since I've been in here?"

I didn't know what he meant, but I nodded anyway, because I didn't want to talk about me. "What prior? I didn't know you had a record."

"I mean. I don't have a record. Just me and a couple of buddies stole some beer from a convenience store back up in Rhinelander once. I had just turned eighteen, so it stuck. We got caught. That's it."

"I'll try to get a meeting with Pete and Donald too. I'll try to figure out what's going on. We're going to get you out of here."

I didn't know if that was true; I didn't know if it was possible. I knew I had to say it, though, and I was glad I did, because Leif nodded and kept picking my hairs off his palms, which were still sweating badly, and he dropped them one by one, and we watched them float to the cement floor.

Leif reached into the pocket of his jumpsuit and pulled out a stack of tattered postcards. He slid them across the table. "All from Erik," he said.

My heart leaped. "Does he know—?"

Leif shook his head. "He hasn't mentioned her once. He sends about one a week. He's on the West Coast. It's his handwriting. I'd recognize it anywhere."

"What do they say?" I rifled through the stock photos on the opposite sides—glossy panoramas of the muddy Mississippi, the Badlands, the snow-covered Rockies, Sun Valley, Idaho. The middle of America did not seem like a safe place for a gay man, but then again, Milwaukee hadn't been either. I wished more than anything that Dee was with him.

"Mundane shit, mostly. You can take them. Give them to police? Maybe it will help."

"Maybe," I told him. I took the stack from him. I turned over the one from Idaho. *I love you, Leif,* it said.

"There's something else," Leif told me. He leaned in. I thought we might get yelled at. "He's seen the photo too."

"How do you know?"

"One of the postcards," Leif choked out. "It says, *Now I know who you really are.*"

I shook my head. "That could mean anything," I said, though I had the feeling he was right. A tear fell down Leif's cheek and he wiped it away quickly. He rolled his shoulders back and set his spine up straight.

"That's not who I am," he said. "The photo."

I felt at the time it was intensely, absolutely, unequivocally important to ignore this.

"If he has seen it," I said, "we need to find him."

Leif shook his head. "He's gone."

One of the odd things about the Milwaukee County Jail is that it shares a parking structure with the Milwaukee Public Museum. After I left Leif, I came out into the lobby of the parking structure and stood in front of the doors to the museum. I had a sudden urge to go inside and sit somewhere quiet and fake. I paid for my ticket (I didn't want to see the exhibit on the *Titanic*) and then stood beneath the massive blue whale skeleton screwed to the ceiling of the museum's lobby.

I spent most of the rest of that afternoon there, and I never told Peter or Ma or Suze. I suspected they'd be indignant and judgmental, like I was taking a day off from Dee's disappearance. I guess I was. I wandered through the exhibits aimlessly. I read nothing and I learned nothing. I bought rock candy from the candy shop in the *Streets of Old World Milwaukee*, which re-created the streets of Milwaukee as they looked one hundred years ago. I sat inside a fake igloo and stared through thick glass at the plastic Inuit family as they went about their icy lives, spearing seals, swaddling babies, sewing skins. I went deep into the bowels of the ocean, descending dark ramps to stare at watery exhibits full of fake lantern fish and giant squid and feel the weight of the rushing water soundtrack. I stood beneath a full-size T. rex as it ripped the guts out of a perpetually unlucky stegosaurus; the entrails hung from the massive plastic teeth, and the prehistoric jungle noises played on repeat. The Milwaukee Public Museum never changed. I was surprised to learn, though, that they'd begun to offer tickets to a butterfly room. This was an uncomfortably warm room in which cases of butterfly larvae hung on the walls until they metamorphosed. These butterflies lived out their short, beautiful lives inside the museum's warm room for the pleasure of the visitors. There was a fake rushing stream with tiny bridges, a wall of fake rock, a trickling waterfall running over it all, real vegetation, some stunning flowers, and of course, butterflies everywhere. They landed on children's shoulders and heads and fingers; they fluttered around the room, knocking against the glass again and again.

I wondered how many of these poor things were crushed under careless boots or in the hands of overeager children. I'm sure there was a great amount of scientific value in the room, but there was also something very dark about the setup. I stood in that room for a very long time, my lungs wet with the humidity and my legs aching from standing in one place, and I thought I had been very careful. I thought I'd been the most careful one in the room. But on my way out, I noticed my sneaker squishing loudly against the museum's marble floor. I lifted the sole of my shoe to find one of the butterflies, folded in half, wing to wing, pressed tight to the bottom of my foot. I scraped it off with my fingernails.

Back at the house, Peter and Ma and Suze were sitting on the front stoop. We spent long hours there that summer and fall, waiting, and waiting, as if maybe Dee would waltz up the block, and we'd all wrap her up, and laugh, and pretend she'd never been gone. Suze was chain-smoking, by the looks of the ashtray next to her. Ma's disapproval of Suze's smoke was obvious, but she looked too tired to protest. I felt their eyes on me as I came up the walkway. The front yard always got me thinking of Dee. In summer we used to run bare-chested, in matching pink-and-white underwear, through garden sprinklers, and we were so beautiful, such blurs of girl and skin, that once someone called the cops on us and said there were naked women in the front yard. The cops came and our parents threw our swimsuits at us; we were six and seven years old. We used to pretend we lived outside, underneath a big pine tree at the edge of our front yard; we pilfered pots and pans and took them beneath the boughs, where we mixed up needle soups and grass stews. Ma used to find her cookware underneath the tree and run after us, shaking heavy soup pots at us as we screamed. This memory made me smile, and when I looked up at Peter, and Ma, and my aunt, and they saw me smiling, I blushed. I couldn't even smile without raising suspicion. I wanted to say, *Listen, I was thinking of Dee. I was thinking of when we were little girls, when we used to play out here, do you remember, do you remember.* But I just straightened out my lips so they didn't have any interpretable shape to them at all. Suze slid over on the cement stoop to let me in. I was grateful for this kindness. I sat down with them. I wanted to ask Suze for a cigarette, but I knew my mother would have a hernia. I couldn't believe how many things she didn't know about me. How does that happen?

"How's Leif?" Peter asked. He reached across Suze to squeeze my shoulder and got a handful of bone. Peter's concern for Leif was jarring to me; three weeks ago, he'd wanted to bash Leif's skull into our record player.

"They're going ahead with the other charges," I said. "The drugs and the gun."

Ma's face collapsed, and I guessed what she was thinking. *I knew you two were mixed up in some bad stuff.*

"But how is he?" Suze asked.

"He's alive," I conceded. "He gave me these." I handed Ma the stack of postcards.

"What the hell are these?" she asked.

"Leif's brother, Erik, he sent them."

She rifled through them, much as I had done, looking for any mention of Dee. Finding nothing, she threw them all back at me. They fluttered pathetically in the air and landed at my feet. I kicked at them.

"These are no help at all, Margaret. This whole time. I haven't understood any of it. And I don't understand you at all. You're focused on all the wrong stuff. You're almost as bad as the police. If I didn't know any better, I'd think you were trying to ruin this for us. I swear to God."

She leaped up from the porch stoop in a swirl of long skirts, pushed the screen door open, and let it slam shut behind her. Later, I understood Ma felt guilty too. She blamed herself for not protecting Dee or me, or for not raising us up to know the difference between a good man and a bad man. As if there were a checklist she'd failed to provide us. *Does he smoke cigarettes and/or marijuana? Does he own a gun? Does he own a bowling ball? Does he hit you during sex? Do you like it?* I wondered if the victims' families felt this guilt. Was there any kind of list that could have prepared those men for the serial killer? We were all just guessing at the risk of our relationships. God, it still makes me so sad and debilitated to think about Dee in that moment—the moment she needed us, needed me. Isn't that the most terrifying part? Imagining her fear. I don't indulge in those kinds of thoughts for long, because it produces a paralysis in me; I can't move or think for minutes, or hours, or days.

"Ma hates me," I said to Suze and Peter. I was hoping they'd contest this, but they stayed quiet. Peter stared at his shoes. Suze blew smoke up to the sky, which was just beginning to go dark. Bats swooped through clouds of mosquitoes above us.

"She wants to find Dee," Suze said.

"Jesus, I'm sick of everyone pretending like I don't want her back too."

Peter was biting his lower lip so hard, the entirety of it had disappeared into his mouth.

"But I'm not under any delusions. Frank—"

Suze slapped me on the back of my head. "Jesus, Margaret. For your mother's sake, can you please carry on as if she's alive."

"You're driving her crazy," Peter added.

"Pete," I tried to reason. "You saw his apartment. Why would he leave his dog there like that? Why would he take all of his stuff with him?"

Peter shook his head at me, and then he left me and Suze alone on the stoop. She patted the back of my head, the stinging place she'd hit me only moments before.

"I'm sorry, baby," Suze said.

"You're not," I told her.

I felt like a child again, or worse, as if I were reliving my teenage years, those dark thrilling years in which it's possible to convince yourself that no one understands you. This time I didn't have Dee as a buffer between me and the rest of the family. A phrase rang in my head: *The course of conflict is not determined by the person who initiates but by the person who responds.*

Suze shrugged it off, and I loved her for it. I resisted the urge to bring Frank up again. To my mind, the only interview worth conducting was one with Frank. The police had botched their chance, and Peter and Ma hadn't even bothered speaking with him. No. That wasn't fair. It wasn't that they hadn't bothered. He'd disappeared from Milwaukee. I knew Suze didn't want to hear any of this, so I bit my nails instead. Isn't it funny? That's Ma's conditioning in me, I think. The daylight lingered in cotton candy–colored swaths of low clouds, but the streetlights were already casting pools of garish light in the gutters. Suze squeezed my knee.

D r. P wedged her trowel between the coffin's lid and one of its walls. She pried on the lid and it gave way easily. Her movements suggested she had done this many times before, which was strange to consider. The coffin's hardware left bright orange stains in the earth. The color gave the soil a sick radioactive look. I smelled the harsh acid of iron in the air. Some of the coffin's wood crumbled underneath Dr. P's trowel. She pried the entire lid off and we all peered in. The coffin was clogged with mud, but a glint of fabric shone through. Dr. P had gloves on. She lifted thick layer upon thick layer of fabric. Someone had buried ten or twelve evening gowns inside the coffin. I heard Wolski make a choking noise. The sniffer dog barked loudly.

"Is she in there?" Wolski asked for us.

Dr. P lifted up the heavy layers of fabric—they were muddy and moldy and crumbling in her gloved hands, but I could make out the glint of glitter, sequins, sheer fabric in all colors, pale blue, yellow, emerald green. I had an image again of swaths of fancy dresses, some with the tags on, hanging in Dee's dorm room closet at Mount Mary.

"I . . . I don't know what to make of this," Dr. P said.

"I might have something," one of the archaeologists said. He was screening all the dirt they had pulled out of the pit. He held up a tiny fragment. "Looks cranial. I can't be sure it's human, though." He handed it to Dr. P, and she placed it gingerly in a paper bag. I stared at those dresses packed tightly inside their grave. The sniffer dog continued to pull against his leash. He whined and whined. What did the dog want? What was he trying to say?

The archaeologists began to pull more fragments from their screens—finger bones, and toes, and maybe pieces of ribs, I heard them say. Small bones.

"It could be her, right?" Pete asked Dr. P.

"It could be," she said, though her voice suggested she didn't think there was much chance. "They're very fragmented, though, and they look quite old."

"Can I see one?" Pete asked. The younger archaeologists looked ready to refuse him, but Dr. P nodded. A young man handed Pete a few crumbling pieces of bone. He rubbed them between his thumb and forefinger. I imagined the oil in his skin shining the mud away. He looked up at me and gestured toward the field outside the woods. I followed him to where Ma was wilting in her wheelchair.

"There was a dog," Pete told Ma. She nodded like she'd known. Thomas Alexander's eyebrows went up just slightly. "And a coffin with dresses. And they're finding some bone fragments." He knelt down and handed Ma three pieces of bone. She took the fragments in her hand. They were so deteriorated, I worried they might crumble into her lap. She looked up at the sky.

"Thank you, God," she said. "Thank you for bringing her home. For putting us back together." She clutched the muddy fragments to her chest. Dirt rolled down her dress.

"Mama," Pete said. "We still can't be sure—"

"Hush. Hush. Come here, now," she said. "Both of you." I went to her and knelt next to Pete in front of the wheelchair. The day was warm, and the clouds moved over us like lush cotton in the sky. I often forgot how beautiful Wisconsin could be. Ma put the fragments in her lap and reached for our hands. Someone in Thomas Alexander's crew snapped a photo of us: heads bent like we were praying together, and maybe in a way we were. I kept my eyes open. I tried not to stare at the muddy bones. I knew they were Dee's.

Ma asked if she could bring the bones back to the Lutheran Home with her, and that's where Dr. P drew the line. Legally, she said, that wasn't possible. The archaeologists would take the fragments back to the lab for analysis. I saw her speaking with Wolski as we loaded Ma back into the van. Thomas Alexander stayed behind, trying to get some action shots with the archaeologists who had the unfortunate job of reburying the dead dog.

I rode back to the Lutheran Home with Ma, Peter, and Suze. Maybe Ma's hope had spread among us: a wildfire we hadn't bothered to fight. Did it matter? Back at the cemetery, Ma had rubbed her face with her dirty hands, so her cheekbones were streaked with mud. Suze tried to rub them clean with a wet wipe, but Ma shrugged her off. She smiled a half smile at her sister with her good side. "Suze," Ma said.

"Hmmm?" My aunt was watching the city rush by. I remembered that as a small child, Dana had been very afraid of freeways. She would complain when we began to accelerate too quickly.

"I want you to call Forest Home and start making the preparations."

"Okay," Suze said.

Pete frowned. "Should we wait to be sure?" he asked Ma.

Half her body began to shake convulsively. "I have waited," she said. "Now you want me to wait longer?"

"No, Mama," he said. "I just thought . . . I don't know."

There was a bout of silence in the car. I felt compelled suddenly to confess something, though I'd never really been able to explain what I felt most guilty about, and I sensed then that even if I had ever been capable of saying it, no one in my family would have understood.

In the end, Ma was forced to wait anyway. Though DNA testing on the fragments could be done in a matter of days, the state crime lab in Madison, which was the only accredited lab in the state, had a backlog of more than eight hundred samples. Most of the samples were from untested rape kits. They said it could take months, even years, for us to get a definitive answer. Pete, Ma, and I sent in our own samples for comparison.

n September, authorities found hundreds of tiny bone fragments in an Ohio woodland near the serial killer's childhood home. They identified one man by a vertebra and a molar. But there were some remains they could not put to a name. This meant there were many families out there just like mine. The serial killer was charged with sixteen separate counts of murder, and though some people suspected he'd killed many more men, he said he had confessed to all his murders. His lawyers began to pursue a guilty but insane plea. They rounded up all kinds of experts—psychologists and psychiatrists who argued that he suffered from borderline personality disorder, alcohol dependence, schizotypal personality disorder, necrophilia, and psychotic disorder. They said he was driven by impulses he could not control. I didn't understand how this was a defense. I wasn't alone.

Pete was the one who first saw the announcement. The new firefighting recruits were holding their annual inauguration at the end of the summer. There was a list of names—men who were to be inducted into the Milwaukee Fire Department. Frank's "real" name was on that list. I couldn't believe it. There was little else, not his sleazy demeanor, or his lack of alibi, or what I believed had been his attempt to frame Leif, or his summer disappearance, that made me more suspicious than that announcement.

We did not tell Wolski we were going; we'd lost almost all confidence in him by that point. They held the inauguration in a grassy clearing at Lake Park. There were white plastic chairs set up in tight rows, red streamers strung from a stage, and long banquet tables filled with cupcakes. Lake Michigan shone hungry at the bottom of the bluff like a massive blue cenote waiting for a sacrifice. Dee had once shown me a picture of the cenote at Chichén Itzá into which she said the Mayans used to throw virgins. I imagined the gracile skeletons piling at the bottom of the well. I never asked if the women were alive when they were tossed into the well.

The guests milled about the park, slapping backs and kissing cheeks and shaking hands. Seagulls cried and picked through garbage. The day was still except for the hot energy I could feel pulsing in Peter's body beside mine. We stayed in the car and watched the clearing fill in with men in black uniforms and white caps. The heat rose in shining waves from their patent-leather shoes. The crowd began to take their seats. There was a feeling of great promise and pride in the air, and I breathed it in from inside the car; I hoped it would renew something that was molding inside me. We waited for Frank.

Peter saw him first, and I knew only by the way Pete went rigid like a rabbit caught unawares. He stayed perfectly still, except his eyes were tracking. I traced Peter's gaze to the banquet tables, where Frank helped two children pile cupcakes onto a paper plate. One of the children stuffed an entire cupcake in his mouth. Frank laughed. He wiped frosting from the corner of the boy's mouth and licked it from his fingers. Peter made moves for the door, groping at his keys, but I steadied him. "After," I said.

Peter nodded. From the car, we watched the class graduate.

When Frank crossed the stage, there was a sprinkle of applause, one man whistled with his fingers, and one woman yelled his real name, Tony, drawing out the O forever, which turned Frank's face so red that Peter and I could see it from the car. He grinned, though, with his big blond teeth.

After the ceremony, the crowd squeezed out of their lawn chairs and celebrated. The smarter guests wandered away to the beer gardens or the bars. I wished suddenly I were one of them; there's nothing like the feeling of celebrating after a stuffy ceremony. While Frank was within sight, Peter swung open his car door and then slammed it so hard, it startled a few of the guests. I followed his lead, but I had the sinking feeling we were making a mistake. As we approached (we were making a wide approach and using tree cover to stay hidden), I saw Frank had hoisted two children up, one on each hip. They had their legs wrapped tight around his waist, and one looked like he might fall asleep; his limbs were limp against Frank's body. A woman, maybe Peter's age, had also fitted herself into Frank. His arms stretched long around all three of them. The woman was stunning, tall, bleached blond, tan, and smartly dressed in a floral shift dress. Her white pumps were sunk into the wet grass. I craned my neck, and my suspicions were confirmed: Frank and the woman wore matching wedding bands. I mimed the wedding ring at Peter, and doubt clouded his face. We stopped at the tree line, watching people tousle the boys' hair, and laugh at their frosting-caked faces, and beam at Frank's fit form, and admire the woman's dress. She had beautiful toned legs.

"What's the plan?" I whispered to Pete.

He didn't turn to me, but he licked his lips. "He's got a family," he murmured. "Kids. I mean, Jesus Christ."

The boys shared Frank's long nose. Peter attempted a step toward Frank but fumbled and caught at a low branch. It snapped loudly, and Frank turned toward us. Peter straightened in the trees, his body poised to approach but seized, and I was reminded again of city rabbits, paralyzed by their own fear of human footsteps. Frank met Peter's eye. The men had never met, so there was no flash of recognition on Frank's face. I expected the recognition when he turned to me, but there was no change. His face was steady, a twinge of confusion, maybe, but he did not blink; he was a good actor. The woman had noticed nothing. I kept my eyes on Frank and waited for him to show that he knew me, or to show a shot of pain or regret, but his face stayed solid. He put the boys down and shoved them behind his large frame. Pete began to move, and my heart felt large, heavy, and impossibly wet in my chest.

"Pete," I whispered. "Stop."

"Why?" he hissed at me. "Why would I?"

He strode confidently over to the family, and I hung back for a minute. Now I felt paralyzed, unsure what I should do with my feet, my face, my hands. I wanted to be bodyless. I followed my brother.

Pete stuck his hand out to Frank, who looked at it like a snake.

"Congratulations, Anthony," Pete said. "Really well done, man." A few of Frank's friends looked on. His wife frowned. Pete's hand hung awkwardly between them. I made eye contact with the wife from my spot behind Pete. She did a once-over of me and then stepped back, dragging her kids by the hands some distance away from us. Frank slowly offered his hand to Pete in return, and the two shook once before letting go quickly. Pete coughed and then hawked a thick glob of phlegm a few centimeters away from Frank's freshly polished shoes. "Can we talk for a minute?" Pete said.

"I really can't," Frank said. "We're about to leave."

"When was the last time you saw my sister Candace McBride?"

"I'm sorry, man. I don't know who you're talking about."

"Like hell," I said. "Where is she?" I leaped at him and Pete caught me.

Frank's wife kept moving with the children farther and farther away. "Go get in the car," Frank shouted at her, and she hurried across the field to the lot on the other side of the park.

"You piece of shit," I said. "People know about you. Dee's roommates, her boss."

"I don't know you. I don't know your sister. If you have any further questions, you can speak to my lawyer." He held out a business card from some fancy law firm, but Pete and I just looked at it. He dropped it on the ground and then went after his wife and kids.

I stayed quiet in the car while we drove back to Ma's house. I swore to let Pete do all the explaining. I couldn't let them know I felt vindicated. I couldn't let them know I was relieved by our discovery of Frank's double life. I couldn't let them know the immense guilt these feelings created. I knew what this meant—Frank had gotten rid of Dee so he could have *that* life. The shiny, polished click of his standard-issued shoes across the stage. I wondered if Peter knew now too.

When we were kids, our parents used to make us help with the yard work on weekends. One of our assigned tasks involved picking up large sticks and branches that had fallen down, so our father could mow the lawn, and also because our mother clearly believed the front lawn looked much better without them. Dee and I collected the branches in tall creepy stick piles that were spread across the grass. Peter would bring the wheelbarrow around and collect each pile to take to the local dump.

We dreaded these yard-work Saturdays, and one hot afternoon I announced loudly to Dee that I'd never force my own children into such pointless tasks. I must have been thirteen. She turned to me and pointed a spiky, forked branch at my chest. "You said you were never going to have children," she said. She prodded me, and I pretended to be mortally wounded. I fell backward into one of our piles of sticks. She looked down on me.

"You can always change your mind, dummy," I told her. She shrugged, broke the stick she was holding across her knee, and threw it into the pile.

Once Peter forgot to collect one of our piles, and in the morning, we woke to find someone had used the sticks to spell out Dee's name in the long grass. We could see it from our bedroom window on the second floor. I thought Dee might be embarrassed, but she went outside in her baby nightgown (white cotton tank dress with faded rose hips on a hem that fell to her shins) and re-collected all the sticks herself. She threw them into Peter's wheelbarrow and then stood on the front lawn with her hand above her eyes like a surveyor. She was looking for him, as if maybe he'd hid out beneath one of the old pines to catch a glimpse of her reaction, but there was no one there. From our window, I saw the thin impressions of bike tires in a trail down to the street. We never found out who did it, although I suspected Dee knew. She didn't tell us, but she had many admirers even at eleven.

When Peter and I got back to Ma's house, I noticed the lawn. There were so many fallen branches that the grass was hard to see. The grass that was visible was long and in need of a cut. The whole yard had a sad tornado-torn look about it.

"We should do something about the yard, huh?" I said to Peter.

"I swear to Christ, Margaret, I don't know where your head is half the time." He got out of the car, slammed the door, and went into the house.

I vowed not to say anything else for the rest of the night. This was my punishment. My head was gone. I was already, at the time, living in the world of memory. I think I realized right then, when I was thinking about the sticks, and as I'm writing this now and comparing my own story to Thomas Alexander's sad story, that I would live there for the rest of my life. That's where my head would stay. I wanted to tell Peter, but I didn't trust myself to say the right thing. I'd never been able to say the right thing. I stayed outside and started collecting sticks. It was still light out, plenty of light left in the day, and I knew I could finish the task. I moved methodically across the whole yard, piling sticks just like Dee and I used to, and I could feel Ma's and Peter's eyes on me for as long as it stayed light. When I was done, there were piles of sticks spread all across the yard, and I chose one right in the middle, no tree covering, and I spelled Dee's name out with the sticks, just like the lovesick kid had done years ago, and underneath her name I wrote, *I love you*.

Everybody knows the longer a person is missing, the less likely it becomes that they will be found. I listened to an NPR story on missing persons in America. There was some academic on the show to report on the "surprising fact" that most missing-persons cases in the United States are solved quite quickly. The guy cited all kinds of statistics, lots of feel-good numbers to prove that most people who go missing are returned to their families within days, if not hours. It didn't seem fair, because these were old people with dementia or general confusion who wandered away from their home or their local grocer and didn't make it very far before they were tracked down. What he didn't say was that most children who go missing are not found quickly, and sometimes they're never found. Many women are never found either. I cringed when he repeated what Wolski had said and what the other MPD officials had said of the boys on the back door of the bars: *It's not a crime in this country to leave your life and start another one someplace else.*

Article VI. Witnesses

RULE 612. WRITING USED TO REFRESH A WITNESS'S MEMORY

a) Scope. This rule gives an adverse party certain options when a witness uses a writing to refresh memory: (1) while testifying; or (2) before testifying, if the court decides that justice requires the party to have those options.

After the excavation, Dana came to see me. Her parents had enrolled her in a new school for the fall, and she'd already started practicing with their swim team. She said she loved being in the water now. Over the past month or so, I'd noticed she had built some bulk in her shoulders. I tried to push away the memory of her heaving in my car, her soggy clothes fogging up the windshield while we drove in silence.

I said, "You look strong."

She rolled her eyes. "Thanks," she said. She sat down on my couch and took some papers out of her backpack. They looked like files from my boxes, but I couldn't be sure.

"How are you feeling?" she asked me. I eyed her. It was an uncharacteristic question. "About the case, I mean? Do you feel ready?"

"I hope so," I said. "But there is a lot I don't remember." It pained me to say this out loud. I sensed Dana knew.

"I can look through what you've got again," she said. "If you want."

I shook my head. "I've got it," I told her, and I squeezed her knee. She allowed this. "How are things? At home?"

Dana shrugged. "Dad is—" She paused. "He's frustrated." I

nodded. They were still giving us the runaround at the crime lab. They said they were doing everything they could to process our samples expediently. Pete had asked Charlie Makon to write a piece for us, but he said he was busy with a bigger story. He'd said it more sensitively, of course, but that's what he meant. There was always a bigger story. Dr. P said the only way our samples might jump the line would be if there was some public pressure. We had never been capable, it seemed, of drumming that up for Dee.

"The whole thing is taking longer than we thought," I said.

"It's not just that," Dana said. "I don't know if I should tell you this. But I think he's losing hope."

"What are you talking about?"

"I don't think he thinks it's Aunt Dee anymore."

"Why do you say that? Did he tell you that?"

She shook her head. "I can just tell."

I didn't agree with this assessment, but I didn't want to argue. "I'll talk to him," I offered.

She shrugged. "Okay. Are you sure you don't want me to read through the case again? I've been going through all the transcripts you've got. I might be able to piece a few more things together for you."

Maybe I gave in because of fatigue. Maybe I gave in because I loved her and I wanted her to love me back. Did I believe she would be able to see something I couldn't? I don't know. I think above all else, I wanted, even if temporarily, to let go. I pushed a stained stack of legal pads toward her, and I was rewarded with a kiss on the cheek.

When we told Wolski about the inauguration, about Frank's wife and kids, he said he would go see about the guy after all. He got Frank's real address, using his real name, from a buddy over at the MFD. Peter wanted to go too, but Wolski said we'd already risked too much when we'd unlawfully entered Frank's apartment. He'd said he'd had to fudge too much paperwork to make that all go away. Pete was irate. Did I think Peter was capable of killing Frank? I'm convinced now that we are all capable. Over millennia, our brains have gotten very large, and very complex, but I know that the simple animal portion of our brains is still powerful. *Why did he leave his dog alone in his apartment? Where was he the whole summer? How long had he lied to Dee about his wife and family in Ohio? Where was he the night she went missing? When was the last time he saw her? Did he send the picture of Leif and me to Wolski?*

Wolski met us at Ma's to report back on all of Frank's dumb answers. Frank had thought of everything. This was not impressive. He'd had a long time to formulate these answers—he'd effectively been missing since Dee had been. Apparently, Frank had asked his buddy to take care of the dog while he was back in Ohio, but the asshole had forgotten and abandoned the animal. Frank had allegedly spent most of his summer in Ohio, where his family lived.

He had the apartment in Milwaukee as a sublet while he was train-ing for the firefighting exam. I thought it was a hell of a nice place for a firefighter in training. He planned to move the whole family up from Ohio after the inauguration. His wife had a good job at GE and was waiting to be transferred to the Milwaukee branch. The kids' names were Samuel and Joshua. They were five and seven years old. Frank said he barely knew Dee. He said it was true they'd met at a bar, but they hadn't had a relationship. It was his word against ours. He said he was at a cookout in his Ohio neighborhood on the Fourth. Wolski said he didn't act suspiciously or seem per-turbed by the interview; Frank said he was happy to help.

We sat at the kitchen table to receive the news. My grandfather had made that table when he was a young man, and though it was worn by the time he passed it on to Ma, my father had refinished it beautifully. He'd polished it in the garage until it glowed amber. I rubbed my thumb into a whorl of wood until it shone with grease. Ma only nodded at Wolski's report as if she'd been briefed already. Peter stared at his hands folded tightly on the table. When Wolski was done, he let us be quiet for a minute, and I admired the space he left for silence. He occasionally showed a gentleness and a com-passion that I never would have believed he was capable of when I'd first met him. After some long minutes, he asked, "Do you folks have any questions?"

I was certain Ma would (she had so many questions for us), but she only shook her head and stood up. She put her arms out to receive Wolski, and he pushed his chair back brusquely, and they hugged. I caught Peter's eye and he shook his head at me just slightly. I didn't know what he was trying to communicate. Ma climbed the stairs and we heard her bedroom door shut with a click. Wolski had a line of sweat running down the right side of his face. I had an urge to dab it away. He jerked his head toward the door and motioned for me and Pete to follow him.

Outside, he lit a cigarette and offered one to me. Pete didn't flinch when I accepted, and Wolski lit it for me. Maybe Pete figured I was black on the inside anyway. He was maybe right. We had learned all kinds of secrets about each other that summer. I'd learned that Pete was seeing one of Dee's friends during our informal investigations into her disappearance. He'd met her at Dee's dorm. I'd never heard of the girl, but she claimed that she and Dee were in drawing together during the spring semester. I saw Peter with the girl in his car outside of Ma's house late one night. It was dark out, but the sky was purple, and the streetlamps flooded the inside of the car so their faces were lit up. They were arguing. Peter kept tossing anxious glances toward the house. The girl had her hand on the car door. When the argument ended, Peter put his hands on the sides of the girl's face and drew her into him. They kissed gently, and then he started the car back up and drove her maybe back to her home, or maybe back to the dorm, or maybe to someplace where he could be sure there weren't any eyes on them. Peter never mentioned the girl to me or Ma.

I inhaled deeply on the cigarette and blew the smoke up to the sky. Wolski was eyeing the sad stick shrine I'd made on the lawn, and sweat rolled from his temples.

"She's a strong woman," Wolski said. Pete and I nodded, and Pete motioned for him to go on. "I couldn't do it to her, though."

I was getting impatient. "What is it, Gary?" Pete asked him. He almost never used Wolski's first name, and finally, Wolski wiped the sweat from his temples.

"Frank, or Tony or whatever, tried to tell me that your sister was a . . . an escort or a call girl type of what have you . . ."

"Fucking ridiculous," Pete said. "What was his evidence?"

"He showed me bank statements, money he'd paid her, I guess. And . . ." His face was pinched. "Pictures . . . of her all dressed up . . . and in compromising . . . situations."

"First he says he doesn't know her and that he never had a relationship with her, and now he says she was a call girl," I protested. "He's got so many different stories." I had a memory of Dee on the bus with her Walkman. I had a memory of opening her closet to stacks of SlimFast cans behind which hung long shimmery dresses. Why hadn't those dresses seemed suspicious to me? Where had she gotten them? Why did she have them? Maybe I'd assumed they belonged to her absent roommate.

"Well, he didn't consider it a relationship. Now, I have to be honest. I felt compelled to investigate this, so I had one of my buddies who has ears in a couple of those . . . agencies ask around." I wanted to ask Wolski if this was the first time he'd actually done any investigative work by himself, but I held my tongue and let him continue. I knew what he was going to say. *People with that kind of lifestyle go missing all the time.* "The girls all have fake names, but one company said they had a woman with Candace's description working for them this summer. They haven't seen her in about a month, though."

Peter shook his head. "You're an incompetent asshole, you know that? Fuck you, Wolski. Fuck you. I should have believed Peg."

I felt my face flush. I could see Wolski was hurt, and I suddenly felt for him, though I hated myself for it. "What description? Did you send her picture?" I asked him.

He shook his head. "I didn't want to risk it. The fucking *Journal.* They're pariahs over there. That's the last fucking thing you need is for someone to leak the photo, and then there's a whole news story about how she was a . . ."

"So what . . . Five-seven? Dark blond hair? Brown eyes? You know that describes half the white girls in this damn city," I said.

Wolski shook his head. I still had a hard time looking at the man without seeing the twitching St. Bernard at his feet. Blood does not flow like any other liquid I've ever observed. "Dee thought they were going to get married. She thought they were serious. He's a fucking liar. Why would he agree to meet me? To meet my boyfriend?"

"He says he never met you either."

"We hung out twice!"

"Now, look, I'm not saying I believe him. I'm just telling you. And there's something else. Frank was acting so smug the whole time, I thought I'd test him a little bit. Asked if he'd mind if I took a look in his car. He's no fool. He read me the whole riot act about warrants and reasonable suspicion and what have you. Gave me his lawyer's card. The whole thing. And then he surprised me. He laughed, said he was just joking, clapped me on the back, led me out to the garage, and handed me his keys. Everything was pretty tidy—a couple of atlases in the glove box and a pack of Marb Reds on the dash. It reminded me of the way his apartment looked— sort of sanitized, you know. But then I looked in the trunk and found a whole bundle full of shovels." Wolski paused.

"Fuck," Peter said.

"He said his parents own a cemetery, and he helps them out from time to time. We already knew that, though." Wolski scuffed the toe of his shoe against the stoop. "Look. This guy. I mean. If he didn't do it, he had something to do with it, and he's lying through his teeth. I know that. Believe me, I know that. I just want you to know that . . . without a body—"

"We know," I interrupted him. "No crime."

"I'm sorry, Pete," Wolski said.

"I've been thinking," Pete said. "Maybe we should get some more help. I've made some appointments with private detectives. I know you've got other cases. I'm not saying you're doing a bad job. I just. I thought we should exhaust all our options. We have to."

Wolski inhaled deeply. His eyes narrowed. Pete hadn't said anything about this to me. Maybe he'd discussed it with Ma.

"Those people will suck you fucking dry. I'm telling you right now. They are disgusting. They hang around grieving families and sell you a whole bunch of bullshit. I'm not kidding, Pete. Listen to me. They'll get you on a retainer and they'll give you less than nothing."

Peter turned his back and went inside without a word. I walked Wolski to the car. He seemed surprised by this gesture. I stood on the curb rocking back and forth on the balls of my feet. He turned the engine over, and it hummed awake. He rolled the car windows down and clenched the steering wheel. I leaned into the open passenger window.

"What about the photo?" I whispered, as if Peter and Ma could hear me from the house over the noisy engine idling.

Wolski shook his head. "You don't know Frank sent it," he said. "There's no evidence of that."

"Who else could it have been?"

"Honestly, I thought you'd had enough of that photo," he whispered. "I was ready to let you forget about it. Let it go." I slammed my fist down on the hood of the police car. Did he think he was protecting me? "That is official City of Milwaukee property, Margaret. Step away from the vehicle." I took my keys out—I had a key to my place with Leif, which I was sure, as I stood there on the curb, was collecting so much dust and grime that it was now inhospitable to life, and my house keys, which I never used because our house was always unlocked. I jabbed the end of my apartment key into the passenger side of Wolski's car and dragged it across the door. The noise broke something inside my ear. He put the car into a jerky first and sputtered away, and I stood there on the curb with the keys clenched in my fist. Across the street, a woman I didn't recognize was watching me with her hose running at her feet. The water ran to the curb and swirled down the sewer.

I was embarrassed that I'd keyed Wolski's car. Peter and I had treated Wolski badly that day. He was an easy target. Hell, he was the only target. He called later that night and left a long voicemail on the home phone. He didn't seem to care if Ma heard it. Maybe he wanted her to hear it. I think his intentions were good, but much like the rest of us, he never had any idea what he was doing. In the message, he said he wished he was better at his job. He said he wished the department had given him the resources he needed. He said he wished they'd tracked Frank down that first week. He said there was only one piece of knowledge he could pass on to us that might put our souls at ease. He said humans are not so complex as we'd like to believe. They are weak and easily consumed by their own thoughts. When someone commits a crime like murder, it will eat, and eat, and eat away at every part of them, at every part of their life, until it has ruined them and everyone near them. I wished this were true, but I really didn't know.

And honestly, I didn't know how that was supposed to comfort us. Pete said before we'd seen the kids, Joshua and Samuel (Pete got in the habit of saying their names), and the leggy woman at the graduation, that he'd had fantasies about killing Frank. I remember Dee's pained voice on the phone when I'd told her I'd tell Pete about Frank's infidelity. *Don't,* she'd said, *he'll kill Frank.* My brother was capable of this. I had no doubt. He said that sometimes, in order to keep from getting too sad, he'd dream up different ways of killing Frank. He didn't elaborate. I didn't want to know. But he said after we saw the kids, Joshua and Samuel, that he began to force himself to quit. He couldn't believe he'd turned into the kind of man who would ruin a family. But he said it was hard to control the fantasies, and he doubted they'd ever go away completely. Now I was scared of him too.

When the results did come in, Ma refused to believe them. I'll admit I also had a difficult time accepting the data. The state crime lab in Madison reported that there was absolutely no overlap in our DNA samples and the DNA of the bone fragments they'd analyzed. There was no chance the fragments belonged to Dee. Dr. P corroborated this assessment when she noted that, given the advanced decomposition of the fragments and the associated coffin, the individual was likely interred between 1870 and 1920. Further, given the soil strata, the grave had likely been disturbed and the coffin's original remains scattered. Apparently, someone had emptied the coffin of most of its original contents and buried the dresses and the dog there more recently. Dr. P said she would not conjecture beyond that.

Months later, when a backhoe stripped that same plot of land and they excavated a thousand tightly packed graves, including some coffins that had been stuffed with medical waste—parts of humans, and waste from dissections, and other unspeakable things in jars—they didn't know who those people were either. Milwaukee had a bad problem with losing track of its people, the living and the dead alike.

Ma didn't care. She wanted the bones buried next to her anyway. She believed they were Dee's. We didn't know what to do. Over and over, she called Dr. P, who told her there was no possibility that they could give the bones to her because it was illegal to do so. Ma called the *Journal Sentinel,* who refused to engage. She called our congresswoman, who said what politicians always say— *I'll see what I can do.* Ultimately, what she could do was very little. Ma became irate and inconsolable. She would throw things at us when we visited her. She smashed all of our photos except Dee's. The nursing home tried to put her on sedatives, but she refused to take them. She felt she'd come closer than ever before, and now she was being deliberately denied solace. Most days I felt the same way. I had also believed the results would be conclusive, because I'd sunk so much energy into my case against Frank. But I knew I couldn't and shouldn't believe any of it now. Still, it wasn't easy to accept.

Alexis Patterson's case came to my mind. Alexis was seven years old when she disappeared on her way to school. The *Journal Sentinel* covered her story, but there was no outpouring of support from around the world, and there was barely any national coverage. In fact, a white supremacist, who was later arrested (but not prosecuted), posted hateful flyers near America's Black Holocaust Museum in Milwaukee asking why any white person would care about the disappearance of a Black child. The national outlets seemed, largely, through apathy, to endorse this hateful man's perspective.

Alexis Patterson was never found. Her family endured far worse than mine: racism, national indifference, bogus tips, and futile citywide searches. Divers skimmed the muck of the Milwaukee River's bottom: nothing. Much later, an Ohioan claimed his wife, who had no memories of her childhood, was Alexis Patterson. The

Sentinel covered this development, too. This woman had a scar under her left eye that matched the scar seven-year-old Alexis had. The *Sentinel* called this woman, who by then had two children of her own, and she said only, "I am not that girl. That is a ridiculous question." Police said that, given the woman's age (she was seven years older than Alexis would have been), it was unlikely this Ohioan was the missing child. But Alexis Patterson's mother said, "My heart is telling me this is my child. My baby is coming home."

I understood this sentiment perfectly. So did my mother.

In the wake of the results, I realized that my case against Frank, especially without Dee's body, was exactly as Dana had described: very weak. It wasn't that I no longer believed Frank was guilty; I believed it more strongly than ever. But in this retelling, I saw that I had somehow exposed my own complicities more than I had indicted Frank. As I reviewed the pages I'd lent to Dana, it occurred to me that I'd almost built a case against myself.

What emerged most clearly from these memories was that I'd kept Dee's relationship with Frank a secret; I'd never explicitly tried to deter her from seeing him; and perhaps even more unforgivable, I'd acted badly in the days and weeks and months after her disappearance. First I'd been incredulous, then I'd been distracted and confused, and finally, I'd zeroed in on Frank in a way that had left my family frustrated. Against my own will, this was the narrative that had taken shape. Dana corroborated this assessment when she came by to return the pages I'd lent her. She handed them back to me with an old transcript stapled to the top. I didn't recognize it.

"Would you be okay if I asked you a few more questions?"

I shrugged. I'd promised myself in the days after we got the results that this time I was really done. Maybe I'd go through the study and clear out some of the files. Maybe I'd finally clean up the apartment. Maybe I'd even try to leave the bounds of the city. (I knew this was all a reach.)

"I don't know what else there is to ask," I told her.

"Does anyone else know about the photo you showed me?"

"Wolski. It's in the police records. That's it."

"Has my dad ever seen it?"

Even decades later, I blushed. I shook my head. "Not that I know. Thomas Alexander, he seemed to know about it. Not sure how. Leif thought Erik had seen it too. I don't think so, though."

Dana thought on that for a minute. "The photo. What happened that day," she said. "It's why you blame yourself . . . for what happened to Dee."

"Oh, baby," I said. "I mean. It's complicated. I don't really blame myself."

"You do, though," she said. "I know. I've seen it."

"What are you talking about?"

"They made a transcript with you too. I found it."

"A transcript?"

"An interview like they did for everybody else . . . Leif and Dee's roommates and her friends. I found yours too."

"I don't remember any interview," I said.

She pointed at the transcript she'd stapled to the top of the case. "Read it," she told me.

"Okay, okay, I will," I assured her.

NAME: Margaret McBride
RELATION: Dee's sister
DATE: July 29, 1991
INTERVIEWER: Suze
LOCATION: Ma's House

SUZE: You're sure you want to do this now?

PEG: I'm fine. I'm good.

SUZE: Okay. Why did you keep Dee's relationship with Frank a secret?

PEG: She asked me to. She said she knew you and Ma and Pete wouldn't like it. Wouldn't like him.

SUZE: Why did she think that?

PEG: He's older. He's a player, you know? Honestly, he's a piece of shit.

SUZE: Why do you say that?

PEG: He's a liar and a cheater.

SUZE: You met him?

PEG: Yeah, twice.

SUZE: When was the last time you saw him?

PEG: I don't remember. Beginning of the summer, maybe? I didn't like him. Leif didn't like him, so we didn't hang out. Leif and him got into a fight.

SUZE: Okay. So when was the last time you saw Dee?

PEG: The Fourth of July.

SUZE: What did you do on the Fourth?

PEG: The day before, Dee called me to say that Frank was cheating on her and she was going to confront him. I convinced her to wait on it and to come spend the Fourth with me and Leif. But before that, we went down to the lake for the fireworks. Just me and her. Smoked some joints. Nothing crazy.

SUZE: And what happened on the Fourth? When did she leave? Did she say where she was going?

PEG: Leif and I dropped acid. We thought Dee did it too, but now . . . I'm not sure. I don't think she did. She walked in on me and Leif having sex. She had my camera. She took a picture . . . while we were . . .

SUZE: She took a picture of you having sex?

PEG: Worse than that.

SUZE: Worse how?

PEG: We were being rough. With each other.

SUZE: He was hitting you?

PEG: She didn't see what she thought she saw.

SUZE: What do you think she saw?

PEG: Leif beating me up.

SUZE: What did she see?

PEG: I told you. We were messing around. But rough.

SUZE: He hit you?

PEG: He didn't mean to.

SUZE: But Dee didn't know that, right?

PEG: I mean. No. That's why I said she . . . she didn't know what she saw.

SUZE: Was she upset?

PEG: I don't know.

SUZE: You didn't see her face? Her reaction?

PEG: I . . . I don't know. I don't remember. I can't remember.

SUZE: Okay, it's okay. So she saw . . . this. And she took a picture. And she left after that? Did she say where she was going? Did she say if she was going to find Frank?

PEG: She said . . . she said . . . I can't remember.

SUZE: Do you remember if she said anything at all before she left? Do you remember what time it was when she left?

PEG: Oh my God, I can't remember, Suze. I can't remember.

I was embarrassed that my niece had read this. Dana had highlighted the last part and drawn a green star next to it: *Oh my God, I can't remember, Suze. I can't remember,* as if it were the key to the case, as if it explained something crucial about me, about what had happened. Maybe it did. The scariest part about the interview was that I had absolutely no memory of it at all. I couldn't even drum up a picture of it in my mind—where Suze and I might have sat, what time of day it was, if we were drinking coffee or wine, if there was light in the kitchen left over from the day, or if it was dark and we'd lit the kerosene lamps Ma had always loved because they reminded her of her childhood. I couldn't recollect a single detail.

The serial killer's trial was the first of its kind televised live. Seventy different news organizations attended, and it was shown on national cable news networks and broadcast live on WDJT, our local radio station. This station obtained record ratings. These legal proceedings would eventually cost the city of Milwaukee more than any other court case in the city's history. The serial killer's lawyer, an infamous prosecutor turned defense attorney named Gerald Boyle, had appeared in a highly publicized case during the 1980s. Dee and I were only girls at the time, but since that case made the national news and the lawyer was on TV and in the newspapers, I recognized him. He had previously defended two cops who murdered a Black man named Ernest R. Lacy they'd falsely accused of rape. They were acquitted. He had also defended the serial killer once before, when he'd stood trial for molesting a thirteen-year-old boy. Boyle told the judge, *We don't have a multiple offender here.*

This time, though, no one wanted to hear the defense Gerry Boyle had cooked up for his client. Even then I knew we couldn't have it both ways. We wanted the serial killer to be sick, an inhuman aberration, because this was an explanation we could live with, one that meant we were sound and healthy. This explanation, however, allowed him to skirt responsibility for his crimes. We could not live with this. People in Milwaukee wanted the serial killer to, as one family member put it, "stand up and take his justice like a man." So we were caught; on the one hand, we wanted to hear what those experts had to say—*This is a sick man, a defective man, a man who cannot control his sick impulses, a man who is himself a victim of terrible diseases.* And yet this allowed him to escape culpability, and we needed him to be completely, unequivocally guilty. And so we were forced to admit that his behavior existed on the terrifying human spectrum of that which we are capable of doing to one another. And listen—everywhere in the country, people were reading the details of his crimes, and listening to his interviews from prison, and watching the trial, and consuming his story with such appetite that, really, it was not hard for me to believe his behavior was human. We are a terrifying bunch.

Leif was in prison but on work release, and I was spending my days watching the clock until I had to pick him up at prison, drive him to Ambrosia, and then drop him back off at prison. Leif tried to carry himself more stoically than ever, a performance for my benefit, perhaps, but a performance nonetheless. He spoke in fragments. Monosyllables. And he seemed to grow thinner and more wiry every day.

We listened to the serial killer's verdict on the radio during one of the drives. Though Gerald Boyle had argued vigorously that the serial killer needed mental health care, not prison time, the judge and the jury did not agree. He was found guilty and sane on all fifteen counts of murder. He was sentenced to fifteen life terms. Three months later, he was extradited to Ohio, where he was found guilty of a sixteenth murder and sentenced to sixteen consecutive life terms in prison: sixteen hundred years behind bars.

Leif was loudly chewing a cheeseburger I'd bought him. He rolled the window down and tossed out two pickles. "Peg," he said. "You know I hate these." He motioned at the car radio and shook his head. "That guy will not last in there."

He was certainly right about that.

Before they took the serial killer away, the judge allowed the victims' families to give what he called "Victim Impact Statements." Some of the families spoke directly to the serial killer. Others spoke about or to their loved ones. Reporters said Shirly Hughes, Anthony Hughes's mother, held up the sign language symbol for *I love you*.

After the trial ended, the national news outlets packed up and left. They'd begun their slow exodus from the city back in September when national interest in the serial killer's case sharply declined. After the trial ended, when they were all finally gone, it was clear that they'd done a lot of damage: They'd tampered with and harassed witnesses and their families, they'd stolen privileged court documents, and perhaps worst of all, they'd made a celebrity out of the serial killer. Everyone in America now knew his name.

After they left, the city felt empty of people but full of quietly boiling fear. The news had done that to us, although we were complicit. Outside the courthouse, the trash cans overflowed with weeks of reporters' garbage, and no one seemed in a hurry to tidy the street. Instead, they held a candlelight vigil to heal the community, but no one was impressed. I stood at the end of North Avenue, where the street spilled over the bluff and ended above Lake Michigan, and watched the sidewalks flicker awake with white light as people came out of homes and restaurants and bars and coffee shops and lit candles. They weren't lighting them to honor the men and boys whom the serial killer had murdered. They were lighting them as a weapon against their own fear of one another.

Some days while Leif was in prison, if we had extra time before I had to take him back, we'd find an empty spot off the highway or behind an abandoned gas station, and I'd give him a blow job. I liked to make him beg when he asked for head. This was never as satisfying as I thought it would be.

During those days when he was in prison, and Dee was gone, and Ma was complacent, and we were all setting ourselves up for the long wait of the rest of our lives, which we knew was coming, I didn't feel much of anything at all. Some days I could tell how bad he wanted it, but he couldn't seem to get hard no matter what I did. I knew all his favorite spots. I knew what he liked and how he liked me to act, and still, he'd be limp in my mouth. I got the sense that he wanted badly to get rough with me, maybe even hit me, because I knew how this turned him on, but he stayed restrained. He'd lift my chin up and away from his crotch and kiss me so soft and sweet, the length of his tongue brushing against my open lips. It was like a threat.

Other days I drove aimlessly around Milwaukee's sprawl. I had an overwhelmingly painful rush of nostalgia for the beginning of last summer—before Walker's Point, before Erik was hurt, before Dee got serious about Frank, when Leif and I would walk for hours around the city, not concerned with the next shifts we had to work, talking about poems and writers we admired, about our childhoods, about our favorite foods. I drove under the sweeping highway overpasses and saw the homeless camps—people living their lives in the places the city hadn't yet figured out what to do with. There were a dozen tentlike structures and the smell of burning plastic. During the brutal Wisconsin winters, homeless people congregated around the massive steam tunnels for warmth. Sometimes the city sent police on horses to clear out these camps.

After the reporters left, the police strutted around the city with their chins a millimeter higher, but their shoulders sagged. They felt as if they'd been dragged through the mud. If they had, I didn't think much of that mud had stuck. In the fall, more demonstrators marched on the *Journal*'s offices and the MPD to protest the way the city had handled the serial killer. They said this case was proof that the police had never been concerned with the safety of minorities in Milwaukee and that the media cared more about glamorizing the serial killer than respecting his victims.

People said their sons' disappearances would have been taken seriously if they'd been pretty white women, not gay men of color. I wholeheartedly agreed. I only wanted to add two words— pretty, *rich*, and *good* white women. I knew my family was at an advantage—at least we'd gotten a report filed for Dee, at least we had Wolski, for whatever he was worth. I knew it was more than some families ever got. But it turns out you often have to be a lot of things to make the news care about you *and* to make you worthy of search and rescue. This is why you've heard about that woman who got kidnapped in Utah, but you can't name a single man the serial killer murdered. Or why you've probably never heard of Alexis Patterson.

I think Frank hoped to doom Dee's case immediately, and in many ways, when he cooked up his story about her "night job," he succeeded. The shoe fit, even if our family knew it was ridiculous. I knew Dee wouldn't have kept that a secret from me, if only because she would have loved to lord it over me: *Look at how dangerous I am now.* No, she wouldn't have been able to keep that a secret. From our perspective, it was a lie. But I saw how the lie answered a lot of questions, especially for Wolski, whose efforts to find Dee began to flag significantly after his conversation with Frank. Not that his effort level before was impressive, but it had been somewhat steady. Maybe, in his eyes, Dee became a little less worthy of finding. Or maybe he just felt like it explained, to his satisfaction, why she had disappeared. The media had done something similar to the people murdered by the serial killer— they said these men and boys were criminals, they were prostitutes, they were drinkers and drug addicts, they willingly posed for nude photographs—as if this helped people to make sense of the cruelty of their deaths. No one wanted to admit that nothing could help us make sense of that.

The night the serial killer special aired, someone nailed an effigy of Thomas Alexander to an old post in the middle of the empty lot at 924 North Twenty-fifth Street and set him on fire. TMJ4 sent a reporter down there to film the burning Thomas Alexander, and the video went viral.

The national popularity of this video also subsumed the story that followed in Milwaukee. The effigy eventually started a fire in the apartment building adjacent to the lot where the serial killer's building had been. It became difficult to get everyone out and to contain the fire. TMJ4 captured an image of two toddlers in pink footed pajamas standing in the middle of the street. This was the same street where once, decades ago, a child had escaped from the serial killer's apartment, bleeding and confused, and the police had returned him to the killer's apartment. The death toll of the fire, officially, was seven. The news anchor interviewed one woman, a resident, who stared into the camera and said only, "My life is over."

Leif left while we were waiting on the lab results. He said he hadn't intended to stay as long as he had, and he needed to get back on the road. I wanted to be snarky and short with him, but I couldn't muster the strength. He asked if he could take a box of my files with him—something he'd found pertaining to Erik—but when he noticed my discomfort, he said he'd scan them and leave the originals. I called him a week or so after we got the results. Maybe I thought he had a right to know. Maybe I just wanted to hear his voice one last time.

"I'm sorry, Peg," he said. "I really am."

I heard some relief in his voice. Had he worried that if the bones were Dee's, Erik might have been named as her killer? Did he believe his brother capable? Do we, any of us, know anything about one another at all? *It's impossible*, I thought, *to say what we know*. I hated him.

"Thanks," I said.

"You still think Frank did it?"

Did it. I hated this construction. Because we'd never had an *it*—done what, exactly? Had he murdered her himself and burned her body in his parents' crematorium? Had he had someone else murder her for him so his hands would be clean and he could climb the ladder in the MFD? Had he tortured her? Had she suffered for a short time? A long time? Every question mark like a lash. I rarely let myself ask so many at once because it could easily induce vomiting. Paralysis.

"Of course," I said. "But I blame myself more and more too now."

"For what?" he asked.

"For everything," I admitted. "I failed her. I failed my family. Even you. In a way."

"Don't say that. I was the one who fucked up. You know? Sometimes I wish I hadn't left. When I did, I mean. Or how I did. I'm sorry," he said. "I still loved you. But I was scared."

"Yeah," I said. "Sure."

"I mean it. I shouldn't have left like that."

"We wouldn't have ever worked again. We couldn't."

"Yeah," he said. "Maybe you're right."

There was a long pause in which I thought he would hang up, but instead he said, "I've told you about my book, yeah?"

"Not much," I said.

"Well, I'd love if you'd read it when I'm done."

What did he think I still owed him? "Goodbye, Leif," I said. A wave of regret washed over me. Briefly, I could see a whole other life, not this wasted, warped march of days ahead of me. Then it was gone.

The Ambrosia chocolate factory did shut down, about a year after the *Journal* broke the news that the serial killer had worked there. People had begun to look at those deep drums of chocolate with newfound horror. During his confession, the serial killer revealed that he sometimes brought his victims' body parts to work with him. Many people, including Leif, were now out of work. It was just like Erik had said. Before the factory closed, they sold hundreds of tons of cocoa bean shells to the city on the cheap; Milwaukee used the husks as mulch around their city trees, so even after the factory closed, the sidewalks smelled of chocolate.

The day Leif got out of prison, we didn't go to the apartment. We hadn't paid rent in months, and we were definitely in breach of contract. I hadn't worked consistent hours at the library in so long, and Leif and I had been pooling our money to pay for his work release program, so we were beyond broke. (I'd never understood that part of the program—you pay to be able to go to work.) I didn't know what we would do. Leif always said the same thing when I was dropping him back off at the prison: *We'll figure it out.* I knew enough by then to know no one ever figures it out.

When I picked him up, he threw himself into the Spitfire like the thing was a coffin. I wasn't sure he'd ever move again. He was skinny, and his body was limp in the bucket seat. He had always been quiet, but he was quieter than ever now. I drove us to a tiny spot of beach north of the city. We walked down a steep, winding path to the rocky beach. There was an old cement pier crumbling into the lake, rainbows of beach glass glinting in the sand, whole tree trunks' worth of driftwood washed up on shore. The lake was seven different hues of blue. Some people said you could see part of an old shipwreck from this beach, and fragments of the ship still washed up here after storms. The lake was glass that day, though. Leif sat down on a log and cried. I did not hold him even though I could tell it was what he wanted. I went to the lake and skipped stones. I wished there were loud waves so I couldn't hear him cry. He should have been alone to do that. When it sounded like he'd calmed down, I went to sit with him on the log.

"We're never going to find Dee," I told him. "I know Frank killed her."

He shook his head. He picked up a piece of smooth brown glass and rubbed it between his fingers. "You don't know that," he said.

"What happened to you?" I asked him.

"You happened."

I allowed this. "What are we going to do?"

He turned to me and held my chin. I closed my eyes and wished we could be living in any other time except now. I knew this was delusional. If you think about the cumulative coincidences too often, it will ruin your mind. Maybe I wanted him to keep holding my chin. Maybe he wanted me to hug him. Maybe I liked it.

"When I'm off parole, I've got a buddy who's gonna set me up with a truck-driving gig. It's good pay, you get regular time off, and the best part—I'll get the fuck out of this city." It was far enough away from the smokestacks to the south, and the ambulances wailing in the north, and the constant whirl of traffic, to feel as if we were out of the city.

"Jesus. Truck driving?"

He didn't say anything. I began to panic.

"Please don't leave me too," I begged. My throat was suddenly dry, and my tongue stuck to the top of my mouth. I was embarrassed to beg.

"You can come with me," he offered. "You should."

I shook my head. "You know I can't," I choked. "Dee . . ."

"You just said it yourself . . . you think she's gone."

"Don't say that," I cried. "Don't *you* fucking say that."

I pushed him as hard as I could. I wanted him to fall. I wanted to hurt him, but he merely teetered backward off the log. Still, he scrambled to stand up and step away from me. His eyes were wide and wild. Maybe he thought then that I was gone too. Maybe I was. Maybe I was just then beginning to feel beyond the shore of my own deep despair. I thought maybe, in the weeks before, I had been feeling Dee's missingness like something too hot or too cold to touch—carefully, tenderly, barely at all—and now I was beginning to understand the intensity, the insanity, even, of really feeling it. I could see then the huge, monstrous shapes of the feeling forming inside me.

"Give me the keys," he said. "I'm sorry. I can't. Stay here. With you." I dug in my pocket for his car keys and threw them at him. He didn't blink, and then he started back up the bluff. I stayed on the log and tried to listen for the car's engine to start up, but all I could hear was the soft lap of the lake on the beach. I listened and listened. I felt Dee's absence growing wider and wider inside me.

I had to walk three miles to a pay phone to call Peter to come pick me up. When I got him on the phone, he was out of breath and confused. *What did we tell you Margaret? You've got to tell us where you're going. Who you're with. How long you'll be. Always.* The shortest bouts of silence from me could throw him and Ma into a panic. I had started asking everyone because I truly didn't know the answer.

"Pete," I said. "What are we going to do?"

"Where the hell are you?"

I told Pete about Leif leaving, and Pete called the man I loved a degenerate, and I clenched my jaw. The phone cut out. I was out of money.

Thomas Alexander expressed some disappointment that he'd been unable to come up with the right location, but he was saved from any publicity (good or bad) regarding his recently botched case for two reasons. First, his serial killer episode would turn out to be his most watched to date. It aired to record viewership and garnered millions of streams. Some critics, even the ones who'd awarded him the truly terrible television award, called this show *thrilling* and *utterly engrossing*. It reenergized his career, they said. Even if we'd had access to the national outlets that covered the psychic, there wouldn't have been any interest in or room for our story. His publicity people did an excellent job controlling that narrative. Though, as Dana later pointed out to us, we could have tried publicizing it ourselves, on social media. But we hadn't been fluent in that language, and we hadn't allowed Dana to teach us. Pete and Helena had severely restricted Dana's access to her social media accounts in the wake of the incident with Cal. And who knows if any of it would have caught on, given the sheer amount of Internet content the serial killer episode generated—GIFs, memes, spin-off TV shows, public appearances, tweets, viral photos. The content seemed endless. I found myself avoiding the news and the Internet just so I didn't have to see or hear anything about the show.

Second, our story about Dee and the psychic was doubly subsumed by the piece that Charlie Makon published in the *Journal Sentinel*. This piece enjoyed widespread acclaim and was covered on all the major news networks. Makon went on the circuit: the morning shows, the cable news shows, the late shows. It was jarring to see his baby face pop up all over the news. The piece's popularity grew. He stretched his fifteen minutes. And in some ways, it turns out, the piece deserved it.

It was true what Makon had tried to tell me that day at the nursing home—his piece was tangentially about my sister, though her name was never mentioned. In essence, the article covered the long reign of a powerful prostitution empire in the city of Milwaukee. For decades, beginning in the eighties, the business had offered, among other services, discreet escorts for high-profile men in Milwaukee. A number of famous Milwaukeeans had used these services at one time or another before the business collapsed: former mayors and police chiefs, important businessmen, and the like. Frank's real name (Anthony Cavelli), embarrassingly for the Milwaukee Fire Department, of which he was now chief, was on the list that Makon had acquired. But in the end, rich men seeing prostitutes was not news. Most of the men had their lawyers put out statements denying any knowledge of or involvement in this business. Statutes of limitations were invoked.

Rather, the most controversial and most discussed aspect of the article concerned the MPD's involvement in the business. These revelations came at a particularly bad time for the police. Makon alleged that several detectives and beat cops were paid a weekly stipend (the amount varied) in order to provide information that helped the service elude police investigation, and in order to derail investigations that could threaten the business. Most disturbingly, Makon reported that a handful of MPD detectives had neglected and, in some cases, even sabotaged active missing-persons investigations, especially if these cases involved (a) a client of the business or (b) a young woman. Makon had a source inside the department. I knew immediately, if there was a conclusive list of the detectives that this business had bought out, that Wolski's name would be on it.

I understood then that Frank had made up his story about Dee and that Wolski had either believed him, or been paid to believe him, because Frank had a history of soliciting prostitutes from this business. Wolski saw what he wanted to see. Whether he would admit it or not, he had used Frank's story to justify Dee's disappearance to us, then to protect himself and Frank from any further investigation. These revelations had an odd effect on me. I felt certain memories begin to sew themselves together: Wolski was not just a so-so cop, he was a corrupt cop, and there had never really been a chance he would find Dee because he'd never really looked for her.

I called him as soon as I'd finished the article.

"So, you made a whole bunch of money hiding these people's shit?" I yelled at him. "Good for you. You're fucking disgusting, you know that?"

"Watch your tone," he said. His voice was hushed. Hoarse. "It's a bad system. I'll admit that. I was doing my best with a bad system."

"Oh, fuck you," I told him. "A bad system? You made a choice. I always, always knew you were a piece of shit."

"You know I'm not," he said. His voice became disgustingly whiny, desperate. I felt sick. "You know me. You know me. I didn't have a choice. You don't understand."

"I do. Do you remember when you first took my statement? Do you remember when you got the photo? You never believed me. You never trusted me."

"Don't blow this out of proportion, Peg. I've always cared for you. I wasn't the one who hurt your sister." I had a memory of him saying the same thing in 1991, upset when people began scrutinizing the MPD alongside the serial killer: *Jesus H. Christ, it's like these people forget who the actual criminal was.*

I hung up on him while he was pleading his case, asking if we could meet to discuss this, if he could tell me his side of the story.

Next I called Pete. I needed to hear a calm, rational take on the piece. He picked up immediately, and I knew I would not get that take from him. He was animated, loud, rambling. I had to tell him to slow down.

"Don't you see what this means, though?" he said finally, exasperated that I was struggling to keep up with him.

"Yeah, Wolski botched our case."

"Of course," he said. "But also, it might give us probable cause to pressure the DA to reopen her case. All the cases he worked could be reviewed now."

I closed my eyes. This was not what I'd wanted to hear. I don't know what I expected. Maybe an apology? I felt like my family had, at times, blamed me for Dee's disappearance *and* for the way her case had collapsed so early. Worse, Wolski had then cast doubt on my version of events. From the first interview, he'd treated me with such suspicion, I'd begun to think of myself as a suspect. He'd made me doubt myself. So of course my family had doubted me. I had been hoping Pete would see this too.

"I'm so tired, Pete," I said. "Even if they do reopen it. There are statutes of limitations and all that."

"Not on murder," Pete said with too much enthusiasm. I recoiled at this response. His position couldn't have been further from my mother's. She no longer cared to pursue any legal avenues related to Dee's case. She had maintained one goal for a long time: to find Dee's body. And after the psychic's botched reading, I began to understand. What would we gain by knowing? What would it change? Nothing.

"We'll see," I told Pete. I wasn't at all hopeful: Nothing had ever moved the dial before.

wanted to die, and I wanted my death to be slow and painful. Emma Bovary's death came to mind. I told Pete this when he picked me up from the side of the road on the day Leif left. He said, *Don't you ever fucking say something like that again, Margaret, Jesus Christ.*

At Ma's, I took off all my clothes except my underwear and my T-shirt, and I climbed into bed. I fell asleep for fourteen or fifteen hours, and when I woke, I lay still and I remembered. Leif called the home phone for me, but I refused to touch it, so Ma would bring the phone into the bedroom and lay it on my stomach, where I could faintly hear his voice speaking into my belly button. *Peg? Baby? Should I come back for you? I want to come back for you. Will you come with me? Please, baby. Come with me. I didn't mean what I said about us breaking up. I was in a bad way. I'm better now, and we should be together.* I'd let him go on for a while before, with effort, I'd hang up the phone. Sometimes when my mother came with the phone, I'd listen a little longer to Leif as he talked about the books he was reading, about what he was seeing and feeling. I never said anything, though. I stayed in bed and refused all food for two and a half weeks.

My mother began whispering with Suze and Pete about having

me committed to a place where they'd force a tube down my throat and pump me full of liquid food. I stayed in bed and watched the way light moved on the leaves of the trees outside my window. I tracked the shadows in my childhood room and learned to love the reality slippage that occurred in my hungriest, saddest states—I could remember with such lucidity in those states: Dee and me playing underneath pine trees, riding bikes together; later, drinking wine and running from men; watching her paint, watching her put on makeup; the night I met Leif, the first time we had sex, the way he held me at night, how he smelled just fresh out of the shower or just home from work. I wanted to stay in these memories for good, and this seemed possible only if I stayed hungry and shadow-watching.

Once, some three weeks or so after I'd climbed in bed, Pete, Suze, and Ma came into the bedroom with a bowl of creamy root soup, which I used to love as a child. Instinctively, I curled myself up into a ball and rolled toward the wall. I put my hands over my head to protect my mouth. Protect the slippage. Pete grabbed my hands and pushed them down to my sides. He rolled me onto my back. Suze held my head. I looked into her eyes, and she was crying but not making any noise. Even after Dee had been gone, after we'd known, because it is known when things like this happen that after a certain time, the person you love is dead, even after we'd admitted, separately to ourselves but never openly to one another, that Dee was probably dead, that Frank or Tony or whatever the hell his name was probably killed her or had her killed, and probably put her body in the incinerator at his parents' cemetery, even after all that, I still hadn't seen Suze cry. But now long, contiguous tears rolled down the slopes of her cheeks and into my face. I spit and bit at Ma as she moved toward me with the soup. She had brought a spoon, but eventually, she abandoned the utensil and just dipped her index finger deep into the bowl. I squirmed and fought the three of them, but I was not strong then, I had never really been strong, and I was tired, very tired, and Ma was able to run her soup-filled finger up and down my gums. I tried to spit it out, but I felt myself swallow some of it, and I could feel it go down my throat and into my stomach, where it ate away at the memories and the slippage so that I was yanked, by my brother's hands, and my aunt's wet cheeks, and my mother's fingers, back into the reality of our lives. This was our routine every day for almost a week before I was fully back in reality and I could smell the smelliness of my own body.

"I won't live without her," I said. My thoughts became bright crystals in front of my eyes; I could see my life clearly now, spinning out ahead for years and years, without Dee. It was unbearable.

My mother put a wet washcloth to my face. It shocked me awake. "There is no other choice," she said. "Let's get you cleaned up." I rubbed my arms where Pete's hands had bruised me through the skin and into the bone.

I had been forced awake, and once out of this sleep, I realized, for the first time but not the last, that I had disappointed my family. I had acted like a child in the face of this disaster, and I would be treated like a child until I proved myself otherwise. So it was at this time that I committed myself to proving that, no matter what the police said, Frank had disappeared my sister. Yes, I'd failed my sister, but Frank, he was the monster. I needed him to be the monster.

After her final stroke, both sides of my mother's face sagged like she was a robot that had been completely unplugged. At the hospital, I kissed her lightly on the forehead, and then Peter dragged me back out into the hallway. The girls and Helena stayed inside and crowded around Ma's bed.

"We have a problem," Pete said.

"Okay," I said.

"We're not going to have any money to bury her," he said.

"Jesus, Pete, she's still breathing in there," I said. "Do you think it's really appropriate?"

"I know. I know," he said. His shoulders were hunched around his ears. He rubbed his face. "But we don't have a lot of time."

"You don't have anything left?" I asked him.

Pete gave me a hard look, his eyes narrowed. "Do you?" he growled.

"Okay," I said. "Fair enough." I knew that Pete had footed most of the psychic's exorbitant forty-thousand-dollar bill. Suze and I had tried to help, but I had been unemployed and draining my savings dry for the past few months, and Suze had almost no savings to speak of. "What do you want to do?" I asked him.

He studied his fingernails. I had an image of him rubbing those bone fragments between his fingers. I wondered if he'd loved those bones the way I had when I'd first seen them.

"I think we should sell off the plot Ma bought for Dee," he said.

I nodded. It made sense. It also made no sense. It was the best solution, but I never would have said it.

"You're right," I said.

"Am I?"

"We don't have any other choice, right?"

"Right," he said.

"She can't know, though," I said.

"She won't know," he said.

He squeezed my shoulder.

The night Ma died, she repeated Dee's name over and over again. We were there with her, Pete and me and Suze and Helena and the girls. I felt, irrationally, that Ma's incessant repetition of Dee's name was an attack on me. I felt, that night, that what Ma was really saying was: *How could you have lost her? How could you have let this happen to her? How could you do this to me?* I cried hard, dry sobs through the whole thing.

Some of us tried to get her to drink water, but all she did was gasp and say her youngest daughter's name on a loop through and into the night until she pulled me close and waved the rest of them off. She whispered. I strained to understand.

"You know."

"Know what, Mama?" I cried.

"I lost two babies," she said. "What kind of mother. How did I lose two . . . Dee, and there was another, and Dee . . ." And then the loops started again, and all she could do was say Dee's name until early in the morning, when she died with her teeth bared and her mouth open in the shape of the sound Dee's name makes.

Though Ma had worked for most of her adult life as a unioned typist, and then for the union itself, and her savings were once substantial (she had planned to divide this among Dee, me, and Pete), by the time she died, she was absolutely bankrupt: She'd paid the second largest chunk of the psychic's bill. Pete was still working on those installments, on the verge of bankruptcy, and Helena told me she thought they might lose their house.

In the end, we didn't have enough. Pete went to speak with the funeral director, who offered to buy back the plot that Ma had purchased for Dee, in order to cover the costs of our mother's coffin and interment. Pete, Suze, and I all voted to sell the plot, which we knew was a kind of betrayal of Ma's trust, and of our commitment to bringing Dee home. Pete said if it happened (we never said *when* anymore), we would find a spot for her. Suze cried for the first time in a long time, and though she'd voted for this option too, she would remain permanently angry with us all for following through with the sale.

At the funeral, I felt as if I should climb into Ma's cheap coffin and be buried alive with her. During the burial, we tried hard not to look at the empty plot next to our parents' graves.

At the wake, Dana showed me videos of the cathedral of Notre Dame on fire. Did I know, she asked, that parts of it had caught on fire last spring? I did not know. Apparently, the most recent attempts to restore the cathedral had caused the fire. Dana clicked the button on the side of her phone so the screen went black.

"Everybody says Paris is overrated anyway," Dana said.

"Who says that? Nobody says that," I told her sharply.

She eyed me. "Dad says you're stuck here," she said.

"I've found it harder and harder to leave," I admitted. "So I guess that's right."

"Well, I'm leaving as soon as I can."

I nodded. I remembered what Erik had said. *I've got to get out of this fucking city.* I thought about Leif at Erik's funeral, where he'd met Erik's husband: They'd been married ten years. I thought about Leif's son, who, he'd told me, was only a couple of years younger than Dana. I thought about Ma's body, pumped full of chemicals, stuck under the ground. I thought about how far Ma had come: All she'd wanted was Dee under the ground with her, and now she'd never get that either.

"I hope you do," I told her, even though I hoped nothing of the sort. She smiled and rubbed the insides of her wrists absently. Then she took up my hand and squeezed it.

The truth was, if there was a truth, I loved Milwaukee the way I suspect many women "love" their bodies. I am intimately, painfully aware of the city's flaws, occasionally obsessive even, but aware also that it's the only one I'm ever going to get. We can't ever really know what it's like to live in another body, to have a different family, to be born into another time, in another city.

Dana leaned in to me. "I have something else to show you," she whispered. She unlocked her phone again, swiped and scrolled for a few seconds, and then handed it to me. "Read it," she said, and then she went to keep her sister, Sophie, company.

Dana had left her phone's Web browser open to an online petition, one that had already garnered millions of signatures. The petition demanded that the current Milwaukee mayor, the district attorney, and the attorney general's office reopen the cases of five MPD detectives. Each of these detectives, the writer argued, had been in the pocket of an illegal for-profit enterprise, and their cases, particularly the cold cases that remained unsolved, should be reopened and investigated with renewed vigor and integrity. Of course, Wolski was one of the five. He'd been on paid leave since the article had come out, and he would remain there until, the police said, they had time to investigate the allegations internally.

There were links to Instagram posts that had gone viral. People were reposting the petition as I spoke. I watched the numbers climb as I sat there. *Jason just signed. Alex just signed. Robert just signed.* Were these real people? The petition prompted me to sign too, and I clicked the button and saw my name appear briefly and then disappear, and then the website was asking me for money and I locked Dana's phone. I scoured the funeral crowd for her. She was rubbing shoulders with Sophie, both in prim funeral attire, sipping kiddie cocktails. Dana handed her little sister her maraschino cherry. There was something about the language of the petition: I knew Dana had written it. She had just turned fifteen.

About a year after Dee disappeared, Suze moved in with Ma and me. I don't think Ma asked her to do it, but maybe Pete did. He was trying then to make up for lost time in law school at Marquette, and he felt guilty for leaving us alone more and more often. When Pete helped Suze move a pickup truck's worth of her belongings in, she explained that she was worried things were getting a little bit too *Grey Gardens* at our house.

The day Suze moved in, Ma and I looked around, and we were shocked to discover that she was right. We hadn't cleaned the house, really at all, since the summer Dee went missing, and in that year we'd allowed everything to pile up: newspapers, catalogs, recyclables, files, bills. I had a hunch Ma was frightened to throw anything away because the possibility always remained that there was something we might need, something pertinent to Dee's case, in all this stuff.

Suze came in and set about trying to organize some of the chaos, though I noticed she was careful, very considerate, with what she threw away, and she always, always cleared it with either Ma or me first.

But even as we continued to hoard documents, Dee's case became colder and colder, and the files seemed more and more useless.

There was never anything new to learn. This was all we knew and (we would eventually accept) all we would ever know: Dee left me in Riverwest and no one, that we knew of, ever saw her again. One anonymous tip put her in Frank's parents' cemetery late on the Fourth of July. Frank, though he'd clearly been cheating and had lied about his name, had an alibi for the Fourth of July (he'd spent the day at a big block party where at least twenty people had seen him), and he was, apparently, living in Ohio at that time. The police told us so many times, *No body, no crime*. And though we all worked overtime over the years pursuing increasingly far-fetched leads, and trying to get publicity for her case, and drum up interest in the media or within the police department, one by one we began to let things go.

One of the first things to go was the hotlines, which we disman-tled in part because they became heinous. People are very cruel. Sometimes the callers would leave prank tips: kids calling in to say they knew where Dee was, leaving addresses to adult video stores, and the like. More insidious were the people who pretended to be Dee. Sometimes they would say things like *I left because I never loved you. Any of you.* Sometimes I fantasized about finding these people and killing them or torturing them. Once, right before we shut down the lines, we got a call from a local psychic offering us unlimited, unfiltered, absolute access to our loved one for the very low fee of only ten hundred-dollar monthly payments.

"The absolute nerve of these people," Ma said to me. I nodded and Suze unplugged the phones.

After Ma died, I received a manuscript in the mail. It was from Leif. He had, despite my substantial doubts, finished his book. The novel was a fictionalized account of his relationship with his brother. Leif had stuck a yellow Post-it on the cover page that said only, *Thoughts?* And though I began to read it, I couldn't make it through the whole thing. I couldn't bear to have Leif's voice living inside my head for two hundred and fifty pages. All I could hear was what I'd lost.

I skipped to the end where Leif had reimagined the months before his brother's death: a whole chapter in which Erik had finally called Leif and invited him out to Cali. Lance cooked elaborate vegetarian meals for the three of them, and they took the dogs for short walks around the property; they made up for lost time. I was crushed by these depictions, especially the sugariness of them, and they left a bad taste in my mouth as if I'd eaten too much candy. My tongue felt as if it were coated with chemicals. It seemed unfair of Leif to worm his way into the end of his brother's life, even fictionally, because Erik had been so adamant that Leif stay away. Though I was curious if this imagining had comforted him: How much had it soothed his guilt? I waited for the part at the end where this fictional Erik would tell this fictional Leif what had happened to my fictional Dee. But, at the end of his life, this version of Erik never said anything about Dee.

In another section of Leif's book, I found the story of the last Fourth we spent together. I was astounded to discover that in Leif's telling of this story, Dee, though mentioned, is merely a backdrop for our acid trip. And though he mentioned the photo, he did so only to explain that somehow he knew Erik had seen it and that, after seeing it, Erik disowned Leif altogether. Leif didn't even mention that Dee was the one who took the picture. And according to Leif's book, it was incidental that she was there but crucial that I was there, when really, it was so obviously the opposite. How could he tell it this way?

I realized then that we must choose to believe the stories we're told. Even the stories we tell about one another. We dedicate ourselves to our own versions, and yet we are slow, reticent even, to admit how much we participate in the creation of these stories we tell about our lives and about the lives of those we love. Sometimes now, for practice, I tell myself all of the stories at once. I say, *Here are the scenarios; here are the possibilities*. What does it mean that each and every one could be made to seem as probable as the next?

Sometimes, for example, I let myself fantasize that Dee had left with Erik, and that they'd gone to live somewhere warm near the ocean. That they'd grown old together. Sometimes I lived in this reality—where Dee and Erik were still alive and moving through a different, better world that didn't need so desperately to hurt them. Other times I imagined the kind of scenarios I never used to, before the psychic, before the article—the ones in which maybe Frank killed her or maybe he didn't. Maybe it was a stranger. Maybe it was an old boyfriend we'd never known about. Maybe it was Frank's wife. Or maybe it was an accident. Maybe she'd gone for a swim and been carried away in a river or taken out to the middle of Lake Michigan, where she'd sunk into the shipwrecks that were decomposing in the deepest beds of the lake. I allowed myself these possibilities and more. But even so, I was never able to shake my belief that the most compelling possibility, that Frank had murdered my sister and destroyed her body, was also the truest.

t was a year or two after Charlie Makon's article came out, and during a period of intense scrutiny of police departments nationwide, that public pressure to reopen several cold cases finally drove Wisconsin's attorney general to make a statement: The Milwaukee Police Department would be revisiting a few of these detectives' cases. Dee's case had made the list. Dana, who had just gotten her driver's license, came to my apartment to tell me the news. I was too tired to react, even though I felt something rising quickly and then falling inside me. She asked if I wanted to go to the beach. I said yes.

I was expecting Bradford, but we drove north in the bright, hot Wisconsin summer. The heat from the highway rose in great shimmering waves. The cornfields were wide washes of green in our peripherals. The whole world took on a comforting blurred quality: everything soft and rushing by. Dana watched me with sharp, darting eyes as we edged closer to Milwaukee's outskirts. I expected her to get off at each exit (because truthfully, this was the farthest outside Milwaukee I'd been in thirty years), but she kept going past Cedarburg and Watertown until we got to Sheboygan, and I said nothing. I checked my pulse. It was surprisingly steady. The farms became less green, less bountiful, and more desperate, like they were hanging on by the spindliest of threads. I knew what that was like.

When we got off the highway, Dana glanced at me again. "You good?" she asked.

I nodded, but I was unsure.

"Dad says you don't want the case reopened."

"That's not true," I told her. I sensed she was fishing for a thank-you. She wanted me to tell her she'd done a good job with my files, with the petition, and with the pressure. I wasn't capable.

"Well, why would he say it?" she asked me.

"I don't know," I said. "Maybe I'm in a different place than I was before."

"So you accept it? You accept what happened?"

I stared at the side of her face. Her cheeks were flushed. "No," I said sharply. "Don't ever think that."

"Well, then, we have to keep trying, right? You should give them your files."

I thought about the stolen law books, the reports, the transcripts, even the newspaper clippings I'd kept on the serial killer. In the end, it hadn't added up to anything. "I thought you said there was nothing there."

"No." She paused. "I see the whole picture now. After the article. I think there's plenty on him."

"I'll think about it," I said, but without conviction. I'd been drained of so much already—I couldn't lose anything else.

We drove past strip malls and half-planted cornfields and truck-stop diners. The temperature dropped ten degrees. Finally, we arrived at an old state park with wild grassy dunes and long winding stretches of eroded beaches. My parents had taken us to this park once or twice when I was a girl, though the beach had been grander and less eroded then. There was so little left now: The parking lot ended mere feet from the water. Dana parked the car due east, and ahead of us, Lake Michigan churned up frothy whitecaps for miles. A song our mother used to hum to us, and which Dee had loved singing aloud during car trips, rang in my head. *Oh, Agnes, won't you go with me? We'll be married in style / And we'll cross Lake Michigan, so blue and so wild / Oh yes, love, I will go with you, leave Wisconsin behind* . . .

On what was left of the beach, I spread my sweater out for us to sit. The sand was warm but damp, and the air smelled like pine, granite, exhaust. I thought Dana would sit down next to me, but she stripped down to her bra and underwear and ran straight into the waves. I heard her laughing and screaming at the cold shock of the water. I wanted to stop her or tell her to be careful; I wanted her to come back. But I was also proud and grateful that she was unafraid. She swam laps and did handstands: Her pointed feet bisected the watery horizon.

After she was done swimming, she sat at the shoreline and let the waves lap at her feet for a few minutes. Then she began to dig a hole, on her hands and knees, as if she were a little kid again. I thought maybe she was going to build a moat and castle. All of her selves flashed in front of me. She was a child, she was a woman, she was my sister, she was not my sister, and then she was exactly what she was: a sixteen-year-old girl digging a hole in the sand. It meant nothing to me. Lake Michigan shone behind her. I shielded my eyes and was seized with the sensation that she would be swallowed. I called to her, so she stopped and stood. She peered down at the sand, and her long, thin body cast a huge oval shadow over the hole.

"Come and see," she shouted. "Look what I found, Auntie Peg."

I shook my head at her, comfortable where I was and fatigued from the drive. The sun had built a comforting circle of warmth on the top of my head. "Bring it to me," I shouted at her.

She jogged over and plopped down next to me, spraying cold lake water on my shoulders. Goose bumps rose all over her arms and legs as she stretched out.

"What is it?" I asked her.

"What's what?" she said. She put the crook of her elbow over her eyes as she lay down. I felt then, for the millionth time, the pull of the long, thin thread that tied this girl to my sister. I held this thought as long as I could, but eventually, it dissolved into the heat of the day.

"What did you find?" I asked Dana.

She laughed. "Oh, there wasn't anything there."

I looked back toward the hole she'd dug and saw she was right. Already the depression had been washed away.

AUTHOR'S NOTE

To reiterate the warning at the beginning of the book: this is a work of fiction. That being said, the narrative intersects with a very real place and a very real set of circumstances, and where it does, I did my best to honor the city of Milwaukee, its people, and those specific circumstances the city found itself in during the summer of 1991. In doing so, I relied heavily upon the following resources: the *Milwaukee Journal*, Anne E. Schwartz's *The Man Who Could Not Kill Enough*, Richard Tithecott's *Of Men and Monsters: Jeffrey Dahmer and the Construction of the Serial Killer*, Dirk C. Gibson's *Serial Murder and Media Circuses*, the Wisconsin LGBT History Project, and the *Wisconsin Light*. A special thank you to Don Schwamb for the invaluable work he does and for connecting me to Jerry Johnson. And a very special thank you to Jerry Johnson for our conversation and for letting me use the edition of the *Wisconsin Light* that appears in the book. This blending of fact with fiction necessitated some massaging, and any factual inaccuracies that result from this massaging are mine and mine alone.

ACKNOWLEDGMENTS

Getting this book into the world was no small feat, and it was certainly not something I could have done alone. I am full of gratitude to all those who helped—in big, in small, and in wine-related ways—along the way. A huge thank you to my editor, Sara Nelson, for taking a chance on this book, right before the end of the world no less, and also to Mary Gaule and the whole team at Harper for giving this book a home. So much love and gratitude to Samantha Shea, who has supported this project from the very beginning and beyond, through its many, strange iterations. I am so grateful to have such a generous, sharp-eyed reader of my work. You truly are, as someone once said to me about you, "One of the good ones." I would also like to thank my advisor at UWM, Professor Valerie Laken, whose guidance, support, and dedication helped usher this book into its final form. Thank you also to professors Liam Callanan, Rebecca Dunham, Kristie Hamilton, and Joe Rodriguez for reading the book and discussing it with such enthusiasm at my dissertation defense. A special thank you to the whole family at Thief Wine in Milwaukee, especially Phil Bilodeau and Aimee Murphy, and all my thiefsters, for the laughs and the love, for your friendships and encouragements during difficult times, and of course for all the wine that fueled this book and beyond. I would also like to thank all of my writing teachers from years past, without whom this book would not have been possible: Kai Carslon-Wee, Amaud Johnson, Judith Claire Mitchell, Marilynne Robinson, Ethan Canin, Kevin Brockmeier, Nimo Johnson, Charles D'Ambrosio, and Bennett Sims. Thank you to the Iowa Writers' Workshop, the Truman Capote Trust, and especially Lan Samantha Chang, Connie Brothers, Deb West, and Jan Zenisek, who have taken good care of writers, myself included, since forever. Thank you also to Jennie Lin for your friendship and for reading very early drafts of this book and reporting back with encouragement. Thank you to two of my oldest, and dearest friends, Aaron Raasch and Tess Snodgrass, for sticking with me, even and most especially when I didn't deserve it. I'd also like to thank my family for their continued love and support. Every single one of you shaped me and shaped this book. To my siblings: Simone Bruhy is an inspiration, a living superwoman and still the coolest wearer of an eyebrow piercing I've ever met; Amanda Bruhy, whose art inspired what appears in this book, is a hell of a strong woman; Nicholas Richards, who is a talented musician and a man with a powerful and beautifully strange brain; and Emma Richards, who is a powerhouse of a human, a tender lover of sweet things, and my best friend always—you are all my home, I love you all. A special thank you, (and apology?) to Emma Richards for reading every single draft of this book. Your contributions to these drafts, and our conversations about them, were invaluable to me. To my nephews, Emmet Johnson, Aidan Johnson, and Langston Bruhy-Hale, thank you for being lights in my life. To Aidan, thank you for teaching me so much about love, beauty, and loss at such a young age. I still think of you often. To my parents, Dr. Patricia B. Richards and Dr. John D. Richards, you have given me everything, so many gifts, my siblings included, and I will be forever grateful. Thank you especially for your support during this process, and for always, always, listening. I love you both. Finally I would like to thank J. M. Holmes whose belief in this book has never wavered, even when mine had begun to do so quite dangerously, and whose love and light and bravery and beauty have expanded the scope of my life and my work, quite literally, as Joan Didion once said, from a short story to a novel.

WILLA C. RICHARDS is a graduate of the Iowa Writers' Workshop, where she was a Truman Capote Fellow. She earned her PhD in English from the University of Wisconsin–Milwaukee. Her first story, "Failure to Thrive," was published by the *Paris Review* and won a PEN/Robert J. Dau Short Story Prize for Emerging Writers.